Nathan Burrage lives in Sydney, Australia with his wife and two daughters. He is the author of *FIVEFOLD*, a supernatural thriller first published by Random House and subsequently translated into Russian, and *Almost Human* a collection of short fiction published by IFWG.

A graduate of Clarion South—an intensive, six-week residential writing program based on the famous US workshops of the same name—Nathan has been shortlisted for both the Aurealis Awards and the Ditmar Awards in Australia.

Intermittent transmissions can be intercepted at www.nathanburrage.com

T0118841

Praise for *The Hidden Keystone*

"A rich and vivid historical fantasy grounded in meticulous research, *The Hidden Keystone* is a powerful tale of political machinations, terrible persecution, and the indomitable hope of the human spirit. Against the bloody backdrop of the First Crusade of 1099 in the Holy Land and the shocking oppression of the Templars in the 1300s France, this masterful work pits the cosmic forces of Mercy and Severity and their human agents against each other in a never-ending battle for the human soul, holding the reader in its grasp well beyond the last page."

- Dr Karen Brooks, author of *The Brewer's Tale*, *The Darkest Shore*, and *The Good Wife of Bath*.

"A marvelous blend of the historical and the fantastic."

- Keith Stevenson, author of *Horizon* and *The Lenticular Series*

"*The Hidden Keystone* is a fascinating historical fantasy story that blends the reality of the Crusades with a mystical tale that hooks the reader into its world, and Burrage leaves them wanting more in the inevitable sequel."

- Joseph Sullivan, Aurealis Magazine (Issue 164)

The Final Shroud

Book 2 of the Salt Lines

by
Nathan Burrage

IFWG Publishing International
Gold Coast

www.ifwgpublishing.com

For Glad & Merv,
and Betty & Bob

A *Cast of Characters* can be found on page 243

A *Glossary of Terms* can be found on page 247

The Story So Far

In *The Hidden Keystone*—Book 1 of *The Salt Lines* saga—Godefroi de Bouillon's quest to reclaim the holy city of Jerusalem for Christianity is finally realised in July 1099. After the long crusade, the sacking of the city is swift and brutal.

Amidst the ensuing chaos, a fraternity known as the Salt Lines pursues its secret agenda. Led by Godefroi's personal chaplain—Hugues de Payens—Godefroi's 'five sacred points' are searching for an artefact that pre-dates even King Solomon. Known by many names, Hugues' search for the keystone takes them into forgotten places beneath the Temple Mount. In the bowels of Jerusalem, Godefroi is forced to fight a member of the Arabic cabal who are the current custodians of the keystone.

While the fractious elements of the Christian army and clergy vie for control of the city, Godefroi's bodyguard—Achambaud de St. Amand—is attacked and grievously injured. Godwera—the wife of Godefroi's brother, who was thought to have perished during the siege of Antioch—is forced to tend to Achambaud while Etienne—the fifth and final member of Hugues' sacred points—struggles to unlock the secrets of a box bearing the five-pointed seal of Solomon.

Godefroi's adversary, Count Raymond de Toulouse, who was appointed by Pope Urban to lead the crusade, presses his claim to rule Jerusalem. While Godefroi rallies his supporters to counter Raymond's claim, Hugues is approached by one of the surviving members of the Arabic cabal. Knowing his quest for the keystone is doomed without their guidance, Hugues allows them to smuggle him out of Jerusalem amidst a cartload of corpses. But on their way to Khirbet Qumran, the ancient settlement of the Essene on the shore of the Dead Sea, Hugues and his captors are ambushed by assassins and Gamaliel, a fallen angel and one of the five Lords of Severity. Only Hugues and Umayr—the leader of the Arabic cabal—survive the attack.

Just over two hundred years later in 1307, Bertrand de Châtillon-sur-Seine is initiated into the Brotherhood of the Temple of Solomon. During his solitary vigil, a vision of an ethereal tree shaped like a candlestick with three branches appears in the stained-glass window of the small chapel. Unidentified brothers accost Bertrand and give him an ultimatum: either defile the cross and join the Salt Lines, or remain forever ignorant of the true purpose of their Order.

The next morning, Bertrand is anointed as a chevalier—or knight—of the Order. Meeting with Everard—the Commanderie's Preceptor—it becomes clear that Bertrand's family are prominent members of the Salt Lines. That evening, Bertrand and Rémi—his bodyguard and mentor since childhood—are roused in the middle of the night. Dressed for battle, they sneak out of the Commanderie via a tunnel in the company of two strangers, one of whom Bertrand can tell is a woman.

The brutal suppression of the *Ordre du Temple* has begun in France. Roustan—an agent of Guillaume de Nogaret, Keeper of the Seals and chief adviser to King Philippe IV—arrives at the Commanderie in search of a woman called Salome. Roustan pursues Everard's men and a pitched battle takes place near the Marne River. Overwhelmed by superior numbers, Salome magically transports the few remaining survivors of Bertrand's Commanderie along a leyline to a new location.

Mortally injured, Everard urges Bertrand to protect Salome. Salome's bodyguard also dies in the aftermath of battle and she binds Bertrand as her new 'Shroud'. Rémi argues against aiding Salome, deeming her a witch, but he refuses to abandon Bertrand.

Travelling across country to avoid the King's soldiers, Bertrand's small party stumbles across the estate of Justine de Fontette, Bertrand's former lover and the reason he was assigned to the chaste Order. A fraught reunion takes place, during which Bertrand learns that his brethren are being rounded up across France. Despite the risk to her position, Justine eventually decides to let Bertrand and his companions go, although Roustan descends upon her chateau and burns it to the ground.

Watching the bonfire of Chateau Fontette from a distance, Bertrand struggles with guilt, assuming Justine has been killed for aiding him. With his former life in ashes, he agrees to take Salome to England, where she believes the secret of the keystone can finally be laid to rest. However, Salome remains vague on how this might be accomplished, and indeed the true nature of the artefact. Bertrand becomes determined to unravel her tightly held secrets, if only to make sense of the grievous losses he has suffered since crossing her path.

First comes the Shroud,
Second the Keystone,
Third the Test,
Unto eternity,
'Til we may rest.

Translated from Hebrew.
Author unknown.

CHAPTER 1

24 July 1099

The fortress of Alamut

The Imam of Alamut shuffled across the rooftop of his tower to keep warm. Flesh was weak: he had known this when he had decided to bind his spirit to a youthful body so long ago. It had placed limitations upon him, but he had learned much from the experience.

Knowledge was the only key that could unlock his prison. This he knew beyond doubt. Brute force, manipulation, even begging for absolution had all failed. Understanding was the key. And to understand, he needed to be human...for a time.

A small patch in the night sky bulged, and after a moment of resistance, the darkness tore open.

Ordinary human eyes would not have detected the tear. At best, a man might glance up at the sky, inexplicably unsettled by something far beyond the realms of his five senses. With innate ability and the appropriate training, a mortal might learn to detect the subtle rift. Perhaps they would notice a slight blurring as the gateway opened, but no more than that.

The Old Man was anything but ordinary.

The tear in the fabric of Malkuth stabilised into a slit of intense emptiness. The darkness of the night sky paled against this searing absence.

The Imam stared up at the gateway. Even in human form, the emptiness of the broken sphere called to him. That absence was not sentient. It was not aware in any way he could comprehend. And yet...

...it seemed to whisper his name.

Not the one he had adopted in this life, but his true, ancient name. The emptiness called to him now, reeling him in with frightening remorselessness.

The Old Man clung to his tired flesh like an exhausted warrior clutches his shield. To succumb to the call of Abaddon now would waste the years of effort and sacrifice he had made in enduring a human lifetime. This body could not sustain him much longer though. Now that the Franj had arrived, it was imperative that the plans he had laid were put in motion. He must deny his essential nature for a little longer.

A speck appeared within the gateway. It expanded rapidly, resolving into the figure of a man wreathed in fog. The visitor squeezed through the gateway and the tear in Malkuth snapped shut. The Old Man sagged against the parapet in relief as his stumbling heart lurched in his chest.

No, it would not be long before he returned to his natural form.

The cloudy figure drifted down to the tower. Fog coiled around its head and body, shrouding the man's features. Beneath the mist, the Old Man caught glimpses of mottled skin. The patchwork flesh belonged to people of a dozen different races. A deep cut, only partly healed, oozed blood along his left shoulder.

"I see your form is waning, Sammael," the visitor said. "It won't be long before you re-join us from your little exile."

"Don't use my name while I remain tethered to this world, Gamaliel. I am simply the Imam in this place."

A gap in the fog drifted across Gamaliel's face and his blistered lips sneered. "I still don't understand what's to be gained from this sad little experiment." Mist coiled about his arm and wove through his crooked fingers as he gestured towards the fortress beneath them. "If it's earthly power you seek, you could claim something grander than this."

"Clarity can be found in solitude," the Imam countered. "Given the nature of your corruption, Gamaliel, I can hardly expect you to appreciate that."

Gamaliel's green eyes glittered between whorls of mist. "Of course, how foolish of me." He gave the Old Man a mock bow. "While the course of history is changing, your solution is to hide in an isolated fortress and bind yourself to a body that should have expired years ago." His laugh was as cold as the emptiness of the broken shells. "Forgive me if I don't worship at the altar of your brilliance."

"As usual, Gamaliel, your imagination extends to only what you see." The Old Man's pulse was taking a long time to slow. "The time of testing is not yet upon us. However, the Christians represent a new spoke in the wheel."

"They're an irrelevance." The fog writhed around Gamaliel. "The cycle of testing is a constant. It grinds us all into oblivion."

"Perhaps not."

The Old Man gazed towards the west. He could almost see the tide washing across the Moslem world. Humanity was so limited, yet those limitations had provided a fresh perspective. He understood mankind, and how it could be manipulated, better than ever before.

"Let us go inside if you wish to debate philosophy. Dying from a chill now would be inconvenient." The Old Man moved to the top of the stairs.

Gamaliel shook his head. "In all honesty, it's disturbing to see you reduced to this."

"We've already been cast down. What's one further rung?" The Imam took the steps down to his private chamber. A fire burned in the hearth and candles glimmered in sconces around the walls. The blue rug was dull in the dim light and its silver star little more than a suggestion within the weave. He shuffled over to the fire.

"You've taken a wound," he said, assuming Gamaliel had drifted silently after him. "For once, it doesn't appear self-inflicted."

"I met with some resistance."

"Really?" The Old Man turned. Here, in the warm candlelight of his chamber, Gamaliel seemed less substantial. He was more of an absence, a blurring at the edges of sight, than a presence. "I trust you were still able to dispatch the old cabal as I requested."

Gamaliel's left hand clenched around a tendril of mist. "Only one survived: the Qāḍī."

"That's...unfortunate. The Qāḍī is dangerous. How did he manage to escape?"

"I don't have to explain myself to you, Sammael." Gamaliel drifted across the chamber. "Especially when you failed to tell me you sent your own assassins. Your little fortress is an irrelevance, not even a thread in the tapestry of history."

"What I've built here," the Old Man replied in a flat voice, "will long outlive my death. Ideologies are much harder to destroy than fortresses." He jabbed a finger at Gamaliel. "Even now, Imams and Emirs are falling beneath the blades of my most trusted servants. Every execution will occur in a public place so the masses can witness the slaughter. Fear sweeps through Damascus and Aleppo. The most enlightened cities in the world will learn that faith can be tempered into a hard edge that strikes down all who oppose it. It is a lesson that will echo throughout history."

"More words, as usual, Sammael." Gamaliel approached the Old Man. "Yet we're still bound to our prison in Abaddon. You promised me release if I helped you, but all I hear is petty human politics."

5

The Old Man moved to the blue carpet and sat at the point of the star dedicated to Hod. "Will you sit and indulge me in my exile?"

Gamaliel hesitated and he glanced at the stairs leading back up the tower.

"I know Lilith and the other Lords await your report," the Old Man said with a smile. "If nothing else, staying a while longer will keep them guessing."

Gamaliel laughed. "Sometimes I think you would do better to hide your cunning, Sammael."

The Old Man inclined his head.

Gamaliel settled on the carpet, the fog blanketing his limbs. "You have a proposal, I take it."

"I do. You know what the Christians seek."

"Baphomet: Mercy's half of the keystone."

"Yes, although they do not grasp its essential nature. The hints I have left them were not that specific."

"Hints? What hints?"

"As I said, Gamaliel, you must look beyond the obvious." The Old Man threaded his fingers together. "These Christians are far more susceptible to manipulation than the educated Saracens or worldly Byzantines. Precipitating their invasion only required patience and time."

"What did you do?" Gamaliel demanded.

The Old Man gave him a dry smile. "Massacre a few Christian pilgrims here and there. Convince the Caliph al-Hakim to destroy the holiest church in Christendom. And plant the suggestion of a fabulous treasure pre-dating Christianity in the minds of the great Counts in the west." The Old Man spread his hands wide. "And so, here we are."

"To what end?"

The Old Man leaned forward. "The vessel must leave this land where the old lore is still remembered. Let the Christians take possession of it and return to their homeland. They are ignorant of its purpose and power. Only then will we be successful in wresting it from the grasp of Mercy."

Gamaliel mulled it over and eventually nodded. "Yes, I see the wisdom in not trying to possess the vessel as it is moved. If we wait until the testing, the servants of Mercy won't have time to counter us."

"My thoughts exactly."

A burning log popped in the hearth. The Old Man said, "But we'll need someone to infiltrate their fraternity from the outset. Someone who can corrupt their organisation from within."

"No." Gamaliel recoiled. "I won't bind myself to one flesh as you have done."

"You must," the Old Man replied. "My time in this body is almost over. And if not you, then who? Would you recommend Tagiriron, with his temperamental outbursts and the subtlety of a battering ram? Or perhaps Lilith, with her insatiable passions that warp her judgement. Even worse, Orev Zarak, who would split the fraternity asunder before they thought themselves safe." The Old Man shook his head. "No, it can only be you, Gamaliel. Decay and corruption have always been your way. You must form the rotten core."

"No. Existing solely in the sphere of Malkuth is too limiting. It is an unnecessary sacrifice."

"Yes, your powers will be limited," the Old Man replied, "but you'll also escape the scrutiny of Mercy. It's the only way to ensure our plans remain undiscovered."

"Even so." Gamaliel's outline rippled. "Sammael, you can't ask this of me."

"Why can't I?" He thumped the carpet with the flat of his open palm. "I ask nothing that I haven't already given." The Old Man reined in his anger. "Gamaliel, we're so close. Another century, maybe two, and we'll be free. What are a few decades in mortal form against that?"

Gamaliel absorbed this in silence. Even the tendrils of fog that wound around his body stilled. Eventually he said, "You've chosen my target, I presume."

"Of course." The Old Man could not suppress his grin. "Someone young, ambitious and well-placed. An intelligent soul, yet riddled with doubt. Taking possession of his flesh should not prove taxing."

"And my reward?" Gamaliel asked.

"Once the two halves of the keystone are reunited, you and I will be the first to ascend from Abaddon."

The fog parted to reveal Gamaliel's startling green eyes. He searched the Old Man's face for long, uncomfortable moments. "If you deceive me, you will account for it. I promise you that."

"Do you really think I would suffer in this body for so many years just to deceive you?"

"Tell me the target's name," Gamaliel replied.

CHAPTER 2

24 July 1099

Godefroi's quarters

Godefroi woke to sunlight streaming through the window of his chamber. His breath was sour, his mouth parched, and an impressive headache pounded against his temples. Perhaps he had drunk more wine than he first thought.

His exchange with Godwera the night before returned to him in a rush.

Godefroi groaned and rolled onto his side. It seemed he had slept on the floor of his bed chamber.

"Ah, you're awake. That's good."

Godefroi blinked. Etienne's pale, earnest face slowly came into focus. The engineer was sitting on the windowsill of his bedroom. Dark circles ringed Etienne's eyes and unruly curls tangled around his ears.

"Water," Godefroi croaked.

"Yes, messire." Etienne turned to a silver carafe on the floor next to him, poured water into a delicate cup, and offered it to Godefroi.

Godefroi downed the fresh water with a grunt of gratitude.

"Here." Etienne offered a platter of food. "Eat these grapes. They're ripe and should help quell the nausea. The bread was only baked this morning and these dates will aid your digestion."

Godefroi sat up and accepted the food. The smell of fresh bread was delicious but the pounding in his head intensified. "How is Achambaud?" Godefroi asked, glancing towards his bed.

Achambaud was propped up on pillows and bathed in sunlight from the open window. A web of blue veins was visible beneath his waxy skin. Sweat plastered his black hair to his brow and temples.

"His condition remains unchanged," Etienne replied. "Godwera told me to make him drink water at regular intervals throughout the night, although I fear he hasn't taken much." Etienne's glance slid away from Achambaud, as if he could not bear the inevitability of what he saw.

"Where is she?" The memory of what he'd said to her was a bruise upon his conscience, unsightly and sensitive to the touch.

"She's resting." Etienne shifted on the floor. "I think she means to heal Achambaud today because she said she needed to gather her strength."

"Let her rest then." Godefroi tore off another piece of bread and chewed it savagely.

Etienne nodded and said tentatively, "Messire, a great number of people have gathered downstairs to petition you."

Godefroi sighed and rubbed his eyes. "Can't Gaston take care of such things?"

"He's organised each petitioner according to their status." Etienne stood and adjusted his brown tunic. "Some of them are quite important."

"The hounds already vie for scraps from my table." Godefroi stood and relieved himself in the chamber pot. The food and water had helped a little. Instead of feeling ghastly, he was now approaching merely indisposed.

"Some of the nobles include Provençals," Etienne added. "It might be wise not to keep them waiting."

Godefroi glowered at Etienne. "I already have a Chaplain who meddles in politics on a regular basis. I don't need more counsellors cut from that cloth."

Etienne bowed but stood his ground.

"What now?"

Etienne's gaze dropped to his feet. "I've discovered something about the object you retrieved from beneath the mosque."

Godefroi stilled. "Have you divined its purpose?"

"Yes, I believe so. Perhaps I can demonstrate?"

"Quickly then." Godefroi waved him over.

Etienne withdrew a leather sleeve from inside his tunic and upended it to reveal the grey spike they recovered from beneath the āl-Aqsa Mosque. Silver flecks glittered between the irregular grooves and symbols that marked its surface.

"Well?" Godefroi asked impatiently.

"I believe it's a key." Etienne's dark eyes sparkled with excitement.

"Impossible," Godefroi replied. "It has no teeth with which to turn a lock."

"None that we can see," Etienne countered.

"Explain."

"Even better, I can show you." Etienne withdrew a small pouch and tipped a pile of metal shavings onto the floor. "Watch what happens when the key approaches."

Etienne pressed the tapered end to the pile of shavings. Flakes of metal stuck to the surface. Etienne rotated the spike but the shavings didn't fall off.

"Is it a lodestone?" Godefroi asked in a low voice.

"I think so, although it's unlike any I've seen before." Etienne admired the spike in a shaft of sunlight. "So, if the lock it belongs to is also metal—"

"It will be drawn to it," Godefroi said.

"Precisely," Etienne said with a pleased smile, "but there's more." He wiped the iron filings from the spike and drew his belt knife. Holding the blade close to the edge of the spike, he said to Godefroi, "Watch closely".

Etienne touched the blade to the spike. As with the flakes of metal, the two were drawn towards one other. Once they were touching, Etienne slowly prised the knife away. "Do you see?" he asked in a low voice. "Just there, along this channel next to the knife."

Godefroi squinted. A section of the spike had lifted fractionally, coaxed out of hiding by the blade. Once Etienne's knife was removed, the raised section dropped back into its shallow channel.

"Why does it fall back like that?" Godefroi asked.

"I'm not sure," Etienne admitted. "Some internal mechanism draws each tooth inwards so that they remain hidden."

"Each tooth?" Godefroi asked. "You mean there is more than one?"

"Of course. There are five in total, one for each channel." He showed Godefroi the shallow grooves. "Each has tiny script written upon it that I can't decipher. And each tooth lines up with one corner of the star." Etienne tapped the cap at the end of the spike.

"One for each element of the soul," Godefroi mused.

"Just so." Etienne weighed the key in his hand. "Messire, it's my belief that if we orient the key in the correct fashion, each tooth shall be drawn outwards and the lock will open."

"And where is this lock?" Godefroi asked.

The delight dropped from Etienne's face. "I pray that Hugues is discovering this as we speak."

As always, the next step depended upon Hugues. Not so long ago the thought would have frustrated Godefroi, but today he had no heart for it. "Let me see it," he demanded.

Etienne handed the key to Godefroi. It was surprisingly heavy, and its surface was smooth like polished marble. Godefroi traced each groove with the tip of his index finger. What secrets would it unlock?

He had hoped for some kind of reaction, perhaps a thrill of recognition like the one he had experienced in the Holy Sepulchre or beneath āl-Aqsa. Instead, the key lay inert in his hand.

"Certainly it's a wondrous thing," Godefroi said thoughtfully, "but is it worth a man's life?" He handed it back to Etienne, who placed it back in the leather sleeve.

"You've done well," Godefroi said. "Find Godwera and bring her to me. And tell Gaston I'll receive the Provençals once I have observed my prayers at Terce."

Etienne bowed and left as Godefroi prepared to shoulder the burdens of rulership.

◆━━━━━━━━━━━◆

Godefroi splashed his face with warm rosewater left in a bowl and smoothed his blonde hair. His beard needed a trim, but having overslept, he lacked the time. He wore a simple linen tunic, finely made with bold black stitching, over well-cut hose. A bliaut might have been more appropriate, although the heat made them impractical except for the most formal ceremonies.

Achambaud had not stirred throughout his preparations, even though Godefroi spoke to him as if he were awake. Perhaps he should ask for the Duke of Flanders' physician: the man was rumoured to be highly skilled.

Godwera knocked on the doorframe. "Come in," he said awkwardly. She trudged past him, head bowed beneath her cowl. Godefroi closed the door and leaned against it. She turned to face him, removed her cowl, and cradled one hand in the other.

"This disguise will not serve for much longer," Godwera said. "Now that you've been appointed the Defender of the Holy Sepulchre, your household will become full of people we can't trust."

She was right. Without Hugues to shelter her, it was only a matter of time before her identity was discovered.

"Can Etienne hide you somewhere?"

Godwera shook her head. "He doesn't know who the other members of the Salt Lines are. Hugues kept them secret. And even if Etienne did, how long am I supposed to hide?"

"Only until Baldwin leaves. Once he's back in Edessa, we can bring you out of hiding. Maybe invent an identity for you. In Constantinople, I saw women who had changed the colour of their hair with dyes. We could—"

"Please stop," Godwera said, raising her palm. "I would be recognised.

Your enemies, especially Count Raymond, would use me to undermine you. Whoever becomes Patriarch would have no choice but to denounce you." She squared her shoulders. "I have thought deeply on this. For both our sakes, you must let me go."

"No!" Godefroi reined in his sudden anger. "With Hugues gone and Achambaud barely clinging to life, I need you close. You know what's at stake, probably better than I. Or don't you care?"

"Of course I care. I'm not suggesting we...abandon our vows." Godwera shook her head. "But our success depends upon your position, and my presence here is a threat to that."

Godefroi had no response to that. She was right. He knew it, yet he couldn't abandon his feelings for her.

"What do you intend?" he asked heavily.

She searched his face. "For now, I must attempt to heal Achambaud. If I'm successful, it will take me time to recover. I'm not sure how long. After that, and if Hugues hasn't returned, I think it best that I return to the Salt Lines. Someone must explain what's happened here."

"Of course," Godefroi snorted in disgust. "They demand everything I have and then ask for more."

"And yet look at what they've given you." Godwera gestured to the open window. "The Defender of the Holy Sepulchre."

Godefroi rolled his eyes. "And I thought debating with Hugues was difficult."

Godwera laughed, the sound light and breathless, with a note of uncertainty beneath it. Would he give up his new title for her? Cede his rule to Baldwin?

No, he would not. Nor could he. And they both knew it.

"You've thought this all through, haven't you?" Godefroi couldn't look at her. He couldn't bear those knowing eyes.

"Yes. Many times. I have more opportunities for reflection than you. And I can't find a way for both of us to have what we want."

That statement was like a killing blow in single combat. The struggle was over: Godwera would not be part of his life, not if she was to find any fulfilment. And how could he deny her that if he truly loved her?

"Very well." He gathered his courage and dignity. "Petitioners are waiting downstairs. What do you need to heal Achambaud?"

She swallowed at his distant tone. "Nothing but privacy. The effort will likely exhaust me. If you could send Etienne to watch over me perhaps. Hopefully while both Achambaud and I recover."

"I'll send for him," Godefroi promised. "He'll make sure no one enters my chamber."

"I wish Hugues were here." Godwera shot an uncertain look at Godefroi.

He did not have the energy to be angry. "So do I."

Godwera smoothed the habit over her hips. "To heal Achambaud, I must tap into the power of Netzach, one of the Sephirot." Her pale cheeks flushed. "The connection is more powerful when I'm...close to him."

"Go on," Godefroi said with a frown.

She avoided his gaze. "The healing process requires direct contact. The more, the better."

"I don't understand."

"Skin to skin," she said, a flush rising up her neck.

Jealousy seethed through Godefroi and it took him a moment to wrestle it under control. "Then do it. I would permit almost anything to save Achambaud's life."

Godwera took two quick steps towards him, grabbed his hand and kissed the back of his fingers. "Thank you, Godefroi. For everything." Suddenly self-conscious, she released his hand and stepped back. He hated this awkwardness between them.

"Help Achambaud," he said. "But do it now. I'm not letting Etienne watch this."

Godwera hesitated, saw the expression on his face, and nodded. With a shy glance at Godefroi, she lifted the hem of her cassock and shrugged out of the coarse wool. Beneath the austere clothing she wore a thin linen shift and a chemise that were almost transparent in the sunlight. Strips of linen had been wrapped around her chest, flattening her breasts to make her figure appear more masculine. Godefroi ached at the silhouette of her curving hips and the way her breasts bulged sideways.

She knelt next to Achambaud and drew the blanket back. Sweat saturated his bandages. Godwera touched his brow. "Achambaud, it's Godwera. I'm going to make you well, but I need your help."

Godefroi moved to the far side of the bed and knelt opposite Godwera. He took Achambaud's hand and squeezed his fingers. Achambaud did not react.

"Achambaud, I need you to focus on my presence." Godwera glanced at Godefroi. He gave her an encouraging nod.

Achambaud's breathing was shallow.

"What I'm about to attempt is dangerous," Godwera said to Godefroi. "Especially for someone so close to the veil. Don't interfere, no matter what happens."

"How dangerous?"

"It doesn't matter. I have to try." She brushed the dark hair back from Achambaud's forehead. "He'll die soon if I don't."

Godefroi weighed the options. "How can I help?" he asked reluctantly.

"Close the curtains and carry me to my sleeping chamber," Godwera replied. "It might be some time before I wake. I trust you'll honour my modesty."

"Of course." Godefroi pulled the heavy drapes closed. He lifted the divan and carried it over to the bed.

Godwera cut away Achambaud's sweaty undertunic. The bandage wrapped beneath his sword arm was caked with old blood, but the wound appeared to have closed over. The deeper injury to his thigh was much worse. When Godwera cut away the linen strips, she discovered the wound was inflamed and red with infection. Achambaud flinched and moaned beneath her gentle touch.

"Are you sure you can help him?" Godefroi asked.

"I have to try." Godwera removed her linen shift and chemise. Using the knife, she cut away the strips of cotton that bound her figure. Her skin was pale with a light dusting of freckles across her breasts. Lean muscles shifted along her arms and shoulders. Godefroi's mouth was dry again and his breath fluttered in the back of his throat like a trapped bird.

Godwera boldly met his stare. "You must forget this, Godefroi. It may seem like a moment of intimacy, but I assure you that it's not." She lifted her chin. "This is for Achambaud, not you."

Godefroi dragged his hungry gaze from the mesmerising curves of her body. "I understand," he said in a thick voice. He averted his gaze reluctantly and focused on Achambaud. The image of her was branded into his mind. He knew it would torture him for many nights to come.

Godwera stroked Achambaud's forehead. "Reach out to me, brother." Godwera lay down on her side next to him and pressed against his clammy skin. She closed her eyes and her lips moved soundlessly. Achambaud remained still, oblivious to her presence. Godwera moved her right hand over Achambaud's wounded leg. This time he did not stir or cry out.

Godefroi squinted at the two of them. A pale, yellow nimbus surrounded Godwera's abdomen, just beneath the sternum. With the heavy drapes drawn, it could not be a shaft of sunlight.

Godwera drew a shuddering breath. Pressure built inside the room. It gathered at the back of Godefroi's eyeballs and squeezed against his eardrums.

Sweat beaded across Godwera's brow and her breathing became ragged. The pressure shifted, compressing into a single point. Godefroi felt a pushing sensation above his solar plexus, as if his ribs were attempting to crack open. His breathing became fast and shallow, but he did not feel any pain.

A silver tendril emerged from Godwera's navel. Godefroi gaped in astonishment. The stem lengthened as it quested towards Achambaud, and it reminded Godefroi of a snake tasting the air.

Godwera's tendril hovered over Achambaud's wounded leg and a bud appeared at its tip, pulsing with yellow light. The bud sprouted open into a flower with five petals. Godefroi leaned closer. In the centre of Godwera's flower, where the ovary and stamen should be, was a silver whorl of light. It was tiny, little more than a pinprick.

She placed her hand above the flower and pressed it against Achambaud's leg. He arched upwards, his mouth open in silent agony. Godefroi grabbed Achambaud's shoulders before recalling Godwera's warning: *Don't interfere, no matter what you see.*

He released Achambaud, hating feeling so helpless.

Convulsions wracked Godwera's body and her grip on Achambaud's leg tightened until her knuckles were white. Achambaud writhed beneath her grip, his spine arching until it seemed only his shoulders and heels pressed against the bed. Blue veins stood out at Godwera's temples.

What if Achambaud's hurts were beyond Godwera's skill? Perhaps he should interfere? Godwera's attempt to draw him back might kill her.

He loved them both, but he needed Godwera more. Godefroi moved around the bed, intending to break the connection between patient and healer. Before he could reach her, Godwera released her grip and the yellow flower withdrew from Achambaud's leg. Its petals folded inwards, hiding the whirling light. The tendril retracted into Godwera's navel and the yellow nimbus faded. It all happened within two heartbeats, maybe three.

Achambaud sank back to the bed with a long sigh. His breathing steadied and became regular. Godwera slumped against the mattress, her head lolling to one side. With infinite care, he gathered up her boneless figure and placed her on the divan. Her eyelids fluttered and her breathing was fast.

"Godwera," Godefroi breathed. "Can you hear me?"

She did not respond. He took a blanket and covered her nudity. In that moment, she seemed so small and fragile. Yet she possessed a power he could not begin to understand. A fierce protectiveness tightened in his chest. He would not summon Etienne or Gaston. The petitioners, noblemen and clergy alike, could await his pleasure. His place was here, by her side, whether she wanted it or not.

Godefroi checked on Achambaud. The wound on his leg was not as ragged as before and it looked as if the skin had begun to knit together. Achambaud's forehead felt cooler to the touch and he was no longer sweating.

"You're going to be all right," Godefroi whispered. "Both of you. I promise."

CHAPTER 3

24 July 1099

Khirbet Qumran

Hugues followed Umayr for two nights through the arid, empty landscape of the Judean foothills. They travelled mostly at night, seeking shade and rest when the sun rose. Hugues burned with questions, but the Qādī remained grim-faced and rebuffed all attempts at conversation. Hugues choose not to press Umayr out of respect for the man's loss.

They slept in caves during the day where the heat couldn't reach them. Hugues' dreams were plagued by shadows and the prickle of a thousand fiery needles. The memory of the terrible demon that had slain Umayr's cabal was never far from his thoughts.

By night, they travelled through ravines or skirted dry watercourses. Once, when they had no choice but to cross a ridge, Umayr insisted they wait until clouds blocked out the moon. Using strips of cloth, he muffled the horses' hooves and demanded silence. They crossed without incident, although the sense of being watched—whether real or imagined—was constant.

During the second night after the attack in the ravine, Umayr led them into a narrow gorge. The starlight leached the colour from the yellow and beige stone, and outcrops reminded Hugues of broken bones protruding from the ground. The gorge ended in a steep drop to a plain dotted with palm trees. Beyond that, moonlight glittered across water. They had reached the shore of the Dead Sea.

Hugues glanced at Umayr. "I take it Qumran lies below."

Umayr nodded, although he didn't appear pleased they had finally reached their destination.

Hugues stroked the neck of his mount. "What now?"

"Now we walk." Umayr dismounted and led his horse down a narrow path that was little more than a goat track. It was only wide enough for one at a time and switched back half a dozen times before reaching the edge of the palm trees.

The shore was at least a hundred yards distant when they reached the bottom. Umayr remained tense and silent as they remounted and passed through the palm trees. Hugues felt a mounting sense of excitement. The Essene had once lived on the shore of the Dead Sea. Was Umayr taking him to one of their fabled sites?

They crested a gentle rise and emerged from the trees. Hugues caught a glimpse of low, crumbling walls. Broken masonry and fallen stones littered the ground. The original buildings had been sizable, large enough to accommodate a community of perhaps a hundred. The sea was closer here. It was only a short walk to the black mud that marked the shoreline.

"Khirbet Qumran," Umayr said. "In Arabic, the ruins of Qumran."

"This was a monastery." Hugues spotted cisterns and the foundations of what could have been a refectory. On the far side, a tower had once stood watch. "It belonged to the Essene."

"Yes. The Romans destroyed it after the Jewish War more than a thousand years ago."

The horses trotted closer and Hugues searched the weathered stone for signs of habitation. Somewhere hidden amid these ruins was the essence of wisdom that Firyal had promised. Hugues licked his dry lips. Another step closer. Another link in the chain that joined him to the artefact.

The horses picked their way through the debris and entered a gap in one wall. Umayr dismounted and gave his horse an affectionate pat. He untied the straps of his saddle and dropped it on the ground.

Hugues dismounted as well. "The Essene, they were holy men who lived separate to the rest of Jewish society. Why would the Romans destroy them?"

Umayr snorted as he removed his saddle blanket and placed it on the dusty ground. "They weren't as isolated as you think. Once, in a time that's still remembered, one of the gates of Jerusalem leading to Mount Sion was named after the Essene."

"They had a community on the outskirts of Jerusalem?"

"They possessed more than just a gate." Umayr's mount whickered as he brushed its coat with long, practised strokes. "The inheritors of Abraham's wisdom had an entire quarter in the south-west of Jerusalem, although they were careful never to wield too much influence during the Roman occupation."

Inheritors of Abraham's wisdom. Umayr spoke those words so casually, yet Hugues understood their significance. Abraham was said to be the father of the Kabbalah, the keeper of divine secrets.

"Is that so?" Hugues said in a neutral tone as he unsaddled his horse. "So large numbers lived inside Jerusalem then."

"Not large numbers, no." Umayr moved to the far side of his steed. "Like any sect, only a few were initiated into their mysteries."

Hugues stilled. "You mean they knew how to wield the five chambers of the Pentemychos."

"Of course." Umayr checked the hooves of his horse. "You didn't think the Salt Lines were the only ones who knew about them, did you?"

Hugues circled around his horse so he could see Umayr's face. "Of course not. I have studied the sacred geometry of Pythagoras' Pentemychos and the hidden Seal of Solomon. I know they symbolise the five lower Sephirot in the Tree of Life."

Umayr grunted. He tethered his mount to a large rock and gestured to Hugues. "Come. If we're to have this discussion, there's a more appropriate place."

Hugues hastily secured his mount and followed Umayr through a maze of broken stone. Shards of pottery crunched beneath his sandals and dust coated his feet. They stopped at what had once been a long, rectangular chamber in the heart of the ruins.

"This was their Scriptorium," Umayr said. "Sometimes I like to come here to imagine what this place must have been like. I can almost feel their bright hopes for their future." Umayr's expression became bleak. Hugues was struck again by the man's enormous capacity for sadness.

Umayr sat on a broad, flat rock and gestured for Hugues to sit. Unable to find a suitable seat, Hugues sat in the dirt.

A stillness settled over the ruins as Umayr gazed into the distance. The night was waning. Despite his impatience, Hugues was content to sit at Umayr's feet and wait. A sense of peace stole over him. He had not felt this way since leaving Champagne.

Whatever claims the Holy Roman Church might make, Hugues knew Umayr was a deeply spiritual man. His sense of honour and morality was as finely honed as any sword. How could he fail to respect such a man?

"Umayr," Hugues said softly, speaking on impulse, "I'm sorry for all that we have inflicted upon your people." A breeze sighed through the ruins. "Please forgive me. And those I represent."

Umayr bowed his head.

Guilt twisted through Hugues and a terrible self-loathing, like none he had ever known before, churned in his gut. The need to repent, to ask for absolution, was a physical demand. Hugues shuffled onto his knees, head bowed, and silently begged for forgiveness.

After a moment's hesitation, Umayr placed one hand on Hugues' head. The connection was light, but an instinctive recognition resonated through Hugues. Umayr, so different in culture and upbringing, was still a kindred spirit. They both valued knowledge and believed in the intrinsic nobility of humanity. In every sense of the word, they were brothers.

Emotion glistened in Umayr's eyes as he studied Hugues. The wrinkles carved into the hard planes of his face softened, as if some internal belligerence had finally collapsed.

"You don't need to apologise," Umayr said. "It's the nature of history, the great cycle we are doomed to repeat." He drew in a deep, steadying breath. "If you would honour the memory of my cabal, and the legacy of my people, then do not seek the wisdom eternal for personal gain. Remember that it belongs to all the people of Creation, and you are but a temporary guardian. This is the only way to repay your Christian debt."

"I swear it to you," Hugues murmured.

"Very well." Umayr glanced towards the east. "It will be light soon. Ask your questions now so your mind is clear when your trial begins." He folded his gnarled hands in his lap.

"The demon that attacked us," Hugues said. "How did you repel it?"

Umayr leaned back against the stone. "If you know of the Tree of Life, you must be aware that the Fallen are five archangels who fell in punishment for forcing Daat, or knowledge, upon the lower part of the tree." He lifted a cautionary finger. "So, they are not demons but a manifestation of the emptiness between the spheres. As empty husks, the Fallen abhor the life granted to mankind. Where there is light, they are the darkness. Where mercy is offered, they dispense only severity. The Fallen seek to corrupt that which is best in us."

Hugues shivered at the memory of the demon's touch. "That doesn't tell me how you repel such a creature."

Umayr sighed. "You don't repel emptiness. You fill it."

"I don't understand."

"A Lord of Severity can only be thwarted by summoning its counterpart, one of the Lords of Mercy. Rarely though, do they heed our call."

"Then what was that pillar of light?" Hugues asked.

"An aspect of the Beni Elohim, the angelic choir that corresponds to the Sephirah known as Hod." Umayr gave Hugues an appraising look. "If you retrieve the essence, the summoning incantation will become clear to you. It's effectively the same for each of the lower five Sephirot. Ask your next question."

"Firyal spoke of a resting place," Hugues said. "If the artefact isn't here, where is it hidden?"

Umayr shook his head. "You must retrieve the essence first. Think! What do you need to know right now? Here, in this place." He gestured towards the ruins surrounding them.

Hugues thought for a moment. The only thing that mattered was finding the essence, whatever it was.

"How do I locate the essence?"

Umayr gave him a gap-toothed smile. "That's better. At dawn, you must leave on foot. You may take whatever possessions you deem necessary. The essence is hidden somewhere in the hills overlooking the Dead Sea. You must return it to me here, in this scriptorium, before the first star is visible in the night sky. You have one day. No more."

"That's ridiculous," Hugues cried. "The coastline runs for miles and I don't even know what the essence is. You've set an impossible task."

"It's not impossible. And you'll know the essence when you see it. I was as ignorant as you when I undertook this trial."

Hugues stilled. "You found the essence?"

"Long ago. Longer than you can imagine." A smile hovered at the edge of Umayr's lips.

"Didn't you protest?"

"Of course." Umayr chuckled. "Not that it made any difference. My predecessor was as intractable as you'll find me to be."

"But what if I don't find it?"

Umayr's expression hardened. "Then Ein Sof, He who is unknowable, does not wish for the guardianship to pass to your people."

"Are you sure it isn't *you* who doesn't wish me to succeed?" If their roles had been reversed, wouldn't he blame Umayr for the deaths of Firyal and the other members of the cabal?

Umayr rose to his feet, his expression unreadable. "The gift of Hod is clarity of thought. I suggest you embrace it." He strode off through the ruins.

◆━━━━•━━━━◆

Hugues could find no sleep in the quiet ruins of Qumran. The ground was hard and his mind was restless. Hugues offered a prayer to the

Trinity, but it was half-hearted, and he derived no comfort from it.

Giving up, he tossed the saddle blanket over his shoulders and pulled it tight around his Saracen robe. A breeze wound through the ruins and dust devils whirled in the corners of broken walls like the questions that spun through his mind.

He wondered whether Godwera had been able to save Achambaud. Was Godefroi crowned ruler of Jerusalem, and if so, would he ever trust Hugues again? And what of these Lords of Severity? Why had the Salt Lines failed to prepare him for such a thing? The more he learned, the more ignorant he felt.

A new doubt crept into his mind.

What would happen if he were successful? There could be no triumphant march back to Rome with the artefact on display. Did the leaders of the Salt Lines, the great Counts of Champagne and Anjou, and others whose identity remained a closely guarded secret, understand the ramifications of success?

Look for the patterns in history, the scholars had said.

Umayr had said something similar, yet his observation was not drawn from fragments of ancient texts. No, it was drawn from personal, and clearly painful, experience.

What if the artefact was indeed a burden, as Umayr had suggested? If that were true, perhaps the Salt Lines were mistaken in thinking they could wield it.

In the emptiness of Qumran, where the breeze whispered of ancient times, Hugues dared to ask a question he had never voiced before.

"Lord, am I truly serving Your Will?"

The words were little more than a murmur in the night. Yet they were offered with an open, penitent heart. Never had he offered a prayer so pure in its absolute humility.

Hugues waited, straining for an answer, for any kind of sign to guide his way. Dust spun and settled in eddies. Hard stones pressed into the soles of his feet while cold points of light mocked him in the vast canopy of the sky.

Profoundly alone, Hugues shivered and wrestled with his doubts in the dark.

CHAPTER 4

26 July 1099

Caves of Qumran

It was a relief when dawn finally stained the eastern horizon.

Hugues had packed his provisions, a flask of water, some hard bread and goat's cheese, candles and flint, and a sturdy coil of rope. Umayr had given him a rough hemp sack, which Hugues had tied off with a cord and slung across his back. Hugues' only weapon was the assassin's knife, which he carried in the sheath of his old belt knife.

"Here, drink this." Umayr offered him a leather flask. "According to the ritual, I can offer no help during the daylight."

Hugues took the proffered drink without comment. The brew was dark brown in colour, and he thought he detected cinnamon and cloves. Hugues swallowed quickly and grimaced at the bitter aftertaste.

"That's enough." Umayr retrieved the flask and stoppered it. "The victuals should sustain you until early afternoon."

"Thank you." Hugues rubbed his bleary eyes as an odd warmth spread through his stomach.

"You slept badly."

Hugues nodded, although it was a statement, not a question.

Umayr clapped him on the shoulder. "So did I the night before." The horizon was brightening. "Hugues, there's one last thing you must do before you begin."

Umayr had never used his name before.

"Follow me." Umayr led him through the ruins to what had been a small building on the edge of the monastery. Only the foundations and a set of steps descending into the dusty ground remained.

"This was once a cistern filled with water," Umayr explained. "The Essene would purify their bodies by washing here every day. They would pray at each step before moving on to the next."

"Seven steps," Hugues said. "The number of the divine."

Umayr nodded. "The final step would see them totally immersed in water, a literal and spiritual purification. I think it's fitting you begin your journey at the bottom, don't you?"

Hugues moved down to the seventh step. He offered a short prayer that asked for guidance and made the sign of the cross. He repeated the gesture at each step.

Hugues scanned the range of foothills running parallel with the shore. Where should he start?

"Sometimes it doesn't matter how you begin," Umayr said, "only that you do." He folded his hands together. "Go now. I'll be waiting."

Hugues nodded and strode out of Khirbet Qumran.

The range of hills was clearly too extensive to explore in a single day. He had to find a way to narrow the focus of his search. Hugues strode across the rough ground, thinking hard.

The best place to start was with what he knew for certain. First, Umayr had told him the essence was hidden somewhere in the hills overlooking the Dead Sea. Second, he only had a day to find it. Why? Was sunlight essential to locating its hiding place? Perhaps, although this notion was troubling. What if it could only be found at a certain time of the day? If he was not in the right position at the right time, he could miss his opportunity. Then again, having the trial take place during the day could be merely symbolic. A rejection of the absence of Daat, perhaps.

Hugues kicked a small stone in frustration. It tumbled across the ground and out of sight. He fought to remain calm.

Given the precious nature of the essence, it made sense that it would be stored in a safe place. Not only that, it was probably difficult to reach to prevent accidental discovery. Although on the other hand, the Essene must have had a means of reaching it when needed.

He scrutinised the steep foothills. A cave would be a secure repository, but over half a dozen of varying sizes were visible and he had barely left the outskirts of the ruins. He would never have time to search them all.

Two foothills met to form a shallow gully not far from the ruins. The infrequent rains must wash down from the foothills here and drain into the sea. Perhaps that was why the Essene had settled here. With no better option, he followed the watercourse.

Umayr said that he would need the clarity of Hod to discover the essence. But his mind was anything but clear; far too many possibilities raced through his skull.

Hugues stopped where the watercourse emerged from the gully. A jumble of loose rocks blocked his way. The sun was climbing behind his shoulder on the far side of the Dead Sea. He could feel its heat on his back. Soon it would become unbearably hot. He did not have all day to figure this out.

———————◆———————

The day wore on as Hugues continued to search for some sign in the cliffs. This arid landscape was nothing like the fertile lands of Champagne that he was accustomed to. All life and colour seemed to have been bleached from the soil. The occasional bush, black and stunted, provided the only relief from the beige and ochre rock that marked the edge of the Judean foothills.

The air shimmered with heat. Hugues paused in the shade of an outcrop and sipped from his flask of water. Little remained and he resisted gulping down the last precious drops. The sun rode high overhead and he was no closer to determining the location of the essence.

He had walked in both directions from Khirbet Qumran, hoping for a landmark that might provide a hint. Many caves dotted the steep slopes. In the heat of summer, they would be the only places that offered any respite. But there were so many. He could easily exhaust his energy exploring only a few of them.

No, there had to be a simpler way to locate the essence.

Hugues slumped to the dusty ground, drained by his journey from Jerusalem and lack of sleep. Umayr had made it plain he could not help in any way. A sudden thought struck Hugues: perhaps Umayr had, in his own inscrutable way.

Hugues recalled the ritual purification of seven steps. Clearly the Essene venerated water, which was not surprising in this dry land. And they had built their monastery next to a watercourse. Had they drawn the water for their cistern from it? And if so, would they view the gully the water cascaded down as a sacred place?

Perhaps.

Hugues hurried back towards the watercourse. The sun pounded his unprotected head and sweat dripped from his face as he shielded his eyes. He could see at least half a dozen openings that were large enough to be considered a cave. Which was the right one?

Hugues recalled what Umayr had said.

This was a test of Hod, the eighth Sephirah on the left pillar of the Tree of Life. Just as Godefroi had fought the old Saracen for mastery of Malkuth, now it was his turn to master Hod, the realm of the intellect. And if that were so...then the correct cave might be the eighth one to the left of Khirbet Qumran.

Hugues waited a moment, testing his idea for any flaws. Only someone indoctrinated in the mysteries of the Kabbalah could have made this connection.

With his back to Khirbet Qumran, Hugues counted the caves he could see. The eighth opening was high up the slope, not far below the summit, and smaller than some of the other caves. Was this the right one? The slope was steep and the last thirty yards were almost sheer. He did not have time to search another cave before sunset.

Hugues took a deep breath. Faith was what he needed now.

The incline was gentle at first, although it soon steepened as he reached the main rock face. Hugues squinted up at the cave. A direct route was impossible. He would need to switch back and forth up the slope, using the natural shelves of rock to rest. The last section, some ten to fifteen yards to the lip of the cave mouth, was a sheer climb. At that height, one slip would likely prove fatal.

Hugues shrugged off his sack and spread its contents on the rock. He had no appetite for the bread but took a final swig that emptied his water flask. He looped the coil of rope around one shoulder.

By the time he began his ascent, the sun was dropping towards the Judean foothills.

◆━━━━━━━━━━━━━━━━━━◆

Between the climb and the relentless heat, Hugues was drenched in sweat when he reached the final section. Blood trickled from a profusion of scratches that had scored his legs and arms. Dust caked his mouth and nostrils so that every breath he took seemed to suck a little more moisture from him, and dehydration had left him dangerously light-headed.

He rested for a moment, pressing his cheek against the warm rock and refusing to look down. The lip of the cave was tantalisingly close. To reach it, he would need to climb the sheer face with only small fissures in the rock for purchase. Hugues took ten long breaths.

"Please, God," Hugues mumbled through cracked lips, "don't let me fail now. By Your Grace and Will, lend me the strength to serve You. Amen."

He squeezed his eyes closed and gathered his determination.

He would not fail. He would not fall.

Hugues tested his first foothold. The crevice he had chosen was not quite wide enough, so he angled his shoe into the gap. Once he felt secure, he pushed with his leg and grasped the handholds he had picked immediately above his head. His fingers wedged into smaller cracks.

Climbing was not a pastime he had indulged in as a youth, but he had met monks who had spent their childhoods on the slopes of the Pyrenees. According to them, the golden rule was to ensure the climber's weight remained centred above their feet. Hugues immediately saw the wisdom of this advice. While his hands could steady his torso, his arms lacked the strength to drag him up the rockface. Finding secure purchase for his feet was critical.

He examined the next section of rock. Picking the best handholds, he pushed off from his braced leg. Hugues' left hand tightened around a knob of rock. His right dug into a small depression. Once he felt steady, he jammed his free foot into another crack.

Another lift and grasp. Followed by another. And another.

His arms trembled from the strain and his feet ached from the contortions he forced upon them. The lip of the cave was close. Almost within reach. The only problem was he could not see another foothold.

Hugues searched for cracks or natural shelves of rock. Wind and rain had eroded the cliff, creating a smooth face. A few ridges marred its surface, but the accompanying troughs were no deeper than his fingernails. He could not trust his entire weight to such a tenuous grip.

A scream of frustration welled inside Hugues.

"Help me!" Hugues cried out in despair. His appeal drifted down the gully and was lost amidst shimmering waves of heat. Nothing moved inside the cave. Not that he had expected anyone. He could not imagine a more remote or desolate location.

What if he gave up and returned later, with horses and men and ropes? Why risk his life in a futile gesture? No. Umayr had been adamant that he must return to Khirbet Qumran by nightfall. How would he face Umayr's contempt if he returned empty-handed?

So up then.

A final surge, hoping for a handhold that he could not see.

A leap of faith.

Hugues examined the rockface through slitted eyes. Yes, it might work. If he pushed off hard, he should be able to just reach the edge of the cave mouth. Only God knew if there was something to hold onto. No time for prayer. The trembling in his arms was worsening. His left foot, wedged in a crevice, ached from the strain.

Hugues inhaled deeply while his heart raced.

Rock scraped against his chest as he pushed with all the strength in his left leg. His hands slapped over the edge of the rock platform at full stretch. His body teetered, delicately balanced on his extended leg.

The rock beneath his hands was too smooth to provide any purchase. No depressions, no ridges or knobs to hold onto. Hugues' fingertips scrabbled as his weight began to pull him backwards. Incredibly, they found something solid. He grasped the warm, curved object in desperation.

Was it metal?

His fingers threaded through a hole and suddenly he had a firm handhold. Using his right foot, he strained for purchase to relieve the weight on his arms. He found the edge of a plane of rock and braced his right foot against it. As Hugues pulled his left foot free, the rough stone tore open his leather shoe and claimed a layer of skin.

His right foot slipped as the plane of rock splintered. Fragments of stone tumbled down the slope and Hugues swung free, anchored only by the metal circle. With a supreme effort, he pulled his body up the lip of stone. His legs were a dead weight, dangling in the air. Each inch forward was a tiny victory.

Lungs heaving, arms burning, Hugues dragged himself into the cave mouth. When he finally swung his legs over and rolled onto his back, he collapsed, utterly spent. Air rattled through his heaving lungs and his body demanded water. But he was alive.

Hugues laughed. The wild, manic sound rattled in his chest and ended in a wracking cough. Death had stood in his shadow. Its cold fingers had almost closed around his neck.

His breathing slowly returned to normal. Hugues opened his eyes. The ruins appeared much smaller from this elevation. He could not see Umayr, but the Dead Sea glittered in the westering sun.

Hugues sat up and massaged his aching calves. Blood welled from his torn foot. Every joint from the tips of his fingers to the balls of his feet throbbed in complaint.

A rusted iron bolt ending in a circle had been driven into the rock. Tied to the top of this ring, where his fingers hadn't reached, was a frayed length of rope. The hemp was dark and weathered. The rope had been severed about a hand's span from the ring.

Hugues shrugged the coil of rope off his shoulder. He tied one end securely to the ring that guarded the entrance and left it coiled on the rock shelf. If all went well, his descent would be much easier.

The cave was a dark mystery that beckoned.

Hugues stepped inside to escape the breeze and used his flint and tinder to coax a small flame into life. The candle he had carried in his pouch had broken in half during his climb. He lit one end and ventured further into the narrow cave.

The opening was too low for him to stand upright. Crouching, he shuffled forward. Bird droppings littered the floor. The meagre light of his candle revealed a jagged ceiling. He saw no sign of tool marks, carvings or paintings. The tunnel narrowed as he penetrated deeper, forcing him to edge sideways.

Had he chosen the wrong cave? It appeared too small to contain anything of importance.

The cave ended in a fissure barely wide enough for a man. His candle revealed a large space on the other side. The air was cool and darkness congealed beyond the candlelight. Hugues squeezed through the gap and something crunched beneath his sandal. Squatting, he saw it was a shard of pottery.

The silence was deep and forbidding as Hugues explored the chamber with his small pool of light. He found the shattered remains of earthenware jugs and pots along one wall. In the centre of the chamber, he was surprised to discover a low bench made from ancient, pitted wood.

Scraps of rotten leather and feathers had been scattered across the table. Hugues picked one up and examined the quill. The tip was broken and covered in a dark brown stain.

"This must be the place," Hugues said under his breath. "Where *are* you?" he asked in a louder voice.

He explored the rest of the hidden scriptorium in desperation. Towards the back of the cave, he discovered a sleeping pallet of dusty straw and mouldy fragments of what may have been a blanket. Beady eyes glinted in the candlelight, so he chose not to disturb the nest.

Hugues completed another loop of the scriptorium, searching in vain for anything he might have missed. He found a crude mortar and pestle carved from stone. Smears of white paint streaked a section of rock. The remains of a fire, grey with age, had singed the stone near the fissure.

"There's nothing here." Hugues slumped to the floor and pressed his forehead against the edge of the ancient bench.

He had chosen the wrong cave.

And with sunset fast approaching, no time remained to rectify his mistake.

Hugues hammered his head against the wood in misery.

CHAPTER 5

25 November 1307

Cistercian Abbey, south-east of Fécamp

"Wait here with the horses." Bertrand handed his damp reins to Rémi. "It's better if I go alone."

Rémi grunted in agreement. The ground had turned to mud after the heavy rain. Clouds whipped through the night sky on a stiff breeze that carried the tang of the ocean.

Bertrand quickly checked on Salome. The effort of transporting them and their horses along the meridian had exhausted her, and she had lapsed into unconsciousness moments after their arrival. All attempts at reviving her had been unsuccessful, so they had no choice but to drape her over a saddle and tie her in place. Placing an ear next to Salome's mouth, Bertrand was relieved to find her breathing remained slow and regular.

Emerging from the forest, Bertrand approached the pilgrim gate set into the wall of the abbey. The main entrance was locked, so Bertrand rang the bell three times, once for each aspect of the Holy Trinity. The sea-breeze plucked at his cloak and sheets of rain billowed across the ground.

A small panel in the pilgrim gate slid open. "Who's there?"

Bertrand couldn't see the speaker as a lantern glowed through the open shutter. "A pilgrim," Bertrand replied. "From the south. My friends and I humbly beseech your hospitality in the name of the brotherhood of Christ."

"You're on a pilgrimage at this time of year?"

"As penance." Bertrand dropped his head. "My Abbot insisted I depart immediately, such was my sin."

"Which abbey?"

Bertrand hesitated. Even revealing where he was from might be unwise. "Brother Bernard of Troyes told me to seek shelter at your abbey. He said Abbot Guillot was a kind man and would look favourably upon my pilgrimage."

"Perhaps," the monk replied, "but not until morning. The Abbot has retired for the night." The light from the lantern receded. "Follow the wall to the north. When you reach the corner, you'll find a barn on your right. You and your companions can stay there for the night. If you reach the river, you've gone too far."

"No!" Bertrand forced the urgency from his voice. "I beg pardon, but I must see Abbot Guillot. He's expecting us."

"No one informed me," the monk replied. "Have patience and you can pay your respects on the morrow."

"I can't wait. One of my companions needs tending."

"Is he ill? I'll not have you bringing sickness into the abbey."

"No, not ill," Bertrand replied hurriedly. "Only injured. He needs shelter and warmth." Bertrand remembered Salome's instructions. "Please, I'm sure the Abbot will see us if you pass on the following message: the sun sets over the Anastasis."

"What's that supposed to mean?"

"Please, just tell the Abbot. It's very important. I was assured he would come in person."

"This is most unusual. Show me your face."

Bertrand pulled back his hood. "My name is Bertrand, and I swear to you upon the name of our Saviour that I was sent here in good faith. Please, take the message to your Abbot. I wouldn't trouble you if it wasn't urgent."

"Wait here." The panel slid home.

Bertrand pulled the hood back over his head. They could not tend to Salome if other pilgrims were already staying in the barn. He knelt in the mud, bowed his head, and clasped his hands together. "Please Lord, if You bear any love for me, let the Abbot come. And I...pray most fervently that in protecting Salome, I am about Your work. Please watch over my family and keep them safe. And when this task is over, I pray that You will reunite Rémi with his family. For Thine is the power and the glory everlasting, Amen."

Bertrand stood. He could not shake the feeling that God would not look kindly upon his prayer. The sense of abandonment he experienced while watching Justine's castle had not abated. At least the rain eased.

The sound of bolts sliding in their housings intruded upon his brooding. He moved aside as the pilgrim gate swung outwards. The first monk carried a lantern, and by its light Bertrand saw a birthmark covered the left side of the monk's face. A second monk had joined him. The newcomer was tall and thin, with kind eyes pinched in wariness. Both monks wore the white habits of Cistercians.

"I am Guillot," the taller monk said, "and this is indeed a foul night to be travelling." He glanced past Bertrand. "You spoke of companions?" He gave Bertrand a look full of meaning.

"Father." Bertrand sank to one knee and kissed the back of his fingers. "Thank you for coming. My companions are waiting under the shelter of a tree. I'll collect them if it pleases you."

"It does." Guillot turned to the other monk. "Thank you, Ernaut. You may return to the gatehouse. I'll see our guests to their accommodation."

"Yes, Abbot." Ernaut ducked his head and gave Bertrand a curious sideways look before retreating into the abbey.

"Collect your friends," Guillot said in a low voice. "We're unlikely to be disturbed, but after the last few months, I prefer to take no chances."

Bertrand hurried back to the edge of the forest. He returned quickly with Rémi and the horses in tow. Salome still hadn't stirred.

Guillot raised his lantern and quickly took in the situation. His mouth thinned as he assessed Salome's condition. "This way. Hurry."

After bolting the pilgrim gate behind them, Guillot led them along a path of stone that wended through neatly tended grass. Bertrand and Rémi made sure the horses kept to the turf to minimise the noise of their hooves. They passed a rushing fountain and a large pool dimpled by rain drops.

"I'm sorry to take you the long way," Guillot said to Bertrand, "but we would be seen passing through the cloister."

Bertrand glanced to the left where Guillot nodded. A few candles burned in the dormitory windows beyond the cloister.

A large building appeared ahead and Guillot nodded at their destination. "The forge. It will still be warm and it's large enough to stable your horses." He glanced at Bertrand. "I presume you won't be staying long."

"No, but I'm concerned for...my companion." It was hard to read Guillot's expression in the dark.

"Your concern is shared by many of us. I didn't think I'd live to see such dark times." Guillot opened one of the large doors and ushered them inside.

The smithy was warm, dry and spacious, just as Guillot had promised. The hearth still glowed with deep red embers that cast ominous hues over racks of hammers and tongs. The smell of wood smoke and cooling metal filled the air.

Bertrand and Guillot untied Salome from her horse and carried her close to the cooling forge.

"I can't believe she's actually here, in my abbey," Guillot murmured in wonder. "How long has she been like this?"

"Since we arrived at the ring of stone on the hill to the north-east," Bertrand replied. "She warned me this might happen. Something to do with crossing two salt lines."

Guillot's eyebrows lifted. "She crossed two salt lines with all of you *and* four horses?"

Bertrand nodded.

"She must have been desperate."

"We barely evaded capture twice." Bertrand gently removed her damp cloak. "With our pursuers closing in, she said it was the only way."

"I take it you're her Shroud."

"Yes." Bertrand smiled ruefully. "Roard died after the first attack and she didn't have much to choose from." He shrugged.

"You do seem a little young, if you don't mind me saying."

"Maybe so," Rémi interrupted from hobbling the horses, "but he's kept her safe where others failed."

"I see." Guillot gave Bertrand an appraising look. "I'm honoured that you have sought shelter at my abbey. What else do you need?"

Bertrand brushed wet strands of hair from Salome's face. "Does she need a physician? She doesn't wake, no matter what I try."

"I cannot say for sure, but she doesn't seem in distress, merely exhausted." Guillot shrugged. "She will wake in her own time." He frowned. "But you must leave before Matins, otherwise the brothers will discover you."

"Is there somewhere else in the abbey we can hide?" Bertrand asked. "Surely the King's men wouldn't dare search here."

Guillot's expression darkened. "Until recently, I would have said the same of the Commanderies of our Templar brethren. Now many are merely smoking ruins."

Bertrand resisted the urge to ask for news. "Have you nowhere to conceal us? As you said, we have no idea how long it will take Salome to recover."

Guillot thought for a moment. "There is a small grange at the edge of our eastern fields. It's not occupied during winter, so it should be safe."

Rémi walked over and squatted next to them. "We need more than a place to hide. We need to take ship to England."

Bertrand nodded. "Salome told me you could help."

Guillot stroked his beardless chin. "I use a merchant captain by the name of Malbert when trading our wool. Given it is nearly December and the inclement weather, it's likely he's in port at Fécamp. He could be trusted if I provided a letter of introduction."

"Nearly December," Bertrand repeated. "What date is it?"

"The twenty-fifth day of November," Guillot replied. "Why do you ask?"

Bertrand and Rémi exchanged a look of astonishment.

"It was late October when Salome...moved us," Bertrand said.

"Extraordinary." Guillot rubbed his bare chin thoughtfully.

"So that cursed Nogaret has had more time to widen his net," Rémi growled.

"Rémi's right," Bertrand said. "All the ports will be watched."

"That's probably true," Guillot said with a slow smile. "But no-one is looking for three Cistercian monks, are they?"

Bertrand swapped a look with Rémi. "Go on."

"I still have some bundled fleece to sell from spring. No one would take any notice of three monks from our abbey transporting it to Fécamp. We do that all the time, although not usually so late in the year."

Bertrand grinned. "What do you think?" he asked Rémi.

"Could work," Rémi conceded. "No armour or weapons though. We would be helpless if caught."

"We'll never fight our way to England anyway," Bertrand replied.

"The wool will buy your passage with Malbert," Guillot said, rubbing his palms together. "Tell him the profit is his in exchange for his silence."

"Thank you, Abbot," Bertrand said. "Salome didn't exaggerate your kindness or generosity."

"No, Bertrand. Thank you for bringing her to me in the autumn of my life. It will be a comfort in the grim days ahead to know that I have helped, albeit in a small measure, to realise the vision of our forebears." Guillot stood. "I'll make the arrangements for your departure." He looked down at Salome. "May I bid her farewell?"

"I...of course." Bertrand sat back on his haunches.

Guillot knelt on one knee, carefully took Salome's limp hand, and kissed the back of it. "May He whom we all worship finally bring you peace, gracious lady. We all pray for you." He gently placed her hand back by her side and stood.

"Thank you, Bertrand. I will treasure the memory of this moment. May God keep you both." Guillot departed with moist eyes.

Rémi waited until Guillot left the building. "Bertrand."

"I know." Bertrand raised one hand for silence. "She hasn't told us everything."

"Not even a tenth of it judging by how that Abbot was honoured just to kiss her hand." Rémi shook his head in disgust and stalked off to collect their bed rolls.

Bertrand clasped her hands in his. Normally they were warm, but now they felt chilly. He chafed her skin and studied her face in the red glow of the embers. Guillot clearly expected something extraordinary from her. Was it her knowledge of Baphomet's location or was there more to it?

Bertrand considered asking Guillot, then dismissed the idea as his ignorance might raise difficult questions. What was Salome hiding? And why was she hiding it from him? Once they were safely aboard ship, he would demand answers.

CHAPTER 6

28 November 1307

Port of Fécamp

Malbert's ship turned out to be a single, square-masted cog about eighty feet long. Called *Le Blanc Écume—The White Foam*—it was anchored some distance from the dock. After making discreet enquiries, Rémi eventually located a sailor willing to row him out to the ship in exchange for the promise of cargo.

Bertrand remained on the busy dock in his white habit. Salome had eventually woken at the remote grange Guillot had ushered them to. Apart from a ravenous appetite, she seemed unaffected by her ordeal. When she learned they were but a day's ride from Fécamp, she had beamed at Bertrand in triumph.

Sailors rushed about their business, chattering in a variety of tongues. Bertrand caught snatches of Spanish, or possibly Portuguese, and English, although he could not follow what was being said. Fishermen offered their catch from makeshift stalls. The fish were so fresh they still flopped limply in crowded pails of sea water. A blustering merchant shouted directions as barrels were unloaded from the belly of a cog at the dock. Gulls circled overhead, their constant cries adding to the clamour.

True to his word, Guillot had arranged a cart and a donkey to transport the fleece. Even though Bertrand had left their horses with the Abbot in exchange for his help, he still thought of the wool as the abbey's property.

"I hope we can trust this Malbert," Bertrand said to pass the time while they waited. He felt naked without his armour and sword. They had already passed one patrol of the city guard. He wondered whether the garrison had been given descriptions of their appearance.

"We've little choice," Salome replied from beneath the cowl of her cassock. "If Guillot says he's reliable, then we must accept his word. Besides, a steady income is a powerful incentive. I'm sure Malbert would be unwilling to risk his tenure with Guillot."

Another patrol appeared at the far end of the dock. They stopped two men, one tall like Bertrand, the other shorter and stockier. Bertrand hooked his arm with Salome's and casually led her behind some stacked wine barrels. They were too exposed out here for his liking.

The patrol moved further down the dock and Bertrand stopped to haggle over some fish. The guards passed them without a sideways glance. Bertrand purchased a cod to preserve the illusion and drew out the transaction deliberately.

Rémi returned a short while later in a rowboat manned by two sailors who strained at the oars. A third man sat in the prow, his curly grey hair tousled by the sea breeze. Bertrand guessed this must be Malbert. The man in the prow leapt from the boat without waiting for the sailors to moor it and clambered up the wooden steps. Rémi followed more carefully, not as certain of his footing and clearly uncomfortable in his white habit.

Malbert was not much taller than Rémi. Startling blue eyes full of wit twinkled in a weathered face. He wore a tunic the colour of storm clouds and faded brown hose tied with a coil of hemp.

"This is a strange time of year to be trading fleece," Malbert said without preamble. His gaze flickered between Salome and Bertrand. "And a dangerous time to be seeking a crossing."

"Good fortune may find a man at any time," Bertrand replied. "Especially when he is a faithful servant of God."

"Amen to that." Malbert crossed himself and gave Bertrand a grin that was full of broken teeth. "Now then, your *brother* here with the surly manner says you require passage along with your cargo. That true?"

"It is," Bertrand replied. "We're to visit our sister abbey at Fountains, north of Leeds. How far north can you take us?"

Malbert grimaced. "My cog sails fine in calm seas, but she wallows in a storm. You can have your choice of the nearest English ports like Bournemouth, Eastbourne or Portsmouth, but I'll risk no further."

"I can't prevail upon you to take us further up the coast?"

"No, you can't." Malbert crossed his arms and ignored the scowl this earned from Rémi. "But I don't wish to seem ungrateful to the good Abbot. I have contacts in Portsmouth, where I trade most frequently. If you wish, I could ask about. One of them will find you the quickest, and no doubt safest, way to Leeds. For a fair price, of course." He shot a sharp glance at Salome. "I take it you're in some haste."

"Yes, we're anxious to be united with our English brethren," Bertrand replied. "As a token of his appreciation, the Abbot said you could retain the profit from the sale of our cargo when we arrive safely."

"Ah." Malbert tilted his head and scratched behind his ear. "If we had started with the Abbot's generosity, we could have avoided this little dance. No reward, no risk, see?" He gave Bertrand a wink before sending one of his sailors in search of the Harbourmaster to seek permission to dock.

"And what do I call you, friend?" Malbert asked.

"Brother Bertrand. You've met Brother Rémi and Brother Henri here has taken a vow of silence."

Malbert flashed them another splintered grin. "Well, brothers, we'll have you on board and rolling with the swell as soon as we're able. I'm sure pious men such as yourselves wouldn't welcome the company of rough sailors, so you can take my humble cabin."

"Thank you, captain." Bertrand bowed, partly to hide his relief.

"You can come aboard *Le Blanc Écume* once we dock. It will take me some time to prise most of my crew from the local taverns, or similar establishments." Malbert gave Bertrand another wink and trotted back down the steps to his rowboat.

CHAPTER 7

28 November 1307

The Draper's Lament

Bertrand closed the back door to the inn and let his eyes adjust to the darkness. A small courtyard separated The Draper's Lament from the stables. Drawing back his cowl, he searched the shadows for movement.

The sound of drunken laughter carried from the tavern behind him. He was glad they were only staying one night: Malbert had promised to set sail the next day.

Bertrand moved down the steps quietly and stopped at the edge of the courtyard. After weeks in the countryside, the stench of open gutters and rotting fish was overpowering. Bertrand pulled a face and breathed through his mouth.

Light glimmered behind drapes in the tavern. Bertrand peered up at the top storey, trying to gauge which window was Salome's. He disliked leaving her alone, although she should be safe.

Besides, he had something that needed taking care of.

Bertrand walked over to the stables and slipped through the main door. It was dark inside, but a half-shuttered lantern glowed at the far end of the stalls. Bertrand glanced up. Nothing moved in the loft, but it was impossible to tell if any of the stable hands remained awake.

Bertrand moved closer to the lantern. Rémi was leaning over their cart, checking its contents. He whirled around but relaxed when he saw Bertrand. "What are you doing here?"

"I'm checking to see all is well, *brother*." Bertrand tapped his ear and pointed to the loft overhead.

Rémi's eyes narrowed. "Is it wise to leave *Henri* alone?"

"He's comfortable for now and it was urgent that I speak with you." Bertrand nodded meaningfully outside.

"Fine. I'm finished here anyway."

"I hope the Abbot's goods remain unsullied." Malbert might refuse them passage if the wool was stolen or damaged.

"Seem to be." Rémi shrugged.

"Praise be to God," Bertrand said.

"Yes, all praise to Him." Rémi followed Bertrand outside. "What's all this about?"

"Keep your voice down." Bertrand led Rémi away from the stables to the far corner of the courtyard. The moon was partially shrouded by cloud, and only a single lantern hung above the rear entrance to the tavern, illuminated the courtyard.

"Now that we've reached the coast," Bertrand said in a low voice, "I think you should return to your family, like you promised."

"I promised to *consider* it," Rémi replied. "Why are you in such a rush to be rid of me?"

The answer was simple enough: if something happened to Rémi, Bertrand would never be able to live with it. "What of Renier, Aude and Gueri? Don't your children deserve a father?"

Rémi snorted. "I know their names, cub. And frankly, you need me more than they do right now."

"Rémi, you've something to go back to. I don't." Bertrand squeezed his shoulder. "I'm not questioning your loyalty or your friendship. You've gone beyond anything my father could have asked. And yes, I'll miss your charming disposition, but this is your last chance to go home. Take it. I beg you."

Rémi was silent for a moment. "You should know by now that I always finish what I start." His voice was gruffer than usual.

Bertrand ground his teeth together. Why did Rémi have to make this more difficult than it already was? "I will always be grateful for all that you've taught me, and I won't repay your generosity by leading you to an early grave. Go and live your life. You deserve it."

"Since when did *you* start taking care of *me*?" Seeing Bertrand's expression, Rémi growled at the back of his throat. "You're not very good at giving a man options, are you? How do I decide between abandoning a man I'm closer to than my own children, and forsaking my family?"

"It's not abandonment if I insist you return home," Bertrand replied. "God knows your family needs you."

"Dung-head!" Rémi cuffed Bertrand's head. "You're part of my family, regardless of your father's coin. How many times do I have to say it?"

"But you're not part of the Salt Lines." If demeaning Rémi was the only way to make him leave, so be it.

"Now you sound like her," Rémi replied with an accusing stab of his finger.

"This is my family's burden, not yours," Bertrand snapped. "I have to avenge Everard and the others."

"Bloody Everard." Rémi shook his head. "Why let a dead man do your thinking?"

"We've been over this." Bertrand folded his arms across his chest. "I can't break my promise to him."

"Pah. Just when I think you've gained some sense you start bleating again."

Bertrand grabbed Rémi's arm. "You're not sailing with us tomorrow."

Rémi twisted free. "Think what you like, but I make my own decisions. I made a commitment to your father and I intend to keep it."

They glared at each other in the dark courtyard.

"You're a stubborn bastard, I'll give you that," Bertrand said.

"And you're an idiot if you think I'll leave you alone with her, and that's the end of it." Rémi pushed past Bertrand and stomped up the steps to the tavern.

"Rémi," Bertrand called. "You may never see your family again."

His shoulders dropped. "Do you think I don't know that?" he said over his shoulder. "That thought gnaws at me every day. But I've two brothers that keep an eye on my Maura and the little ones. And your need is greater than theirs."

"I told you before, there'll be no returning to France."

"So you keep saying, but perhaps you're just expecting the worst."

"You taught me to think that way!"

"Only when weighing your options. Now our course is set, no point moaning about it."

"You're impossible." Bertrand didn't know whether to hit Rémi or hug him.

"And now you sound like my wife." Rémi grinned.

"Are your family truly cared for? If by some chance we did return, and something had happened to them..."

"Then the blame would be mine." Rémi pressed his hand to his forehead. "Please, enough of this. My head aches." He walked up the steps and entered the inn.

Bertrand sagged against the wall of the tavern. It was a relief to know Rémi would accompany them to England, but he felt guilty as well. If the trail of destruction that had followed them from the Commanderie ever reached Rémi's family, Bertrand would never be able to forgive himself.

Too tense to sleep, Bertrand decided to check on the Abbot's wool again. Rémi would have undoubtedly seen to everything, but he needed something to keep him occupied.

Bertrand entered the stable and stopped in confusion. What had happened to Rémi's lantern? The stables were in almost complete darkness. Had the wick burned down?

Feet shuffled on the cobblestones behind Bertrand. He whirled to one side, lashing out with an elbow. Someone grunted as his blow connected. A second person crashed into Bertrand from the opposite side, throwing them both to the floor. Bertrand brought his knee up into the belly of his assailant. At least two more figures loomed over him. Bertrand wrestled the man off him and struggled to rise. A boot caught him in the chest and tossed him onto his back. Men fell on top of him and a sack was pulled over his head. He struggled, but the weight of numbers pinned him to the ground. His hands were tied behind his back and he was dragged further into the stables.

Bertrand shouted for help. This earned him a kick to his side that left him gasping for breath.

Light flared, visible even through the coarse weave of the sack. "Are you sure it's him?" a woman's voice asked.

"Yes, Seigneuresse. I got a good look at him when he left the tavern."

Bertrand stilled. "*Durand*? Is that you?"

"Remove the hood." He knew that voice, didn't he?

The sack was torn from Bertrand's head. He blinked at the bright lantern shining a few inches from his face. Half a dozen men surrounded him. They parted to allow the woman to approach. Bertrand caught sight of her narrow feet and simple skirt first. An impossible thought occurred to him as he looked up at her face.

Bertrand stared into narrowed blue eyes. Long brown hair, touched with a hint of grey, framed a familiar, aristocratic face.

"Justine?" Her name came out as a gasp. "You're alive! How...how did you find me?"

"Abbot Guillot told us where to look for you."

Bertrand shook his head. "I thought...after the fire..." Durand, her captain of the guard, and a handful of her other servants watched on impassively.

"You thought what, Bertrand?" Justine bent down so she could stare into his face. "After the King's men slaughtered more than half of my household and left my chateau in smouldering ruins, tell me, what did you think? Were you satisfied?" He belatedly noticed she was clutching a knife in one fist.

"I thought I'd lost you forever. That's what I thought." Justine was alive. He could scarcely believe it. Tears welled in his eyes.

"So, you knew they destroyed my chateau," Justine said through clenched teeth, "and you did nothing."

"No! I wanted to ride back, I wanted to fight."

"Dressed like a priest," she said, gesturing at his cassock with disdain.

"This is just a disguise. I would have ridden back; I was going to."

"Then why didn't you?" The tip of her knife pressed against his chest. "Why, Bertrand?"

He wilted beneath the accusation in her eyes. "Salome said that's what they wanted. That it was an ambush."

"So, you left me to burn. Even though I warned you against her."

"I never meant for any of this to happen." He met her furious gaze. "Please, Justine. Not a day has passed without me wishing I could change what happened. To know that you still live is a blessing beyond anything I could've asked for."

"This is not living," Justine snapped. "You chose *her* over me, and it cost me everything." Her voice dropped. "Did you know they executed your father and brothers as well?"

Bertrand trembled in shock. "What? I—that's impossible. The King—"

"The King branded them heretics for being part of the Salt Lines after Nogaret's men finished razing my estate. They burned at the stake, and now I'm landless with no lord to appeal to. Thanks to you, I'm an outcast with only vengeance to sustain me." The dagger tip pierced his skin and a bright red spot appeared in his cassock.

Bertrand bowed his head. His family were dead because of him. The pain of Justine's dagger was nothing compared to that.

"Go ahead then," Bertrand murmured. "Like you, I've lost everything I cared about. Even your affection. Death would be a relief."

"Don't think I won't!" The dagger in Justine's fist trembled.

He gazed directly into her eyes. "You never left my heart, Justine. Not when I joined the Order, not when I met Salome, even now as I face my end. If your face is the last thing I see before my soul parts ways with my body, I count it a blessing."

"It's far too late for pretty words, Bertrand." The pressure of her knife didn't slacken.

"Seigneuresse, let me do it," Durand said. "The sin should not be upon your hands."

"Silence," she hissed. "This is my right." Her fierce gaze searched Bertrand's face.

"I know I have no right to ask anything of you," Bertrand said. "My life is yours to claim, if you wish it. I think, perhaps, it always has been. But we are victims of the same enemy. They want Salome for some reason I am yet to fully comprehend. By taking her to England, I can thwart their plans. I know this means little to you, but once she's safely delivered to her refuge, I swear I will return and submit to your judgement."

Justine's eyes narrowed. "I don't believe you."

"Please Justine, I swear upon the souls of my father and brothers."

Her eyes misted over. "Your father...he refused to tell them anything. He spat at the feet of the King's emissary, Roustan de Toulouse. They tortured him terribly before they burned him at the stake as a heretic."

Bertrand closed his eyes as another sharp pain twisted through his chest. His father had been a stern and critical man, but he had refused to betray Bertrand. And his two older brothers — Armand and Reynald — were gone as well. He must find some way to honour their sacrifice.

"Cut me loose, Justine. If you don't believe I'll keep my promise, you must know I'm honour-bound to avenge my family."

Her dagger traced a line down his chest as it dropped to her side. Tears ran freely down her cheeks and she brushed them away angrily with the back of her hand. Rising to her feet, she turned her back on him and said, "Cut him loose." Her voice was steady but her shoulders trembled.

Durand reluctantly obeyed. Bertrand stood and rubbed his wrists. He took a half-step towards Justine.

"Don't touch me," she warned. "I have cousins in Troyes. You'll find me there. Now leave, before I change my mind. And tell that strumpet of yours never to set foot in this country again."

He searched for the words that might bridge the gulf between them, but it was useless. Mere words would never be enough.

"I will return, Seigneuresse," Bertrand murmured.

CHAPTER 8

26 July 1099

Caves of Qumran

Hugues' candle eventually burned out on the wooden bench of the abandoned scriptorium. Too exhausted to move, he cradled his head between his drawn-up knees as darkness enveloped him.

He had failed.

Despite all the trials that he had endured over the three thousand miles of this pilgrimage, it ended here in an abandoned cave looted of any value long ago.

He could not even muster anger.

Clearly God had forsaken him for his heresies, for his presumption in assuming to know His Will. Like the scriptorium, Hugues had been abandoned.

What a fool he had been. The Salt Lines had sent him here to die. Even now, they were probably planning other campaigns, chasing down other hints and rumours. No doubt they would recruit others with the promise of ancient wonders.

And yet...he *had* witnessed miracles. He had penetrated further into the mysteries of the artefact than any other Christian. Surely that counted for something?

Perhaps Umayr only required a token from this place as confirmation that Hugues had reached it?

No. He had said Hugues would recognise the essence.

A stubborn part of Hugues' mind urged him to think. What if this abandoned chamber was part of the trial, a test of his character and faith? Could the essence be metaphysical? Not an object as such, but a state of mind? Could it simply be faith, the essence that drove all men to seek the divine? If so, perhaps all he need do was simply return to Umayr before nightfall, empty-handed yet enlightened.

It was either that or admit defeat.

Hugues stood. With his eyes squeezed shut, he pictured the shape of the scriptorium. To reach the fissure that connected to the cave, he would need to skirt the table and take four, maybe five, steps to the far wall. From there, he could feel his way to the narrow tunnel.

Trailing his hand along the edge of the bench, Hugues shuffled around it, let go and stepped blindly into space.

The ground dipped slightly beneath his feet and he raised his arms for balance.

A second step. Then a third.

The wall should almost be in reach. Hugues took a fourth step and reached out blindly. Something sharp stabbed him through the rent in his shoe. Hugues dropped into a crouch and felt around his foot. Pottery shards, maybe a piece of rough glass. Nothing of importance.

He rose from his crouch and froze. A faint, silver outline glimmered in the rock directly in front of him: two circles surrounding a five-pointed star. As with the Holy Sepulchre, Hebrew markings curled around the edge of the inner circle. He inched closer, staring in astonishment.

The numeral for ten had been inscribed above the top of the star. If he spread his arms wide, he could just touch the second and third points of the star. Next to the point on his right hand was the numeral for nine; on his left, the numeral for eight. The lower points of the star were even with the floor, so that the circles appeared to be cut off at the ground.

How did he miss this when he first arrived? The wall had been blank. He was certain of it. Even as he considered the mystery, the faint silver lines began to fade. Perhaps they had absorbed the candlelight, and once cut off from further illumination, they slowly released that light. He had heard of crystals in deep caves that possessed similar properties.

Hugues tentatively touched the edge of the seal. The stone was rough and dusty, although the outline of the circle was noticeably grittier. A sediment had been rubbed into the stone and tiny granules stuck to his fingertips. He licked his index finger and a sharp, mineral taste stung his palate.

The silver glow continued to dim. Already it would be invisible in direct sunlight. Soon it would vanish entirely.

Hugues thought rapidly. The Seal of Solomon inverted the Tree of Life by placing the tenth sphere on top. The eighth Sephirah dedicated to Hod was positioned on the upper left.

Umayr said he would need the clarity of Hod to solve this test. Hugues had assumed he was speaking metaphorically. Now he wondered whether it had a literal meaning as well.

Hugues felt around the left point of the star. Just below the numeral for eight, a small piece of stone, no bigger than his palm, shifted beneath his fingers. Hugues' pulse quickened.

Using the tips of his fingers, he traced the perimeter of the stone. The loose stone fit the wall so well only hairline cracks betrayed its presence. Even if he had known where to look in bright light, Hugues doubted he would have found this hiding place.

Perhaps that was the point? This discovery required him to acknowledge his ignorance, his blindness.

Hugues drew the assassin's knife from his belt and gently eased the tip of the blade into one of the tiny cracks. It just fit. A quick twist of the hilt prised the stone loose and it dropped into Hugues' free hand. He sheathed the knife and examined the stone by touch. The front was rough like the rest of the cave but the back was unnaturally smooth. He carefully placed one hand inside the cavity.

The recess was not deep, less than a forearm in length. Standing on his tiptoes, he found a shallow depression at the back of the cavity. Hugues' fingers brushed against something dry and rough. Trembling with excitement, he drew the object out of its hiding place.

It felt like a pouch made from animal skin, sealed by a leather cord tied around the neck. Hugues would need light to explore his find.

"Thank you," Hugues whispered into the still chamber. He replaced the small stone in its fitting. The silver seal had vanished and the scriptorium was plunged back into darkness. How long until sunset?

Hurrying now, Hugues located the fissure by trailing one hand along the wall. He shuffled back through the cave as quickly as he could manage. A low hanging outcrop scraped the side of his head and he felt a trickle of blood run into his tonsure. The gloom eventually gave way to the orange glow of the setting sun.

Hugues emerged from the cave mouth and sucked in fresh air. Rather than triumph, he felt only an overwhelming sense of relief.

Vivid shades of red and violet streaked the sky. Hugues glanced at the pouch in his hand. The animal skin—probably goat or sheep—was old and dry. A leather thong had indeed been tied around the neck. Judging from the thick layer of dust, this pouch had not been opened in a long time. A hard object nestled inside the pouch. He longed to open it, but Umayr's instructions were explicit: *return before nightfall*. The ruins weren't far below, but the descent was steep and he was weary.

Patience. He could wait just a little longer.

Hugues tested the knot of the rope he had tied through the metal ring. It was still securely fastened. The rope was not long enough to reach the bottom of the gully, but it would see him past the steepest part of the rockface. He wrapped the rope around his waist, tied a slipping knot, and threaded the loose end through it. Using his knife, he cut strips from his robe and wound them around both hands. Finally, he tucked the precious pouch into his breeches.

When he was ready, he leaned out from the cliff-face and fed the rope through his hands. At first, he simply walked backwards down the cliff, carefully placing each step. He was acutely aware of the sun dropping towards the western horizon, which had already plunged the gully into shadow.

Growing more confident, Hugues pushed off with both feet, trying small jumps as the rope blurred through the rags binding his hands. Hugues reached the main slope without mishap. Despite the rags, his palms and fingers were raw from the rough hemp. Every part of him ached. He set his body's complaints aside and focused on his goal: *Umayr. The scriptorium. By nightfall.*

The words became a mantra to channel his dwindling strength.

The descent was much easier than the climb. Deceptively so. He stumbled and nearly pitched headfirst at one point. Pebbles slid down the slope and Hugues fought for balance. He over-compensated and fell on his bottom. Stone scraped against his buttocks and a sharp outcrop brought him up short. Hugues caught his breath and felt beneath his tattered robe. To his immense relief, the pouch was still there.

He needed to move quickly yet carefully. Hugues continued his descent, concentrating on his footing.

The sun had dropped beyond the foothills by the time he reached the watercourse. Hugues scrambled down the shifting pile of rocks. Long fingers of shadows stretched towards the Dead Sea and Hugues shivered as he recalled the ambush in the ravine.

He set off at a run once he reached level ground. His tired muscles protested and he was forced to drop back to a fast jog. His breath rattled in his dry throat. When did he last have a sip of water?

The twilight deepened.

Hugues' pace slowed to a shuffle and he cursed his weakness. Sunlight twinkled on the far side of the Dead Sea and Khirbet Qumran loomed at the top of a rise on his left. Summoning the last of his strength, Hugues lurched up the final slope.

The muscles in his legs burned and each step sent hot needles lancing through the soles of his feet. A low wall appeared before him. He stumbled and caught his balance with one hand on the warm stones.

His other hand clutched the pouch in a death-like grip. A voice called his name. Hugues staggered towards the sound.

Dark spots floated across his vision. He tripped on a worn block of stone and stumbled to his knees. A jolt of pain lanced up one leg.

"When you left," a rasping voice said, "I doubted whether you would return in time." A light flared in the ruins.

Hugues lifted his head.

Umayr sat in the shadows, his back to the ancient stones. He rose to his feet, an unshuttered lantern in one hand. "I confess that I am curious to see what you have brought, if anything at all."

"Here." At least that was what Hugues intended to say. The word was little more than a croak. He dropped the pouch into Umayr's outstretched hand and sank to the ground.

Umayr set the lantern down and retrieved a water skin. "Drink this." He pressed the skin to Hugues' mouth.

"Slowly, slowly," Umayr admonished, as Hugues gulped the water. "I don't have so much that you can sick it up again." The water was warm and sweet. Hugues took another, more measured draft.

"Wait here." Umayr disappeared into the shadows and returned a few moments later with a carafe made from thick glass. "Water from the Dead Sea," he explained. He weighed the pouch in his other hand. "Do you know, I hoped to never see this again. After all this time, I should have known better." He picked at the leather cord. "At least the skin has endured."

Hugues frowned. "You—" He cleared his throat.

"Yes," Umayr replied. "The pouch has been waiting in its hiding place for a long time. Over one hundred and fifty years at my last reckoning."

"What?" Hugues gasped.

"Baphomet bestows long life upon those it deems worthy." Umayr untied the knot and Hugues leaned forward to get a look. The inside of the pouch was stained a dark, mouldy brown. The Qādī removed a small, circular jar of polished black marble. He cut away the wax seal with his knife and removed the lid. The jar contained a pile of dark brown flakes. Hugues squinted at them, confused and vaguely disappointed.

The flakes were not thick enough to be chips of rock, nor were they pieces of wood. For a moment, Hugues had wondered if they might be fragments of the True Cross. Umayr took a pinch of flakes and dropped them into the carafe of sea water. He tightened the lid back on the jar and dripped wax from a candle to reseal it.

Hugues forced a question through his cracked lips. "What are you doing?"

"You'll see." Umayr swirled the contents of the carafe. The flakes quickly dissolved into the salt water and the liquid turned dark brown.

"This is the essence of knowledge," Umayr said. "The sweat of those who toiled upon the shores of the Dead Sea." He unstoppered the carafe and offered it to Hugues. "Drink."

Hugues hesitated.

"Drink," Umayr urged. "You have disturbed the ancient balance. Now you must bear the burden."

Hugues opened his mouth to ask a question. Umayr forced the edge of the carafe between his lips. The liquid was warm and bitter as it poured into his mouth. Hugues swallowed, fighting the reflex to gag on the salty brew. A fleeting aftertaste of copper soured his mouth.

"What was that?" Umayr's explanation made little sense and Hugues' stomach rumbled in complaint.

"Sleep."

"I—"

"Sleep," Umayr repeated. "It will be the last time you can ever truly rest."

Hugues tried to form a question, but the words fled before a burning sensation swirling through his guts. Sweat beaded across his face and a deep chill shivered down his spine.

Hugues was on fire...he was freezing...he was falling...

CHAPTER 9

27 July 1099

Khirbet Qumran

It was still night when Hugues woke. He could not tell how long he had slept. A few hours might have passed, or it might have been days. He had no sense of the passage of time.

His body ached everywhere and the muscles in his legs were stiff. One knee throbbed and his stomach had seized into a knot that protested at the tiniest movement. His mouth was parched and his throat raw.

Hugues lay still and licked his cracked lips. The air was cold, although Umayr had covered him with a blanket. He tried to piece together the events of his ordeal.

Umayr had made him drink the essence. Why? What purpose did it serve? How would drinking a mysterious brew give him access to secret knowledge?

Hugues rolled onto his side and sat up with a groan. Someone shifted in the shadows and a low voice called out in Arabic.

Who was that?

Hugues froze. Where was Umayr? Another figure emerged from the deeper shadows of the ruins, moving almost silently over the hard ground.

"Hugues, don't be afraid," Umayr called softly. "It's only my servant. I asked him to watch over you while I made the final preparations." He emerged into the loose rectangle of stones surrounding Hugues. A shorter Saracen, dressed in a dark robe that blended with the night, accompanied him. The man had wrapped the end of his turban about his face so that only his dark eyes glittered in the starlight.

"How long have I slept?"

"A day." Umayr squatted next to Hugues. "You need more time to rest, but I'm afraid this is a luxury we can't afford. Roll over. My servant has a special unguent. It will make your body limber enough so that you can ride."

"Ride?" Hugues glanced at the newcomer. Why was he hiding his face? "Where are we going?"

"Back to Jerusalem, of course."

"Who is this man? Where did he come from?" After the secrecy of their journey, the sudden arrival of a stranger was unsettling. Were there more servants nearby that he didn't know about?

"A simple servant," Umayr repeated. "He does not speak your tongue, so you have no use for his name." Umayr glanced between Hugues and the silent Saracen. "As for why he hides his face, it's safer for him that way. Once he takes you back to Jerusalem, he will be released from my service. You can trust him to lead you truly."

"You're not coming," Hugues observed.

"Turn over." Umayr spread a saddle blanket across the stony ground and rolled Hugues onto his stomach. The servant knelt next to Hugues and quickly cut away his tattered Saracen robe. A chill spread across Hugues' skin and his muscles tightened in reflex. Hot filaments of pain drew taut across his back. Hugues doubted he could even walk in this state, let alone ride.

Hands slapped together and rubbed vigorously. The strong smell of cloves, softened by honey and olive oil, drifted on the air. The servant placed his hands on Hugues' legs.

"This may hurt," Umayr warned, "but my people are skilled in the art of relieving tired muscles. Surrender to his hands and it will go better for you."

The unguent was cold at first but became warmer as it penetrated Hugues' skin. Umayr's servant kneaded his tired flesh with strong fingers. Hugues ground his teeth and endured the treatment, trying not to tense, as this only seemed to make it worse as Umayr had warned.

By the time the servant had finished with his neck and shoulders, Hugues' body pulsed with heat and he was lathered in sweat.

Hugues rose from his stomach tentatively and was astonished to find his body did not protest as he stretched. He even found he could stand without assistance.

"Here," Umayr said. "Put this fresh robe on."

Hugues shrugged the robe over his near naked body. "That was amazing." Hugues turned to the servant. "Thank you." The man nodded briefly, gathered the remains of Hugues' old clothes, and slipped back into the ruins.

"Where is he going?" Hugues asked.

"Tending to the horses." Umayr sat cross-legged on the ground. "Sit." Hugues joined him, still marvelling at his recovery.

"How much of yesterday do you remember?" Umayr asked.

"Most of it, I think." Hugues massaged his temples. "Only the last part is hazy. I was half mad with thirst." A yawn caught Hugues by surprise. It seemed nothing could cure him of weariness.

"That's good," Umayr replied. "Do you remember the essence?"

Brackish, salty water. The strange, dry flakes.

"Of course."

"Do you know what it is?"

"No."

"When an Essene elder died, it was said that he looked upon the face of God. After his death, his body was carefully prepared. Once the ancient rites were completed, a small incision was made in the back of his skull. The blood from his brain was collected in a chalice. Through alchemical means, this blood was dried and preserved."

"The brown flakes," Hugues said in growing horror. "Are you saying they were the remains of—" He could not finish the sentence.

Umayr nodded. "The secrets of Abraham could never be written down. Instead, the Essene adopted an oral tradition for imparting their knowledge, a tradition they inherited from their forefathers." He picked up a handful of dry soil and let it crumble between his fingers.

"As their numbers dwindled," Umayr continued, "the Essene developed new techniques to pass on their sacred knowledge. A more radical approach that guaranteed only the worthy inherited their sacred trust. When the Romans finally wiped them out, they died knowing their secrets had been preserved. Literally."

"That's barbaric."

"Is it?" Umayr gave him an amused look. "I'm surprised to hear a priest of Christ, who serves His body and blood at every communion, should think so."

"That's different," Hugues protested. "The Eucharist is part of the holy sacrament."

"Well, it does not seem so different to me," Umayr replied, lifting an admonishing finger. "Christ broke with the Essene after His falling out with John the Baptist. However, that did not prevent Him from adopting some of their customs. Fortunately, your Scripture never revealed the full truth, although the metaphors are there for those willing to look."

He may have a point, Hugues reluctantly conceded. "If this blood I swallowed is supposed to contain the knowledge of the Essene, why don't I feel any different?"

"You're not the vessel," Umayr replied, "only the messenger."

Hugues paled. "This Baphomet, does it require my blood?"

Umayr glanced towards the Dead Sea. "You must locate the tomb of David. That is where the artefact rests."

"How do I find it?" Hugues asked with a frown.

"Search your Scriptures. They detail the path to the tomb." Umayr removed a leather cord from around his neck and offered it to Hugues. "I have something I must give you." A dull shard of crystal hung from the cord, almost the length of Hugues' little finger. "Wear this at all times. It will shield you from the gaze of Severity."

Hugues examined the crystal. It was almost clear and ended in a sharp point. "Thank you, but won't you need it?"

"Not anymore."

Hugues accepted the rough necklace, holding up the crystal shard in the moonlight.

Umayr stood and cold realisation crept over Hugues as he clutched the pendant. This was a parting gift. "No." Hugues rose to his feet. "Come back to Jerusalem with me. I still need you. The Salt Lines can protect you."

Umayr smiled, the expression bitter and desolate. "I no longer wish to be protected." He drew his scimitar and offered the hilt to Hugues.

"No, I won't do it." Hugues backed away from the proffered hilt. "This is unnecessary, just as your friend the ālim Sharif didn't need to fight Godefroi."

Umayr shook his head. "In time, you will come to understand why this must be. The world constantly renews itself, spinning the future as the past falls away. But our threads are not forgotten. They will be gathered up and woven again. So it will be for you, one day."

Hugues shook his head. "No, we must learn from the past so that a new future can be written. That's why I've come all this way to find you."

Umayr smiled. "I once thought as you did, and it is right that you think this way now. Perhaps you will remember what I have said and say a prayer for my soul in times to come. And so." He offered the hilt to Hugues again.

"Too many have died already." Hugues turned the hilt aside.

"You cannot bring me with you." Anger tightened in Umayr's worn face. "Doing so would expose those you wish to protect. And you cannot leave me behind. Severity has marked me. Without the crystal, it will not take them long to find me."

"I won't take your life," Hugues said. "There must be another way."

Umayr thrust the hilt into Hugues' hand. "Now that you carry the essence, my role is finished. Every one of those I care about has gone before me. A change is coming, and I do not know if my people, whom I have loved and served, can withstand it." He closed Hugues' fingers around the hilt. "Will you not offer me this one mercy?"

Hugues trembled. "Umayr, I can't. Please, I beg you. Don't demand this of me."

Umayr's expression darkened. "Now is not the time for weakness. You have proven you possess fortitude. Don't be afraid to draw upon it now."

The scimitar was light in Hugues' hand. The Frankish broadswords and maces that he was used to were much heavier. It would be so simple. A single, true stroke.

"Come back with me," Hugues pleaded.

Umayr shook his head. "The past cannot abide in the future."

Hugues let the scimitar fall to the hard ground. "I won't take your life."

"Then you risk everything you hope to achieve."

"I'll find a way to keep you safe."

Umayr's shoulders slumped. He turned and called out in Arabic.

"What are you doing?"

"Calling for the horses," Umayr replied. "We must leave."

From the darkness, Umayr's servant replied in Arabic. Hugues could not follow the quick string of syllables, but he thought he caught a questioning note. Umayr responded with a tone of command. His servant emerged from the ruins, his eyes wide and staring beneath his wrapped turban. Umayr spoke again, punctuating his words with a sharp, chopping motion. The servant strode forward and thrust a dagger into Umayr's chest just below the ribs.

Umayr collapsed to his knees with a gasp and a dark, red rose bloomed across his robe. The servant dropped his knife, wailed in Arabic, and tore at his clothes.

"No!" Hugues caught Umayr as he slumped to the ground.

The Qāḍī's gaze settled on the night sky, and his green eyes narrowed for a moment, as if he had caught sight of something up there.

"*Allāhu akbar*," Umayr whispered in wonder before he left his limp body in Hugues' despairing grasp.

CHAPTER 10

29 November 1307

Port of Fécamp

"How much do you think he knows?" Bertrand asked.

Salome steadied herself against the roll of the cog by bracing one hand against the wood panel of Malbert's cabin. "More than I'm comfortable with, but I think he's smart enough not to be overly curious."

"Let us hope so." Bertrand glanced around the tiny cabin. "It'll be a long voyage stuck in here."

Salome gave him a patient smile. "I'll welcome the rest. Besides, Malbert senses I might be a risk to his crew."

Bertrand frowned. "How can you be sure?"

She shrugged. "Call it instinct."

Bertrand gazed about the small cabin. A hammock had been strung between two walls and a small bureau was fixed to the starboard wall opposite the narrow door on the port side. Two lit lanterns swayed from the ceiling.

"I have questions," Bertrand said.

Salome smoothed her hair back with her fingertips. "Yes, I know."

Bertrand opened the door and peered down the corridor leading up to the deck. Rémi was still guarding the entrance. He shut the door. "We won't be interrupted."

Crow's-feet pulled at the corners of Salome's eyes as her gaze narrowed. He had wondered about her age before. At times, he had assumed she was only a few seasons older than him. Now, the gap seemed far greater.

"What do you wish to know?"

He sat on the floor of the cabin in the hope that it might reduce the rolling motion of the ship. A queasy feeling was already uncoiling in his gut. "Guillot said something while you were unconscious."

"Did he?" She sat down on the hammock, clearly at ease with the swaying of the boat.

"He's expecting you to do something that involves the vision of our forefathers. I assume that means the Salt Lines. What did he mean by that?"

"Ah." Salome folded her hands together and considered them. "Bertrand, please understand. The knowledge I possess is dangerous. If I hold something back from you, it's because I hope to protect you from what I have suffered."

"That may well be, but there is something you must understand about *me*." Bertrand bit off each syllable in a low voice. "My family kept secrets from me until the day I left for the Commanderie. Now they are dead, and I'll never get a chance to understand why unless you tell me. Justine has lost everything because of me, and probably regrets not taking my life back at The Draper's Lament. So, don't insult me by this talk of suffering. While I might be young, I've known my share."

"Bertrand, I'm sorry." She leaned forward to touch him, but he brushed her hand aside.

"I don't want to be patted on the head and told to run along," he said through clenched teeth. "I deserve more than that."

Salome's expression hardened. "Then let me tell you something about me. I once felt as you did. I once believed it was my right to demand knowledge. In the end, I got what I wanted. I wasn't ready and it brought disaster upon those I cared about." She rolled up the sleeve of her Cistercian cassock and brandished her forearm. "You want to know how I earned these scars? Pride and wilfulness. That's how."

"So, they *are* self-inflicted."

Salome twisted her fingers through the netting of the hammock. "In a manner of speaking, but not from any blade." She looked up at the ceiling. "The point is this: consider very carefully what you wish to know. I will not keep anything from you if that's what you truly want, but there is always a price. I wish someone had warned *me* of that as I'm warning you now."

"I've already paid your price, whether I chose to or not."

"Very well," Salome said. "We'll talk once we're at sea and sure there is no sign of pursuit." She stood. "I'm tired. Why don't you take some air before the sea becomes too rough?" She smiled. "Your stomach is sloshing about almost as much as this boat."

Bertrand stalked from the cabin, strode down the short corridor, nodded at Rémi and emerged onto the aft deck. Malbert was yelling a stream of instructions from the upper deck as the crew made ready to sail. Sailors bustled about the cog, loading provisions and the bundled wool.

Bertrand moved to the stern where there was less activity. As always, no matter how he tried to pin Salome down, she always evaded direct questions. He gripped the wooden railing and stared at the bustling port.

His family had been burned at the stake as heretics. Images of his father and brothers writhing in the flames haunted him. Did his father curse his youngest son before the end?

Tears trickled down Bertrand's face and dropped into the dirty green water sloshing against the hull.

He recalled his last private conversation with Everard at the Lodge: *We can't escape what we are, Bertrand. The lines of history that lead down to us can never be erased, much as we may wish to. You'll find your path in life will become easier if you accept that this is so.*

"I won't forget," Bertrand murmured, "and I swear that I will find a way to avenge you all."

His gaze wandered across the docks and up to the roofs of Fécamp. Despite Rémi's uncharacteristic optimism and his promise to Justine, he knew this might be the last time he would look upon his homeland. So be it. He was an orphan now, with no land or title to claim.

Whether he liked it or not, Salome and the remnants of the Salt Lines were the only family he had left.

CHAPTER 11

30 November 1307

Le Blanc Écume

A day after sailing out of Fécamp, Bertrand knocked on the door of Malbert's cabin. The cog rolled alarmingly in the heavy swell of the Channel. He caught his balance in the narrow passage with a grimace. His stomach growled, but he could not bring himself to eat; not after having brought up his breakfast earlier, much to the amusement of the crew.

Salome cracked open the door. Seeing Bertrand in his white cassock, she stood aside and let him slip into the cramped cabin. With a sharp glance over his shoulder, she shut the door behind him.

"You've been sick."

"I'll be fine once we're back on land." Bertrand leaned against the stern wall, slid down onto his bottom, and pulled his legs up to his chest.

Salome smiled. "Is this your first time at sea?"

He nodded miserably.

"You'll get used to it." She undid the hammock, rolled it up with practiced ease and placed it in one of the drawers of the bureau. "What have you told them about me?"

"That you're ill." Bertrand grimaced. "Worse than me. None of the crew will go near you for fear of catching it."

"That's good." Salome grinned and sat on the groaning planks opposite him. "Thank you for being so convincing."

She chuckled at his scowl.

"You seem in good spirits," he said sourly.

Her amusement faded. "I'm just relieved to be leaving France. Champagne was a haven for a long time, but I nearly stayed too long. We're fortunate to have made it this far."

"It was your magic that saved us." The ship lurched beneath them and Bertrand threw out a hand to catch his balance.

Salome shook her head. "I can't wield it without a Shroud. You are the half that makes me whole, whether you realise it or not."

He looked deep into her eyes. "I need to understand."

Salome sighed. "Those are the very words that started me down the path that ends in today. Are you absolutely certain? Ignorance is far more comfortable than having everything you believed torn apart."

The queasiness in Bertrand's gut hardened into a knot. "Everard once told me we can't escape who we are. I think I'm finally beginning to understand what he meant." He did not try to explain. He was not sure he could.

Salome nodded. "He was a wise and generous man. And he thought highly of you." She shrugged. "You will recall that I told you the great mysteries could only be unravelled in layers. Don't expect everything to become clear at once. You must progress step by step, like any adept."

Bertrand nodded. "I remember."

"Good." Salome cupped her hands in her lap. "To understand the ancient lore, one must study the divine power of numbers. For some, this is the work of a lifetime. Others progress far more quickly." Salome rose and placed her ear against the wooden panel. "Is Rémi watching the corridor?"

"Of course."

She sat down again and crossed her legs. "Your ancestors were astrologers and mathematicians of great skill. How else could they have mapped the meridians that run beneath the earth? Yet despite their learning, much of their lore was derived from even more ancient sources."

The cog plunged down a wave, forcing them to catch their balance.

"In the time of your Saviour," Salome continued, "there was a sect known as the Essene. They were monks and ascetics who lived in remote places, such as the desert and the shores of the Dead Sea. Spurning the company of ordinary men, they wore white robes, tended their flocks of sheep, and laboured to the glory of God."

"They sound like Cistercians."

"Exactly," Salome replied. "Your Cistercians are the modern incarnation of that ancient order."

Bertrand rubbed his bearded chin. "I don't see how. The Cistercians were established by the great Bernard of Clairvaux who gave our Order its monastic rule. We learn about Bernard as part of our training to become chevaliers."

Salome nodded. "Would you be surprised to learn that Bernard was a member of the Salt Lines? After all, he was closely related to the Counts of Champagne who are one of the foremost families in the Fraternity."

Bertrand absorbed this thoughtfully. "So, what happened to these Essene?"

Salome bowed her head. "They were destroyed during the Bar Kokhba revolt against the Romans. Almost nothing remains of them, apart from their writings hidden in secret scriptoriums scattered near the Dead Sea. These scrolls spoke of preparing for a great war with a terrible enemy. One might assume this was a reference to the Romans, but there are references to the 'legions of Severity'."

"Severity?" The knot in Bertrand's stomach tightened. "Are you saying that the men pursuing you are part of the same group that destroyed the Essene so long ago?"

Salome's eyes glistened like water on onyx. "If the Salt Lines have endured ever since the few surviving Essene escaped to western shores, why is it impossible for their enemies to have done the same?"

This is absurd, he wanted to say. But the existence of the Salt Lines could not be disputed. And if the Fraternity had existed in secret for so long, why not its enemies?

"So the battle that the Essene fought over a thousand years ago is still being fought today."

"Yes, Bertrand. In secret and under a different pretext, but in spiritual terms the opponents remain the same. Now you understand why your Order is being persecuted."

"But why? What do they hope to gain?"

Salome traced a circle in the air with her finger. "So, we come full circle."

The *Écume* plunged into another trough. Bertrand grimaced. "What do you mean by 'full circle'?"

"The forces of Severity understand the power of divine numbers, as did the Essene. While your Scripture refers to the Word of God as the spark that ignites all of Creation, the Essene believed it to be a series of sacred numbers reflected in the Tree of Life. The Lords of Severity fractured the tree by offering forbidden knowledge to mankind. This split the keystone in half, one for Mercy and the other for Severity. If they can join the two halves together, the Lords of Severity can unravel the divine sequence and free themselves from their prison in Abaddon. If that were to happen, all Creation would be perverted."

Not much of that made sense to Bertrand, so he focused on the part he did understand. "So you're saying the men hunting you hope to destroy our world." Bertrand didn't bother to hide his scepticism. "How is that of any benefit to them?"

"Those men are merely foot soldiers," Salome replied. "They have no concept of the broader consequences of their actions. Only their masters, the five Lords of Severity, truly understand."

Another heavy wave thudded against the hull. Bertrand's elbow collided with the doorframe and even Salome appeared unsettled.

"Why does none of this appear in Scripture?" Bertrand asked, rubbing his elbow.

"It does, Bertrand." Her lips quirked. "It's all there, only hidden in metaphor and allegory. I've already spoken of the Tree of Life. The tree is the key to the divine sequence of Creation."

"I don't follow."

"Close your eyes," Salome said. "Picture the tree that you glimpsed in your chapel. Do you see it?"

Bertrand summoned the image: a silver tree captured in stained glass. Three branches spread from a narrow trunk, each rising vertically up a separate pane, before angling inwards to rejoin the central branch at the crown. Embedded in the branches were ten silver circles, starting at the foot of the tree and rising up each branch. The image reminded Bertrand of the trikiron, a candlestick with three arms used in some church services.

"Do you see the three pillars, Bertrand?"

"If you mean the two branches spreading out from the central trunk, then yes." He kept his eyes closed to hold onto the image.

"Good. From left to right, they are Severity, Unity and Mercy. See how the middle pillar of Unity is the tallest?"

The middle panel was indeed the tallest and the crown of the silver tree almost reached the stone arch framing the glass. "Yes." Bertrand frowned. "But how—"

Salome gripped his wrist and the picture in Bertrand's mind brightened. The tree expanded from the stained glass, growing in size and clarity. The ten silver circles he remembered were no longer inert. They spun so fast it was only possible to see blurring colours.

"What's happening?" Bertrand cried. He opened his eyes, but it made no difference. All he could see was the unearthly glowing tree.

"You asked for knowledge," Salome said. "These are the ten Sephirot, or spheres of existence. See how the upper three are separated from the lower seven? This is the first of the divine sequence. The trinity, the aspect of God that is Unfathomable, separated from the rest of His Creation. This is Ein Sof, the joining of the masculine, the feminine and the Shechinah, or holy spirit. Together they create the spark of life that descends the tree."

In Bertrand's mind, a pulse of light sped down the tree, zigzagging its way to the bottom. It reminded him of a lightning flash.

"Let go." Bertrand pulled away from Salome. The tree vanished and he was back in Malbert's tiny cabin. "How did you do that?"

Salome made a calming gesture. "That's not important. Focus on the numbers. Second in the sequence is the seven remaining Sephirot. As you saw, the spark passes through each sphere. As it does so, the divine impulse takes form until it reaches the tenth Sephirah, which is the physical world as we know it. That is why the spiritual number of the angelic choirs is seven. They are the bridge between Ein Sof, whom we can't comprehend, and our material existence."

At least that made sense. In Scripture, angels were often the emissaries of the Lord or the bearers of visions. "These...Sephirot." Bertrand stumbled over the unfamiliar word. "What are they exactly?"

"They're states of being. How best to explain it?" Salome looked at the ceiling of the cabin in thought. "Think of an artist asked to paint the wall of a church. He doesn't just begin to paint. He waits for inspiration. A vision if you will, of what he might paint. Next, he sketches the image, trying to capture what he glimpsed in his vision. After that, he considers the wall itself, seeing the possibilities and limitations of his chosen materials. Finally, he selects his tools and assistants. Only then does he begin to paint." Salome arched her eyebrows. "Do you see?"

Bertrand nodded. "The painting begins with a vision of what might be and slowly takes form."

"Exactly."

Another wave crashed into the hull of the *Écume*. Was the storm worsening? Bertrand pressed his back against the doorframe and tried not to think about the fact that he couldn't swim.

Salome gestured about the cabin. "The world around us is the final form of the painting. But it begins with a vision that we can't possibly comprehend, and that is Ein Sof."

"So, the bottom of the tree is our world and the top is heaven. Is that what you're saying?"

"No." Salome raised an admonishing finger. "That's your priests talking, twisting the ancient wisdom into something that even the simplest can understand. But let me finish the sacred numbers. Next in the sequence is five. This is the spiritual number of man and is represented by the five lower Sephirot. It's no coincidence that Christ suffered five wounds before his death. Each of those wounds symbolises the death of an aspect of the human soul."

Bertrand frowned. "The soul has five parts?"

"Yes." Salome smiled. "Surely you don't think the urge to survive comes from the same place as the ability to create music or art?"

"No, but—" Bertrand ran his fingers through his curly hair as he thought furiously. "How can a soul be divided into parts?"

"I'm not dividing it," Salome explained, "I'm simply naming the elements that make it whole. The five lower Sephirot represent a different aspect of our soul. The Salt Lines refer to them as the Mysteries, because they are the key to understanding our existence."

"I see," Bertrand said. But he didn't. Not really.

Salome patted his knee. "I told you it would take time to understand. For now, it is enough to remember the divine sequence: ten states of existence in all of Creation; three for the trinity of Ein Sof; seven for the angelic choirs; five for mankind."

"Ten, three, seven and five," Bertrand repeated. "I still don't see why these numbers are so important."

"It's what they represent," Salome said with a sigh. The lanterns swayed overhead as the *Écume* continued to roll through the heavy swell.

"Remember, we're talking about the design of Creation. First there was nothing. Then the keystone was cast into the void and the first Sephirah formed around it. The vision of the painting if you like. The other nine Sephirot followed. For a brief time, Ein Sof and His Creation were in harmony, but then mankind became aware of Mercy and Severity. This is the forbidden knowledge in your Old Testament. An absence appeared in the central pillar called Daat. It created a rift between Ein Sof and the rest of Creation, and it brought Mercy and Severity into conflict. Until the two opposing pillars are unified with the central pillar, Ein Sof and His children will remain separated."

Bertrand stared at Salome. Her explanation would see her burned for heresy in any part of the Holy Roman Empire. Yet some of it did seem to overlap with the teachings in the Bible. "This Daat sounds like the expulsion of man from the Garden of Eden, but the rest of it?" He shook his head.

"I know it must be overwhelming," Salome replied. "Just think on what I've said. I'm sure you'll have more questions."

The *Écume* pitched heavily to starboard. How could anyone stay upright in this weather? "Your magic. The way you moved us along the meridians. Does it come from this tree?"

Salome gave him an appraising look. "You're a quick student. Yes, Bertrand. I can move us along the meridians by manipulating the tenth Sephirah. It is called Malkuth and it governs the physical world."

"What else can you do?"

"I think that's enough for now." She brushed a lock of hair from his face. "You look pale. Some fresh air might do you good."

"Assuming I'm not washed overboard." Bertrand staggered to his feet. "We'll continue this once I've had some time to think on what you've said."

"Of course." Salome smiled. "Before you go, would you like to know why they're called the Salt Lines?"

Bertrand gripped the doorframe and nodded.

"In ancient times, salt was one of the few ways known to preserve food. In some lands, it was so precious that it was even used as a form of currency. Trading routes were established to transport shipments and towns sprang up along these routes. So salt became synonymous with prosperity and the preservation of life."

Salome lifted her hand to prevent Bertrand from interrupting.

"What is *less* well known, however, is that salt is also used in certain rituals of purification. You'll witness this once we reach our destination."

Her last comment raised more questions, but judging by her pursed lips and the tightness pulling at the corners of her eyes, she was unwilling to say anything further. At least the mystery surrounding the origin of the Fraternity's name had been dispelled. That was more than his father or brothers had ever told Bertrand. "Thank you, Salome. I'll check on you later."

She dipped her head in response. Bertrand tried to gain a sense of what she was feeling through their link, but she must have anticipated the attempt, as she was shielding her emotions.

Bertrand closed the door to her cabin and shuffled down the corridor to the ladder where Rémi waited. His mind was awash with everything Salome had told him, and he was not sure it would ever settle into any kind of sense.

CHAPTER 12

5 December 1307

Portsmouth

Bertrand watched the boats jostling for position in Portsmouth harbour from the deck of *Le Blanc Écume*. Most were small fishing vessels. Only one other vessel rivalled theirs in size. Dock rats from the Harbourmaster's office rowed between the ships, assigning docking rights according to precedence and the occasional clink of coin. A light rain fell from the overcast sky and a cold breeze skimmed across the whitecaps. After the crossing they had endured, the harbour felt as flat as glass. Gulls circled overhead, screaming at each other, and swooping down upon floating refuse.

"Doesn't look so different from home," Rémi noted. Having dispensed with their disguise as monks the previous evening, Rémi had reverted to his customary leather armour. His axe lay propped against a wooden bulkhead within quick reach. Bertrand had not donned his chainmail, but he would once they disembarked. England was an unknown, and since he did not speak the language, he felt a show of strength might help avoid any trouble.

"It's similar," Bertrand agreed. "The buildings are a bit meaner, but only marginally so." He shrugged. "Given all the stories about the English, I expected more dramatic differences."

"It'll be the people, not the buildings," Rémi muttered.

They only had to wait until noon before they were able to dock. Malbert took the helm of the *Écume* and shouted for the mainsail to be reefed as they approached the pier. It did not take long before the ship was securely moored.

Malbert joined them at the stern. "Welcome to England, my martial brothers. The ale here is thick and almost as sour as its women. It rains more often than not, and the further north you travel, the more barbaric the locals become. I'm sure you're in for a fine stay." His bright gaze took in Rémi's armour and axe. "I imagine you'll be wanting to meet my factor as soon as you're able."

"Thank you for your hospitality, Captain," Bertrand replied. "The sooner we're off your boat, the better for all concerned."

Malbert clapped Bertrand's shoulder. "With your delicate disposition, brother, I can understand why you say that. Let me collect a few members of my crew and we'll go ashore. The rest can unload my cargo."

"I'll collect Brother Henri from your cabin." Bertrand gave Malbert a nod and went below deck. Salome was already dressed in her white Cistercian habit. Bertrand donned his chainmail with her help.

Malbert was waiting on the main deck with two crewmen armed with cudgels. He raised one eyebrow when they approached. "Lo, a miraculous transformation has taken place. The sick rise from their deathbeds and a monk wields the sword of the righteous."

"That's enough of your foolery," Rémi growled.

"Careful, friend," Malbert replied with a smile that didn't reach his eyes. "You've made the crossing without getting too wet; it would be a shame to toss you over the side now."

Bertrand cut in before the simmering dislike between the two men could escalate. "Captain, you don't need questions about your passengers and we don't want to be giving answers. Take us to your factor and we can go our separate ways. That's all Abbot Guillot asked, remember?"

Malbert gave him an appraising look. "You've dealt fairly with me, *Brother* Bertrand, so you can expect the same from me. Whatever trouble you're sailing from, it's no business of mine. But if I were you, I'd hide that symbol." He pointed at the pommel of Everard's sword.

Bertrand flushed when he realised the Beauseant was in plain view. Rémi hastily found a scrap of canvas and tied it around the pommel with a piece of twine.

One of the crewmen slid a plank onto the pier and they disembarked the *Écume*. Bertrand staggered on the timber beams of the dock. It felt like the ground was still rolling. Malbert noticed his unsteadiness. "Once the sea has got hold of you, it takes a while to let go. The land will settle soon enough."

The crewmen chuckled but Bertrand kept his temper in check. Malbert liked provoking reactions, so Bertrand was determined not to give him one.

They marched up through narrow alleys that stank of rot and sewerage as much as those in Fécamp. Malbert was clearly familiar with the way, as he never hesitated through the maze of streets. Bertrand tried to remember their route but it soon became impossible.

For the most part the street folk ignored them. Vendors hawked their wares from carts and stalls. Merchants hurried about their business, seamstresses sewed in open windows, fishmongers brandished their latest catch. It was remarkably like home, except Bertrand couldn't understand anything they said. Occasionally he caught a snatch of conversation in French, but it was alarmingly rare. How would they cope on their own if none of them spoke the language?

He cursed the limited education he had received.

Eventually they stopped outside a modest two-storey wooden home. As they moved uphill away from the docks, the streets had widened and the class of people improved. While none of the homes in the district were built from stone, they were well-tended and obviously belonged to merchants and affluent burghers.

"Here we are," Malbert said with a wink. "Bet you thought I was lost." Malbert banged on the solid timber door and yelled something in English. Someone yelled back from inside the house. A few moments later a panel in the door slid open. Bertrand couldn't tell whether it was a man or woman.

"Open up, Tristan," Malbert said in French. "This is no way to treat your business partner."

The door swung open. A short, florid-faced man dressed in a cream-coloured tunic with navy stitching stood in the doorway. He scratched his ample belly and replied in French, "Malbert, you knave. What are you doing here? I didn't expect you until March at the earliest."

"I accepted a special cargo from the Abbot." He nodded at Bertrand and Rémi, who flanked Salome.

"Oh." Tristan stepped down from the doorway and squinted at them. "Why would Guillot send a brother and two armed guards during winter?"

"You'd best ask him that," Malbert replied with a flick of his wrist. "Although perhaps such matters should not be discussed on the street, eh?"

"No. Of course not." Tristan's chin wobbled as he glanced about to ensure they were not overheard. "What was I thinking? Please, do me the honour of coming inside." He led them inside the town house.

Bertrand and his companions shrugged out of their cloaks. Salome remained hooded and hunched over, as if she was unwell. A small fire crackled in the hearth and Tristan ushered them to a low bench that occupied the front half of the room.

"Beatrice!" Tristan called out something in English that Bertrand couldn't follow. A woman stamped down the wooden stairs that ran up one side of the main room. She was short and stout like Tristan, with light brown hair that hung loose almost to her waist. Beatrice frowned at her visitors, but a burst of words from Tristan sent her scurrying into the buttery.

"Please, sit," Tristan said in slightly accented French. "My home is modest, but I know Cistercian brothers have no taste for luxuries. Even so, Beatrice will serve us some warmed cider in just a moment." He gave them an ingratiating smile.

"Thank you for your hospitality," Bertrand replied. "Brother Henri is unwell and has taken a vow of silence until we reach Fountains Abbey. I am authorised to speak for him."

"I see." A frown creased Tristan's forehead. "I'm very grateful to the Abbot for using me as his factor here in England. Nothing's too much trouble for any member of his abbey."

"Good," Malbert interrupted, "because they're your problem now. I promised them passage to England and I've kept that promise. I'll come see you in a few days, Tristan. For now, I have a cargo to sell, and then coin to spend in your taverns and elsewhere as it pleases me. Farewell, Brother Bertrand. I sincerely hope our paths don't cross again." He gave them a wave and strode outside.

"Malbert?" Tristan rushed to the doorway. "Wait! Come back here! Malberrrt!" After a few moments, Tristan slowly closed the door against the rain and leaned against the doorframe. He muttered something in English that sounded suspiciously like a curse.

"Impossible man," Tristan said, switching back to French. "Who are you?" He held up a pudgy hand. "No, don't tell me. I don't want to know." He sank on to the stool and regarded them warily. He had turned pale apart from blotchy red spots on his neck.

Salome sat on a stool, her head bowed and hands in her sleeves so her scars were hidden. Beatrice appeared in the entrance to the buttery, watching with a concerned look. Empty tankards hung loose from each hand.

"What do you want?" Tristan asked.

"Safe passage to Leeds," Bertrand replied. "We'll need three horses and some equipment. We can pay, of course."

"Be that as it may," Tristan glanced uneasily between the three of them, "it doesn't explain why Malbert is so keen to be rid of you."

Rémi crossed his arms. "Let's just say we prefer the company of those who revere the Temple."

"Ah. I see." Tristan threaded his fingers together and bit his bottom lip. "Personally, I've always held that honourable Order in high regard. But times change."

"So it seems," Bertrand replied. "What's the situation here in England? Does King Edward follow the French example?"

"Not yet. But there are rumours, of course." Tristan avoided Bertrand's questioning look. "The King was only crowned in July, as you know. He's still establishing his rule, so offending King Philippe would not be high on his list of priorities, I shouldn't think."

"There has been no seizure of property or arrests then," Bertrand said.

"Only nominal gestures so far." Tristan glanced at Salome's bowed head and hurriedly averted his gaze. "Nothing to rival the brutality of your countrymen."

"Can you help us or not?" Rémi demanded.

"Yes. I believe I can." Tristan glanced at Rémi. "It might take a little time, however."

Bertrand leaned his elbows on the pitted surface of the table. "How long?"

"A few days, at least." Tristan shrugged. "One doesn't just buy three mounts with a snap of one's fingers, you know. Besides, you would be safer travelling with others. Perhaps I can locate a caravan that's heading...where did you say you were going again?"

"Fountains Abbey," Bertrand replied.

"Ah, well, you'll want a caravan bound for Leeds." Tristan's ingratiating smile returned. "That *will* take some time," he said with a sympathetic look. "It's hardly the time of year to travel."

"Well, if that's the case," Rémi said, "where do we sleep?"

"I beg your pardon?" Tristan drew back in astonishment.

"You said it would take a few days." Rémi shrugged. "So we stay here until then."

"But you can't," Tristan said in growing horror. "I don't have the space. This is my home, not an inn."

Salome disguised a laugh with a cough.

Bertrand gave Tristan a hard look. "Did you not just say nothing was too much trouble for members of our abbey?"

"Yes, but I—"

"But what?" Bertrand asked. "You didn't mean what you said?"

Tristan squared his shoulders and looked offended. "No, of course not."

"Well, there's no argument then," Bertrand said reasonably. "We stay here until you've found us horses and there'll be no need for us to inform the Abbot that his good opinion of you is unfounded."

Tristan spluttered at their stony expressions. "Perhaps I *could* expedite the process," he said slowly. "Yes, if I make certain enquiries— discreetly, of course—we might be able to have you away quicker than I first thought."

"Good, that's settled then." Bertrand moved to the fire and warmed his hands. "What happened to that cider?"

CHAPTER 13

31 July 1099

The Tower of David

For the first time since Godefroi had entered Jerusalem, a new day dawned with the promise of rain. Admittedly the thin wisps of clouds were so high overhead they brushed against the very bulwarks of heaven. If the baleful sun did not burn them away, the wind would surely scatter them. Even so, Godefroi clung to the notion that it might rain.

"No sense in hating him," Baldwin said next to Godefroi. "After his failure to win the crown, and the humiliation of his trusted Bishop ceding the tower to you, what choice did he have?"

As usual, his brother wore a half-smile on his face. The comment was pitched so that the other lords standing near the parapet of the Tower of David wouldn't catch it.

"I suppose I'd do much the same in his shoes," Godefroi replied. Now that Baldwin had called him back to the moment, it was impossible to ignore what was happening below. The main thoroughfare that led south to the Gate of Siloam writhed with men and horses, carts and camp followers. The massed, undulating body of the Provençals was pouring out of Jerusalem. Once through the main gate and free of the city, they would head south before swinging east to explore the River Jordan. Or so Raymond had said.

"But?" Baldwin prompted.

Godefroi smiled, despite his troubles. "But it feels like sacrilege to abandon this Holy City after the oaths we swore."

Baldwin trailed a hand across the worn battlements. "You're worried about a counter-attack from Cairo."

"It's inevitable," Godefroi replied. "Raymond's departure was expected, but I did not expect Robert of Normandy to leave as well. If āl-Afdal does attack, we'll be heavily outnumbered." He watched the procession gloomily. "The Egyptians could be outside the walls before the end of August."

Baldwin nodded thoughtfully. "If only the threat could be confirmed."

"Before the Provençals travel beyond reach," Godefroi added.

"Then the Count and Normandy could not refuse your summons," Baldwin concluded. "The defence of Jerusalem must take precedence over any other dispute."

"The Egyptians prefer the sea route," Godefroi mused. 'so it's likely they'll make for the port of Ascalon. If we could send someone to scout the souks, perhaps we might winnow the truth."

"They'll need to be a native," Baldwin said. "Or perhaps an Armenian. I'll make some discrete inquiries."

"Thank you." Godefroi tore his gaze from the Provençals and gave Baldwin a smile. "Our presence here is still precarious until reinforcements arrive from Constantinople. How fares your County of Edessa?"

Baldwin's smile faded. "I'm not sure. News is hard to come by. I fear that if I'm gone too long, the Armenians will appoint their own ruler."

"I understand." Godefroi leaned on the battlement as he peered over the rooftops. "So you'll marry then. One of their princesses, to strengthen your claim to the throne."

"I suppose." Baldwin shrugged. "With Godwera in God's care, I am free to choose."

"Do you miss her?" Godefroi asked softly.

Baldwin gave him a strange look. "Not particularly, in truth. From the first, it was clear she did not care for me. Nor did she bear me any sons." Baldwin stroked his chin as he considered the question. "Now that we're here in the Holy Land, I doubt she would have taken to this life. Her soul was more suited to the convent than the castle." Baldwin crossed himself for speaking of the dead.

"Perhaps it's for the best then."

Baldwin gave Godefroi a frown. Thankfully any further conversation was interrupted by the arrival of a royal page.

The youth was dressed in the new livery designed for members of the royal household. His tunic of black wool bore a red cross over the heart. The hose were looser than usual in Lorraine, a concession to the formidable heat of the Holy Land. Even though the page was young, he panted from the long climb up the steps. A bead of sweat dripped from the tip of his nose after he bowed.

As Seneschal of Godefroi's household, Gaston approached the page. After a quick conversation, Gaston sent the youth scampering back down the steps. Gaston wore an anxious expression as he joined Godefroi and Baldwin. "Messire, a visitor begs a private audience with you. Ordinarily,

I would have sent him to join the rest of the petitioners but—" Gaston shrugged apologetically.

Godefroi cocked his head. Gaston was not usually given to uncertainty. "But not in this case."

"No, messire," Gaston said with a deferential nod. "Not when the supplicant claims to be Hugues de Payens."

"Hugues! Are you sure?"

"I haven't seen him myself, but surely your page would recognise him." Gaston's frown deepened. "Apparently he's dressed like a Saracen and hardly in a fit state to be received in your court. Perhaps I should check before—"

"No, I'll see him alone." He stabbed a finger at Baldwin. "I need you to stay until the end of August. Promise me."

Baldwin pressed his lips together.

"Promise me," Godefroi repeated. "There'll be rich pickings in the Egyptian camp."

Baldwin exhaled through his nose and his shoulders dropped. "As your vassal and a devoted Christian, how could I refuse?" He sketched a courtly bow.

"Exactly." Godefroi approached Robert of Flanders. "Robert, I'm grateful for your unwavering support. When time and opportunity allow, I'll be sure to reward your loyalty. As will God, no doubt, when you're eventually called into His presence." Godefroi waited long enough to acknowledge Robert's bow before dashing down the steps, two at a time.

Where had Hugues been all this time? Had he ventured forth alone or in the company of the Salt Lines? And had he discovered the artefact?

The questions raced through his mind as Godefroi hurried down the stairs.

On the first landing, the page beckoned Godefroi towards a private antechamber. He brushed past the page and strode into the room. A travel-stained figure stood next to an arrow slit overlooking the Jaffa Gate. The muddy, loose-fitting robe he wore had much in common with Saracen clothing, although the battered shoes were of Christian design. A rude, black cross had been stitched into the back of the robe between the shoulder blades. The man's head was covered by a hood of light damask.

Without turning, he said, "Close the door, Godefroi."

Godefroi's hesitation evaporated. Despite the exhausted note that infused the timbre of those words, there was no mistaking Hugues' voice.

"No one is to disturb us," Godefroi told the page. "And if I catch you, or anyone else listening, I'll have their head mounted on the battlements." The boy backed away and bowed low.

Godefroi slammed the door closed and leaned against the timber frame. "Hugues?" Godefroi breathed. "Where in God's name have you been?"

Hugues turned and drew back his hood. Whatever he had experienced during his absence had left a mark. Dark crescents underscored his eyes and his slightly hunched shoulders hinted at a heavy burden. Thick stubble covered his chin and brown hair bristled where his tonsure was growing out.

Hugues leaned against the stone wall. A shard of dull crystal hung from a leather cord around his neck. "They've turned you into a ruler, I hear."

"They have, but what have they made you into? You seem quite different."

"A humbler man." Hugues gave him a wry smile.

"What's that supposed to mean?" Godefroi pushed away from the door, suddenly furious at the way this conversation was unfolding. "You've been gone for eight days without a single word the whole time. Achambaud and Godwera nearly died. Raymond and Robert of Normandy are abandoning us as we speak and you—" Godefroi took a steadying breath. "And you greet me with more evasions."

"You're quite right. Please forgive me." Hugues rubbed his eyes with a dusty hand. "Let me do you the courtesy of trusting you as much as I've insisted you trust me."

Godefroi's gaze narrowed at hearing his old complaint.

"I know the resting place of the artefact," Hugues said softly. "And I carry the essence with which to animate it."

"You're sure?" Hope flared within Godefroi. Perhaps the artefact could be used to defend Jerusalem? "You have it on your person?"

Hugues gripped Godefroi's elbow. "The Egyptians *are* coming, but they're not whom we need fear." Hugues touched the curious piece of crystal that hung around his neck.

"I don't understand. Who are you talking about?" This drawn, intense man was not the priest Godefroi remembered.

"I'll explain everything once we gather the others. We must find the tomb of David before our enemies arrive."

CHAPTER 14

31 July 1099

The Latin Quarter

Hugues stopped in the narrow alleyway. A pair of cats watched him from the flat rooftops overhead and the stench of sewerage fouled the air. He was surprised to discover he missed the stillness of Khirbet Qumran.

"This isn't the way to your residence," Hugues noted.

Godefroi had shed his royal garb and concealed his identity beneath the black habit of a simple monk. The deception would only survive a casual glance. Godefroi's frame and bearing were not suited to devotion.

"I had them moved," Godefroi replied. "My household has grown since my elevation." He glanced about the alley. They were alone, apart from the cats prowling the rooftops and rodents scrabbling through the refuse. "I couldn't risk having them discovered. Not so early in my rule."

Hugues frowned. "I can understand why you would conceal Godwera, but why Achambaud?"

Godefroi grimaced. "I made the mistake of allowing my physician to examine him. The fool was convinced that Achambaud would die. He recommended I turn him over to the priests so they could usher him into God's care." Godefroi spread his hands in resignation. "How then could I explain why he was still breathing?"

"By the grace of God?" Once, not so long ago, Hugues would have been absolutely sincere when he made that suggestion. Godefroi responded with a noncommittal grunt.

"So he *has* recovered then," Hugues said. At last, some good news.

"See for yourself. We're almost there." Godefroi trudged to the far end of the alley, glanced both ways down the cross street, before waving Hugues on.

Godefroi led him to a modest home eclipsed by taller buildings on either side. Constructed from stone blocks weathered by the elements, it appeared solid without being imposing. A simple, yet sturdy-looking door provided the only entrance from the main street. Godefroi banged on the timber and glanced about again.

Hugues shifted uneasily on his feet. He was acutely aware that much had changed during his absence. "Who do you think would spy on us?"

"Arnulf perhaps. His ambitions have grown." Godefroi shrugged. "Or Raymond. Even my allies." He banged the door again. This time Hugues caught the shuffle of footsteps on the other side. "When I catch a spy," Godefroi said with a hard smile, "I'll be sure to put the question to them."

Hugues rubbed at the stubble on his chin. It had been too long since he last shaved. "I suspect we were watched well before your ascension. When Firyal smuggled me out of Jerusalem, her people were attacked. At the time, I thought those soldiers might have been yours."

Godefroi shook his head. "They weren't mine. I was at Council when you disappeared."

The door was unbolted and swung open into a dimly lit room. Godefroi entered the house and Hugues quickly followed. The curtains had been drawn, so it was difficult to make out much in the gloom. Hugues had the impression of a crude table and chairs, rough sleeping pallets, and a row of spears stacked against one wall.

A man dressed in a leather jerkin and stained hose quickly closed the door behind them and bolted it again. Despite his rude garments, his fair hair and beard were neatly trimmed. He dropped to one knee before Godefroi.

"Thank you, Frederik." Godefroi touched the guard's shoulder. "I don't think we were followed but stay alert."

"Yes, lord." Frederik rose and retrieved a spear.

Godefroi led Hugues deeper into the dwelling. "Part of my household guard," Godefroi murmured. "I couldn't trust Godwera and Achambaud to anyone else."

"Very wise." Hugues was pleased to find Godefroi had not been idle in his absence.

They emerged from the narrow corridor into a second, larger room. The furniture and fittings were noticeably finer, yet hardly fitting for nobility.

Godefroi strode outside into a surprisingly large, walled courtyard. Tall palm trees quartered the square and a pond glistened in the centre.

Hugues caught sight of golden shapes darting through the depths.

"Hugues? Is that you?"

A familiar figure dressed in a knee-length linen tunic and matching hose emerged from the striped shadows cast by the palm fronds. Achambaud was thinner than Hugues remembered and paler too. He still favoured his injured leg, but his smile was broad and his embrace full of vigour.

"By God, it's good to see your face again." Achambaud clapped him on the shoulder. "Even if you look half-Saracen."

"Not as good as it is to see you on the mend." Hugues stepped back and shook his head in wonder at Achambaud's condition. "We nearly lost you."

Achambaud's expression darkened. "It was Godwera who saved me, although I almost wish she hadn't."

"Where is she?" Hugues asked.

Godefroi's jaw tightened. "In the far corner where the sun is fiercest. She's always cold, if you can believe that. I'm hoping your return will rally her spirits."

Hugues nodded. Godwera must have tapped into the power of Netzach to heal Achambaud. She had literally drawn upon her own life to save him. "Take me to her."

"This way." Godefroi passed through a screen of palm trees and into a secluded pool of sunshine. Achambaud trailed after them, limping slightly across the flagstones. Godwera lay on a divan in a loose-fitting gown with a woollen blanket drawn up to her waist. Etienne knelt at her side with a flask of water.

"Dearest sister." Hugues sank to his knees and took Godwera's limp hand. She was as pale as her linen and he could trace the delicate blue veins beneath her skin. She tried to sit up but lacked the strength to do so. Godefroi waved Etienne away and lifted her gently by the elbows so that she could sit upright. Hugues nodded at Etienne as Godefroi made her comfortable.

"I see time has not been kind to either of us," Godwera said softly.

"Unfortunately, I must agree with you." Hugues rubbed her hand gently. Her fingers felt like ice beneath his weathered grip. "Tell me, are you cold? Your skin is chilly to the touch."

Godwera sighed and closed her eyes. "I'm always cold, even in the sun. Isn't that strange?"

Tears welled in Hugues' eyes. She had overreached and he had allowed her to do it by following Firyal. "I grieve to see you like this."

"Then like Godefroi, you focus on the wrong thing," Godwera

replied. "How could I let Achambaud die? Especially when his conscience is the keenest of us all?"

Achambaud leaned against a palm tree, a look of misery etched into his face.

"You're right," Hugues replied with a wan smile, "but what you did took courage nonetheless."

She gazed at him, her eyes slightly unfocused. "You're different." A statement, not a question.

"Yes." Hugues leaned forward and said in a stage whisper, "I've discovered the location."

Godwera's eyes widened. "Truly?" she asked. "You found it out there?"

"No," Hugues replied, "although I carry the last element we need to claim it."

"Where is it?" Etienne asked excitedly.

"It's good to see you again, brother." Hugues clasped Etienne's hand in greeting.

Etienne grinned in delight and pulled the grey spike they had retrieved beneath the āl-Aqsa Mosque from his tunic. "It's a key: one that attracts metal to it. If you know the site, we'll be able to unlock the gate that must guard the way." His fevered excitement reminded Hugues of how he had once felt, although those emotions belonged to a man yet to understand the true nature of the responsibilities he was assuming, a man who had not yet met Umayr or Firyal.

"Put it away, Etienne!" Hugues glanced at Godefroi in concern. "Is it safe to speak freely here?"

"We should move inside to be sure." Godefroi lifted Godwera without any discernible effort and threaded through the trees back to the main house. Hugues threw an arm around Etienne's thin shoulders, hoping it would take the sting from his rebuke.

"I'm sorry, Hugues," Etienne said. "It's just that we're so close. After all this time."

"I know," Hugues murmured, "but now we must be more cautious than ever."

Once they were settled inside, Godefroi summoned Frederik and his men-at-arms. He divided them into three pairs. Frederik and one guard were ordered to protect the front of the house. A second pair was sent to patrol the courtyard, while the third pair roamed the upper storey.

"We won't be disturbed," Godefroi said, "but I'll have to return to the Tower soon. You had best explain quickly, Hugues."

Godwera lay on a makeshift pallet, propped up by pillows. Godefroi refused to sit and prowled about the room. Etienne took a stool and sat next to Godwera. Achambaud was content to sit on the floor with his back to the wall and his healing leg stretched out.

"As Godwera would have told you," Hugues began, "I left Jerusalem in the company of Saracens. Firyal, the woman who nursed Achambaud, was part of a cabal, much like our sacred points. They were very old. Far older than the spans granted to most men or women." He suppressed a pang of loss at their deaths.

"We were ambushed on the way to a place near the Dead Sea," Hugues continued. "Only my guide, a man called Umayr, and I survived." He faltered at the memory of the demon's attack.

"Attacked by whom?" Godefroi asked.

"Assassins, a rival faction of Saracens," Hugues replied. "And a... demon. Umayr called it a Lord of Severity."

Godefroi exchanged a worried glance with Achambaud.

"Umayr was able to drive it off, although our party was decimated. At the shore of the Dead Sea, I succeeded in locating what Umayr called the essence. I still don't fully understand what it is, but I believe it's required to use the artefact."

"This essence," Etienne said, "is it some kind of device?"

"Not really," Hugues replied. "It's difficult to explain."

"Can I see it?" Etienne asked.

"No," Hugues replied with a shake of his head.

"And the site of the artefact?" Godefroi asked. "How far do we have to travel? It will be difficult for me to leave the city with Arnulf's priests constantly plucking at my hem. The city's defences must be repaired too. Especially if āl-Afdal is sending an army."

"The artefact is located in the tomb of King David," Hugues replied.

"Isn't the tomb of King David said to be buried beneath the Church of the Apostles where the Last Supper took place?" asked Achambaud.

Etienne frowned. "The Saracens destroyed that church. One of the Provençals told me only rubble remains." He gazed out towards the courtyard. "And it seems a very obvious choice to hide an artefact of great value. Surely the tomb, if it's still accessible under the ruins, has already been robbed."

Hugues frowned as he fingered the crystal shard hanging against his chest.

"You have doubts," Godefroi noted. "Do you think this Umayr lied to you?"

"No, Umayr's integrity is beyond question, although I agree with

Etienne," Hugues replied. "It seems too obvious a choice. Umayr said David's resting place is described in Scripture. I must study the verses that detail David's life, as much can change in two thousand years."

Godefroi stopped prowling around the room. "I'd come with you, but that would draw too much attention. At least with the Provençals gone, you won't have Raymond looking over your shoulder."

It was clear Godwera was not in a fit state to help with the search and Achambaud was still recovering. "Etienne and I will search for his resting place," Hugues said.

Achambaud made a noise of protest.

"No, Achambaud." Hugues shook his head. "It's better if you remain with Godwera. The two of you need to regain your strength as quickly as possible."

CHAPTER 15

31 July 1099

The Holy Sepulchre

Gamaliel was hidden in a narrow side alley when the three men he had been stalking finally emerged from the town house. He had chosen the body of an Armenian merchant. Waiting until the merchant left his companions to relieve himself on the road from Jaffa, Gamaliel had invaded his flesh and quickly conquered his mind. Entering Jerusalem in spirit form would have been simpler, but the city had always repelled the Lords of Severity. The only way to locate his quarry was by walking in the flesh of ordinary men.

Just as Sammael had said.

Gamaliel focused on his prey. The warrior stood half a head taller than his two companions. He had attempted to hide his identity beneath a black cassock, but it was a poor disguise. The priest had changed from his dusty robes back into the garb of a monk.

The three men did not loiter in the street. Separating without a farewell, the warrior strode back uphill towards Gamaliel's position. The priest and the engineer headed east at a slower pace. Gamaliel eased into the deep shadow of the alley. The warrior was alert. His gaze swept both sides of the street and lifted to the balconies overhead.

Gamaliel gathered the emptiness that defined the Fallen and projected it outwards: *this alley is empty. Nothing of interest lies within. Pass by. Pass by.*

The warrior continued up the street without a glance in Gamaliel's direction. Even so, he waited twenty heartbeats before emerging from his lane. No sense in risking accidental discovery. Besides, he knew where his quarry was heading. The rituals of Christianity made their priests predictable.

Men and women were emerging from the homes they had seized as the day cooled and shadows lengthened. Knots of Christians formed on the street, talking in a range of languages. Grim-faced women collected their laundry from lines their Moslem predecessors had fixed to the balconies. Cats mewled in the hope of a scrap of food.

Gamaliel drifted among them. Their chatter was like the lowing of cattle or the bleating of sheep. The two men he was following wove through the growing mass of people with a determined stride. He trailed at a distance, sometimes stopping to admire the wares on display to preserve the charade. The finest items for sale were always of Moslem origin.

The Christians had enthusiastically adopted the souks. Makeshift stalls sold fruit and grain, silks and fabrics, even the odd trinket. A bell tolled in the distance. It was not the muezzin that Gamaliel's host was accustomed to, but he recognised the summons just the same.

His prey hurried through the twilight crowd to attend the dilapidated church so many had died for. Fortunately, other pilgrims were rushing to attend Vespers, so his presence did not draw attention. Feeling more confident, Gamaliel closed the gap.

The only real concern was that the priest might sense his presence. Gamaliel had nearly torn the priest's soul from his body during the ambush in the ravine, so he would recognise the touch of Severity. The only way to avoid discovery was to withdraw totally into the flesh of his host, as any overt manifestation of power would give him away.

The bell tolled again, calling the faithful to the Holy Sepulchre. Gamaliel shifted closer to his target with the general press of people. The two men shuffled through the ruined basilica with the rest of the pilgrims. Gamaliel was jostled as the crowd surged towards the courtyard, each vying to get the best view of the ceremony. He suffered these indignities with a forced smile. After all, this was supposed to be an ecstatic moment for the character he was playing.

His quarry joined the rest of the clergy assembled outside the Anastasis. Each man genuflected towards the High Altar set before the apse of the rotunda. After crossing themselves, they each received a candle, which was lit from the one taper.

Gamaliel noticed the other monks cast odd looks at the priest. It seemed his absence had been noted. What had he done after the ambush? And why had he returned to Jerusalem?

Taking its cue from the clergy, the pilgrims produced candles or small lanterns. Monks moved among the crowd with burning tapers and lit the candles in the front row. These pilgrims shared their flame with their neighbours, so that small pockets of light dotted the darkening courtyard. Gamaliel had not thought to bring a candle with him. When the woman next to him offered him one, he shook his head.

He would not embrace the light. Not under any circumstances.

"Blessed children of God," called a squat priest. "We have gathered here, on the very site of the resurrection, to meditate upon the sacrifice of our Lord and Saviour, Jesus Christ. For He is the light that washes away our sins." The priest wore a satisfied smile on his face. Gamaliel sensed this one craved power and privilege above all things.

He shifted his attention back to the priest and the engineer. The younger, curly-haired man in the brown tunic picked at the melted wax on his fingers in a distracted manner. The priest was cut from an entirely different cloth. When Gamaliel seized him in the ravine, he was met with a level of defiance that belied the man's mild appearance. This one possessed a formidable intellect. If a threat existed to Sammael's plan, it would come from this man and not the warrior.

So, a choice was required.

Gamaliel could follow Sammael's instructions and allow the Christians to retrieve the keystone. Or he could act as he thought best.

Sammael was not here. He had not witnessed the nature of these Franj. Yes, they were unruly, poorly educated and superstitious. They were also determined and resilient. He suspected they might prove more difficult to manage than Sammael believed.

Gamaliel scrutinised his quarry as the service droned on. At the appropriate junctures, he mouthed empty platitudes. Much depended on his choice. Perhaps even more than Sammael had foreseen in his isolated fortress.

If only he had more time to observe, to ensure he made the right decision.

Gamaliel's gaze flicked between the two men and he relished the feeling of uncertainty. The choice he made now could well shape the future of the world. And if that were true, was he not one with God at this very moment?

The priest's head snapped up as the prayer finished, his expression rigid as he searched the crowd facing him.

Gamaliel dropped his head. He must be careful, especially now that his choice had been made.

CHAPTER 16

6 December 1307

Portsmouth

Salome woke Bertrand in the small hours of the morning by placing her hand over his mouth. The fire had burned low, and when she saw he would not cry out, she removed her hand. Rémi's snoring continued, undisturbed.

Bertrand sat up. "What's wrong?" he whispered.

"You don't speak English, do you?"

Bertrand shook his head.

"I do." She shifted on her knees and glanced at the wooden steps. No sound came from Tristan and Beatrice upstairs. "Obviously I can't treat on our behalf, so I must teach you."

Bertrand rubbed the sleep from his eyes. "We hardly have time for me to learn."

"You misunderstand. I can give you my knowledge of the language. It will seem as if you've always spoken it."

Bertrand stared at her. "How is such a thing possible?"

"By manipulating the eighth Sephirah known as Hod, which governs the realm of the intellect, including language." She sat on the floor next to him. "Close your eyes and bow your head. You'll experience a moment of disorientation. Remain still. The feeling will pass."

"Wait. Is this safe?" That was not the question he wanted to ask. Just having her so close made his breath shallow and set his pulse racing.

"Of course." Salome smiled. "I've done this with other Shrouds before."

"Other Shrouds?" Bertrand pulled back. "How many have you had?"

"Quiet." Salome glanced towards the stairs. "I would prefer no one knew about this."

"How many?" A wave of irrational jealousy flooded through Bertrand.

Salome hesitated, perhaps realising her mistake. "Too many,

Bertrand. I truly hope you're my last."

"Can you never answer a direct question?"

"The truth is I've never counted. Doing so would be too... distressing." She drew her knees up to her chest and wrapped her arms around them. "Now tell me, does complete honesty make you feel better or worse?"

He gazed into the embers. "You've had that many you need to *count* them?" How was he supposed to respond to that? The revelation left him feeling insignificant. He tightened the blanket around his shoulders.

"And now you prove my point," Salome said in a low, passionate voice. "Knowledge is both a blessing and a burden."

"And they all died." Bertrand scrutinised her in the dark. "Didn't they?"

"Yes," Salome admitted. "Most, like Roard, were victims of those who served Severity. A few died of natural causes, including my first Shroud."

"Every time I think I'm beginning to understand you, I discover that I'm mistaken."

"You're not the first to say that," Salome replied. "Now please, let me bestow the blessing of Hod upon you. I fear we'll be travelling a long way today. You should try to sleep while you can."

"Is that your way of ending the discussion?" Bertrand asked.

"No," she snapped, "it's my way of focusing on what's needed."

Bertrand met her angry gaze. "Very well." He shrugged off his blanket. "What do I do?"

Salome knelt in front of him. "Close your eyes and relax. It's more difficult if you're tense."

Bertrand lowered his head. Her fingertips pressed lightly against his temples. A strand of her charcoal hair brushed against his face. Even though it was irrational, an erotic pulse beat through his body.

Salome was using him just as Rémi had warned. Any affection given was intended to ensure his compliance. Yet he could not shake his desire for her. If he just lifted his hands, they would brush against her breasts. Desire and anger circled each other endlessly until they became inseparable.

"Relax, Bertrand."

The air shivered with a thousand feathers that fluttered through the air and brushed against his skin. The fine hair on his arms and neck lifted. His throat felt like it was swelling impossibly wide and his breath came in short, staccato bursts.

Salome released him and the sensations ceased immediately.

Bertrand blinked. He lifted his head and rubbed his face. Surely his hair was standing on end. "I feel strange," he said. "Did it work?"

"Yes, the blessing was successful." Salome tilted her head and watched him with her almond-shaped eyes.

"How can you be sure?"

Salome grinned. "You just replied in English."

Bertrand's hands dropped to his side in astonishment. She was right. He had not even noticed when she switched from French.

———◆———

"Seigneur! Seigneur Bertrand? I have someone I wish you to meet." Tristan came bustling into his town house with a pleased look on his chubby face. He removed his cloak and tossed it to Beatrice, who had been sweeping the floor whilst casting sullen looks in Rémi and Bertrand's direction. Only an hour before, Bertrand had used his newfound English to convince Beatrice that Salome was sick. She was now resting comfortably on a pallet upstairs, still disguised in her white habit.

Tristan ushered a second man into his home. "This is Sir William of Salisbury. I think you'll be most pleased to make his acquaintance." Sir William was almost as tall as Bertrand. He was broad across the chest and thick through the arms and shoulders. Like Bertrand and Rémi, he wore his light brown hair short with a full beard. Chainmail glinted beneath his grey cloak, but he bore no tabard. A sword hung from his belt, almost identical to Bertrand's.

"A pleasure to meet you," William said in a halting French.

"The pleasure is ours," Bertrand replied smoothly in English. He suppressed a flash of amusement at the look of surprise on Rémi's face. "This gaping fellow here is my companion, Rémi. Brother Henri is unwell and has retired upstairs."

Tristan's mouth dropped open. "You speak English?" He paled.

Bertrand grinned. "Passably well."

William frowned at this exchange before turning back to Bertrand. "That's a relief. My French is appalling, as you've no doubt noticed."

"Thank you for the courtesy, though." Bertrand inclined his head.

"Tristan here tells me that you're bound for Fountains Abbey," William said. "Is that correct?"

"It is. Despite the season, we were hoping to travel in good and honourable company."

"What's he saying?" Rémi asked in French.

"We may have found a company to travel with," Bertrand replied quickly. "Just be patient." He turned to William and switched back to English. "Forgive me. Rémi doesn't speak English."

"I can hardly criticise him," William said with a rueful grin.

Bertrand decided he liked this Englishman.

"Tristan tells me you share a...reverence for the Temple," William continued carefully. "Is that so?"

"It is indeed," Bertrand replied. "Although admitting this in my homeland has become an offence to the crown."

"So I'd heard." William shook his head. "Did you know they arrested the Grand Master—God bless Jacques de Molay—and the Preceptor of Normandy?"

"Surely not," Bertrand protested. "Even King Philippe would not dare assault their persons without Papal consent."

"I have it on good authority they're imprisoned in the Temple in Paris," William continued. "Rumour has it they're to be tortured until they confess to crimes authored by Philippe's Keeper of the Seals."

"How can the Pope allow such travesties?" Bertrand asked.

William shrugged. "You should listen to the gossip on the street. There's not much sympathy for our Order among the common folk. They believe we've grown too wealthy and arrogant. I fear good King Edward will bow to pressure and seize the Order's holdings here."

"Is that why you're heading north?" Bertrand asked. "To escape persecution."

William glanced at Tristan. "I fear our time is over and I'll not see my men punished for crimes they are innocent of. Scotland does not bow to Rome. It's said Robert the First, King of the Scots, will welcome any of our brethren."

"How many men do you have?" Bertrand asked.

"My company numbers just over forty," William replied. "That includes squires and sergeants, of course. Another chevalier and his sergeant would be welcome on such a dangerous journey."

"That's kind of you," Bertrand replied.

William smiled. "In times such as this, safety lies in numbers."

"Exactly so." Bertrand tried not to appear too eager. "When do you intend to depart?"

"On the morrow," William replied. "Tristan here found me while purchasing the last of our provisions."

"And a fortuitous meeting it was," Tristan interrupted. "Gentlemen, please sit. It seems you've much to discuss. I'll bring wine and cheese." He hurried off to the buttery, obviously keen to be rid of his unwelcome guests.

CHAPTER 17

8 December 1307

Portsmouth

Roustan estimated at least two dozen ships bobbed in Portsmouth harbour, although it was hard to be sure with visibility limited by the sleet falling from thick, grey clouds. The majority of the boats were small fishing vessels, which could be safely ignored. His quarry could have landed at any number of different harbours along the English coastline, but only a handful of the closest ports made sense during winter. Added to that, only larger vessels would risk the dangerous voyage.

The water was choppy and reflected the dull grey sky. Roustan was saturated from a combination of sea-spray and sleet. An icy wind swept across the water and its cold fingers plucked at his cloak and leather cap. Yet despite the inclement weather, he remained ensconced in the prow. It was possible, however unlikely, that he might identify the vessel that Salome had used in her crossing. And while he was actively searching for her, the fiery barbs of Gamaliel's compulsion left him alone.

Pain: he had never thought of it as having a personality until Gamaliel showed him its various moods. Sometimes it was brutal and savage, like a club pounding Roustan's body. Other times it was fine and delicate, like the tip of a heated knife carving excruciating lines of fire into his flesh.

Gamaliel had visited during the crossing from Le Havre.

Roustan quailed at the memory of the demon's foul touch. It had slid into his mind as naturally as a man draws breath. He had been asleep at the time and woke screaming. His cries were so intense that Gilles, the Captain of Guillaume's guards, had knocked on his cabin. By then Gamaliel had taken complete possession of Roustan's body. When Gilles inquired whether he was well, Gamaliel had snarled an order to never disturb him again.

Roustan closed his eyes. Gamaliel proceeded to explore the limits of his tolerance for agony. Where an ordinary man might pass out, Roustan had no such escape. Each time he slipped towards unconsciousness, Gamaliel had drawn him back.

He had wanted to die, but Gamaliel refused. Instead, the demon had somehow strengthened the compulsion it had woven into the fibres of his being. Now Roustan's every waking moment was consumed with thoughts of Salome.

Unlike Guillaume, Gamaliel was not content to capture her at the cathedral. The demon wanted her now. Roustan could not be certain, but he suspected Gamaliel had his own plans.

He trembled again. Judging by the demon's hatred for Salome, whatever he had endured was nothing next to what it would inflict upon her person. The mere thought of it was almost enough to elicit sympathy. Almost.

"Seigneur?"

Roustan turned. The first mate was waiting uncertainly at the stairs leading up to the prow.

"What?" Gamaliel's compulsion allowed no room for courtesy. Unless Roustan was actively engaged in locating Salome, it was either a bludgeon or a whip. Sometimes both at once.

The first mate cleared his throat. "The captain says we've been granted permission to dock."

"Well, tell him to get on with it."

"Perhaps you'd be more comfortable in your cabin?"

Roustan stared at the first mate in silence. The man ducked his head and hurried off. He returned to peering at the ships through curtains of sleet. The sooner he found her, the sooner this misery of an existence ended. One way or another.

◆━━━━━━━━━━━━━━━━◆

A delegation was waiting when Roustan disembarked. The contingent included a score of soldiers and an anxious-looking official. Judging from his black cloak and finely made doublet, he was probably a canon lawyer. Roustan strode down the walkway followed by Gilles and the rest of his escort.

The nobleman was a plain-faced fellow with pale blue eyes and the slightly sallow look of someone who spent too much time indoors. He bowed from the waist. "My name is Andreu le Court," he said in fluent French, "assistant to the Lord High Chancellor. We received a letter from your master advising of your visit. At the Chancellor's request, I've been dispatched to offer whatever assistance you might require during your time in England."

"I am Roustan de Toulouse. I need to see the Harbourmaster immediately."

"The Harbourmaster?" A look of surprise at Roustan's abruptness flashed across Andreu's face. "Wouldn't you prefer a fire and dry clothes? This abominable rain is typical of this time of year, I'm afraid. However, I've secured a fine inn for you and your men at the crown's expense."

"Thank you for your kindness," Roustan replied. "You can send my escort there, but I must see the Harbourmaster now. Do you have a mount for me?"

"I—yes. Of course." Andreu gestured to his men. A spare mount was brought forward.

Roustan swung up into the saddle. "Gilles, I'll meet you at this inn shortly. What's it called?"

"The Courtesan's Fancy," Andreu supplied.

"Let me accompany you, Seigneur," Gilles responded.

"I'll be quite safe with Monsieur le Court," Roustan replied. "See to your men and equipment. We may need to leave without much notice. I'll join you soon." He turned to Andreu, who had mounted a grey mare. "Which way?"

"Follow me." Andreu led Roustan and their escort through the rain-drenched alleys of Portsmouth. Few people were about in such dire weather.

"The letter from your master neglected to mention the reason for your visit," Andreu said over the clatter of horseshoes on cobblestones. "Perhaps if you were willing to disclose it, I might be able to assist."

"I'm here on a private matter for his lordship," Roustan replied. "It's an extremely sensitive matter, so I must exercise a degree of discretion. I'm sure you understand."

Andreu pressed his lips together and maintained the courteous demeanour of a true diplomat.

After a few minutes twisting through the narrow streets, they arrived at the Harbourmaster's office. The two-storey timber building commanded a good view across the harbour. A narrow path— unsuitable for horses—led down to the water and piers designed for smaller craft. With the heavy layer of cloud, twilight was descending earlier than normal. Candlelight glowed through the thick windows of the office.

Roustan dismounted and handed his reins to one of Andreu's attendants. He strode up the worn stone steps and banged on the heavy timber door.

"Aye, just a moment," someone called out in English. A tall, lean fellow dressed in a worn grey tunic and dark green hose opened the door. He had the weathered look of a career sailor, with callused hands and a heavy brow. Taking in Roustan's bedraggled appearance and the guards behind him, he said, "What can I do for you, good sir?"

"Is the Harbourmaster here?" Roustan asked in fluent English. He had not known more than a handful of words before Gamaliel had stuffed the language into his head.

"Aye," the sailor responded. "Can I ask who's come visiting?"

"An emissary from the King of France," Andreu said from behind Roustan. "The Lord High Chancellor has guaranteed him every assistance, so you'd do well to make way, goodman."

The sailor retreated reluctantly. Roustan strode into a room with a low ceiling and a fire crackling in the grate. A staircase rose to the upper level on his left. On his right, a wide desk had been positioned beneath the main window looking out across the harbour. Scores of leather-bound journals had been stacked tightly in thick shelves set into one wall.

A greying man with a white beard pushed back from the desk and rose to his feet. He was dressed in a grey doublet with burgundy hose and fine leather shoes. In his fingers he held a quill. Black ink beaded from the tip. "Who is this, Jim?"

The tall sailor gestured towards Roustan and Andreu. "They say they've been sent by the King of France."

"Are you the Harbourmaster?" Roustan demanded.

"I am. My name is Edward Shipworth." He placed the quill carefully in the ink jar. "Whom do I have the honour of addressing?"

"I'm here on urgent business for his majesty, King Philippe," Roustan replied. "First, I need to know the name of every ship that has arrived in this port from France in the last two weeks. Second, whether any remain berthed here. Third, their next destination." He ticked off each requirement on his fingers.

"I see." Edward looked Roustan up and down. "Do you have any papers that support your claims?"

"I can attest to his identity," Andreu interrupted. "He's just arrived on *The Sea Falcon* out of Le Havre. My instructions come direct from the Chancellor himself." Andreu removed a piece of parchment from a pocket hidden inside his doublet. "You'll recognise the King's seal, I'm sure," he said pointing to the crest embedded in the wax.

"Indeed I do, sir," Edward replied. "Still, it'll take some time to approve this gentleman's request."

"I don't have the luxury of time," Roustan snapped. "Show me the ledger and I'll look myself."

"Out of the question," Edward replied. "These records are kept for the King and his representatives. It's against the law to—" Edward stumbled to a halt as Roustan drew his dagger.

"Show me the register now!" Roustan snapped.

"Seigneur!" Andreu made a calming gesture with both hands. "There's no need for threats."

Roustan rounded on Andreu. "Either you're here to help or impede me. Decide now: which is it to be?"

Andreu's pale eyes were huge in his face. "There's no need—"

"There is every need," Roustan snarled. "You know whom I represent and the matter is urgent. I swear you'll suffer if you cause me any delay." The dagger trembled in his fist. "You all will."

"Do as he says," Andreu said slowly. "This man is under the protection of King Philippe. I'll answer for any complaint you might have, Shipworth. Get the records."

Edward reluctantly retrieved a journal and laid it out upon his desk. A seagull's feather jutted from the stitched pages of parchment. He turned to the page with the feather and stepped back warily. "There. That's today's date. The first column is the date of arrival, the second the name of the ship. Beneath the ship's name is a brief description of its cargo. Date of departure appears in the next column, followed by intended destination. That's all I have."

Roustan sheathed his dagger and skimmed the records, working backwards. Given the time of year, it was hardly surprising that only a few ships had arrived from France in the last fortnight. Of those that had originated from France, only one remained in port: *Le Blanc Écume*, a cog out of Fécamp, apparently carrying wool.

Roustan tapped the entry. "This *Écume*. Did you inspect the ship?"

Edward frowned. "No, why should we? It regularly docks here, transporting cargo for the Cistercian brotherhood. The captain is well known to me and honest enough."

"Don't you think it's a strange time to be peddling wool?"

Edward shrugged. "Perhaps there was a shortage and he accepted a special commission."

"My thoughts exactly." Roustan stroked his beard. "You say the captain is well known to you. I need a description of him and the location of his berth. In writing." Roustan seized a blank piece of parchment from the desk and handed it to Edward.

Edward glanced at Andreu, who nodded. He took the parchment

from Roustan with a scowl. "What will happen from here?"

"That doesn't concern you." Roustan took Andreu by the arm and led him outside. "I need to recruit men who can take orders, wield a sword, and not ask difficult questions. Where can I find them?"

Andreu stared at Roustan. "Just how many mercenaries are you talking?"

"Two score at least."

"I'm not sure," Andreu faltered. "Truth be told, I don't normally deal with such folk."

"But you could make inquiries."

"Yes, of course," Andreu replied. "If I may ask, why do you need such a large force?"

Roustan considered the sallow Englishman. "Our King is very anxious to recover something stolen from him. That will have to be enough for you." Roustan re-entered the office and waited for Shipworth to finish his description of the *Écume*'s captain and its dock.

For the moment at least, Roustan was free of pain.

CHAPTER 18

1 August 1099

Godefroi's safe house

"**Y**ou're restless." Godwera lay on a divan in the deep shade cast by palm fronds. A thick blanket covered her, even though the day was suffocatingly hot.

Achambaud stilled his drumming foot and shifted on his bench of stone. Sweat beaded on his forehead and his tunic stuck to his ribs and back. Godwera had urged him into the shade but he had refused, wary of the new and disturbing feelings her proximity elicited. Besides, heat and hardship were things he understood. Enduring them was like being reunited with old friends.

"I'm sorry if I disturbed you, ma dame."

Godwera laughed. Her dry, throaty chuckle became a hacking cough. Achambaud retrieved a carafe of water and poured it into a flask.

"Such...formality," Godwera wheezed, "is...hardly...required...between us."

"Drink."

She swallowed obediently and regained her composure.

Achambaud remained in the shade of the palms. Seeing Godwera so diminished, and knowing he was to blame, was excruciating. He had learned not to give vent to such feelings, however. His guilt only caused her more pain.

A bond had formed between them the day she had risked her life to heal him. Achambaud did not understand it, but at times he could feel her emotions stirring. He suspected she could sense his moods too.

Whenever Godefroi visited—which thankfully was infrequently— their connection only intensified. Godefroi's presence always drew conflicting emotions from Godwera. Her emotional state would shatter into jarring shards of desire, defiance, and an ache that Achambaud could not name.

"You wish you had accompanied Hugues," Godwera said, "instead of tending to me." She rolled onto her side and her blanket dropped down to her waist, revealing the swell of her breasts beneath her shift and the pale curve of her neck. Desire threaded through Achambaud and drew painfully tight. He felt guilty for feeling this way, but he was powerless to prevent it. Thankfully she pulled the blanket back up to her shoulders.

"I no longer seem to know what I want," Achambaud replied, "assuming I ever did." He did not bother to hide the bitterness. There was little point. They were attuned. Impossibly, perhaps ruinously, so.

"It's strange, is it not," Godwera said, "that we should arrive at the same point from such different journeys."

"I'm not sure I understand, ma dame."

She *tsked* at his insistence on addressing her so formally. Did she not understand it was his sole defence against what lay between them?

"You can't decide which path to choose," she explained, "because you've lived a life of service. Only now, you realise that neither Hugues nor Godefroi can offer what you crave." She closed her eyes and Achambaud felt an echo of her frustration.

"As for me, well…" She spread her hands in a self-deprecating gesture. "Now that I've finally been offered the freedom to choose, I find that I'm unable to do so. Circumstances won't allow it. And so here we are." Achambaud caught the flash of her smile. "Adrift and rudderless, although not alone. Where will the tides take us, I wonder?"

Achambaud knelt at the foot of her divan. "Godwera." He stopped. His voice was too husky and the emotions stirring inside him were too deep and dangerous. The thing that lay between them was no longer inert. It stirred and wound around them. "I would serve you, ma dame, if you wished it." Another path, one he had not dared consider, opened before him. It was narrow and treacherous. One stumble and he might never recover, but he sensed it was worth the risk.

Godwera sat up and a purple cushion tumbled onto the flagstones. Neither moved to retrieve it. Achambaud could not drag his gaze from her face. She brushed a dark strand of hair aside and gazed at him intently. "We're companions, you and I. Not servant and master. Don't you feel that?"

Tears welled in his eyes and his fingers cracked as they curled into fists. Old, unhappy memories threatened to break free. All he had ever truly wanted was to belong. Not to a lord's household or an Order, but to *someone*.

She sank back against the divan and he clasped her delicate hand in his rough, scarred ones and sobbed.

"Dear Achambaud, this is my gift to you. Are you listening?"

He nodded, far beyond speech.

"If we're to experience any grace in this temporal life, then it must be we who grant it to ourselves." She gently lifted his chin so that he saw her tremendous compassion for him. "Healing you has taught me that lesson, so it is *I* who must thank *you*."

He clutched at her fingers, unable to bear letting go.

Godwera smiled. "I think you're the best of our sacred points, Achambaud. Accept the gift of embracing that truth, and whatever path you choose will serve God."

Achambaud bowed his head. "You don't wish me at your side."

She sighed and Achambaud felt an echo of her disappointment. "I wish for you to be free," she replied, "as I have wished so long for myself. Choose to serve Godefroi or Hugues if you must, but do so because you *want* to, not because you *need* to." She gently withdrew her hand.

Achambaud rocked back onto his haunches and stood. His leg flared with pain, but he did his best to ignore it. He could not look at her. Shame burned through the fibre of his being. "After—" he stopped, wanting to find the right words. "When this is done, where will you go?"

"If we're successful, back to the Salt Lines." A smile tugged at the corners of her mouth. "Lost among their dusty secrets, someone must remind them of the importance of grace."

Bells tolled in the distance to mark the hour of Sext. Godwera cupped her hands together. "May I have a moment alone to pray?"

Achambaud left Godwera's sanctuary and circled the pond. He should feel humiliated by her rejection, but her words had lodged deep inside him. He must make peace with his conscience before he could choose his path. Besides, the overriding emotion he sensed from Godwera was regret, not disdain at his advances.

Yet again, she was a mirror to his heart.

CHAPTER 19

2 August 1099

The Pool of Siloam

The Pool of Siloam was a deep, rectangular trough cut into the earth and bordered with weathered stone. Hugues descended the steps and removed his shoes at the water's edge. Etienne slumped onto the cracked stone paving next to him. Sunlight sparkled across the clear water, which was only ankle-deep. During the height of the siege, it had been completely exhausted by the parched Christian army. After a questioning look at Hugues, Etienne removed his shoes as well.

"You're wondering why we've come here," Hugues murmured as he gathered up his habit and tucked the folds into the cord around his waist.

Etienne glanced over his shoulder.

They were not alone. Four water bearers were filling two large urns near the foot of the stairs. Once finished, they would portage their sloshing cargo back to the souks in Jerusalem for sale.

Etienne shrugged. "I assumed you would explain when you were ready."

Hugues untied Etienne's pilgrim sack and shoved their shoes inside. "Umayr said it was all chronicled in Scripture. It occurred to me while trying to fall asleep that perhaps he was speaking literally. Sure enough, the second book of Chronicles describes how King Hezekiah, threatened with a siege by the Assyrians, had the foresight to build a tunnel to secure Jerusalem's water supply. Chapter 32, verse thirty reads: *'And Hezekiah himself hath stopped the upper source of the waters of Gihon, and directeth them beneath to the west of the city of David'.*"

Etienne stared at the pool. A slight current rippled across its surface. He turned to the far stone wall and the jumble of rocks that had collapsed at its base. "The pool and spring are connected."

"Exactly," Hugues replied. "So the city of David must have been located above the spring."

Etienne pursed his lips. "And you believe the pool of Siloam is in the western part of the city of David."

"I do, although I found more references." Hugues glanced at the water carriers to ensure they were not eavesdropping.

"Consider Book 1 of Kings, Chapter 2, verse 9," Hugues said. "'*So David slept with his fathers, and was buried in the city of David.*' And in the book of Nehemiah, Chapter 3, verse 16 refers to '*The place over against the sepulchres of David, and to the pool that was made, and unto the house of the mighty*'."

"That must be it," Etienne whispered in excitement. "The sepulchres of kings near a pool. That can't be coincidence."

"That was my conclusion." Hugues smiled. "In those times, it was unusual to bury the dead inside the city for fear of sickness. My guess is that the royal necropolis was placed at the edge of the city, well away from dwellings and the main trade routes."

"So, not close to this pool," Etienne mused. "The book of Nehemiah must be a reference to the Gihon Spring then."

"I believe so," Hugues replied. "And the *house of the mighty* must surely be a reference to God's kingdom."

"To which we always turn east."

"Exactly. The west bank of the Kidron valley looks east and it's not far from the Gihon Spring. I think we'll find David's tomb near there."

Etienne was silent for a while. Eventually he asked, "When did Hezekiah reign?"

"About seven hundred BC," Hugues replied. "Roughly two hundred and fifty years after King David."

"And you think some kind of marker has been left in the watercourse."

The water bearers had almost filled their urns. "I think for the defence of any city to be viable, they must control their water supply." Hugues nodded towards the water. "Aren't you thirsty?"

Hugues lay flat on the warm stone platform and scooped up handfuls of water. The liquid was cool and refreshing. A hint of minerals played across his palate.

Etienne copied Hugues, slurping water from his cupped hands and scrubbing his dusty face. When he had finished, the curls about his ears were plastered to his neck.

Hugues leaned back against the wall and waited for the water carriers to leave. They waited in silence as the men checked their netting. Once the urn was securely fastened, they braced one pole against each shoulder and lifted it into the air. Eventually the two men reached the top of the stairs, readjusted positions so they faced the same direction, and staggered back towards Jerusalem.

"Finally." Without waiting for Etienne, Hugues stepped into the pool and used his pilgrim's staff to test his footing. The water was soothing against his calloused feet. Etienne waded after him and eddies swirled around their feet.

"The tunnel must be over here." Hugues traced the subtle current back to the far wall. A pile of large stones had tumbled into the pool at some point, blocking off any sign of a tunnel or watercourse. Looking closely, Hugues noticed water trickled through small gaps in the rock. Was it possible the entrance had been collapsed deliberately?

"Quickly, Etienne." Hugues waved him over. "Do you see this large rock? Good. It's braced by this one beneath it. We'll have to move these two up here first." Hugues tapped each rock in turn with the butt of his staff as he spoke. "We must work quickly."

"Let me try. Here, take this." Etienne passed the sack to Hugues and clambered up the main boulder until he was precariously balanced at the top.

"You might want to move out of the way." Etienne jammed his pilgrim's staff into a gap between the loose stones and the rock face. Making sure of his footing, he heaved. The wooden staff snapped with a loud crack that echoed around the pool. Etienne just caught his balance.

Hugues offered his staff but Etienne waved him off. "No, no, it's all right. A shorter piece will be stronger anyway." Etienne wedged the broken end of the staff into the gap. When he could not force it in any further, he used a small rock to hammer the tip in deeper.

Once Etienne was satisfied, he placed a flat rock between the rock face and the broken staff. Bracing his feet as best he could, Etienne levered the shaft. A shower of stones tumbled into the pool with a splash.

Etienne repeated the exercise on the other side of the main boulder, clearing the uppermost rocks. The opening of a tunnel became visible. Etienne scrubbed away dirt and mud. Beneath the detritus, a curved arch of stone was visible.

The gap Etienne had opened was small. Big enough for a child, perhaps even Etienne's slight frame, but it would not accommodate Hugues.

"Well done," Hugues said, "but I'm not sure we'll be able to move that boulder."

Etienne clambered down to the pool. Using the broken end of his staff, he cleared away some small stones beneath the water. Eventually he turned back to Hugues. "The left side is solid and grounded. We would need horses and ropes to roll it away." He moved around to the right side. "Over here, the rock has been worn away by the passage of water. Our best chance is to roll it in that direction."

"What do you suggest?" Hugues asked.

"Put the sack down and come back over here."

Hugues glanced at the stairs. How long would it be before they were interrupted? He had left agents of the Salt Lines to block the path to the pool. They could manage that for a time, but if a chevalier or noble arrived, they would be forced to withdraw.

When Hugues returned to the boulder, he found Etienne had wedged his broken staff between it and a slab of rock that lay at the bottom of the pool. "We don't have the strength to roll this boulder," Etienne explained. "However, with the right amount of force applied at the correct points, I think we can shift it. I'm going to bear down on this staff with all my weight. Hopefully that will allow you to turn it. I need you to jam your staff behind the boulder. As I press down to lift the rock up, you force it to one side."

"Like opening a door."

"Exactly."

Hugues moved into position next to the boulder.

"Ready?" Etienne asked.

Hugues nodded.

Placing one hand against the wall for balance, Etienne stepped onto the broken shaft. Hugues wedged his feet against the wall and pushed against his staff. The boulder shuddered before his staff snapped in two.

Hugues fell headfirst into the pool and a high-pitched whine keened through his ears. He staggered to his knees and gasped for breath. The sound cut out as soon as he surfaced.

Etienne's laughter died as he caught the look on Hugues' face. "What's wrong? Are you injured?" He waded over and helped Hugues up by the elbow.

Hugues withdrew the necklace that Umayr had given him. Leaning forward, he dipped the shard of crystal in the water. It vibrated between his fingers and Hugues caught a high-pitched whine. He jerked the crystal out of the water.

Hugues clutched at Etienne. "Did you hear that?"

"Hear what? Your splash?" Etienne frowned at him in puzzlement.

"No," Hugues replied. "A...buzzing sound, like a wasp, when the crystal dipped into the water." He tried again, longer this time. The vibration made his ears and teeth ache.

"I can't hear anything," Etienne said.

Hugues glanced at the shard. Why did it react like that? He had never heard of crystal responding to water in such a fashion. Perhaps the explanation lay further upstream. Hugues set the problem aside with a shake of his head. "We need to move that boulder."

"I think we're close. I felt it shift before you fell." Etienne seemed relieved by the change in topic.

They resumed their positions and tried again. Hugues used both pieces of his snapped staff to shift the boulder. It was harder with the shorter lengths, but they didn't snap this time. Committing all his strength to the effort, Hugues managed to force the boulder forward a few inches.

Hugues collapsed against the stone wall, breathing hard. Etienne inspected the breach. "You did it. I think we can squeeze through." Etienne retrieved the sack. "Are you ready?"

Hugues nodded and rolled his wrists. "You go first. I'll pass the sack once you're inside."

Etienne squeezed through the narrow gap between the boulder and the rock wall.

Hugues stuffed the sack through the opening and prodded it with his broken staff until Etienne could reach it. He then retrieved the pieces of his broken staff. Using a few well-placed stones, he weighed them down underwater, next to the boulder. With luck, no one would notice what they had done here.

He returned to the narrow opening. "This is going to be tight." Hugues took a deep breath and exhaled. Jagged edges pressed into the small of his back and scraped against his unprotected calves. He wriggled sideways, breathing shallowly to keep his body as flat as possible. Halfway through, a knob of stone grated against his spine. Hugues stilled, fighting to control his panic.

"The stone is wet," Etienne called from the tunnel. "You can slide past it."

Etienne was right. Moisture trickled down his neck and calves. Or perhaps it was sweat. Hugues eased forward, half a finger's length at most. The stone ground into his flesh but didn't break his skin. Rather than trying to avoid it, Hugues moulded his body to the curves and depressions of the boulder. He edged forward again.

"Almost there," Etienne called.

The rock crowded Hugues on all sides, only allowing shallow

breaths. He slid forward again and cracked the back of his head on an unseen outcrop. Blood oozed from his scalp and ran past his ear lobe. Etienne appeared from the gloom. He took Hugues' outstretched hand.

"Slowly," Etienne said. "Relax through it."

Hugues exhaled and squeezed past the last section of the boulder. Stone grazed his shoulder-blades and he stumbled on something below the water. Etienne caught him before he tripped.

"Easy," Etienne said. "I was afraid you might get stuck there."

"*You* were afraid?" Hugues retorted. "I pray there's a way out at the end of this tunnel. I'm not sure I could manage a second attempt."

Etienne fumbled with the sack, unknotted it and withdrew two candles and his tinder box. "Can you hold this?" He handed the candles and sack to Hugues. It was difficult in the gloom of the tunnel to coax a spark. Etienne struck the flint against the metal strike repeatedly before the oil-soaked char cloth caught alight. Fanning the embers carefully with his breath, Hugues dipped the wick of each candle in the flames. Candlelight cast a weak glow through the tunnel.

Etienne doused the char cloth with the hem of his tunic, checked the embers had gone out, and packed everything away in the sack.

Hugues lifted his candle overhead. The tunnel was narrow, wide enough for a man to pass but not two. Moisture glistened on yellow rock that was stained with white sediment. The ceiling was surprisingly high, so much so that even the tallest of men need not bend their knees.

Etienne's eyes glimmered in the candlelight. "I can go first, if you wish."

"Protect your light," Hugues replied. "We mustn't get trapped down here in the dark." He brushed past Etienne and followed the ancient aqueduct.

CHAPTER 20

2 August 1099

Hezekiah's tunnel

A disguise had been necessary.

That much was obvious when Gamaliel tracked them to the Pool of Siloam. The priest had been clever enough to leave peasants blocking his trail.

The arrival of more water bearers was too fortuitous to ignore. Anywhere else, he would have slipped from the flesh he wore and taken hold of one of the muscled slaves, but not here before the walls of Jerusalem.

Gamaliel joined the growing argument between the peasants and the men who made their pitiful living carting water. As the argument escalated, he threatened to report the seizure of the pool to the King's Seneschal. As expected, the priest's men hesitated. They could not afford to attract too much attention.

The peasants withdrew after a round of empty threats. Clapping him on the shoulder like an old friend, the water bearers invited Gamaliel to join them at the pool. He graciously accepted.

It *was* what he had wanted in the first place, after all.

Busy with their heavy urns and the steep steps, the water bearers failed to notice the submerged stones and the tunnel partially visible behind the boulder. Gamaliel followed them down the steps, his gaze locked on King Hezekiah's ancient tunnel.

What had drawn the priest to it?

Bound to flesh, there was only one way to find out. Yet he would have to wait. Filling a water urn seemed to take an inordinately long time.

After a few scooped handfuls of water, Gamaliel settled in a sunny corner and pretended to fall asleep. At least he would not need a light in the tunnel. Even cloaked in human flesh, the Lords of Severity could still see in the dark.

The tunnel proved far longer than Hugues had expected. It wove through the earth, occasionally widening into small pools before narrowing again. Moisture glistened on the walls of the aqueduct. He ran one hand along the sandy-coloured bedrock, his fingertips brushing against pick marks that were almost two thousand years old.

Hugues and Etienne waded through the tunnel in silence. The water was fairly shallow, only reaching mid-thigh at its deepest. It was much cooler below ground. Every now and then the tunnel twisted unexpectedly. The air was still and candlelight glistened off the steadily flowing water. Hugues had hoped for some kind of markings or symbols to indicate the site of David's tomb, but he saw none.

Eventually Etienne broke their silence. "Hugues, can we stop a moment?"

Hugues halted and turned around. "What is it?"

"My candle is burning low." Etienne fumbled with his sack and withdrew a short length of candle. Using the wick of his failing candle, he lit the new one and raised it overhead. "That was my last one, I'm afraid."

Hugues glanced at his candle. Hot wax had already dribbled over his fingers, creating a protective layer. His candle would not last much longer either.

"Do you know how far it is to the spring?" Etienne asked.

"No," Hugues replied. "It's hard to get your bearings underground."

"If we turn back now," Etienne said quietly, "I'm sure my candle will last. But if you don't know how much further we must travel—" He spread his hands helplessly.

"Hush," Hugues said. "Do you hear that?"

Etienne stilled as he strained to catch the sound. A distant splash reached them.

"That's not an echo," Etienne whispered.

"No," Hugues replied in a matching whisper. "Someone is in the tunnel with us."

"Could it be a member of the Salt Lines?"

Hugues shooks his head. "I told them not to approach the pool. So we either confront whoever is following us or we go on."

"God in heaven," Etienne said with feeling.

"I say we keep going," Hugues said.

Etienne nodded.

They moved through the tunnel at a brisker pace, not speaking for fear of being overheard. Hugues searched the walls for the markings in vain. Nor was he able to locate any offshoots from the tunnel. The walls were hewn from seamless rock. In desperation, Hugues knelt and plunged the crystal shard in the water. The piercing vibration was definitely stronger. He could only take a few seconds of its keening before he yanked the crystal out.

"Don't do it again if it pains you so," Etienne whispered.

"The sound is stronger. We must be heading in the right direction."

Hugues ploughed on through the narrow tunnel. The incline began to steepen as his candle finally guttered out. Fortunately, natural light illuminated a bend in the tunnel.

Hugues struggled forward against the strengthening current and rounded the bend. Weak sunlight filtered down from a shaft in the roof. Lying in front of Hugues was a large, roughly circular pool. As he watched, water bubbled up from a subterranean source.

Etienne joined Hugues at the edge of the pool. "This must be the Gihon Spring." He doused his candle. The roof curved into a natural dome. On the far side of the pool, rough steps climbed out of the chamber. They angled up through the rock and twisted away to the left.

"Must be." Hugues glanced back the way they had come. The bend obscured any sign of pursuing lights. "We must be quick." Hugues waded into the middle of the spring. It was much deeper than the tunnel, reaching up to his chest. He struggled to keep his balance on the slippery rock.

When he felt he was in the centre of the spring, Hugues immersed the shard. The pitch of the crystal was much deeper this time. No longer painful, it had a penetrating quality that vibrated through Hugues' fingers, down his arm, and through his body. Ripples radiated outwards from where Hugues stood.

The crystal shuddered in his fingers and a single reverberating chime rose up from the depths. Even though it was far distant, hidden beneath layers of rock, the chime rolled up through Hugues and into the shard. Somewhere deep below, something recognised the crystal and hailed its arrival.

Hugues lifted the shard from the spring. "Quickly," he beckoned to Etienne. "I have what we came for."

Etienne waded through the deep water as quickly as he could. Together they scrambled up the steep steps on the far side of the pool. Hugues stopped at the landing where the tunnel twisted to the left and dropped to the ground, motioning for Etienne to copy him. Lying flat on his belly, he watched the spring for signs of pursuit.

Time trickled past agonisingly slowly. Hugues strained to detect any movement in the gloom. Water gurgled up from below, but it was the only thing that moved.

Hugues licked his lips and waited.

They were being followed. He was certain of it.

Etienne pressed the hilt of a knife into his hand. Hugues wished he had a more substantial weapon, but it would have to do. They had prepared for exploring caves, not combat.

Nothing stirred in Hezekiah's tunnel. Hugues remembered the attack in the ravine where Firyal had died. He knew the darkness could not be trusted.

Hugues waited long beyond the period caution dictated. Eventually he rose cautiously to his feet. "Outside," he said in a hoarse voice.

The sun was high overhead when they emerged from the rock overhang that hid the entrance to the spring. Hugues was grateful for the bright sunlight.

"What happened back there?" Etienne rubbed his arms.

"I think we were being followed."

"Yes, but by whom?"

"I'm not sure." That was a lie. Hugues had a terrible suspicion of what had followed them into the tunnel, but he did not want to unsettle Etienne.

They had emerged on the eastern slope of a lower hill to the south of Jerusalem. The Kidron Valley dropped away directly in front of them. Stubborn bushes and the occasional olive tree clung to the steep slope. Despite their proximity to Jerusalem, no one was in sight.

He closed his eyes and recalled the chime echoing up from below ground. It was deep. Buried a long way beneath the earth, almost directly below them. If Hezekiah's tunnel did not provide access to whatever lay down there, only one other option was possible.

"Where are those ropes?" Hugues asked.

"Here, in the sack." Etienne unpacked them.

"Good. Follow me." Hugues led Etienne across the stony ground to the edge of the valley. The slope was not vertical, but it was steep enough that Hugues wouldn't risk it without a rope.

Hugues gauged their position relative to the Gihon Spring and moved a few feet south. "Secure the rope to something." Hugues wrapped the other end about his waist.

"You're going over the edge?" Etienne asked.

"If I'm right, we all will."

Etienne tied the rope to a large boulder embedded in the ground and donned lambskin gloves so he could feed out the rope as Hugues descended.

"Ready?" Hugues asked.

Etienne braced his feet and wound the loose length of rope about his waist twice. "Let's hope what you're looking for isn't far. This rope won't reach the bottom."

Hugues estimated the length. "It should do." He backed off the edge and started his descent. Etienne fed the rope out, a little too slowly at first but he quickly gathered speed as his confidence increased. Hugues avoided the small shrubs that clung to the slope so the rope wouldn't snag.

About forty feet down, he spotted the mouth of a small crevasse to his left. Brush had partially covered the entrance, so it would have been easy to miss if he had not been looking for it. Hugues yanked on the rope twice. The feed from above halted and Hugues examined the hidden entrance.

Three large steps to the left should do it. But he would need more rope.

Hugues yanked on the rope three times, indicating Etienne should continue feeding out the line. The rope jerked and continued dropping. Once Hugues felt he had enough to work with, he jerked the line twice again.

He took two small steps to the right and then dashed to the left. His first swing brought him to within a foot of the crevasse. Hugues let momentum carry him back the other way, his feet skimming across rock and loose soil. When he completed his arc to the right, Hugues swung back to the left and charged towards the crevasse. He reached it easily and hooked one leg in the opening. Branches scratched his shin and he grabbed the thickest of these with his free hand.

Enduring more scratches to his arms, Hugues wiggled into the tight entrance. Once he felt safe, he yanked the rope three times again to obtain some slack. Etienne fed more rope down, allowing Hugues to worm further into the crevasse.

Tucked safe inside the opening, Hugues hacked away the smallest branches and twigs with his belt knife. The thickest branches proved too challenging, so Hugues untied the rope and fastened it to the strongest of these.

Hugues rolled onto his stomach and glanced into the depths of the tunnel. The opening was wide enough for him to crawl through. A thin trickle of water threaded across the bottom of the fissure. Could this watercourse be connected to the Gihon Spring?

He dipped the crystal shard in the trickle of water. A booming chime thundered through the connection. Hugues yanked the shard back and trembled at the powerful reaction. What was waiting for him at the end of this narrow cave?

Hugues wriggled forward. The fissure widened as it burrowed into the rock. Hugues was able to crouch and eventually stand. It should have been too dark to see, but strange veins in the rock glimmered with a pale blue light. Hugues touched one. The light came from some kind of fungus. He rounded a bend and almost collided with a wall of rock.

"No," Hugues whispered. "This is the place. I know it is." He glanced about to either side, but it was a dead end.

Hugues touched the wall. Unlike the sides of the crevasse, this stone was dark yellow bedrock, solid and unremarkable. Water seeped from the base of the rock wall and trickled out of the watercourse. None of the blue fungus grew on it.

He frowned in suspicion. Hugues rapped the rock with his knuckles. It seemed solid.

"Clever," Hugues whispered to the shade of whoever built this façade. "But you used the wrong type of rock, so the blue fungus never grew back." He was sorely tempted to break open the false wall. However, only the five sacred points could disturb David's resting place.

"I'll return with the others," he promised.

CHAPTER 21

15 December 1307

North of Leeds

"I don't suppose I can persuade you to accompany us." William had stopped at their cooking fire to speak with Bertrand. The tall English knight was already dressed for the day's journey in a plain grey surcoat and a green cloak worn over his chainmail. The rest of his men were breaking camp.

"I'm afraid not," Bertrand replied with true regret, "although I appreciate the offer."

The sun was peeking through the bare branches of the dell where they had camped. It had rained heavily throughout the night, making for a cold and miserable night's sleep. The ground squelched beneath Bertrand's boots and a chill in the air promised snow.

"Thought as much." William's gaze shifted to Salome's hooded figure sitting under a square of canvas tied between trees. "You've more pressing business, it seems."

"We do." Bertrand wished he could confide in the English knight, but Salome had forbidden it.

"Well, perhaps you'll reconsider when your affairs are settled." William glanced around the dell. "My men will need a rest. Depending on the hospitality of the Abbot, we may stay at Fountains for as long as a week. As I've already said, you'd be mad to return to France. And I fear England will become equally inhospitable to our Order."

"Thank you. I'll keep that in mind and I hope we see each other again." Bertrand clasped William's forearms and kissed him on either side of the cheek, as was his custom. "I'll look for you if we do head north."

William smiled. "Farewell then." He nodded to Rémi and lifted a hand to Salome, but she did not respond. William shook his head and mounted his horse. Within a few moments, the rest of his brothers were mounted and riding north out of the dell.

Rémi stood and joined Bertrand as they watched their English brethren depart.

"They'll be at the abbey before nightfall," Bertrand said. "It's only another twenty miles or so."

Rémi grunted. "It was good to have some company, even if they were English."

Bertrand smiled. "I like William. I think we could have trusted him."

"Perhaps." Salome had slipped through the trees without making any noise. Rémi startled at the closeness of her voice, although Bertrand had sensed her approach.

"But he's not of the Salt Lines," Salome observed. "Why take unnecessary risks?" Salome removed her cowl. Her normally olive skin appeared pale in the early light and dark crescents bruised the skin beneath her eyes.

Bertrand ran his fingers through his tangled hair. "Surely we'd be safer among members of the Order than on our own."

"Probably, but we would also be easier to locate."

Rémi frowned. "We're in England now. Philippe and his lackeys have no authority here."

"Gold and privilege recognise no borders." She rubbed her hands together for warmth over the fire. "He'll have factors in England looking for us. Don't doubt it for a moment."

Bertrand switched topics. "You said we were close to our destination."

Salome chafed her arms. "Rooklyn Abbey is another two-day's ride north-west from here on the edge of the Yorkshire Dales. Assuming no delays, we should arrive before dusk tomorrow."

"A roof overhead would be welcome," Rémi grumbled. "I'm heartily sick of this wet English winter."

Salome smiled. "You'll find a warm welcome at Rooklyn, I'm sure. They've been waiting for us to arrive for some time."

"Who are *they*?" Bertrand asked.

"The Abbot and his monks, of course."

"William has never heard of this abbey," Bertrand replied. "Don't you think that's strange?"

"No. Not really." Salome frowned. "Construction was only finished in secret last year. You shouldn't have said anything, Bertrand."

He ignored the irritation that bristled through their link. "I don't understand this."

"Understand what?" Salome put her hands on her hips.

"Why go to the trouble of building a secret abbey when all you need do is to forget the location of the keystone?" Bertrand tilted his head as he watched her reaction. "It seems like a lot of trouble, don't you think?"

"I told you before," Salome replied in an overly patient voice. "The abbey was built on the intersection of two salt lines in the geographic centre of Britain. It's a sacred place."

Rémi scratched his head. "Why is the location so important?"

"It just is." Salome stalked over to her horse and checked her saddle.

"I think Rémi asked a fair question," Bertrand said, refusing to budge. The tiny rose in the webbing of his right hand began to ache. Bertrand stared at it in astonishment. Was Salome feeling threatened?

She turned to face the two men. "The knowledge was granted to me in a sacred place, so it must be taken from me in a similar location. Now are we going to talk all day, or are we going to finish this journey?"

"No need to ask me twice," Rémi muttered. "I wanted this over before it even began." He stamped over to his horse.

Bertrand sensed there was more to Salome's answer, but he let it pass. Like Rémi, he was anxious to end their journey. Especially since the rain chose that moment to make an unwelcome reappearance.

CHAPTER 22

16 December 1307

Rooklyn Abbey

As Bertrand had feared the day before, heavy flakes of snow followed on the heels of the persistent rain. After hours in the saddle, it felt like daylight had just skipped past them, leaving them wreathed in a grey twilight that limited visibility to less than thirty yards in any direction.

Despite the conditions, Salome led them confidently through empty fields, over ice-encrusted brooks, and around rolling hills. Bertrand was content to follow, but he found the emptiness and silence of the landscape unnerving. Perhaps it was the snow that blanketed sound. He had experienced enough winters to know that a heavy downfall could create an eerie stillness in forests. Yet the barren lifelessness of the moors was unlike anything he had seen before.

Towards the end of the day, the landscape became hillier. The snowdrifts were deeper here and the gloom thickened in the narrow valleys that squeezed between low but steep, hilltops. Salome let her horse pick the best path. Despite his best efforts at massaging his fingers and wiggling his toes, Bertrand's extremities were so cold they had stopped aching.

He raised his voice. "Salome, we must make camp."

Close behind Bertrand, Rémi grunted in agreement.

"We're almost there." Salome and her horse were vague shapes amid the flurries of swirling snow. Bertrand sensed both determination and foreboding from her. No doubt she was anxious to reach the abbey before nightfall.

Rémi urged his horse forward. It floundered in snow drifts as it tried to draw abreast. Bertrand shortened his reins to let Rémi catch up.

"We either stop or freeze in the saddle." Rémi waved a gloved hand in front of his face. "My fingers and toes have already started. Cock's probably next."

Bertrand grimaced at the rough humour. Salome had already disappeared into the grey haze ahead.

Rémi leaned over and thumped Bertrand's shoulder. "Listen, cub. There's nothing out here. Not even a goat track. We need shelter."

Rémi was right. Apart from a few mounds of stone that *may* have been deliberately arranged, he had seen no sign of human habitation for hours. It was time to make camp. Bertrand drew in a breath to call out when a spike of excitement from Salome jolted through him.

"Bertrand!" The wind snatched her voice away.

"She's found something." He turned and urged his tired mount forward. The ground rose sharply and his mare struggled for footing. Bertrand was tempted to dismount, although he knew the snow would quickly sap his energy.

The wind was stronger on the hilltop. It howled around him and snapped at his cloak. Bertrand leaned against the neck of his horse and urged her forward. Salome's excitement and trepidation were building. He followed her tracks along the spine of the ridge. The snow was lighter here and his mare made better progress.

Salome and her horse emerged from the billowing drifts of snow. She lifted her hood and gave him a relieved smile. "We've arrived." She pointed towards a steep trail that curled around a bend as it dropped into a hidden valley.

Bertrand stared down the trail. All he could see was carefully arranged stones embedded in the earth. They formed platforms of rock, spaced at regular intervals, almost like giant steps.

"It's best we go by foot from here." Salome dismounted and started down the trail, leading her horse by the reins.

"Where's she off to now?" Rémi had arrived in time to see the rear of Salome's mount rounding the corner.

"Heaven only knows." Bertrand glanced at the sky. Night was not far off. If they did not find shelter soon, there would be no light to set a fire. On the other hand, this ridge was far too exposed for them to remain here. Bertrand shrugged. If Salome was mistaken, he would force her to make camp. He dismounted and followed her.

"She'll get us all killed," Rémi shouted.

Bertrand ignored the warning and concentrated on the descent. Each landing was large enough to accommodate a horse. As he cleared the third platform, his mount suddenly whinnied and reared in terror. Bertrand was yanked backwards as the reins jerked his wrist. He teetered, one arm windmilling to catch his balance. A hoof caught him in the left shoulder and sent him spinning downhill.

He came to a stop, sprawled on the next shelf of rock. His shoulder throbbed through the numbing cold. Bertrand groaned and rolled onto his side.

"Bertrand!" Salome bent over him in concern. Beyond her, the sky was stained with beautiful streaks of lavender and vermillion. The heavy layer of cloud and blinding snow had completely vanished.

He sat up in astonishment, too surprised to pay heed to the pain grinding through his shoulder-blade. "What happened to the snow?" He gaped at the clear sky.

Salome knelt next to him. "I told you Rooklyn Abbey is situated in a sacred place. How bad is your shoulder?" She tried to help him up.

"You didn't tell me the weather is different from one step to the next," Bertrand snapped.

Rémi emerged from the curtain of snow only a few feet away. His mount tossed its head and stamped its hooves, but Rémi kept a firm grip on his reins. He had managed to capture Bertrand's mare as well.

"What in the name of God is this?" Rémi asked in astonishment.

Salome rose from her crouch over Bertrand. "We've arrived at Rooklyn Abbey." She edged her horse back to the side of the trail so they could get a clear view of the valley below. The surrounding hills formed a steep, roughly circular, basin. Pockets of wildflowers bloomed amid the lush green grass that covered the valley floor. A mild breeze blew through the valley and sunlight sparkled across a brook.

A cluster of buildings drew Bertrand's eye. Spires topped the north and south towers of a cathedral. Nestled next to its southern side was the square courtyard of a cloister. Attaching to the cloister was a series of smaller buildings, including what looked like a dormitory and a five-sided chapter house. The brook ran through the abbey, disappearing beneath the cloister before reappearing on the far side to drain into a pond.

Bertrand finally found his voice. "How is this possible?"

Salome smiled. "Rooklyn is protected by the power of the meridians that intersect beneath it. As long as the wards remain, winter's touch will never take hold. Come, our journey is almost over." She turned and led her horse down the switchback trail that dropped to the valley floor.

"Unnatural is what it is," Rémi muttered.

Bertrand shivered. "Would you prefer the blizzard?"

"At least we know what to expect from it."

Bertrand privately agreed, but they could hardly turn back. He followed Salome down the switchback cradling his left arm. After a few moments, he caught the sound of horseshoes as Rémi followed.

For some reason his gaze was constantly drawn to the cathedral. It was hardly the largest or most impressive he had seen. The flying buttresses and eaves of the steeply tiled roof were constructed from dark grey stone. Yet despite the plainness of its facade, the cathedral had a commanding, almost forbidding, aspect.

Another thought struck him.

Where were the monks and lay brethren? A few sheep grazed throughout the basin, but he saw no shepherds tending them. A lone building to the south of the abbey could have been a forge, yet no smoke issued from its chimney.

In France, an abbey of this size would usually be supported by a sizeable community. The absence of any folk was unnerving.

Bertrand concentrated on his footing, knowing his bruised shoulder would punish him if he stumbled again.

Once they reached the bottom, Salome remounted and cantered towards the western entrance of the cathedral. Rémi helped Bertrand back into his saddle and they followed at a more cautious pace. Despite Salome's apparent exuberance, Bertrand still sensed trepidation from her. Something about this place terrified her, although she was anxious not to show it.

Bertrand and Rémi's shadows reached the church well before they did. They dismounted before the twin oak doors where Salome waited impatiently. Her mount grazed at the grass a few yards away and the other horses followed its example.

"I honestly didn't expect to reach this place." Salome's dark, almond-shaped eyes glistened with emotion. "Thank you." She took Rémi's hand and kissed the back of his fingers. Turning to Bertrand, she repeated the gesture.

Shock flashed across Rémi's face before he regained his usual glower. "Are we going inside or not?"

"Rémi, this is no ordinary church."

"That's hardly a revelation," he observed drily.

"It was designed by the Salt Lines," Salome continued, ignoring Rémi's sarcasm. "Only members of the families may enter these doors. It's probably best if you remain with the horses. I'll send Bertrand once the way is clear."

Rémi scowled. "Clear of what?"

Salome smiled. "This is a path only intended for my Shroud and I. To force your way inside would be disastrous. Please. Wait for Bertrand.

I promise all will be well."

"Having come this far, do you really think I'm just going to wait around outside?" Rémi's face turned red.

"Rémi, please," Bertrand interrupted. "Do as she asks. We have no idea what to expect."

"My point exactly." Rémi jabbed a finger towards the cathedral. "Where is everyone? If she's an honoured guest, why does no one receive her? I don't like it, cub."

Bertrand faced Salome. "They're fair questions."

"The monks are inside, waiting for the two of us. Not three." She turned and lifted the heavy latch that held the door closed. Using her free hand, she took hold of the iron ring and pulled. The tall door swung open with a faint shudder. The hinges were well greased and hardly made any sound.

It was dark inside the cathedral. No candles or braziers had been lit. Bertrand had an impression of a vast space, far larger than it seemed the walls of the cathedral could possibly contain. The nearest flagstones were worn smooth, which reinforced his impression of age. He could just make out two enormous pillars that divided the nave. Beyond that, the cathedral was wreathed in darkness.

Salome crossed the threshold and entered the nave. Bertrand followed close behind, peering into the gloom for any kind of threat.

"Call me if you have need." Rémi's voice seemed to come from a long way away.

Salome stopped in the centre of the nave. She closed her eyes and lifted her hands, palms facing the floor. After a moment, she took a half step forward and sank to her knees. "Kneel here, next to me." Her voice was hushed, the words almost breathless.

Bertrand glanced around the still cathedral. "Perhaps we should light a torch?"

"No, that's the point. Emerging from darkness. Kneel. Now."

Bertrand knelt reluctantly, shifting his scabbard so that it would not strike the flagstones. The sound of his chainmail was loud in the stillness. He suddenly thought of his all-night vigil back at the chapel of St Anne. It was hard to believe that ceremony had been only two months ago.

"In the name of the Ishim," Salome intoned, "I embrace Adonai Melech, the root of all creation."

Bertrand's skin tingled as unseen forces brushed against his face and the stone beneath them trembled. The vibrations shot up through his knees and a brief flash of pain stabbed him in the groin. Grimacing, he leapt to his feet.

"What was that?" Bertrand said through his teeth.

Salome rose from her kneeling position. "Malkuth, the tenth Sephirah. Come." She moved further down the nave. She lifted her arms up, palms facing the flagstones with fingers flared. Bertrand was reminded of a water diviner he once saw locating the best place to dig a well.

Salome stopped abruptly. She knelt again and bade Bertrand join her.

"In the name of the Cherubim," Salome said in a clear voice, "I embrace Shaddai el Chai, the essence of imagination."

The air stirred about them again. Half-glimpsed images danced about Bertrand, gyrating so quickly they blurred from one shape to the next. This time pain stabbed Bertrand just above his pubic mound and he bit the side of his mouth in surprise.

Salome stood and moved towards her left. Passing through an enormous arch, she entered the north aisle.

"What are these stabbing pains?" Bertrand whispered as he groped after her in the darkness.

"As we move through the Tree of Life, the different spheres mark different parts of our body," Salome replied.

"I see no tree," Bertrand said in a churlish voice.

Salome turned to face him. "The cathedral *is* the tree, if you look from above. Remember the three stained glass panels from the chapel in your Commanderie?"

Bertrand nodded.

"The nave and the aisles to either side are the same."

In his mind, he pictured the Tree of Life that he had glimpsed in the Chapel of St Anne. Yes, it would be easy to impose the tree over the floor plan of a cathedral. The nave would form the central pillar, while the outer aisles represented the pillars of Severity and Mercy. Suddenly Salome's path took shape in his mind. They were tracing the lightning flash of Creation, following it back to its source.

Salome lifted her hands again, closed her eyes and took a few steps forward. Grabbing his arm, she pulled him down to kneel next to her. "In the name of the Beni Elohim, I embrace Elohim Tzabaoth, the splendour of vision."

Another tremor passed through the floor and words from a dozen different languages passed across Bertrand's lips. Despite the strangeness of each syllable, he knew they were ancient words of devotion. The clarity of his thoughts was interrupted by a fiery barb that pierced his throat. Bertrand coughed, and he felt dizzy, almost disconnected from his body.

"You're doing well," Salome murmured. "Only two more." She turned right and crossed the nave to the south aisle, guiding him by the elbow. Raising one hand, she located the correct position and made them kneel again. "In the name of the Elohim, I embrace Jehovah Tzabaoth, the triumph of harmony."

A burning sensation spread from Bertrand's navel. He doubled over, assaulted by the sudden pain.

"Netzach," Salome murmured, "The seventh Sephirah. Only one more, Bertrand." She helped him to his feet. He staggered and nearly fell. His body trembled violently.

"What's happening?" The words slurred in his mouth.

"You're experiencing the five lower Sephirot in succession," she replied, as she guided him back to the nave. "Adepts normally study the Mysteries for years before undergoing a ceremony such as this, but we don't have time to properly prepare you." She tested the air above the flagstones with her free hand. "Here. It's almost over."

Salome led him back into the nave and they walked further into the cathedral. A strange calm spread through Bertrand. It deadened his senses until he could barely hear Salome's encouragements. His eyesight dimmed and his mouth became parched. He felt like he had been wrapped in black velvet with only his heartbeat for company.

Salome's words drifted across his strange cocoon. "In the name of the Malachim, I embrace Aloah v'daat, the beauty of individuality."

Pain found him, even here in this remote, dislocated state. It drilled through the centre of his forehead, punching through his strange apathy. Colours cascaded over him, shifting from one shade to the next in sudden twists and mesmerising, shifting patterns.

Bertrand, open your eyes.

Salome's voice infused him. He wanted to obey, but the torrent of light was too beautiful. The colours possessed a liquid quality, rippling and shimmering unpredictably.

Bertrand, come back to me. I need you still.

He whimpered at the thought of abandoning such beauty. All that awaited him was ugly and dull in comparison.

Wake now, sweet Bertrand. The sphere of the spirit is not for you yet.

He opened his eyes.

Salome leaned over him. Her expression was drawn and filled with concern.

He blinked. "I saw a light. No, many lights. And colours. So many colours. Yet they were all part of one whole."

"Yes, you did." Her bottom lip trembled as she touched his cheek.

"The lights. They were...each and every one of us."

"Yes." Salome took his hands and drew him to his feet. "You glimpsed the beauty the tree has woven into all of us."

A shiver ran through Bertrand. "No, I have never seen anything as beautiful as that."

Salome smiled. "Everyone has the potential for grace, even if we don't realise it. Bertrand, few could have endured the ordeal you just went through. You burn bright."

He rubbed his eyes with his knuckles. Pinpricks of light still danced behind his eyelids and he was plagued by the feeling he'd lost something important. When he withdrew his hands, the cathedral was no longer dark. Candles flickered from tall iron stands spaced at intervals down the nave. Braziers hung from brackets set into the pillars. They had reached the crossing where the nave intersected the transepts.

Bertrand gazed wonderingly at the cathedral. "What happened?"

"You endured a test of the five elements of your soul."

"I don't understand."

"It doesn't matter now. Come." Salome took his hand and led him down the nave to the walled choir. They passed through the intricately carved wooden door and exited through the far entrance into the apse. The high altar gleamed in the candlelight beneath the dome. Bertrand noticed a five-pointed star within two circles had been carved into the side. He could see no sign of a crucifix anywhere.

Salome and Bertrand genuflected towards the high altar. Rising to his feet, Bertrand followed Salome towards the square chapel at the easternmost point of the cathedral. There she stopped. Her shoulders shook and contradictory emotions surged through his link with her. He sensed both relief and trepidation, delight and grief.

"What is it?" Bertrand hurriedly joined her.

Five monks in white habits awaited them in the tiny chapel. Behind them stood a simple wooden altar covered in scrolls and leather-bound books.

The eldest monk, whose completely bald pate was spotted with age, took a step forward. "Welcome to Rooklyn Abbey," he said in English. "My name is Edwyn and I have the honour of being its Abbot. These are the other members of my cabal." His voice quavered beneath the arched vaults.

"You must be the Lady Salome and her Shroud," Edwyn continued. "Praise be to Ein Sof that you have arrived at last."

Edwyn and the other monks prostrated themselves before Salome and Bertrand.

CHAPTER 23

16 December 1307

Rooklyn Abbey

"Please, take as much as you want." The monk had a kind, round face with bright blue eyes and a ready smile. Like the brothers Bertrand had known in Champagne, he wore the tonsure and white habit of the Cistercians, although the cord about his waist was yellow instead of black.

Bertrand tried to remember his name. *Thomas.* That was it.

"You must be famished after your long journey." Thomas offered the platter of cooked lamb to Bertrand again.

"Thank you." Bertrand took a leg of roasted mutton dusted in herbs and a flat bun of unleavened bread. The meat was almost hot enough to burn his fingers and his mouth watered as he took a savage bite.

"You're welcome," Thomas replied. "The Abbot should join us soon. We're all most excited by your arrival." Thomas moved on to serve Rémi, who still glowered at being 'let in like a servant'.

The calefactory was a plain stone chamber with a low, arched ceiling. Sharing a common wall with the kitchen, the two large hearths radiated considerable heat. A low table had been placed before a stone bench that ran along the wall facing the fires.

Bertrand leaned against the warm stone and let the heat sink into his bruised shoulder. He took another bite of the mutton and chewed slowly. Weariness had settled into the marrow of his bones and he fended off the persistent advances of sleep.

A cold gust of air heralded the arrival of Edwyn and a second monk via a door that connected to the cloister. Edwyn closed it with an apologetic smile. The second monk carried a platter containing a carafe and four goblets.

"Please accept my apologies for my absence," Edwyn said. "Only five of us remain at the abbey, so I cannot delegate chores to others." Edwyn smiled at Bertrand, Rémi and Salome. "Given the conditions you've endured, I thought you might care for some mulled wine. Stephen here will serve you."

Bertrand sat up straighter. Stephen was a large man with a wide jaw, dark brown hair and the shoulders of blacksmith. His hands were enormous and his thick fingers were covered in old scars. Despite his size, he served the mulled wine with gentle grace.

Bertrand accepted his goblet from Stephen. "Thank you for this kindness." He stared directly into Stephen's brown eyes in an attempt to gauge his disposition. Stephen gave him a slight smile, inclined his head and returned to Edwyn's side. Bertrand noticed the cord around Stephen's waist was red, while Edwyn's was blue.

"Thank you, brother," Edwyn said to Stephen. "That'll be all for now."

Stephen nodded and left the room without a word.

Edwyn sipped from his goblet and sighed in obvious pleasure. "Age is truly the greatest test of mortal flesh. The passing of years grants us wisdom yet dilutes our energies and thus our resolve. And what is wisdom without the determination to use it?"

"Wisdom may be shared with others," Salome replied. "Isn't that the responsibility of the wise?"

"Perhaps." Edwyn's smile revealed a mouth full of yellow teeth. "Although the wise know that most will choose not to heed them."

Salome smiled back. "Like Cassandra, the Prophetess."

"Even so." Edwyn regarded his goblet, obviously lost in thought.

Rémi took a swig of wine, met Bertrand's gaze briefly, and arched his eyebrows. The conversation had been in English thus far, so Rémi had been unable to follow it.

Salome broke the silence. "Wisdom comes to those who are ready to receive it. Believing otherwise is to invite despair. I, more than most, can attest to that."

Edwyn nodded his bald head. "I don't dispute that, Lady Salome. But in my lifelong studies, I've often wondered how we are to know *when* we are truly ready."

"When you stop wondering," Salome replied. "When you're content with your understanding and your place in the world."

"Yes, that may be true." Edwyn rubbed his sagging jowls. "Does that make sense to you, Thomas?"

"Perhaps." Thomas' frown suggested otherwise.

Edwyn placed his goblet on the wooden table and folded his hands together. "I take it you still wish to proceed with the ceremony."

Salome glanced at Bertrand, moistened her lips, and said, "Of course. Was there any doubt?"

"No, but it seemed apropos to ask. All the preparations have been made." His gaze darted between Salome and Bertrand. "Forgive me for asking, but are you similarly prepared?"

Bertrand sensed this question was directed at him. "Prepared for what?"

"Why the ceremony, of course," Edwyn replied. "The sacred union will demand much of you, far more than passing through the five lower Sephirot. You must be pure of soul indeed to represent the pillar of Mercy."

"Why do I need to do anything?" Bertrand asked. "Isn't the ceremony supposed to help Salome forget the location of the keystone?"

Salome's gaze dropped to her lap.

Edwyn glanced between them. "You haven't told him."

"No." Salome took a long draft of her mulled wine. Bertrand didn't need their link to feel her surge in anxiety.

"Told me what?" Everyone in the calefactory avoided Bertrand's gaze except Rémi.

"What's going on?" Rémi asked in French. He stood, obviously sensing the tension in the chamber. Bertrand made a placating gesture.

"Abbot Edwyn," Salome said, "perhaps you could give me some time to explain. Both of them deserve better than this."

"Certainly." Edwyn rose to his feet with an effort and Thomas moved to his side. "Much as it pains me to suggest this, perhaps we should consider a delay. If your Shroud isn't ready, then—"

"No." Salome rose to her feet and smoothed her riding dress. "I've waited long enough. Now that we're here, I'll explain everything to Bertrand."

"As you wish." Edwyn dry-washed his hands. "But the union is delicate. Any emotional turmoil, any disharmony, could be disastrous."

"I know that." Salome drew her shoulders back. "All will be well. I promise."

Edwyn bowed. "As my lady commands." With Thomas at his elbow, Edwyn left the calefactory.

Salome turned to face Bertrand and Rémi.

Switching to French for Rémi's benefit, Bertrand said, "Is this another of your 'layers of understanding' or can we finally call it deception?" He knew she could feel his rage.

"Not another layer," Salome replied. "We've reached the heart at last. Rémi, please sit. I'll do my best to explain."

CHAPTER 24

4 August 1099

The Necropolis

Much to Hugues' frustration, it was not until the following evening that the five of them were able to return to the watercourse. Given Godefroi's movements were heavily scrutinised, Hugues had arranged an all-night vigil. If any were to ask, Godefroi was engaged in prayer and could not be disturbed.

Moving Godwera had proven to be a challenge. While she had gained in strength since Hugues had returned to Jerusalem, she remained a shadow of her former self. Certainly, she lacked the strength to rappel down the steep slope of the Kidron Valley. Fortunately, Etienne had devised a solution. He rigged a chair of sorts, using a broad piece of wood for a seat, with holes at each end through which a rope was threaded. Short loops of rope were cinched around her waist and provided stability for her upper body. Godwera's descent into the watercourse had been slow and ungainly, but she had reached the mouth of the crevasse safely.

The other four men had rappelled down the slope without difficulty, although Achambaud was sweating and breathing hard when he finally squirmed into the narrow opening.

"Is this the wall you spoke of?" Godefroi hefted the mallet he had brought.

"It is," Hugues agreed. "Do you see how the blue fungus doesn't grow there?"

Achambaud lifted his lantern overhead to get a closer look at the dull, rock wall. Like Godefroi, he had chosen to wear leather armour with a thick woollen under-tunic. A short sword hung from his belt. "Why does it glow like that?" Achambaud asked.

"I don't know." Etienne moved closer to inspect a patch of the glowing fungus with his lantern. "Perhaps it's the minerals and constant moisture."

"I hardly think that's important right now." Godwera touched Etienne's elbow to draw him away from his study of the fungus. Etienne jumped and nearly dropped his lantern.

"Sorry." Godwera gave Etienne a strange look. "Are you well, Etienne?"

"I'm fine." He backed away from her as far as the watercourse allowed. Godwera frowned at this behaviour. Hugues could not restrain his impatience any longer.

"Godefroi." Hugues indicated the wall blocking their path.

"With pleasure." Godefroi spread his feet wide and tested the swing of his mallet.

They backed up to give Godefroi room. It was crowded in the narrow watercourse. Hugues' heart was beating hard and he gnawed at the inside of his lip. Was this the right place? Had Umayr stood here once, desperate to know what lay on the other side, yet afraid to find out?

Godefroi swung his mallet with a grunt. The façade cracked and chips fell to the floor. Godefroi swung again, harder this time. A vertical crack splintered down the wall, about the length of a man's hand.

Godefroi checked the breach to confirm that it was dry. He swung again, aiming for the base of the fissure. His next three blows lengthened and widened the crack. Godefroi swung again and again, bunching his powerful shoulders and throwing his weight behind each blow. Chunks of rock tumbled into the watercourse. The breach had widened sufficiently for a child to slip through.

"Rest a moment," Hugues suggested. Godefroi leaned the mallet against the wall and wiped sweat from his forehead.

Hugues raised his lantern and peered through the rift. It was dark on the far side and the air was moist and thick. Hugues thrust the lantern through the gap. Two pillars of pale marble gleamed at the edge of his light. They stood like sentinels on either side of a broader tunnel. Flagstones lined the floor and the walls of the tunnel had been chiselled smooth. Water pooled at the foot of the stone façade, but it was not deep.

"What do you see?" Godefroi asked.

Hugues withdrew his lantern. "A wide tunnel lined with marble pillars. A fitting resting place for kings." His voice shook with a tremor of excitement.

"Then we've found it." A grin split Godefroi's bearded face. "The ancient necropolis of the kings of Jerusalem."

"Praise God." Hugues made the sign of the cross. "There's a pool of water on the far side. It'll gush out when the wall is breached, so make certain of your footing." They moved to the sides of the watercourse.

Godefroi struck the façade with renewed vigour. The metal head of the mallet drew sparks from the cracking stone. Entire sections of the wall caved in with loud splashes.

The wall finally gave way and water gushed from the opening. Hugues clutched at an outcrop as muddy water gushed past his calves.

Godwera stumbled and Achambaud caught her about the waist with the crook of his arm, his free hand wedged into a seam of rock to brace them.

The water subsided quickly and Hugues hoped it wouldn't draw any attention.

Hugues joined Godefroi at the mouth of the hidden tunnel. Godefroi said nothing: he simply stared into the darkness, the handle of the mallet forgotten in his fist. The moment of silence between them as they stood upon the brink of the unknown invoked a powerful feeling of déjà vu. It took Hugues a moment to place the feeling, but it was Godefroi who named it.

"It feels just like the morning before the siege of Jerusalem when our fates lay in the balance," he murmured. "By God, that day seems a lifetime ago."

Hugues nodded. The sense of expectation—of recognition even— had returned in full force. Any doubts he had over whether this was the resting place of the keystone evaporated.

The other three joined them at the ruined façade. Godefroi stepped through the breach first, the mallet balanced in one hand. Hugues followed with his lantern, then Etienne. Achambaud helped Godwera over the rubble.

The flagstones had been laid so well the joins were almost seamless. Each stone was perfectly smooth like marble. With water constantly seeping down the sides of the tunnel, it made for slippery footing.

The opposing pillars were only the first of a series that lined the tunnel roughly every twenty strides. The pale marble columns were thicker than a man's torso, with narrow flutes carved into their surface. Hugues ran a hand around one pillar and counted ten furrows in all. The top of each column appeared to merge with the rock, no doubt supporting the roof of the tunnel.

The blue veins of fungus emitted a soft, blue glow. Dark mosses and lichens gathered in small cracks in the side walls as well, although the pale marble pillars and flagstones remained free of any growth.

Godwera clutched Hugues' arm. "Something's wrong," she whispered.

Hugues turned to face her. "With this place?"

"No, with us."

"What do you mean?"

Godwera hunched her shoulders. "I'm not sure," she muttered. "It's just...I don't feel—" She gathered her composure. "It doesn't feel like when we entered the Holy Sepulchre. Something has changed."

Godefroi had stopped and followed the exchange with a frown. Achambaud hovered at Godwera's elbow, unusually solicitous. Only Etienne hung back, his lantern raised so he could explore the carved foot of the nearest pillar.

"Much *has* changed," Hugues agreed. "I, for one, feel different."

"That's not what I mean."

"Then speak plainly," Godefroi snapped. "What are you trying to say?" His angry gaze flickered between Godwera and Achambaud.

"Enough." Hugues raised his palm. "Whatever petty slights or grudges you bear, put them aside. This is not the place for them."

Godwera took Hugues' free hand. "Hugues, if you have ever trusted my counsel, listen to me now. Each step we take is a trespass, a violation of whatever goodwill brought us here. I can't explain why, only that I feel it deeply."

"What do you suggest?" asked Hugues. "Would you have us turn back?"

"Only for a short while. We can return." She squeezed his hand for emphasis, her expression pleading.

"No." Hugues shook off her hand. "We've come too far, and our enemies are closing in."

"Can't you smell the vile stench that surrounds us?" Godwera's lips trembled.

"You were stronger once," Hugues replied. "That's what has changed." Godefroi nodded.

"And you have become more desperate," Achambaud replied. "Which could lead to the greater sin, I wonder?"

Hugues bit back a retort. "A long time ago," he said slowly, "I warned you that we would all be tested. Now, with our goal within reach, I remind you again."

"I'm not turning back." Godefroi rapped the head of the mallet on the flagstones. "Not after all the lives spent to reach this point. I won't dishonour those sacrifices." He spun on his heel and strode deeper into the tunnel.

"If I seem desperate," Hugues said to Achambaud, "it's because I'm afraid that if we falter now, we'll never be allowed to return." He hurried after Godefroi with Etienne close behind.

Another pair of marble pillars loomed out of the gloom. Godefroi gave a cry and darted forward. Hugues rushed over to see what he had found.

Godefroi had discovered a small niche carved into the dark yellow bedrock. Inside the aperture lay a sarcophagus carved from black marble. The casket had been polished until it gleamed. The edge of the lid was inlaid with tiny pearls and strips of lapis lazuli bordered the top of the coffin.

The others crowded in to examine Godefroi's find, including Achambaud and Godwera. Hugues took a step back to give Etienne more room and noticed symbols had been engraved into the foot of the sarcophagus. He knelt down to take a closer look and realised they were stylised Hebrew letters.

Hugues translated each symbol: "H – Z – K – H." He blinked in surprise. Ancient Hebrew was not a language he had ever studied, although Umayr said that the essence would grant him knowledge. Had it allowed him to read the inscription?

A chill prickled across his flesh.

"Not David," Etienne said in a disappointed voice.

"Hezekiah ruled about two hundred and fifty years after David," Hugues replied. "So at least we know this *is* the royal necropolis."

"There are more." Achambaud pointed to a second sarcophagus on the opposite wall further back in the tunnel. Like Hezekiah's coffin, it glittered with pearl and lapis lazuli, although the marble used in its construction was not as dark.

Godefroi shrugged. "So we go back in time."

They continued down the passage, passing sarcophagi on either side. Each seemed pristine and undisturbed, although the workmanship of the coffins became rougher as they progressed.

Eventually the tunnel ended in a small, circular chamber only a few yards wide. The bedrock was undressed and seeped with water. Two niches had been carved into the rock on opposing sides of the chamber. A single, circular piece of grey stone had been laid in the centre of the floor. Carved into it was a design Hugues had come to expect: the Seal of Solomon.

Water trickled down the walls and filled the outline of the five-pointed star and the two circles that surrounded it. Short spikes of iron—orange with rust—jutted from the star's five points where they met the innermost circle.

"The eternal cycle," Hugues murmured.

"What?" Godefroi asked.

"I was just thinking of the symbolism," Hugues replied. "Here we've walked through a corridor dedicated to the dead, only to find the Seal of Solomon, which represents the five elements of the human soul, watered by an eternal spring. It symbolises the journey of life into death and life again."

"Very poetic," Godefroi grumbled. "Where is the artefact?"

"It must be here." Hugues moved into the circular chamber and skirted the edge of the seal. He peered at the tomb on the left. A single name had been inscribed at the foot of the sarcophagus: 'DWD'. "DAWID," Hugues breathed.

Any lingering doubts were washed away by this discovery. They were meant to be here. Hugues knelt on both knees. A silent sob shuddered through him. He would offer a prayer of thanks once they had returned to Jerusalem.

"Forgive me for disturbing your rest," Hugues murmured. He rose and crossed to the second sarcophagus, still avoiding the seal. This one was unmarked. The cavity that housed it was much broader and deeper than the other apertures. Two small columns of marble framed the entrance, one white and the other black.

Hugues moved between the pillars and examined the sarcophagus.

Unlike the other caskets, it seemed to be cast from copper. No jewels or precious stones adorned its surface. The only marking of any sort that Hugues could find was a small hole in the centre of the lid. He knelt down to examine the side of the sarcophagus. Three thick bolts jutted from the side of the coffin, just below the lid. Hugues checked the other side. A matching set of bolts pierced the far side. The casket had turned green where it touched the wet ground.

"Godefroi," Hugues said, "help me move this lid." They tried to slide the heavy cover off but it wouldn't budge.

"I think you need this." Etienne brandished the grey metal key Godefroi had retrieved from beneath the āl-Aqsa Mosque.

"Of course," Hugues murmured. In the excitement of discovering the ancient necropolis, he had forgotten the key. "You do it," Hugues said, motioning to Etienne. "You've earned the right."

Etienne smiled and moved over to the copper lid. Holding the short metal spike delicately in his right hand, he examined the surface of the sarcophagus. "There are no markings," Etienne said with a frown.

"Does it matter?" Godefroi growled. "Just shove it in."

"The angle of entry is important," Etienne replied. "See these grooves? They must align with the lock. If I force it the wrong way, we may damage the key or the mechanism."

Hugues ran the tips of his fingers around the small hole. The surface was indeed smooth. "They must have left some sort of sign to orient the key correctly,"

"The carving," Godwera said in a weary voice. She pointed at the Seal of Solomon etched into the floor. "The key bears the same symbol. I imagine you need to place the key in the lock according to the same orientation as this carving."

Etienne blinked in astonishment. "Could it really be that simple?"

Hugues had already moved back to David's sarcophagus. The presence of two caskets had worried him. However, Godwera's insight had provided the context he lacked.

"What are you doing, Hugues?" Godefroi asked.

"Confirming the orientation of the key as Godwera suggested."

"How?" Godefroi moved closer to observe Hugues, taking care not to step on the seal.

"Do you see how one of the points of the star is aimed at David's tomb?" Hugues indicated the ray that aligned directly with David's sarcophagus.

"How does that help us with the key?" Godefroi demanded.

"Here rests the greatest King of ancient Israel," Hugues said. "Surely King David must be the ultimate symbol of mastery of the physical world."

"Of course," Etienne said in sudden understanding. "The tenth Sephirah must point towards his resting place." He rotated the key in his hands until the point marked with the numeral for ten pointed towards David's tomb. Hugues moved back to the copper casket.

Etienne grinned at Hugues across the lid. "The simplest solutions are the best."

Godwera shook her head but kept her peace. Achambaud took half a step closer to her and drew his short sword.

"Do it," Hugues said.

Etienne inserted the metal spike with its strange grooves into the hole. The key snapped into position with a dull clang and something crunched inside the casket. The metal bolts that had secured the lid shot out of the casket with a screech of metal. Etienne stepped back, his face infused with fierce delight.

CHAPTER 25

4 August 1099

The Keystone

Hugues stared at the copper lid of the sarcophagus. Etienne had stepped back, his eyes wild with excitement. Godefroi dropped his mallet on the ground with a loud clatter and moved carefully towards the lid.

"Wait," Hugues called.

Godefroi gave Hugues a look of pure exasperation. "What now?"

"I don't know what's inside," Hugues said. "The ancient references gathered by the Salt Lines were always vague."

"Hugues," Godwera called, "this search has cost so many lives. I fear only further pain and loss awaits. Walk away, I beg you."

Hugues sighed. "I agree the price has been heavy, yet the past cannot be undone. What matters is what we do from here."

"Oh, Hugues." Godwera shook her head in disappointment.

A strange, sickening feeling spread through the pit of his stomach. Had he lost Godwera's respect as well?

"Has anyone stopped to consider," Achambaud asked, "that there might be a reason they hid this tomb and locked its contents?"

"To prevent grave robbers." Godefroi shrugged. "I agree with Hugues. We've fought for this moment and we've earned the right to open this tomb. All this hesitation is just snivelling weakness."

"Enough," Etienne snapped.

Everyone turned to him in shock.

"If we walk out of this tunnel now without opening it," Etienne said in a voice that trembled with anger, "it will haunt us for the rest of our days. I'm not going to endure that. Not after all that I've suffered. We deserve this."

"Etienne, don't!" Godwera stretched a hand towards him. Etienne grasped the edge of the lid, dropped into a half-crouch, and pushed with his legs. Veins in his neck stood out like cords at the effort.

Hugues moved forward to help. With a grunt, Etienne shifted the lid and shoved it sideways. The curved edge scraped the top of the casket and balanced precariously. Etienne braced his feet against the wall and pushed again. The lid squealed across the rim and toppled onto the stone floor with a loud peal.

Hugues staggered against the black pillar. The sound of the falling lid was identical to the booming chime that he had heard when the crystal shard was immersed in the Gihon Spring.

Everyone was paralysed by shock.

Etienne's chest heaved as he stood staring down at the casket. A look of horror had frozen across Godwera's face. Achambaud raised his short sword, but nothing emerged from the sarcophagus.

Godefroi leaned over the casket and looked down. A strange expression stole over his face. Hugues detected both surprise and anger. Godefroi addressed Etienne in a flat voice. "Do anything like that again without my permission and I'll bury you down here."

Hugues stood in a daze. How had the harmony of his sacred points become so fractured? Etienne had never acted out of turn in all the long years that Hugues had known him.

"Hugues." Godefroi cracked his name like a whip.

Hugues approached the casket. It took a moment for what he was seeing to register. It was empty. No, not quite empty. Hugues lifted his lantern. A narrow set of stairs, cut into the dark yellow bedrock, descended into the darkness. The casket was merely a cleverly disguised door to hide this secondary tunnel.

"Did you know about this?" Godefroi demanded.

Hugues shook his head.

Achambaud and Godwera squeezed into the aperture to examine their find.

"Give me your lantern," Godefroi commanded. Etienne handed over the light without protest.

Godefroi picked up his heavy mallet and hefted it in one fist. "No one comes down these stairs until I call, understood? Especially not you." Godefroi pointed the metal head of the mallet at Godwera.

"We don't know how far they go," Hugues protested.

"Perhaps all the way to hell," Godefroi replied grimly. "Either way, you stay here until I say it's safe. If you don't hear from me, put the cover back on and hammer in the bolts. No one comes down looking for me." This last command was directed at Achambaud.

"You don't have to go," Godwera said.

"Yes, I do," Godefroi replied. "Death has overlooked me countless times on this pilgrimage so I can walk down these stairs." He shifted on his feet, suddenly uncertain. "I think perhaps I finally understand what you've been trying to tell me," he said to Godwera. "Our lives are not ours to spend as we wish."

Godwera's smile was filled with regret.

Godefroi squared his shoulders and turned to Hugues. "You can follow once I know it's safe." Godefroi swung a leg over the sarcophagus and tested the first step. The wet rock took his weight. Godefroi was so broad his bulk filled up the sarcophagus. With the long-handled mallet in one hand and the lantern in the other, it would be a tight fit.

Godefroi began his descent.

◆━━━━━━━━━━━━━◆

Of all the things this journey had demanded of Hugues, allowing Godefroi to disappear down those unexpected stairs was perhaps the hardest. Hugues could barely remain still. Perhaps he had crossed the border into the realm of obsession because he was prepared to die to know what lay at the bottom of those steps.

Seconds squeezed past as water oozed from the walls of the necropolis. The glow of Godefroi's lantern had long since disappeared. Hugues could not abide the waiting any longer. He needed to fill it with something.

Anything.

"It's not like you to be so rash, Etienne."

Etienne had lit a candle to replace the lantern Godefroi had confiscated. The wavering flame cast shadows across his thin features.

"Our will was faltering," Etienne replied. "I had to commit us before it failed."

Godwera was watching Etienne with a puzzled look. He had seen that expression on monks as they wrestled with a particularly difficult translation.

"Taking time to consider our actions isn't faltering," Achambaud replied. "Your rashness could have endangered our lives."

Etienne studied his candle and did not respond.

"Please, we mustn't bicker like this," Hugues said. "Not when we're so close. The unity of the sacred points is paramount."

"You say 'unity'," Achambaud replied, "but you really mean obedience." Godwera nodded in agreement.

"You see?" Etienne said to Hugues. "Our determination falters. The value of everything we have striven for is being questioned."

Hugues ignored Etienne. "You've lost faith in me," he said to Godwera.

"After all that I have confided in you." He leaned against the wall of the circular chamber. Why was everything turning awry?

"It's not that." Godwera shook her head. "With our injuries, we've had time to reflect. This quest has compelled you from the beginning. It compels you still, to the cost of everything that's important. Don't you see that?"

Hugues swallowed, uncertain how to reply.

"Hugues!" Godefroi's voice echoed up the twisting stairs. "Come down...down...down!"

"Stay with me." Godwera gripped his hand. "We don't have to go down there."

"I'm sorry." Hugues withdrew his hand. "I couldn't live with turning back now." He lit a second candle from Etienne's before climbing into the casket. The stairs were steep and slippery. Footsteps followed close behind. Hugues glanced up and saw it was Etienne. Hopefully Godwera and Achambaud would join them, although he was no longer certain of their support.

The staircase spiralled down through the bedrock. Hugues stopped counting after the first thirty steps. It was cold so far below ground. The chill clung to his skin, except for one spot just below his throat. Hugues drew out the leather thong around his neck. The crystal shard Umayr had entrusted to him was warm. For some reason, he took comfort in that.

The flight of crude steps twisted through beige rock streaked with ochre. As Hugues rounded the bend, he saw that they ended in a low passage. Hugues moved forward cautiously. After a few feet, he emerged into a small, oval chamber of roughly hewn walls.

"What in the name of all that's holy is this?" Godefroi gestured towards what he had been staring at.

Hugues lifted his candle and gazed in astonishment. An enormous crystal cut in the shape of a rose was set in a stone plinth almost waist height. Suspended upright in the stem was a dark-haired woman. Her head was tilted back, as if she was gazing at the crystal petals above her, and her arms were crossed over her chest. Her smooth skin was even darker than Achambaud's.

Hugues gaped. "I have...no idea," he said at last.

The crystal radiated a noticeable heat, which would explain why this chamber was dry. The woman—whoever she was—had been clothed in a gown of pure samite. Threads of silver were braided through her long black hair. The netting glittered beneath the crystal. It reminded Hugues of a crown of tiny stars.

Heat flared against Hugues' skin. He cried out and tore the leather thong from his neck. The crystal shard winked in the light as it dangled from the broken strap.

"Who is this?" Godefroi demanded. "What's that in your hand?"

"The final key to unlock her tomb." Etienne directed a look of triumph at Hugues. "Do you see now?"

Hugues gazed at the piece of crystal dangling from his fist. Of course. The colour and texture matched the rose perfectly. The shard was even calling to it, heating up as it drew closer.

"Who is this woman?" Godefroi roared. "And where is the god-forsaken artefact?"

Etienne moved towards the crystal. Unlike Godefroi, he did not seem disappointed by their discovery.

"I don't know, Godefroi. Please, just let me think." Hugues circled the chamber, looking for the cleft he knew must be there. At the base of the rose, near the woman's feet, was a small crack. Hugues cut away the leather thong with his belt knife. The shard was hot to the touch, painfully so, but it did not burn his fingers. Hugues held the end of the shard and twisted it until it aligned with the fissure.

He was distantly aware that Godwera and Achambaud had emerged from the stairs. The beauty of the rose was drawing Hugues in. Deep beneath its surface, light skittered off its planes. Hugues gazed into its depths, trying to divine its purpose.

Without making a conscious decision, Hugues thrust the crystal shard into the crack.

A wave of heat rushed outwards, buffeting Hugues. Cracks spider-webbed outwards from the shard. Hugues backed away as the fractures widened. A chime thundered through the chamber, far more powerful than the one in the Gihon Spring. The ground trembled and dust showered the chamber.

The rose splintered, its surface resembling a million jagged teeth. Light from Godefroi's lantern and the candles twinkled across those serrated edges.

What had he done?

Trapped against the rough stone wall, Hugues could only watch as the crystal rose imploded. Sharp filaments and jagged chunks of crystal pierced the woman's body. They tore through her skin and sank into her flesh. In two heartbeats, three at the most, the entire crystal structure had submerged into her body.

Hugues blinked in shock. Despite all the cuts that scored her body, the woman collapsed on the plinth without shedding a drop of blood.

He took a cautious step closer. Her body was covered in fresh wounds that closed over as he watched, leaving a horrifying web of scars across her olive skin.

"God in heaven," someone muttered. The words were so choked with disbelief Hugues couldn't tell who spoke them.

The woman's robe was shredded and the angry, red mosaic of scars was already fading to white. Hugues stared at the whorls and ridges of scar tissue. The scars were almost like script in their complexity. If he could just touch her, if he could tear away the remaining rags that clothed her, perhaps he could read the message carved into her olive flesh. Perhaps he could finally understand.

Desire thrummed through Hugues, awakening long-denied urges. He stumbled, caught his balance, and staggered again as another convulsion shuddered through him. A hot, urgent need was rising up through his chest. He felt like he was going to climax and be sick at the same time.

"Hugues!" Godwera's voice spun around him. The chamber lurched, everything out of focus except for the scarred woman.

Another spasm threw him forwards like an enormous hand in the small of his back. Hugues' legs trembled and he almost fell. He was going to vomit unless...unless what? His knees crunched into the plinth. His hands slapped against the top of the pedestal.

And the writhing in his stomach instantly died.

The mysterious woman lay directly in front of him. Her beautiful, perfectly symmetrical face drew him in. Dark, arched eyebrows framed the bold curve of her nose. Long lashes curled away from her high cheekbones. Even the faint scars covering her face were tantalising. Hugues was certain they formed an intricate text. If only he could decipher her. She offered knowledge. Wisdom. All the things he craved. Even those other needs he had denied for so long.

She was a riddle.

A compulsion.

A completion.

Hugues bent over the scarred woman and pressed his lips against hers.

His stomach spasmed so hard his muscles seized, paralysing him. He couldn't move, couldn't break free. His abdomen heaved again, higher this time. Something lodged deep inside him broke free.

Hugues dry-retched and the woman's lips parted. A final wrench ripped through Hugues' stomach and the essence coursed into her mouth. His strength fled and he sagged against the plinth. His stomach ached and his throat was raw. Even his vision was blurry. Yet these sensations were a relief after what he had just endured.

Godefroi and Achambaud grabbed him under each arm and dragged him away from the scarred woman.

"What has come over you?" Godwera whispered when the two men had pulled him to safety.

"The essence," he said in a croaking voice. "Umayr said...it was necessary."

The scarred woman on the pedestal drew in a sudden, ragged breath. Her long lashes fluttered and her left hand twitched. Another breath whispered past her lips and her chest shuddered. Dark brown eyes shot open. She sat up abruptly and turned towards them.

Taking a deep breath, she screamed.

CHAPTER 26

16 December 1307

Rooklyn Abbey

"If you want my help," Bertrand said into the silence created by Edwyn's departure, "I'll need the complete truth." He folded his arms across his chest. "No more half-truths or holding back."

"The complete truth." Salome laughed bitterly. "The truth is I've been pursued all my life. Take the last two months and imagine lifetimes of that! Can you fault me for being reluctant to trust too quickly?" She gestured towards the cloister. "Now that we're actually here, I feel warier than ever. Instead of relieved, I'm—"

"Afraid," Bertrand said.

"But I shouldn't be," Salome replied. "This is what I wanted: an end to a burden that should never have been mine." She pulled back her sleeves to expose the inside of her forearms. "An end to these scars."

The misery and guilt that poured from Salome were too raw and painful not to be genuine. However, those feelings had become constant companions, and Bertrand realised she did not know how to be free.

He ground his teeth in frustration. It was far easier to remain angry than to empathise with her. But she was in pain and he cared too much to let it pass.

"We've reached the end of your journey, as you say," Bertrand said. "So let Rémi and I help you carry your burden, if only these last few steps. Can you do that?"

Salome scrubbed tears from her cheeks. He had never seen her so vulnerable before. Bertrand wrapped his arms around her without thinking. She remained stiff for a moment, trembling before surrendering to his embrace. Bertrand stroked her charcoal hair as she pressed her face against his chest.

"In all the years the Salt Lines protected me," Salome said into his collarbone, "this is the first time any of them offered to bear my cross."

"Then let me. You don't need to do this alone. Not anymore."

Rémi cleared his throat. "Listen to the cub. He should know. I've told him the same damn thing enough times."

Salome choked back a laugh. "Thank you. Both of you." She eased out of Bertrand's embrace. "You're right. I can't do this alone. The ceremony requires both of us." Her expression became guarded again.

"Why am I needed to help you forget something?" Bertrand asked.

Salome met his gaze squarely. "I told you that I know the location of Baphomet. That is true because it's embedded in my flesh."

She was not jesting. He could see that from her expression. Bertrand groped for a response. "I thought...I mean, I assumed the keystone was too large to be carried upon your person."

"It is a great burden, but it's part of me just the same." Salome traced the scars on the back of her hand. "That's where I got these from. Joining with Baphomet marked my flesh, just as our joining marked yours."

Bertrand glanced at the tiny rose in the webbing between his thumb and forefinger.

"Baphomet grants me the power to tap into the meridians," Salome continued. "And it has allowed me to live as long as I have."

"And just how long is that?" Rémi asked with a shrewd look.

"By your calendar, over a thousand years, although I remained dormant for many centuries after the destruction of the Essene. It was the first Grand Master of your Order, Bertrand, who woke me."

"Hugues de Payens woke you?" Bertrand could hardly believe what he was hearing.

"Yes, not long after Godefroi de Bouillon captured Jerusalem. Godefroi and Hugues were members of the Salt Lines. Since then, the Fraternity has protected me from the agents of Severity. First in the Holy Land, then as their holdings diminished, in Champagne."

"That's impossible," Bertrand protested. "No one can live that long."

"No ordinary person," Salome agreed. "But Mercy's keystone is seared into my flesh. I cannot die while we remain joined."

"And that's what Guillaume de Nogaret wants," Rémi said. "He wants this keystone so he can become immortal."

"No. I'm almost certain Nogaret is possessed by one of the Lords of Severity. If they capture me, they can merge Baphomet with Severity's keystone that binds them to their prison in Abaddon. If that were to happen, the Tree of Life would unravel, as I've already said. The emptiness of the void would pervert everything that we cherish."

Bertrand remembered the destruction that befell his family and

Justine's estate. "So will the ceremony destroy Baphomet?"

Salome shook her head. "Baphomet can't be destroyed in any sense we understand." She moved closer to the hearth and gazed into the flames. "Edwyn has been studying the Mysteries his entire life. Using the resources of the Salt Lines, he's gathered every scrap of text ever discovered about Baphomet and the paths of wisdom that unlock the Tree of Life. Using that knowledge, he has assembled and trained his cabal. Each is highly skilled in one of the five lower Sephirot."

"You mean Thomas and the rest of the monks," Bertrand said.

Salome nodded.

"To what purpose?" Rémi asked.

Salome lifted her chin. "To separate Baphomet from my flesh. To lay its ancient knowledge finally to rest. For all time."

Bertrand exchanged a confused look with Rémi. "I still don't understand why you need me."

"The tree has three pillars, Bertrand."

"Yes, I know, but there are only two of us." He glanced at Rémi and suddenly wondered.

"For the ceremony to be successful," Salome said, "The two opposing pillars must be in alignment. Since I carry the knowledge of Baphomet, I represent Severity, as it was the forbidden knowledge of Daat that separated Ein Sof from the seven lower Sephirot. You must represent Mercy. And through our unity, we can cleave to the central pillar."

"Our unity?" Bertrand frowned. "Aren't we already bonded?"

The suggestion of a smile twitched across Salome's lips. "Like the two pillars, the genders must be in complete alignment. Masculine and feminine joined to become one."

Bertrand stared.

"Yes, Bertrand. This is the ultimate purpose of the Shroud. You're my counterweight in this world. Not only my protector, but ultimately my other half in a spiritual and physical sense."

A slow flush crept up Bertrand's neck. "You want me to couple with you, in a church, with five monks present. Please tell me I've misunderstood."

A wave of compassion rolled through their shared link. "The ceremony will be held in the chapter house," Salome replied, "not the cathedral. Other than that, you understand me well enough."

"Is this some kind of jest?" Rémi thumped a fist against the stone bench. "Didn't you just promise to tell the truth?"

"I did and I am." Salome moved away from the hearth and leaned against the table. "Separating Baphomet requires a delicate balance. Not only between the masculine and the feminine, but also the five elements of the soul. That's why Edwyn's cabal have been training in the Mysteries. If I don't seize this opportunity now, it may never come again." She gave Bertrand a pleading look.

"What you ask is a profanity of the worst kind." His voice shook with the terrible anger growing inside him.

"I know it must come as a shock, but I did promise you a consummation once. What did you think I meant?"

"Certainly not this!"

She sighed. "Bertrand, you once swore to act as both my defender and advocate. I remind you of that vow."

"If I had known what was being asked of me, I would never have agreed to it. You tricked me!"

"No. Fate threw us together. You were my only chance, so I took it. Please try to understand." She tilted her head as she searched his face. "You feel betrayed and manipulated. Your anger is deep because you believe—" She took a step towards him. "Bertrand, I am not Justine. As my Shroud, you mustn't carry the past with you. The ceremony will fail without your total commitment."

He had not realised the origin of his anger until Salome put it into words, but she was right. He had hoped against all reason that she might come to care for him. Now, however, her true interest in him was revealed. He was a tool. Nothing more.

You must not carry the past with you.

Everard had said almost exactly the same thing. Had he foreseen this situation, or was it merely a coincidence?

He needed time to think.

Bertrand strode over to the door and wrenched it open. A cold wind swirled through the calefactory. The abbey might be protected from the worst of winter, but the night air still held a keen edge.

He strode into the covered walkway of the cloister and slammed the door behind him.

◆————————◆

"I should've known I'd find you here." Rémi's footsteps rang across the stone floor of the scriptorium. They were magnified by the eerie silence of the abbey.

Bertrand remained staring out the narrow, arched window. It was deep into the night. A few lit candles had been placed on the writing bench, but most of the chamber was draped in darkness. Only the barest suggestion of shelves was visible.

"Leave me be." Bertrand watched his shadowy reflection in the glass mouth the words.

"Why?" A wooden stool groaned as Rémi settled on it. A moment later, a second stool scraped across the stone, before his boots clunked upon the seat.

"I need to think."

"If you ask me, you do too much of that."

"I didn't ask you," Bertrand snapped. "Nor do I need one of your lessons." He glared at the thick glass and willed Rémi gone.

"I know that, cub. Especially given the way you've handled yourself these last few weeks."

"Well and good. I still need to be alone." Bertrand pressed his forehead against the stone window frame.

"I reckon a friendly ear is what you need. Left alone, you'll only complicate matters."

Bertrand turned to face Rémi. His face was half in shadow, giving him a lopsided grin. "I don't complicate matters," Bertrand said. "They got that way all by themselves."

Rémi's chuckle came from the back of his throat. "I seem to remember you choosing to make those vows to Salome. Against my advice. Can you recall why?"

Bertrand frowned. "You know why. Everard—"

"Forget Everard." Rémi waved his explanation aside. "You stepped out of the man's shadow the moment you accepted his sword. What convinced you to help her?" Rémi's level stare was unnerving.

Bertrand thought back to when he first met Salome. "I just knew she needed our help. Her grief over Roard mirrored how I felt about Everard. And...well...she needed us."

"No, she only needed you." Rémi chewed on a fingernail and examined it. "And perhaps you needed her."

"What?"

"Think about it. All you've ever truly wanted is a chance to prove your father wrong. No surprise there, given how he treated you." Rémi pointed a finger at Bertrand. "Make no mistake, Salome's that chance. It won't come again."

"I know that."

"Then why hesitate? The woman wants you. God knows you've wanted her from the very first. Why complicate it?"

"It's not as simple as that."

"But it could be. If you let it."

Bertrand scuffed one boot on the floor. "I see what you're saying, but she's using me. Just like Justine."

"And you're using her." Rémi shrugged. "That's how it works, cub."

"How am *I* using *her*?" Bertrand folded his arms across his chest.

"Look where you are." Rémi gestured at the vaults of the cathedral. "Generations of your family have protected her, but none of them are here now. You are. So there's your triumph." He clucked in disapproval. "Do you really think your father sent you to Everard by chance? And if you were Everard, would you have chosen a newly-made chevalier to protect Salome? No, cub. No matter which way you look at it, it's clear that you're *supposed* to be here."

Bertrand bit the inside of his lip. "As usual, your simplistic view of the world does make some sense."

Rémi grinned.

"But if everything you say is true, why wasn't Salome honest from the beginning?"

"As to that, it's hard to say." Rémi scratched his head. "Sometimes if a man wears armour too long, he feels naked without it." He shrugged. "Secrecy and deception are her armour. If she's as old as she claims, perhaps she's forgotten how to take it off?"

"I suppose." Bertrand rubbed his beard. "But what if she's lying? Or at least, still holding something back? How am I supposed to trust her?"

"At this point, trust doesn't come into it, cub. Your choices are simple. Either we leave tomorrow or you give her what she wants. All of it." He grinned again.

Bertrand pulled a face. "Be serious."

"I am. Stay or go. I'll follow you either way."

"That simple."

"Why not?" Rémi stood and slapped Bertrand on the shoulder. "Think too much and you freeze with indecision. Now you should get some rest."

The door to the scriptorium swung open and Thomas appeared in the doorway. After a moment's hesitation, he took a step inside. "Forgive this intrusion. The Abbot sent me to find you." He hunched his shoulders, as if expecting abuse.

Bertrand stood. "What's wrong?"

"The Abbot has received word of a large contingent of soldiers passing through Skipton," Thomas replied. "Most appear to be mercenaries, but a cadre of French soldiers accompanies them. It's rumoured their commander is a representative of King Philippe."

Dread placed the tip of a cold finger on the nape of Bertrand's neck and trailed it down his spine. "What does he look like? Cruel face, dark hair and a neat black beard?"

"I'm sorry, I don't have any more details."

Bertrand traded a worried look with Rémi. "And these forces are heading this way?"

"Yes, although the Abbot believes they won't be able to penetrate the wards that surround the abbey." Thomas wrung his hands together. "However, he wishes to conduct the ceremony at dawn. Will you be ready?"

Stay or go?

Bertrand licked his lips. "Tell the Abbot…tell him, I'll be ready."

CHAPTER 27

17 December 1307

The Chapter House

Bertrand woke well before dawn, uncertain whether he had actually slept or merely lingered on the border of dreaming. He lay on his pallet and tried to imagine the humiliation this day would bring. In the end, it was a relief when Thomas arrived to collect him from the dormitory.

Thomas had foregone his white habit for a flowing robe dyed bright yellow. A belt of woven silver circled his waist. "Please, wear this and nothing else." Thomas offered Bertrand a simple white linen robe. Bertrand shed his outer garments and stripped off his breeches.

Rémi rolled onto his side on his pallet and propped his head on one hand. "Just as well you're a chevalier, cub. Otherwise you couldn't wear the white."

"Very amusing," Bertrand replied with a sour expression.

Thomas examined Bertrand. "Fits perfectly. Please follow me."

Rémi rose from his pallet and pulled on his boots.

Thomas frowned at Rémi. "Not you."

Rémi gave him a dangerous look. "Why not?"

"The ceremony requires Baphomet, her Shroud, and the cabal. No one else is permitted."

"As you pointed out last night," Bertrand said to Rémi with a strained smile, "she only needs me."

"What am I supposed to do?" Rémi demanded. "Sweep the floor?"

"I would be grateful for your prayers," Bertrand replied.

Rémi grimaced before giving him a reluctant nod.

Thomas tugged on Bertrand's sleeve. "Those soldiers will be on the march. We must make haste." He hurried out of the dormitory.

"Thank you, Rémi." Bertrand tried to find more adequate words to express the depth of his gratitude but settled on an impulsive embrace. The look of surprise on Rémi's face was worth it.

"God bless you, cub. I'll be waiting."

Bertrand's throat tightened with emotion. He nodded once and hurried after Thomas.

The monk led him down to the gallery of the cloister. Thomas turned left and walked to the nearest pillar topped with a square capital. He passed through an open archway next to the corner pillar and walked across to the fountain in the centre of the courtyard.

"I thought we were going to the chapter house?"

"You must purify yourself first," Thomas replied. "This is an ancient tradition, dating back to our distant ancestors, the Essene. Perhaps even earlier." He pointed towards the fountain. "There are seven steps to the bottom. However, as Lady Salome's Shroud, you're her connection to the physical world. So you need only reach the fifth step. Pause at each one and follow my instructions."

Bertrand looked at the seething water. No doubt it was freezing, despite the wards protecting the abbey. The fountain was carved from black stone shaped like a fir tree. Water bubbled from the top and trickled down cunningly carved channels, so that it pooled and glistened in ten descending cups, before swirling into the pool.

"The Tree of Life," Bertrand murmured.

"Just so." Thomas beamed at him. "Are you ready?"

Bertrand lifted a foot over the stone lip of the pool. The water lapped just above his ankles and saturated the hem of his robe. It was so cold it stung his skin.

"Stop there," Thomas ordered. "That's good. Don't move until I tell you." Thomas closed his eyes, lowered his head and inhaled deeply. Bertrand watched him curiously.

"In the name of Adonai Melech, I summon the Ishim." Thomas lifted his palms so they faced the sky. "Sandalphon, Lord of the Ishim, I beseech thee to purify this man and speed him along the paths of Mercy. In the name of Ein Sof, let it be thus. Amen."

Thomas raised his head and opened his eyes. "Bertrand, dribble some water over your head."

Bertrand followed Thomas' instructions. Icy water ran down his face and trickled through his thin beard.

Thomas smiled. "You can move to the next tier."

Bertrand took another step down. The water level rose to his knees and he suppressed a shiver.

"In the name of Shaddai el Chai," Thomas intoned, "I summon the Cherubim. Gabriel, Lord of the Cherubim, I beseech thee to lend this man your strength and speed him along the paths of Mercy. In the name of Ein Sof, let it be thus. Amen."

Thomas motioned for him to scoop more water. Bertrand's robe offered no protection against the numbing cold and the shivers set in. The water rose to the top of his thighs as he descended to the next step.

"In the name of Elohim Tzabaoth, I summon the Beni Elohim. Raphael, Lord of the Beni Elohim, I beseech thee to help this man find truth and speed him along the paths of Mercy. In the name of Ein Sof, let it be thus. Amen."

Bertrand drizzled another handful of water over his scalp without being prompted. The sting of the freezing water had given way to an aching numbness. He blinked, trying to focus upon Thomas' face.

He descended to the next step without being prompted. The water level rose to his nipples. A thread of panic pulled tight in his chest. If there were seven steps, wouldn't he drown? Bertrand suddenly realised Thomas was praying again.

"...Haniel, Lord of the Elohim, I beseech thee to nurture this man and speed him along the paths of Mercy. In the name of Ein Sof, let it be thus. Amen."

Bertrand scooped water over his head and lurched forward again. The water rose up to his chin. The stone beneath his feet was slippery. He tried to focus on Thomas, but the frothing water from the fountain was too loud.

"...Aloah v'daat...beseech thee to grant this man grace...Ein Sof... Amen."

Bertrand cupped another handful of water. The water would surely close over his head at the next step. Perhaps this was a test of commitment. If so, he would not fail. He took a deep breath and lifted his foot.

"Wait!"

A new voice cracked across the frothing water. Bertrand blinked. Edwyn peered anxiously at him over the lip of the fountain.

"Come back, Bertrand." The Abbot waved to him frantically. "The sixth and seventh steps aren't part of this ritual."

He gazed into the frothing water. It would be so easy to lurch forward. To let the water close over his head. God knew he was weary. Was there no end to the testing, of continuously having to prove himself?

Bertrand gazed up at the stone tree that loomed overhead. Water cascaded down its black, shimmering face. He remembered Salome explaining the tree was the source of life, a lightning spark that zigzagged down from God. Standing chin deep in the pool, he saw the water was more like a pulse. A current that ran through the veins of rock. He tilted his head back and let the water rush into his mouth.

Freezing water slid down his throat and his bare feet slipped on the step. He fell backwards, submerging beneath the water. Bertrand endured a terrifying instant of disorientation before he landed on a higher step. He surged back to the surface and clambered back up the remaining steps.

Thomas and Edwyn helped him from the pool. Bertrand's chest heaved as he gasped for breath.

"Slowly, Bertrand," Edwyn said. "If your mind is calm, your body will follow."

He concentrated on taking slow, deep breaths. The terrible numbness that had invaded his body retreated to his extremities.

He shivered and gazed into Edwyn's grey eyes. "I'm not afraid of taking the last steps."

Edwyn smiled. "I see that, but it's unnecessary."

Bertrand straightened to his full height. Edwyn was dressed in a robe like the one Thomas wore, except it was dyed a bright blue. He also wore a belt of woven silver.

"Are you ready to continue?" Thomas asked.

Bertrand rubbed his arms and shivered violently. "Yes."

"Good." Edwyn's smile widened. "I daresay you won't be cold for much longer. Not when you see the Lady Salome."

———◆———————◆———

They stopped outside the entrance to the chapter house. A succession of splayed arches, each set inside the other, drew the eye inwards to the entrance. The Abbot knocked on the heavy oak doors. One swung inward, and a monk Bertrand had not spoken to before appeared in the entrance. He was short and older than Thomas, with the hunched look of a scholar. His robe was dyed indigo and he also wore a silver belt.

"This is Brenton," Edwyn said to Bertrand. He turned to Brenton and asked, "Is she ready?"

"Yes," Brenton replied. "She endured the purification of flame without any difficulty."

"Good, good." Edwyn dry-washed his hands. "Then we're ready to proceed." He glanced up at the sky. "Dawn is rushing to greet us." Brenton backed away and Edwyn led them into the chapter house.

A short corridor connected the chapter house to the cloister. Glowing coals in a large brazier warmed the narrow alcove. Bertrand rubbed his arms to stimulate his circulation. His robe was still damp, but a visit to the calefactory had largely dried him out.

Stephen turned to watch their approach. He was dressed in a red robe. Next to him was the fifth member of Edwyn's cabal. He wore an orange robe and was almost as tall as Bertrand, although painfully thin. Stephen moved to one side and Bertrand caught sight of Salome. She had her back to him, her gaze fixed on the depths of the chapter house.

Salome wore a simple linen shift like his, except hers was dyed black so that she appeared almost bodiless. Her long hair was unbound and hung almost to her waist. A delicate silver netting crowned her head and tiny stars glimmered amidst the fine wires. Staring at her from behind, Bertrand was reminded of the night sky.

She must have sensed his scrutiny because she turned and regarded him with her dark, almond-shaped eyes. In that instant, he could not tell what she was feeling. Salome smiled and the moment of uncertainty passed.

"Bertrand." The monks moved aside as she took his hands in hers.

"You're still damp," she murmured.

"Apparently, I needed a bath. You could've told me earlier," he said with a smile. He was pleased to find his voice was steady.

The smile reached her eyes. "Here, stand beneath the brazier while they make the final arrangements." She glanced at Edwyn.

"We're almost ready, my lady." Edwyn gestured to the other members of his cabal. "Let's give them a moment alone." The monks' robes swished across the flagstones as they followed Edwyn into the chapter house.

Salome hadn't released Bertrand's hands.

"Thank you for putting aside your doubts," she said. "Few men I've known could shrug off the weight of their pride as you have. I'm glad that you're here with me now. Truly."

He could tell that she meant it. "How could I not be?"

Salome placed a finger on his lips. "Hush. No explanations. Just accept my gratitude."

Bertrand nodded.

Salome's finger brushed his cheek. "In a moment, they'll take us inside the chapter house. During the ceremony, you must focus upon me. Ignore them. Ignore whatever you might see or hear. Remain focused solely upon me. If it helps, close your eyes."

Bertrand swallowed. His mouth was dry. "Salome." He licked his lips. "I'm not particularly...experienced."

She softened at the embarrassment that flooded through him.

"Sometimes I forget how young you are." She pulled his head down and placed a soft kiss upon his lips. Drawing back, she said, "It's not a question of skill or experience. We are halves of the same whole, Bertrand. That's the nature of the sacred union; the separate branches becoming one."

Edwyn appeared in the archway. "We're ready."

Salome threaded her arm through his. "Walk with me." The side of his arm pressed against her breast. He felt her pulse racing beneath her skin. It seemed to beat in time with his.

They walked down the narrow alcove. Bertrand's breathing became fast and shallow, as if he were about to ride into combat. Edwyn stood aside as they entered the chapter house.

The chamber was built in the shape of a pentagon. Three tiers rose in succession from the floor on each side like an ancient amphitheatre. Normally these would provide seating for the entire monastic community, but they were empty. Narrow windows, not much wider than arrow slits, were spaced at regular intervals above the top tier. The approaching dawn glowed through the east-facing windows.

Edwyn closed the door behind them and bolted it. "Please. Move into the centre of the Pentemychos."

Bertrand and Salome moved into the middle of the chamber. As his eyes adjusted to the gloom, he noticed lines of salt running across the floor. Each line joined one corner of the room to the other four, forming a five-pointed star. A different monk stood in each corner. With their backs to Bertrand and the cowls pulled over their heads, the only way to identify them was by the colour of their robes. A line of salt ran along the foot of the lowest tier, enclosing the star in the shape of a pentagon.

The symbolism of the lines of salt was not lost upon Bertrand. This was his family's legacy, a secret tradition inherited from a time so ancient that perhaps it pre-dated even written history itself. Yet part of Bertrand rebelled at was unfolding here. This was not the intimacy that Salome had once promised him. No, it felt more like a profanity, a breaking of vows. And yet...another part of Bertrand knew that Salome could not be free of her burden without him. He could *feel* her desperation and the pain of all the sacrifices she had made, all the losses she had endured. The terrible weight of them would crush a lesser person. Knowing that—having actually experienced it—how then could he deny her?

Bertrand trembled with the conflict raging inside him.

Salome disengaged her arm from Bertrand, turned to face him, and raised a gentle hand to his cheek. Her gaze was filled with such compassion that Bertrand couldn't hold it for longer than a moment.

Taking a step back, Salome lifted the hem of her shift over her head and let it fall to the tiled floor in one fluid movement. Like Bertrand, she was naked underneath. As he had suspected, her entire body was covered in a complicated maze of scars. His gaze roamed down the curve of her neck, travelled along the ridge of her shoulders and paused at her breasts. They were smaller than Justine's and sat higher. Her nipples were darker too. He glanced at her face, and a challenge flashed in her eyes, as if she knew what he was thinking.

Her stomach was flat and hard, and the bottom of her ribs jutted from her skin. He drank in the curve of her hips and the dark hair that nestled between her legs. The muscles in her thighs and calves moved beneath her skin as she shifted on her feet.

Salome was nothing like Justine. Her body was lean and graceful like a dancer's.

A smile quirked her lips. "Well?" she murmured.

The hint of amusement in Salome's expression was enough to fracture Bertrand's indecision. He couldn't just stand there, staring at her like a fool.

Powerless to halt the flush rising up his face, Bertrand pulled the shift over his head and gathered it in front of his groin. Salome gently removed it and dropped it on the floor. A low rumble echoed around the chapter house. It took Bertrand a moment to realise the monks had begun a slow chant. He strained to catch the words, but they were in a foreign tongue that seemed to run together.

Salome gently turned his head back to her. "Focus on me, Bertrand. Nothing else." She pulled his head down and kissed him on the mouth. Her lips parted and the tip of her tongue teased him. Desire jolted through Bertrand and he grasped her by the hips and drew her close. Her skin was smooth and hot to the touch. He felt damp and cold in comparison.

The intensity of their kiss deepened. Her breasts pressed against his chest and the delicious softness of that contact sent blood throbbing through him. He stiffened, pressing against the firm muscle of her thigh. Salome cupped her free hand around one of his cheeks and ground her pelvis against his leg. Bertrand inhaled through his teeth. Feeling his building pressure, she shifted her stance and Bertrand moaned into her hair.

The chant suddenly ceased. In the sudden silence, a single word rolled around the chamber: "Ateh."

165

Bertrand glanced up at the nearest monk. It must be Thomas, as he wore a yellow robe. Thomas clenched a plain black dagger in both hands. The tip of the blade was level with his forehead. As Bertrand watched, Thomas and the other monks reversed the hilts of their knives so the points turned downwards and they called out, "Malkuth."

Salome turned Bertrand's head back to her. "Don't stop now." She guided his hand between her legs and nipped at the hollow above his collarbone. Her breath was fast and hot.

"Ve-Geburah," resonated through the chapter house.

Despite the long-denied desire coursing through Bertrand, he glanced over Salome's head. Thomas and the orange-robed monk had turned their daggers to the left. They swung the blade to the right and called out, "Ve-Gedulah."

Each intonation was louder than the previous one, as if they too were building to a climax. Salome lifted her head and kissed him again. Her free hand gripped the base of his manhood and she pulled him down onto the cold tiles.

"Le-olam," swirled through the chapter house. The incantations were running together, almost overlapping as they bounced off the stone tiers.

Salome pushed him flat and straddled him. Taking him in both hands, she guided him inside. The monks raised their daggers and plunged them into the tiled floor.

"Amen."

Bertrand closed his eyes at the sudden rush of pleasure. His hands tightened around her hips. Salome descended slowly and the bliss of being inside her was overwhelming. Yet he also shared her delight at the delicious friction through their link.

She rose up and descended again. Pleasure rippled through his body, emanating from the top of his pubic mound. This was not the localised sensation he was used to. It rolled outwards at each stroke. Salome rose and descended again. This time they moaned together.

Light suddenly glared against Bertrand's eyelids. He opened his eyes and squinted. Brilliant pillars of light sparkled where the monks had once stood. Thomas was engulfed by a shaft of intense yellow, while an orange pillar shimmered to his left. Startled, Bertrand rose up on his elbows. Each corner of the chapter house was illuminated by a different colour: indigo, blue, red, orange and yellow.

The strange, rumbling sound of the chant moved to a higher pitch.

Salome pushed him back down. "Look at me, Bertrand. Don't...stop." She thrust against him again. He arched his back to drive deeper. Salome rolled her hips forward and cupped his face to prevent him from looking away.

He ignored the pillars of light and the strange chant. Only Salome mattered, rising and falling above him in an accelerating rhythm. The tide of their shared rapture was carrying them away. He focused on the curve of her neck as she arched her head back. The cascade of charcoal hair over her bare shoulders was mesmerising.

Soon.

He could not stand much more.

The strange light merged and became a brilliant, sparkling silver. It reminded Bertrand of the meridians beneath the earth. The air thickened and the silver glow sped along the lines of salt. Bertrand turned his head to find they were surrounded by a pentagram of rippling silver.

Salome gasped, not from pleasure but shock. Bertrand looked up at her. The scars covering her skin were transforming. The faint white marks widened and silver light poured forth. They were cracks, he realised suddenly. Glimpses of something hidden within her.

Baphomet.

Mercy's keystone that underpinned Creation.

"Keep...going," Salome panted.

He gripped her by the hips as his pleasure tipped over the edge. As Bertrand climaxed, the rush of release coursed through his link with Salome. It triggered her orgasm so that ecstasy ricocheted back and forth between them. The shared bliss merged them into one and Bertrand lost all sense of self. The force of their passion sent them tumbling like a thousand leaves before a storm.

The cracks in Salome's skin widened even further and light speared out from her. A searing agony overtook them as Edwyn's cabal tore Baphomet from the very fibres of their being.

Yet the rending pain was a form of release too. Pain and pleasure entwined, becoming indistinguishable. They felt filled to the brim. Each contraction, each breath, was almost unbearable in its intensity.

Surely, this exquisite agony-ecstasy would be the end of them?

It was too much. No mortal could survive the intensity of the sacred union for more than a handful of heartbeats. A deep, instinctual sense of preservation forced Bertrand from his communion with Salome.

The blistering light from Salome thickened and ran from her multitude of scars. It oozed from her like dazzling silver blood. Those drops that struck Bertrand sizzled against his skin before pooling beneath him. Even as the intensity of his orgasm faded, he felt the mercurial light hardening beneath him.

Salome shuddered and rolled off him. She slumped to the tiled floor, gasping for breath. Bertrand rolled onto his side, wanting to comfort her, but he lacked the energy to do more than caress her hip. Her body had become dull, almost lifeless, compared to the glory it had housed.

He blinked in astonishment. The tiled floor of the chapter house had become the face of an enormous, pale sapphire. Strange letters, as black as the abyss, squirmed across the face of the shimmering surface.

The pillars of light that guarded the five corners of the pentagram brightened and the atmosphere in the chamber shifted. Bertrand felt it in the pit of his stomach. The low, rumbling vibration of the chant intensified into a high-pitched whine. The lettering on the face of the enormous jewel squirmed in agitation.

Salome raised her head. "What are they doing?" She struggled to her knees and screamed at the blue pillar. "Edwyn, stop this!"

The whine became piercing. Bertrand's ears ached and his teeth throbbed. He clamped his hands over his head, but it made no difference. The air in the chapter house thickened and thudded to the pulse of something vast beyond imagining.

Salome rose unsteadily to her feet. "Edwyn, you must stop! All of you! This isn't the way!"

Bertrand got to his knees. Pressure was building inside the chamber. The jewel throbbed, and the walls of the chapter house shuddered, releasing plumes of dust from the ceiling. From the corner of his eye, Bertrand saw the air twist and churn. Unseen apparitions brushed past his naked skin, burning hot or searing cold, sometimes both at the same time. From a great distance, he caught the sound of a thousand screams, followed closely by the answering challenge of a choir. Pain lanced the top of his skull.

"We must stop them!" Salome pulled Bertrand up by the arm.

"How?" Bertrand yelled over the sound of gibbering shrieks and the soaring notes of the choir.

"The pillars!" Salome staggered towards Edwyn's blue column.

The yellow shaft that had once been Thomas was closer. Bertrand lurched into a stumbling run. The air had become so thick it was like wading through water. A hideously deformed shadow, man-sized but with far too many grasping limbs, rose up from the black script inscribed on the face of Baphomet. Bertrand had no time to dodge but careened straight through it. Tendrils of fire scored his flesh and he stumbled, crashing headlong into the swirling pillar of yellow light.

Silver sparks exploded behind his eyes. The pressure in his skull bulged and finally burst. He fell. And kept falling, flailing, desperate

CHAPTER 28

17 December 1307

Rooklyn Abbey

Light flakes of snow settled on Bertrand's face. He blinked and tiny beads of moisture trickled down his cheeks and into his beard.

The sky overhead was full of thick, grey clouds. He turned his head and the roofline of the cloister came into view. It seemed he was lying on his back in the grass courtyard. The gurgle of the fountain was audible behind him.

He sat up with a lurch and immediately regretted it. Pain splintered across the top of his skull. Twisting to one side, he vomited.

"Easy, cub." Rémi squatted next to him and drew up the woollen blanket that had covered him. "You're so green I could lose you in the grass."

Bertrand struggled to focus on Rémi's familiar face. "What happened?" His tongue was thick in his dry mouth.

Rémi scowled. "The whole abbey started shaking, that's what. I was sure the roof would come down on your heads. So I dragged you outside."

"Salome?"

"She's safe. I pulled her out after you."

Bertrand closed his eyes, which only made things worse. The ground felt like it was swaying, much like when he had disembarked from *Le Blanc Écume*. "Help me up." Bertrand staggered to his feet with Rémi's support. He clutched the blanket around his shoulders for warmth, realising he was still naked underneath. "Where is she?"

"Over there." Rémi pointed at a still figure lying closer to the chapter house. "What in the name of Christ happened in there?"

Bertrand hurried over and knelt by Salome's side. She was so still he feared she was no longer breathing. He pressed his ear to her mouth and was relieved to catch a whisper of breath. She was paler than normal and the scars on her face had vanished. He lifted the blanket.

All of her scars had vanished.

The sight of her naked figure triggered a rush of memories. He lowered the blanket to keep her warm.

Something had gone wrong during the ceremony. Salome had been terrified. He remembered that well enough. As well as crashing into the yellow pillar of light that had been Thomas.

"What happened?" Rémi asked again. "The ground shook and I heard…the voices of the damned and an answering choir." Rémi made the sign of the cross with a haunted expression.

"I'm not sure." Bertrand stared at Salome. She seemed too perfect without her scars. Younger too. "Where is the Abbot?"

Rémi hooked a thumb behind him. "In the scriptorium, arguing something fierce with the other monks last time I checked. They won't answer me in our tongue. You did notice it's started to snow."

The implications suddenly sunk in. Bertrand sat back on his heels. "The abbey is no longer protected."

Rémi nodded. "That's my thought. Also explains why the monks are at each other."

Bertrand bent over Salome and touched her face. "You must wake up now." He shook her gently by the shoulder. Her long lashes fluttered. He gave her another shake. "We're in danger. Wake up."

Salome groaned and her eyes cracked open. "Tell me I'm dead," she whispered.

"Afraid not," Bertrand said with quiet relief. "Just feels that way."

"It's gone." Confusion spread across Salome's face. "I can't feel the salt lines beneath us. The Sephirot are closed to me."

He helped her sit up. Now that she mentioned it, he could no longer sense her in the back of his head.

"Edwyn." Salome's expression changed to horror. He saw the significance of the snow register upon her face.

She leapt to her feet and ran to the chapter house, clutching the blanket around her shoulders. Bertrand chased after her, followed by Rémi who swore in surprise. Salome stopped at the entrance. Looking over her shoulder, Bertrand caught the gleam of the enormous sapphire covering the floor. The silver light and black writing had disappeared, but the atmosphere inside the chapter house remained charged, like the air before a storm.

"I can still feel it," Salome murmured. "Faint, but definitely there." She trembled.

"That's behind you now." Bertrand placed a protective arm around her shoulders and drew her outside.

"What, in the name of all the saints, *is* that thing?" Rémi asked quietly. "It was blazing like a full moon when I dragged you outside. The air was thicker than honey."

Salome turned to Bertrand. "We have to find Edwyn. He's made a terrible mistake."

"They're in the scriptorium," Rémi said. "Is anyone going to explain what's going on?"

Salome hurried down the gallery and rushed up the steps to the scriptorium. The sound of arguing voices echoed down the stairway as Bertrand and Rémi followed. Shoving the door open, Salome burst inside. The voices fell silent. Bertrand stopped in the doorway. All five members of Edwyn's cabal sat around the bench used for copying manuscripts. They appeared unhurt and still wore their ceremonial robes. Edwyn had risen from his seat to point a finger at Stephen in his bright red robe.

"Why?" Salome demanded in French. "What made you think you had the right?"

Edwyn sank back onto the bench. He looked exhausted. "We have studied and trained for this all our lives."

"The cycle of testing can't be circumvented." Salome jabbed an accusing finger at Edwyn. "You know this. You know what happened to the Essene when they tried."

"Of course. I studied the scrolls brought back from the Holy Land." Edwyn rubbed his face with a trembling hand.

"We thought it would be different this time," Stephen said.

"We were prepared," Thomas added. "You shouldn't have interrupted us. We could still succeed, even now."

"I told you," Brenton cut in, "that's impossible. Look at Edwyn. He barely survived the last attempt. And poor Patrick is blind." He pointed at the orange-robed monk who wore a bandage over his eyes.

Thomas drew breath to reply, but Bertrand cut him off. "Interrupted what? You separated Salome from the keystone. It's still there in the chapter house."

Salome shook her head sadly. "They tried to use it. Once they drew it from me, they tried to wield its power."

Was that why the black letters had squirmed as if they were alive?

"To do what?" Rémi demanded.

"To communicate directly with Ein Sof," Salome replied. "They tried to use Baphomet to directly petition the Holy Trinity."

"Isn't seeking the great restoration between God and His children a worthy goal?" Edwyn asked.

"It's not a question of worth," Salome snapped. "Ein Sof has withdrawn from us until we find a way to overcome the self-awareness of Daat. That's what the cycle of testing is for. Each time the five chambers of the human soul are measured."

"Many within the Salt Lines believe the status quo should be challenged." Edwyn sighed. "After all, how can we entrust such a burden to untrained, randomly chosen people? Surely you, of all people, see the madness in that."

"It's not for you to decide such things!" Salome cried. "You're not the caretakers of mankind. That role belongs to the Lords of Mercy."

"And where are they?" Thomas pounded the table with a fist. "The Lords of Severity wreak havoc amongst us, but where are the archangels of Mercy? Who will lead the great restoration if not us?"

Salome shifted her angry gaze to Thomas. "Your attempt failed, and in doing so, it has endangered everything we hoped to achieve. Far from laying Baphomet to rest, you've alerted both Severity and Mercy to its location. And snow is falling outside, which means your wards have failed. What do you propose to do now?"

"She's right," Edwyn said. "We've failed and we lack the strength to make another attempt. Those troops will soon be upon us, and we lack the means to defend the abbey."

"Does it matter?" Bertrand asked. Heads swivelled in his direction. He turned to Salome. "Didn't you once say Baphomet couldn't be used without you?"

Edwyn frowned. "The Lords of Severity cannot touch this half of the keystone. That's why they need Salome to carry it into Abaddon, the core of hell. But if she were captured, it's conceivable they could merge it with her flesh again. After being joined together for so many centuries, a natural affinity would have surely developed." He turned to the other monks. "That's why we have but one option."

The monks fell silent.

"What?" Rémi demanded.

"The abbey must be destroyed," Edwyn said in a pained voice. "Burned beyond recognition. Along with all evidence of what we've attempted here. Unfortunately, that includes my brethren and I. Baphomet must not be disturbed again until the time of testing." He drew himself upright. "Is that not so?" he asked, looking around the table. Stephen glowered and Thomas knotted his hands together. Patrick, the blind monk, and Brenton nodded.

"My friends," Edwyn said, "This decision must be unanimous. We all understood the gravity of our undertaking and the price of failure."

"If we could just—" Thomas began.

"There's no time," Stephen said in a flat voice. "Those soldiers will arrive before nightfall. And even if we did have time to make the attempt again, I fear we may do more harm than good. It's over, Thomas."

Thomas searched the faces of his brethren. Seeing their expressions, he lowered his head in defeat. "How?"

"Hemlock," Edwyn replied. "I have a distillation from the roots and seeds. Our last communion together, followed by an eternal sleep in consecrated ground." He sighed. "Are we in agreement then?"

No one protested.

Bertrand stared at them, stunned that they would consider taking their own lives.

"Very well." With a visible effort, Edwyn turned his attention back to Salome. "Please accept my apologies. Our intentions were noble."

Salome nodded. "And what of me? I remain a risk if what you say about my affinity with Baphomet is true."

"You do not deserve our fate," Edwyn replied. "Not after what you have already suffered. Go north. Seek shelter beneath Mount Heredom. It's the only place Severity cannot reach you."

Bertrand frowned. "Heredom? Where is that?"

"It's one of the three sacred mountains," Salome replied. "It's said the Lords of Mercy retired there when their disappointment in mankind became too great to bear. I've been looking for it since I was awoken, but its location has been lost."

"Not true." Edwyn shook his head. "In my studies, I discovered the mountain is located in the heart of Scotland. The local people know it as Schiehallion. This is my gift to you, in compensation for our pride in believing we knew better than our ancestors."

Edwyn rose from his chair and tottered to the nearest shelf. He rummaged through the scrolls before locating a satchel of dried calfskin. "Despite our confidence of success, I planned for failure as well." He tapped the satchel with trembling fingers. "Inside is a letter of introduction from me addressed to the Abbot at Fountains. The Abbot will render whatever assistance you require. It also contains a map to Heredom."

He offered the satchel to Salome. "Accept this with my sincerest apologies. I wish you well in finding peace, my lady. For surely you have earned it."

Salome took the satchel after a moment's hesitation. "Thank you, Edwyn. May you and your brethren be ushered into the benevolence of

Ein Sof." She turned and pushed past Bertrand, a stricken look on her face.

"Is there anything else, Chevalier Bertrand?" Not even the prospect of imminent death could animate Edwyn. He seemed devoid of all emotion, apart from exhausted resignation.

"What of the keystone in the chapter house?" Bertrand asked. "Surely we can't just leave it here to be discovered by those soldiers or looters?"

Edwyn nodded. "A natural cavern lies beneath the chapter house. It's one of the reasons we chose this site. We'll fire the timber beams supporting the floor. Baphomet will sink beneath the ground and rubble will cover it. Even if Severity's agents were to discover it, they cannot access it without a trained cabal, and a vessel that carries the essence of knowledge."

"By 'vessel', you mean Salome."

"Just so," Edwyn agreed with a sad smile. "Your time as her Shroud may have ended, but she still needs your protection. You must see her safely to Heredom."

Bertrand glanced at Rémi who muttered some choice oaths.

"Then our ways part here," Bertrand replied. "I wish you all courage in the hours ahead."

"Thank you for that kindness," Edwyn replied, "although it's unnecessary. Courage is only needed when one lives with purpose. Now if you'll excuse us, we have much to prepare."

Bertrand bowed to the five monks and backed out of the scriptorium without another word.

"We need to leave as soon as you and Salome are dressed," Rémi said in a quiet voice. "With luck, the snow might cover our tracks."

Bertrand nodded. "It seems William was right after all; Scotland is our last refuge."

CHAPTER 29

4 August 1099

The Necropolis

In all the battles Godefroi had fought, he had never heard a person scream like that before.

The anguish in that cry reverberated around the chamber, and beneath it, he caught the brittle, torturous sound of crystal grinding together.

The woman kept screaming, on and on.

Godefroi dropped into a crouch and covered his ears, although it made little difference. The piercing scream overwhelmed everyone except Etienne, who remained on his feet, teeth bared in a grimace.

"Stop!" Godefroi bellowed. "For the love of God, I command you to be silent!"

Incredibly, the strange woman obeyed. Her dark eyes fixed on Godefroi as Hugues struggled upright. Godefroi forced him back down by placing one heavy hand on his shoulder and said through gritted teeth, "Be still. You've done enough."

"My name is Godefroi de Bouillon." He rose to his full height. The last echoes of the woman's unbearable screams died away. All that remained was a faint, high-pitched whine deep in his eardrums. "By virtue of conquest, I am now the ruler of Jerusalem."

The woman swung her feet off the plinth and leapt to the floor in one fluid motion. The shredded robe did little to hide the tautness of her stomach or the curve of her breasts and hips. Despite the fine lattice of scars that now covered her skin, the woman was beautiful in an exotic way. She spoke rapidly in a tongue Godefroi didn't recognise.

"I don't understand," Godefroi replied. "Do you speak French?"

The woman switched to a different language, however Godefroi still could make no sense of it. Pausing only briefly to see if he understood, she rattled off a series of incomprehensible phrases. Her frown deepened at his inability to understand her.

"Do you understand any of this?" Godefroi asked Hugues in a low voice, his gaze not leaving the woman.

"Some, perhaps," Hugues replied. "I think her dialect is archaic."

The set of the scarred woman's shoulders stiffened and her eyes widened in horror. Lifting a shaking hand, she pointed at Etienne and snarled, "Gamaliel!"

While he didn't understand the reference, Godefroi recognised the tone of accusation. Hugues' breath hissed between his teeth as he spun around to face Etienne.

Etienne drew his belt knife and took a step towards the scarred woman. Godwera, who was closest to Etienne, caught his elbow. Etienne pivoted on his heel and slashed at her. Godwera reeled backwards with a cry of pain and clutched at her arm. Dark blood welled between her fingers.

"Godwera!" Godefroi took an involuntary step toward her.

Godwera's face had stiffened in shock. "Etienne!" she called again. Not in anger, but desperation. She sank to her knees, her eyes wide in her pale face.

Godefroi crouched down and wrapped his hand around the handle of the mallet. Achambaud leapt at Etienne and grappled for the knife. Fighting with a wiry strength that Godefroi had never suspected he possessed, Etienne twisted in Achambaud's grip. Hugues drew his knife and moved between the struggling men and the scarred woman.

Etienne slammed the heel of his boot down Achambaud's shin and wrenched his knife free with both hands. Achambaud gasped in agony as he staggered sideways. Etienne changed his grip and swung backhanded. The attack was so swift Achambaud had no time to defend himself. The dagger lodged in Achambaud's shoulder and his left arm went limp. Etienne ripped out the knife and kicked the back of Achambaud's knee.

Achambaud drew his short sword as his leg crumpled beneath him. Twisting his hips, he slashed at Etienne in a sweeping arc. Etienne tried to evade the blow, but Achambaud's blade sliced across his belly. Unable to break his fall with his nerveless left arm, Achambaud crashed face down into the rock and his sword clattered from his grasp.

Etienne teetered on his feet. The white, glistening coils of his entrails bulged against the gash and blood soaked his habit. Despite the injury, he strode forward and kicked Achambaud in the side of the head. Achambaud fell limp and didn't move again.

"You can't have her." Hugues had drawn his knife and taken position between Etienne and the plinth. The scarred woman had backed behind the pedestal, her almond eyes wide in horror. Etienne swung about, his left hand holding his innards in.

"You can't stop me." The voice that emerged from Etienne's mouth was harsh and nothing like his usual soft speech. "I killed the last cabal. Now I'll destroy yours." Etienne shuffled forward, a bloody snarl curling his lips.

Hugues paled at those words. "You have no place here, demon."

Godefroi swung his mallet into the side of Etienne's head before he could reply. Etienne careened into the rough wall, bounced off the stone, and collapsed. Half of his face was crushed and his head lolled at an unnatural angle.

"Thank God," Hugues whispered.

Etienne twitched and took a gurgling, horrifying breath. His thin arms pushed him into a kneeling position and Etienne's head lolled on his shoulders. He gave a throaty chuckle thick with clotted blood.

Screaming with rage, Godefroi drove the mallet into Etienne's back. The blow flattened Etienne and Godefroi caught the crack of breaking vertebrae. Etienne's fingers scrabbled at the rock as his ruined body tried to rise again.

Godefroi hefted the mallet and threw all of his fury into the blow. The metal head crushed Etienne's skull in an explosion of bone and bloodied brains. Godefroi swung again and again, screaming incoherently, until Etienne finally lay still.

He dropped the bloody mallet, his chest heaving. Blood covered his leggings and tunic. Lying at his feet was the unrecognisable remains of one of their sacred points. Godefroi lifted his haunted gaze to Hugues. "What have I done?"

"It wasn't Etienne," Hugues said unsteadily. "The man we knew is gone. He was merely a puppet for a demon."

Godefroi shuddered. He had never slaughtered anyone like that before. Not even in battle, let alone a companion.

"Godefroi." Godwera's voice was weak. He hurried to her side and examined her wound. The cut was deep and oozing blood. She had turned deathly pale, and her breathing was shallow and fast.

"Don't punish yourself," Godwera whispered. "It's this place that's to blame."

"Hush." Godefroi tore strips from the hem of his tunic and bound the gash in her arm as best he could. She needed a physick and clean water. Achambaud still hadn't stirred.

The scarred woman suddenly screeched in warning. Godefroi swung around to find a black mist oozing from Etienne's corpse.

"No," Hugues whispered in horror.

"What's happening?" Godefroi cried out. He drew his belt knife to protect Godwera.

The mist congealed above Etienne's body into a twisting, serpentine shape that ended in an obscene, leering mouth.

A paralysing terror took hold of Godefroi and his legs trembled. How in God's name could this creature still be alive?

The fog thickened as it poured from Etienne's mangled corpse. Godefroi glanced at the stairs leading out of the chamber. He could get Godwera to safety, but that would mean leaving Hugues and Achambaud behind. The scarred woman raced around the plinth and grabbed hold of Hugues' hand, incomprehensible words streaming from her mouth.

"I don't understand," Hugues cried in frustration.

The woman howled a single word: "Shechinah!"

Hugues grasped her by both arms. "Did you say Shechinah? The Holy Spirit?"

The scarred woman nodded vigorously and pointed to the floor.

"Hold it off for as long as you can!" Hugues cried.

Godefroi's grip on the hilt of his knife tightened. It was probably useless against something formed from mist, but it was all he had. He glanced down at Godwera, paralysed by indecision.

"You must help Hugues," Godwera urged. "There's no escaping this."

The fog elongated into a long, twisting column and wove towards Hugues. Summoning his courage, Godefroi moved to intercept it.

He slashed at the mist and his knife sliced through without effect as he had feared. The mist coiled around his arm and Godefroi backed away, frantically trying to scrape it off. It clung to his sleeve and icy needles punctured his skin, deadening the muscles in his arm.

"Hugues!" Godefroi bellowed. He twisted around to find the scarred woman kneeling at the priest's feet. Hugues had placed one hand on the crown of her head and the other was raised overhead. His eyes were squeezed shut and he seemed deep in prayer.

They would need more than prayer to defeat this demon. Godefroi searched the chamber for a weapon in desperation and his gaze fell upon the lantern.

The fog tightened around Godefroi's forearm and crept towards his shoulder. A voice invaded his skull, soothing him like a mother with a newborn babe. That terrified Godefroi more than anything else.

Your mind is not as strong as that of the friend you just killed. Taking you won't present much of a challenge.

Godefroi staggered towards the lantern and kicked it over. The glass shattered and burning oil spilled across the floor. Gritting his teeth, he shoved his mist-bound arm into the flames. The fire scorched his leather armour and seared the flesh beneath, but it did nothing to slow the advance of the fog creeping towards his throat and face.

"Hold on!" Godwera called faintly.

Stupid and stubborn to the end.

The voice in his head was gaining strength. His entire arm was numb now and it refused to heed his commands.

I'm going to make you all suffer, starting with your precious woman before she bleeds out.

The chill reached Godefroi's neck and panic finally seized him. "Help me!" Godefroi screamed.

Hugues turned towards the roof of the chamber and chanted in a loud voice. "In the name of the five mysteries, I summon Adonai Melech, Shaddai el Chai, Elohim Tzabaoth, Jehovah Tzabaoth and Aloah v'daat. Remember your vows. Aid us now in our struggle with Severity."

As Hugues spoke, the scarred woman hummed in a low, resonant tone. The sound trembled through the walls of the chamber and the air crackled. Godefroi felt something deep within him respond, as it had in the Holy Sepulchre and beneath the āl-Aqsa Mosque.

The fog halted just beneath Godefroi's jaw. He sensed its hesitation and hope flared inside him. Perhaps Hugues had found a way to drive it off.

He cannot help you, the voice said in the space behind Godefroi's fore-head.

Cold, ethereal fingers closed around Godefroi's throat. He clawed at the mist, but his fingernails only tore his skin. Tendrils of fog invaded his nostrils and ears. Godefroi screamed and they crept into his mouth too.

Mine, echoed triumphantly inside Godefroi's head.

"I summon the Holy Shechinah," Hugues shouted in desperation. "Please, master of the Middle Pillar. Return to the kingdom of Malkuth. Walk among us again."

I am Gamaliel, the voice whispered to Godefroi. *And I am your one and only master.*

Godefroi convulsed as he fought to retain control of his body. Darkness pooled inside his mind, cold, ancient and merciless. This was not his destiny, he screamed silently.

Shadows swirled around him, thickening into high, circular walls. He was falling into a deep well, forced down into a tiny corner of himself.

With nowhere to retreat, he refused to surrender, fighting to hold onto who he was with every shred of strength and will that he possessed. Yet no matter how hard he rallied, he was forced down.

CHAPTER 30

18 December 1307

The ruined abbey

Roustan let his horse pick its way through the snow as he surveyed the wreckage. The glow of the fire was a beacon as they crossed the moors, although it had largely burned out by the time they had arrived. Only pockets of rubble and the odd timber beam still smouldered amid the fresh snow. Some of the cracked stones glowed with residual heat where the fire had burned fiercest.

Whatever purpose this abbey had served, it had clearly been abandoned.

The captain's expression was anxious as he trotted over on his horse.

"I take it you found nothing of value," Roustan said.

"I'm afraid so, Seigneur. A couple of charred bodies; monks, by the look of their dress. The fire destroyed almost everything else."

"That's what it was intended to do. Any tracks?"

"No. If anyone escaped the blaze, the snow has concealed their trail."

"Widen your search," Roustan commanded. "There may be another way out of this wretched valley."

"My scouts have already—"

"Tell them to look again!" Roustan shouted. Guillaume had promised she would be here. How in God's name was he supposed to find her now? Already his guts clenched in anticipation of Gamaliel's rage.

"Yes, Seigneur." The captain waited patiently.

Roustan fought for calm. "Is there something else?" he asked through his teeth.

"The mercenaries, sir."

"What of them?"

"You promised them spoils when we ransacked the abbey." The captain glanced about to make sure they were not overheard. "There is a risk they might turn upon us if they're not compensated."

Roustan gazed at the men picking through the ruined buildings. The captain had a point. The mercenaries outnumbered his troops four to one. They might pluck up the courage to demand payment.

"Tell them we haven't finished hunting our quarry yet." Roustan stroked his beard. "And give them an advance, as a token of good faith. Three pennies per man should silence their complaints for now."

"They'll want to know where we're going," the captain ventured. "What should I tell them?"

Roustan spat. "You can tell them our destination is wherever I decide. Now locate those tracks."

"Yes, sir." The captain wheeled his horse about and trotted off.

Don't be so hard on the fellow. The voice oozed across Roustan's thoughts like pond scum across the surface of water. He stiffened at the unexpected intrusion.

"Gamaliel."

There's no need to say it out loud. I hear everything, especially that which is left unsaid.

Roustan shivered at the demon's touch. How long had the creature been present? And why did not he sense its presence? Every other visitation had been like an invasion. Was Gamaliel spying on him now? Or was it becoming easier for Gamaliel to slide in and out of the harness he had wrapped around Roustan?

Ah, what gorgeous panic. Please, don't stop. Your questions are quite entertaining.

Roustan quelled his racing thoughts with an effort. "You said Salome would be here. I did everything you asked of me, but she's not here. It's not my fault."

No, she has fled again. Things have...changed. But we still need her.

Roustan sagged in the saddle. He had known the demon was unlikely to let him go without capturing Salome. Still, he had harboured a faint hope that simply reaching the abbey as quickly as humanly possible might count in his favour.

Hope is a cruel mistress, I'm afraid. Despair is a far more reliable master. Less scope for disappointment. Trust me, I should know.

This banter was out of character for Gamaliel. Normally the demon was brutally direct. It was almost as if he was reluctant to address the real issue.

"Do you know where she is?" Roustan asked.

I know where she must be going.

"Where?"

On the north flank of a mountain in Scotland is the entrance to a series of caves. The opening is guarded by a small fortress. Very ancient. Long since abandoned. Occupy the fort and stop her from entering those caves. Kill any who defend her and bring her back to this valley. Do these things and I will set you free.

"Where is this mountain?" Roustan asked. "What is it called?"

Gamaliel hesitated. Roustan could feel his reluctance to say the name. *The locals know it as Schiehallion. It's located in the very heart of Scotland.*

"What's so special about this place?"

A blinding pain lanced through Roustan's skull. Spots swarmed across his vision and he nearly toppled from his saddle. "I'm sorry! Forgive me," he gasped.

The spike withdrew from his skull with a final, agonising wrench. *Get to Schiehallion before Salome. Fail me and you'll suffer far worse.*

"I understand." Roustan waited for a reply but none came. "Gamaliel?"

The demon was gone.

For now.

Roustan massaged his throbbing forehead and choked back a sob.

When it came to Gamaliel, it was dangerous to assume anything. Yet he was certain he sensed...if not outright fear, then trepidation when the demon mentioned the mountain. Perhaps this Schiehallion contained something that could hurt Gamaliel. Or failing that, it might offer a way to break the demon's hold on him.

He rose up in his stirrups and bellowed at the retreating Captain's back. It would be even colder further north, but the faint hope of salvation would keep him warm.

CHAPTER 31

4 August 1099

The Necropolis

The woman howled a single word: "Shechinah!"

Hugues grasped her by both arms. "Did you say Shechinah? The Holy Spirit?"

The scarred woman nodded vigorously and pointed to the floor.

"Hold it off for as long as you can!" Hugues cried to Godefroi.

Gamaliel had taken possession of Etienne. Hugues didn't know how—or when—this could have happened, but he had witnessed firsthand what a Lord of Severity could do.

"You must tell me how to summon the Lords of Mercy." Hugues shook the scarred woman in desperation. "I know it can be done. I've seen it." Umayr's cabal had known the secret of summoning the angelic choirs.

The woman shook her head in frustration. "Shechinah," she replied with matching urgency.

"How?" Hugues spread his hands and hunched his shoulders in a gesture of helplessness.

The scarred woman pointed at Hugues and then at the ceiling. Her brown eyes pleaded with him to understand.

The sound of breaking glass was soon followed by Godefroi bellowing for help. Hugues fought down a rising sense of despair. Achambaud was unconscious, Godwera would bleed to death without help, and Godefroi was locked in a battle for his very soul. He was the only one left.

"Show me how, damn you!"

The woman grasped Hugues' wrist and placed his palm on the crown of her head. Using gestures, she instructed him to raise his free hand overhead.

Was this some kind of invocation? Perhaps a way to summon aid? Hugues fervently hoped so.

Trusting that the words were not important, only the intention, Hugues recited the names of the five lower Sephirot, and binding them all together through the middle pillar of Unity, Hugues summoned the Holy Shechinah.

The chamber rumbled as the words of his summoning died away.

The scarred woman's skull became hot and then searing to the touch. Pain burned through Hugues' hand and up his arm, but he refused to break the connection. The heat shot through Hugues' chest and burst through his upraised arm towards the ceiling.

Godefroi threw his head back and howled into the air. His cry was a mixture of despair and triumph. He staggered, his movements jerky and abrupt. Hugues had a sense of what Godefroi must be experiencing, for he remembered Gamaliel's touch. He spared a brief thought for poor Etienne: succumbing to Severity alone must have been a terrible fate.

Hugues released the woman and drew his knife. He was no match for Godefroi, but if he struck now, it might create enough time for her and Godwera to escape. He took an uncertain step towards Godefroi.

The woman grabbed Hugues' wrist and shook her head. She pointed at the ceiling. Hugues looked up. A silver circle had appeared in the bedrock and liquid light suddenly poured forth from that opening. The radiance had a strange, shifting quality, and it cascaded from the ceiling to pool on the floor in front of them. Hugues and the woman backed away until the plinth jutted into his back.

Godefroi roared in anger and clawed at something unseen in the air.

The pool of light deepened and its surface swirled like a whirlpool. A Nubian materialised in the strange shaft of light. His long black hair was oiled and bound in braids that were tied into a single queue that hung past his shoulders. Dressed only in a linen shift, his dark glistening skin rippled with muscle. This was not like the columns of light Umayr's cabal had summoned in the ravine.

"Enoch!" The woman threw herself at the feet of the apparition.

Hugues stared. Enoch? Was this the same Enoch from the Old Testament who, it was said, ascended to heaven and became an archangel?

"Salome," Enoch replied with a smile. "Please, rise." He gestured with the tips of his long, black fingers. She rose, bowed deeply and touched her forehead, lips and heart in a fluid gesture.

She said in a rush, "You must help me. Gamaliel has infected this cabal." She pointed at Godefroi.

Hugues stared in astonishment. He understood her perfectly now.

Enoch glanced at Godefroi, who was ominously still. "Alas, I cannot intervene," he replied with a sad expression.

"But you must," Salome cried. "Think of the consequences should Severity take me."

"I'm aware of the consequences," Enoch replied, "just as you know I may only walk the earth when the Pentemychos is ready to be judged. You have been woken before your time," Enoch said with a disapproving look at Hugues.

Salome dropped to her knees. "Please, Enoch. After carrying it for so long, you cannot abandon me now."

"Sweet child." Enoch reached towards her, but his fingers pressed flat against the edge of the shaft of light encompassing him. "I cannot interfere until the time of testing. You must choose a Shroud and endure until then."

Enoch's form shifted momentarily to a tall, golden figure, long-limbed and regal in its bearing, before flickering back again.

Enoch turned to face Hugues. "You will form an Order. You and your brethren quartered in Troyes will dedicate your lives, and resources, to protecting this woman and the great burden she carries. You will not rest until such time as she finds peace. Swear you will do this, as will the generations that follow."

Hugues sank to his knees. "I swear to protect her, as will the generations that follow," Hugues said in a voice filled with awe. Enoch's vow hardened into an unbreakable determination inside Hugues. He would protect Salome at all costs with every resource and means at his disposal. Hugues nodded. This was his life's work. Nothing could divert him from it.

"Mine," Godefroi whispered in a voice that was no longer his. He bent over and retrieved the bloodied mallet. He swung it through the air, testing the balance. An unfamiliar leer spread across his bearded face.

"Enoch!" Salome clambered to her feet and threw a desperate glance at Godefroi. "They will rip Baphomet from me. You must help."

"Three times must I deny you," Enoch replied, a look of regret softening his expression. "You must find a way to defeat Severity." The liquid light swirled inside his pillar and its radiance dimmed.

"Still," Enoch said in a fading voice, "if Gamaliel wants Baphomet so badly, perhaps you should oblige him?" The pillar shimmered and scattered into sparkling motes of silver.

Enoch was gone.

"Just the three of us again," Gamaliel said through Godefroi's mouth. He lurched towards them, swinging the mallet in low, menacing arcs.

Salome grabbed Hugues' forearm and dragged him around the far side of the plinth. "You understand me now, yes?"

"Yes." Hugues kept an eye on Godefroi's progress. The pedestal would not keep him at bay for long.

"Listen," Salome said urgently. "I'm going to release the piece of Baphomet that you used to wake me. No time for questions," she said, waving his confusion aside. "When I do, you must strike him with it." Salome knelt and closed her eyes.

Godefroi reached the far side of the plinth and stared at Hugues. "I have his memories now. Did you know that part of him is going to enjoy killing you?" Godefroi swung the mallet in the space between them, testing his range. Hugues dodged back and the blow whistled past.

Salome moaned on the floor. Hugues didn't entirely understand what she was doing, but he knew she was the only chance they had.

"Godefroi, you must fight this." Hugues dodged again as Godefroi swung an overhead blow. The metal head struck the plinth so hard that it cracked. "If not for the brotherhood we shared, then fight for Godwera."

"Keep talking," Gamaliel replied. "He can still hear you, and every word is an exquisite torture." Godefroi jumped onto the plinth, and bracing his weight with his free hand, he kicked out horizontally with one foot. The heel of Godefroi's boot struck Hugues' arm. Hugues collapsed to the floor of the chamber, the fingers of his knifehand suddenly numb with pain.

Salome screamed and the piercing squeal of grinding crystal rent the air. Dropping to her hands and knees in front of Hugues, she vomited blood. Godefroi leapt from the plinth and landed next to Salome.

"That's enough, you witch." Godefroi's boot slammed into the back of Salome's shoulder and Hugues caught the snap of bone. She screamed again, this time in a normal human voice.

"I'm going to rip every piece of it from your miserable carcass," Gamaliel threatened her. "You'll rue your pride a thousandfold. Perhaps then you'll understand my brethren better."

Enoch's command to protect Salome still thrummed through every sinew of Hugues' body. As he gathered himself to tackle Godefroi, something sharp pressed against his good hand. He glanced down and saw a familiar sliver of crystal glinting in Salome's pool of blood.

Gamaliel grabbed a fistful of Salome's hair. "You asked for wisdom," he snarled. "Now you'll learn the price that we Fallen have paid for it."

Hugues clutched the shard in his fist, ignoring the sharp edges that drew blood. As Godefroi threatened Salome, Hugues lunged towards them in a crouch. Godefroi twisted to face him and swung the mallet in a vicious, downward arc. Hugues drove the shard into Godefroi's thigh and rolled desperately to his left at the same time. The mallet-head caught him a glancing blow across his ear and cheekbone.

Black and white spots danced across Hugues' vision, and it felt like a wasp was buzzing through his eardrum. The roughly hewn ceiling slowly came into focus. It took Hugues a long moment to realise that he was lying on his back. Looming over him, Godefroi stared in surprise at the crystal sliver jutting from his thigh. Salome had wriggled free of his grip and backed up against the wall.

Godefroi hefted the mallet and took a step towards Hugues. "Priest, you'll—"

The crystal gleamed and Godefroi froze. Confusion spread across his face, followed by a growing expression of horror. A brilliant light exploded beneath his skin. It poured from his open mouth and burst from his ears and nostrils. His skin became translucent, exposing the complex web of veins and arteries, and the dark outline of another figure nestled inside Godefroi. Nothing could hide from that illumination, and no shadow could survive its scouring light.

Hugues edged backwards across the floor until the chamber wall pressed against his spine. A strange, unearthly keening escaped Godefroi's mouth and it conveyed unimaginable pain and anguish.

Only much later was Hugues able to piece together the events that followed in blinding succession: the shadow nestling inside Godefroi burning away; the light from the crystal shard flaring and winking out; the crystal falling to the floor, inert once again; and Godefroi collapsing in a boneless heap.

Hugues blinked and shook his head in an attempt to expel the dancing afterimages.

Salome released a pent-up breath that became a deep, shuddering sob.

Hugues crawled over to her. Godefroi—or what remained of him— didn't stir. Hugues retrieved the sliver of crystal just in case.

"Are you hurt?" Hugues grimaced at the stupid question. "Beyond your shoulder, I mean."

Salome looked up. In the weak and uncertain light, her eyes were almost black. Unshed tears glistened in their depths.

"You should not have woken me," she said. "Do you have any idea what would happen if Severity ever possessed me?"

"No." Hugues noticed a patch of skin below Salome's throat had become smooth and free of scars.

"Pray that we never find out." Salome took the sliver of crystal, wiped away Godefroi's blood with the tattered remains of her shift, and swallowed it. Tiny white scars spread across the smooth patch of her skin.

Hugues frowned, at a loss to solve this new and unexpected puzzle.

CHAPTER 32

4 August 1099

The fortress of Alamut

Night had settled over the fortress of Alamut when the chill in the air deepened. The Old Man remained in his meditative pose at the top of his tower; legs crossed and palms resting on the opposite knee. Despite his outward calm, anticipation thrilled through the chambers of his heart. News had been scarce. What would this visit bring?

Sammael? The name was a breath on the night breeze.

He stirred. "Is it done, Gamaliel?"

The cold that sharpened the edge of the breeze wavered. Sammael opened his failing eyes. Clouds masked the moon. "Answer me, Gamaliel."

Salome is free and has joined the Christians, Gamaliel replied. *She still carries her half of the keystone.*

"How did she escape?" Sammael asked.

It was the priest, Gamaliel replied. *He used a fragment of Baphomet. Its touch burned me from the body I had seized.*

"What?" Sammael surged to his feet. "Men cannot wield the keystone! Not without a Shroud and a cabal. Cease your theatrics and manifest so we can speak properly."

I cannot, Gamaliel replied. *The fragment nearly burned out my essence. I must return to Abaddon before I dwindle any further.*

Could this really be possible?

"Wait." Sammael shuffled to the parapet. This body had served its purpose and was deteriorating rapidly. Time—that most implacable of adversaries—had almost won.

Sammael squinted across the quiet fortress that he had built. No lights glimmered upon the walls to betray its location. Instructions had been left, subordinates trained. They would continue to create division between the two flourishing branches of Islam, playing off against the Christians where needed. The region would remain in chaos for many,

many years to come.

Throwing his arms wide, Sammael pitched forward and let gravity take him. Air rushed past his face as he plummeted towards the hard ground. At the last possible moment, Sammael slipped free from the shackles of flesh and watched as his former shell bounced on the unforgiving stone. Blood pooled around the broken figure.

Now who is being theatrical?

Even in spirit form, Gamaliel's essence was weak. The fabric of his being billowed in the currents that swirled beneath the physical world like tattered strips of velvet.

Tell me, Sammael commanded.

Gamaliel recounted the entire story, starting with his selection of the curly-haired engineer to infiltrate the cabal, and finishing with the priest plunging the shard of Baphomet into him.

Sammael absorbed the retelling without interruption. In the end, only two points were of significance.

Think carefully, Sammael said. *You're certain that Enoch confirmed this was not the time of testing.*

That's what he said.

And he did not intervene.

Not directly, Gamaliel replied, *although he planted the seed of my demise.*

So Salome walks the earth again and the cabal that woke her is broken. He ascended until he hovered above his former tower. Having spent so long in human form, he could not help but turn west and gaze towards the horizon. Such limitations need no longer constrain him, but they lingered while the memory of flesh was still strong.

Will you try to seize Salome? Gamaliel's presence was a faint echo of his former strength.

They will take her back to France. The Salt Lines will hide her until the time of the testing. Sammael studied the faint outline of his brethren.

We can't allow that, Gamaliel said.

Nor will we. Sammael smiled. Gamaliel could always be relied upon to state the obvious. *We must assemble the other Lords. They must be informed.*

They won't heed you, Gamaliel warned. *Lilith is clouded by the smoke of the poppy and passes her days in fevered pursuit of carnal pleasures. Orev Zarak agitates the tribesmen of the steppes. Soon those hordes will ravage this landscape. As for Tagiriron, I lost track of him in the Orient, but rest assured he pursues his own designs.*

Sammael suppressed a flash of irritation. *Petty diversions*, he replied with a flick of an ethereal hand. *They will respond if the summoning originates from one of the holy mountains.*

How? Gamaliel asked. *Sion is closed to us and Mercy has claimed Heredom.*

Which leaves us with Ararat, Sammael replied. *Salome will travel west. As the ancient knowledge of Baphomet moves, the balance of power will shift. Champagne, Burgundy, Lorraine: these are our new battlefields. It will take time to infiltrate the Salt Lines. We must start now, before they ready their defences.*

Why must you always complicate matters? Gamaliel complained. *Why not simply rally the Moslems, recover Jerusalem from the Christians, and imprison Salome until the time of testing?*

The Moslems are fractious and divisive, as you well know. Any attempt to dislodge the Christians will take far too long to co-ordinate. By the time we take the city, Salome will have slipped through our net. No, the only way to locate her again is through guile, not force. You have demonstrated that, if nothing else.

Gamaliel's form billowed in indignation. *You blame me for this situation? After almost being burned from existence, you lay the blame at my feet?*

Of course not. Who knew a mortal could wield a piece of the keystone? Sammael made a placating gesture with hands he no longer possessed. *We have learned something new.*

I paid a very high price for that knowledge, brother.

I seem to recall that you were eager for the glory, Sammael replied.

The two Lords of Severity faced each other in the darkness. Gamaliel's insubstantial form trembled. *The others might heed you, Sammael, but when they learn of this, they will never trust you again.*

Sammael sneered. *Hollow threats are pointless. You need to return to Abaddon to recover. No one is going to be hearing from you for some time.*

As usual, Sammael, your superiority is your weakness. Have you forgotten that I am the only one who has seen Salome in the flesh?

Not at all, which is why we must find a way to resolve our dispute. Sammael drifted closer to Gamaliel and allowed a note of conciliation to enter his voice. *My original offer still stands.*

I would be a fool to trust you again.

But can you afford not to? Tagiriron might be interested, even Orev Zarak.

Gamaliel studied Sammael with obvious dislike. *What do you propose?*

I will head west and infiltrate the French monarchy while you regenerate. With luck, you will be strong enough to leave Abaddon once I have located Salome. Together, we will drag her back to Abaddon, rip the keystone from her flesh, and destroy our prison. Sammael let the promise hang between them. *What do you say, brother? We can still ascend together.*

I will consider it. Gamaliel drifted higher above Alamut. *You know where to find me.*

Exerting the remnants of his energies, Gamaliel opened a rent in the fabric of Malkuth. The pull of Abaddon was much stronger in spirit form. It took an enormous effort for Sammael to resist its call. Gamaliel slipped through the portal, which snapped closed behind him.

Sammael scowled at the point where Gamaliel had disappeared. If his time as the Imam of Alamut taught him anything, it was that incompetence could not be tolerated. Not in the lowliest servant...or a peer.

Perhaps he should pursue Salome on his own? Could he really entrust the pursuit of his freedom to anyone else?

Sammael ripped open a gateway. His quarry was on the loose, but he would run it to ground. The thrill of the hunt quivered through the emptiness of his being. It could almost pass for a flicker of life. For now, that would have to be enough.

CHAPTER 33

25 December 1307

Mount Heredom

Bertrand hunched over his saddle and flexed his gloved fingers to maintain his circulation. The wind keened from the north, depositing fresh flurries of snow. His mount plodded up the foothill doggedly, its head drooping beneath the bitter onslaught. The journey from Rooklyn to Fountains Abbey, and then on to Scotland, had all but exhausted the poor beast. They were fortunate to have caught up with Sir William and his men at Fountains.

Andrew, the local guide they had paid to locate the ruined fortress on the northern flanks of Schiehallion, was barely visible ahead. Bertrand glanced over his shoulder. A single file of horsemen behind him disappeared into the swirling snow. He wondered how Salome was coping with the cold. Since her separation from Baphomet, her powers of endurance had waned to ordinary levels. If the long journey had drained Bertrand, he could only imagine how she must feel.

A steep shoulder parted the veil of snow. The trail curled around the base of the outcrop and twisted left, out of sight. Bertrand squinted up the steep rock face. Visibility was too poor to make out any landmarks.

He huddled deeper into his cloak and dug his spurs into the flanks of his mare. She tossed her head but kept plodding. The poor animal was beyond goading.

Rounding a jumble of rocks, he entered a sheltered valley. Fresh snow covered the ground, making for treacherous footing. At least the wind had dropped away. Andrew was just visible twenty yards ahead staring up at the walls of the valley. Bertrand guided his mount next to the Scotsman on his sorrel mountain pony.

"There 'tis." Andrew pointed at a mass of toppled stone nestled at the top of the valley. "I'll not be going any closer, not for all the gold in King Edward's treasury."

Bertrand squinted. "Are you sure this is the place?"

"Aye, I'm sure. Now I'll be off, having seen to me obligations. If ye take me advice, ye'll keep goin'. The Gaelic name for this place is '*sidh Chailleann*', which means 'Fairy Hill of the Caledonians'. This place belongs to spirits, I tell ye. It's no place for men." Andrew shivered and crossed himself.

Bertrand scrutinised the ruined fortress. What he had taken at first to be natural rock formations were actually weathered fortifications. The outer wall was largely intact, although a jumble of rocks near the centre of the fortress appeared to have blocked off the main gate.

Salome and Rémi joined Bertrand. Her mount was skittish, rolling its eyes and jerking its head. She tightened her grip on the reins and patted its neck.

"Andrew says this is the fortress." Bertrand pointed to the ruins. "But I'm not sure there's a way in. See how those boulders have collapsed the wall."

"We'll find a way," Salome replied.

"How can you be so sure?" Rémi asked. "Looks abandoned to me."

"Necessity," Salome said with a grimace. She urged her horse forward up the steep slope. Sir William joined Bertrand and Rémi a moment later.

"Rémi, stay with her," Bertrand said in French. "I want to talk to William for a moment."

Rémi grunted an acknowledgement and continued up the slope.

"Where are they going?" William asked.

"Up there." Bertrand pointed. "Apparently this is the place."

William pulled a face. "It's little more than a pile of rocks. Is Andrew sure this is the fortress we're looking for?"

Bertrand turned to question Andrew. The Scotsman had slipped away and was already retracing their path. "Salome seems convinced. And I, for one, wouldn't mind being out of the weather."

William frowned as he surveyed the terrain. "We'll have to make the best of it then. If nothing else, we'll have the advantage of higher ground. If we can free those boulders, they might cause some damage. See how the land narrows into a water course over yonder. That will funnel their attack."

"William—" Bertrand hesitated as he sorted through his conflicting feelings. "You know I'm grateful to you and the brothers who volunteered to accompany us. More grateful than I can express."

William held up one hand. "Spare me your speech, Bertrand. I saw the letter from Abbot Edwyn, so I know he held the Lady Salome in the highest regard. You can't fend off three score or more men on your own and that's the truth of it."

"Even with your brothers, we're still outnumbered at least three to one. Take them further north. If we conceal our tracks, perhaps you can lead them away."

William shook his head and snow tumbled from the hood of his cloak. "We both know that won't work. Every attempt we've made to lose them has failed. Whoever is hunting you seems to know your destination." He gestured towards the fortress. "Let's not let the lady get too far ahead."

Bertrand gave William a pained smile. "I once rode with another party of thirteen like this one. Only Salome, Rémi and I survived that day. And I very much fear the same man is following us."

"Then embrace your opportunity for revenge," William replied with a fierce grin, "for I'll not abandon a fellow member of the Order. Nor will I allow our fate to weigh upon your conscience. It's our choice to be here." He glanced back towards the line of Templar brothers rounding the steep shoulder. "I know you refuse to speak of what happened in France, but it's plain to me your fate is linked to that of our Order. If protecting the lady somehow aids the restoration of our brotherhood, I'll not shirk from that responsibility. I'm sure you'd feel the same if you sat in my saddle."

There seemed little point in arguing with William. Besides, Bertrand was greatly comforted by his presence. He was sure that Everard would have approved of this selfless English chevalier.

Bertrand and William rode up the final rise to the crumbling outer wall together. Despite the impact of rock falls and the erosion of time, the barricade was still formidable. Bertrand searched for a point of entry wide enough to accommodate their horses.

"Over here!" Salome's call was muffled.

William and Bertrand coaxed their mounts over to her. She and Rémi had stopped where a tumble of rocks had brought down a section of the wall. Salome was peering into a gap underneath a large boulder.

"I can see daylight on the other side," she said in English for William's benefit.

"It's not high enough for the horses though," William noted.

Salome rose to her feet and dusted snow off her legs. "Ask your men to scout both sides of the wall for a larger opening. I doubt they'll find one, but it's worth checking."

William gave the order and his men fanned out. "What if they don't find another entry point?"

"We'll have to abandon the horses." Salome glanced at Bertrand. "Sanctuary lies within these caves."

Bertrand quickly translated the exchange for Rémi.

"Releasing the horses means surrendering our only means of escape," Rémi noted.

"The poor beasts are half dead anyway," Salome replied. "Our only hope lies inside that mountain."

A scout came trotting up the hill. The brother dismounted and hurried over.

"How far behind?" William asked. "Will they reach us before night-fall?"

"Two hours at most," the brother replied. "The snow won't hide our tracks in time."

William gave Bertrand a pointed look.

"Very well." William considered his men before gazing up at the ruined fortress. "This is where it will be decided. If we can't find a better way in, have the men assemble here. We have no choice but to abandon the horses."

The scout nodded and hurried back to his mount.

"I'm not waiting." Salome untied her possessions from her saddle, hefted the sack over her shoulder and crawled beneath the boulder.

Bertrand swung out of his saddle and gathered his few possessions. "Rémi, wait to see if they find a better way in. If not, follow us inside."

Rémi nodded. "Keep a careful watch. This place looks deserted, yet so does the cave of a sleeping bear."

Bertrand got down onto all fours. Behind him, William and Rémi discussed defensive tactics in broken French.

The ground was hard and icy beneath his gloves. He crept into the gap, careful not to dislodge any rocks. Salome was a shadow ahead of him, wriggling through the confined space. He avoided wondering how stable the boulder was and concentrated on moving forward. After a few bruises and scrapes, Bertrand emerged into a large courtyard.

The original design of the fortress was much clearer from this vantage point. The outer wall had been organised around the natural foundations of rock. Two barbicans, one at each end of the outer wall, guarded against possible attack from either of the steep slopes.

Unlike typical inner courtyards, this one was triangular as it tapered back into the cleft of the steep valley. The main gate had been in the centre of the outer wall, but it was buried beneath a landslide. Rain and snow-melt had carved a narrow watercourse through the rubble.

Bertrand frowned. Why would anyone go to the trouble of building a fortress in such a desolate spot?

Salome clambered over a mound of fallen rocks and paused to get her bearings. A small inner keep nestled at the point where the two flanks of Schiehallion met at the tip of the triangular courtyard. The blank stone walls of the keep were hewn from the mountainside so that the eye slid past them. Salome hurried towards it.

"Salome, wait!" Bertrand called.

He raced across the uneven stone. Salome disappeared into the lengthening shadow of the western flank. Bertrand increased his pace. It was unlike her to be so reckless, even if she was certain the Lords of Mercy could be found within this isolated mountain.

Salome halted before a wide opening in the wall of the inner keep. A twisted gate of iron lay on the ground. Scorch marks were visible where the stone had cracked and split. Crenelations jutted high overhead like teeth bared at the darkening sky.

"What happened here?" Bertrand asked.

"I don't know." She wrung her hands. "If the entrance to the mountain has been defiled..."

Bertrand put an arm around her shoulder. "You weren't to know."

She looked up at him, her expression twisted with guilt. "What if Edwyn was wrong? I will have trapped us all."

"Then let's hope that Edwyn was not wrong."

Bertrand shrugged his shield off his back and drew Everard's sword. They stopped a few feet inside the keep while Salome lit a torch. Holding it aloft, she examined the interior of the building. Like the outer stronghold, the inner keep was roughly triangular in shape. A wooden platform, partially collapsed now, ran along the wall facing the courtyard. It was clearly intended for archers.

A staircase had been cut into the mountain at the back of the keep. The cracked stone steps spiralled up into the ceiling and descended into the bowels of the mountain. Salome and Bertrand moved forward warily. If a battle had been fought here, no trace of the combatants remained: no brittle bones crunched beneath their feet; no discarded armour rusted quietly in dark corners.

"Down?" Bertrand asked.

Salome nodded. She bent over the edge of the steps and extended her torch as far as possible. The worn staircase dropped away into inky darkness. "This must be the way."

"Perhaps we should wait for the others?"

"No. If the entrance to the Halls of Mercy is sealed, we need to know now."

"Stay close then."

Bertrand descended the steps first, testing his footing before committing his weight. Salome followed, raising the smoky torch overhead to light his way. At first the steps were broad and even. As they descended, the stonework became rougher. The transition from staircase to tunnel was gradual yet unmistakable. Moisture beaded on the walls and dripped onto the hewn rock.

He wondered how deep they were. The tunnel ended with a sudden twist to the right. Rounding the corner, Bertrand confronted a small cavern. He edged into it carefully, sword raised. Salome lifted her torch to reveal stalactites hanging from the low roof. The cavern was roughly oval in shape, no more than ten paces wide. Metal glinted at the opposite end.

Bertrand and Salome moved closer. Five iron bars, each thicker than Bertrand's wrist, were embedded into the rock floor and ceiling. The tunnel continued on the far side. Looking closer, Bertrand noticed an iron wheel with five spokes jutting from the rock next to the bars. A circular hole gaped where the axle of the wheel should be.

Salome dropped to her knees and pressed her face to the ground. "Thank you, Lords of Light and Mercy. I despaired when I saw the state of your house."

Bertrand sheathed his sword and helped her up. "I don't understand. I see no way through that portcullis."

"Exactly." Salome smiled, although tears shimmered in her eyes. "The way is closed, but not lost."

She rummaged through her sack and withdrew a piece of tightly wrapped lambskin. Cutting the leather ties with her belt knife, she unrolled the skin to reveal an odd spike of metal. It was dull grey in colour, although flecks twinkled in the torchlight. One end was flat, while the other end tapered to a dull point.

"Do you know what this is?" Salome asked.

"No. A weapon?"

"It was the key to my prison," she replied. "Now it'll unlock my freedom." She inserted the spike into the axle of the wheel. It clicked into place with a loud clang. Taking hold of the flattened end of the spike, Salome turned it a half rotation. The squeal of long-dormant metal filled the chamber.

"Bertrand, please turn that wheel to your right."

He placed his shield on the floor. Taking a two-handed grip, Bertrand strained to turn the wheel. Heaving with a combination of body weight and raw strength, he managed a quarter turn. The five bars lifted an inch with a squeal of protest. Bertrand kept straining until sweat ran down his back. Each quarter turn raised the strange portcullis higher. Soon they had lifted it sufficiently for a person to crawl underneath.

A distant yell echoed down the stairwell. Bertrand snatched up his shield and drew his sword. Listening carefully, he recognised Rémi's voice in the echoing cries.

"Call them down," Salome said, her eyes wide with excitement. "Sanctuary awaits inside."

Bertrand strode to the foot of the staircase and bellowed for Rémi and William to join them.

CHAPTER 34

25 December 1307

The Halls of Mercy

Rémi watched impassively as the English chevalier organised their defence.

A few brothers had bravely volunteered to guard the foot of the stairwell. William had sensibly arranged a second group to defend the tunnel that passed through the portcullis.

Unfortunately, it seemed there was no way to lower the bars once inside the tunnel. It was a pity the architects of this strange place had neglected this point, because it meant they were all about to die. He had glimpsed the force following them through the foothills. Despite the close quarters, there was no way on God's good earth they could prevail against such numbers.

At best, their defence would slow the assault and inflict heavy losses upon the enemy. In a less determined foe, that might be enough to discourage further pursuit. But if Bertrand was right, the man leading these troops was the same one who had attacked them at the Marne. Rémi shook his head. No number of casualties would dissuade such a ruthless man.

He glanced at Bertrand and Salome quietly arguing near the portcullis. No doubt the cub was anxious to fight. Salome, on the other hand, remained convinced help was to be had in the bowels of this wretched mountain.

Rémi snorted at the notion. For such a smart woman, she had failed to grasp the obvious: this place had been abandoned long ago. They were at least a century too late to seek the assistance Edwyn had promised. Perhaps even more.

He chuckled quietly at the back of his throat. No sense chasing a horse that had already bolted.

So he had a simple decision to make. How did he choose to die? Fighting alongside the English, who had proven to be better companions than he had expected, or a more uncertain death, guarding Bertrand's back as they fled down some godforsaken tunnel. They could fall victim to a cave-in, or plummet down a chasm, or worse still, die of thirst as they wandered endlessly through a vast network of caves.

Easy decision, really.

Bertrand pointed towards the staircase and made a chopping gesture with his hand. Salome shook her head and tugged on his arm. It was clear she wanted to escape into the tunnel.

Despite the inevitable outcome of this battle, he was glad he had stuck with the cub. Bertrand had grown over the course of this journey. It gave Rémi quiet pleasure to witness the man he had become, and to take a measure of satisfaction for his part in it.

Of course, he would give anything to see Maura and the children again. He would sweep Renier, Aude and Gueri up into his arms and apologise for being absent for so long. He would make them understand the sacrifices he had made were for them, and how much he loved them. Then he would smother them all in kisses.

Rémi shook off the pleasant daydream. No sense torturing himself.

He squared his shoulders and marched over to Bertrand and Salome. "You had best be going." The two of them were so intent upon their argument they looked up in surprise.

"We'll do what we can here," Rémi continued, "but the deeper you're in that tunnel, the better your chances. Assuming it's not a dead end, of course."

"You're not coming with us?" Bertrand asked.

"No and don't bother arguing. You're just wasting time. That's all I can give you now." He glanced towards William. "You can't expect me to let the English clean up our mess."

"Rémi, I—"

He cut Bertrand off. "If by some miracle you escape, contact Maura. She'll know who you are." He took a deep, steadying breath. This was proving more difficult than he had expected. Best to finish it quickly.

"Tell her I'm sorry," Rémi said. "And to never doubt that she and the children were ever in my heart. Now go." He gave Bertrand a shove. "Get into that tunnel and don't look back. May God have mercy upon all of us." He made the sign of the cross.

Salome's expression conveyed both admiration and a grim understanding. She, at least, knew this was the correct decision. Lord Above, he still hated it when she agreed with him.

Bertrand wrapped Rémi in a tight embrace. "I'm not delivering that message. You tell her in person," Bertrand whispered fiercely.

Rémi gave him a gentle shove. "If God wills it."

The sound of harsh voices echoed faintly down the stairwell.

"Bertrand, we must hurry." Salome lifted her torch and peered into the tunnel.

Rémi waved him on. "Go."

"We'll find help down there." Bertrand let Salome drag him under the portcullis. Rémi hefted his axe. It would be a relief to finally put it to use.

The attack began in unexpected fashion.

It took Rémi a few moments to identify the rumbling, thumping sound rapidly approaching down the stairwell. It was only just before the barrel struck the sharp bend in the stairs that Rémi realised what it was.

He shouted a warning that was already too late. The wooden ribs of the keg cracked as they smashed into the tunnel wall and the momentum was such that the barrel ricocheted into the cavern, spraying pitch in all directions. A torch was promptly hurled from the stairwell and flames erupted in the cavern.

Rémi retreated before the blaze. Arrows zipped through the flames and William's men cried out in pain. He crouched down behind his shield, presenting the smallest target possible.

How many of William's brethren had already fallen? It was impossible to tell amidst the smoke and confusion.

"Fall back to the portcullis!" he yelled.

William took up the cry in English. A few brothers scrambled back to Rémi's position. One poor fellow crashed about the cavern, desperately batting at the flames leaping up his leggings. An arrow took him in the chest and he fell into a blazing puddle of pitch. More shafts rattled against Rémi's shield and whined overhead.

This was madness. With the fire between them and the archers, they had no way to counterattack.

"We need to move deeper into the tunnel!" Rémi shouted. "Make them come to us!"

"Fall back!" William shouted in English.

The remaining brothers retreated beneath the partially raised portcullis. The passage twisted through the rock, descending the further they went. At least the turns would provide some protection from bow-fire. It would have to be hand-to-hand in these close confines.

The tunnel darkened as the glow of the fire abated. Only two of the brothers carried torches. However, they possessed the foresight to leave two unlit lanterns in the tunnel should they need to retreat. Having lit the lanterns, William placed one man at the front and the other in the rear. Rémi counted five remaining men aside from him and William.

He glanced at the low roof. Not a lot of room to swing a sword. The shorter reach of his axe would prove more effective.

"Which way?" William called.

Rémi pushed forward to find the tunnel forked into three different passages. "No idea. We have two options. Either make a stand here or retreat further and guard each branch."

William's expression was difficult to read in the uncertain light. "Are you sure it's wise to divide the few men we still have?"

"One or six hardly makes a difference. These tunnels are only wide enough for one man to fight at a time." Rémi peered back the way they had come. They did not have much time. "If we retreat into each branch, it'll force the enemy to divide their force as well. If nothing else, it might give Bertrand and Salome more time. That's all we can offer at this point."

William scowled. "That and a measure of revenge."

"I'll take the left fork," Rémi said. "That way you can divide your men into groups of three. God be with you, brother."

"And with you," William replied.

Rémi took one of the oil lanterns and plunged into the left-hand fork. The tunnel narrowed immediately as it wove through the dark rock. The floor was damp and slippery in some places. He resisted the temptation to call out to Bertrand. Hopefully the cub and Salome were far from here. If God was feeling benevolent, they might even discover a way out of this cursed rat hole.

The tunnel curled sharply to the left and flared into a natural cavity. Raising his lantern, Rémi saw it was not wide enough for him to be outflanked, but it gave him room to swing his axe both overhead and sideways. Plus he had room to side-step if need be.

He closed the shutter of his lantern until only a glimmer of light escaped. Darkness pressed in on all sides. He slowed his breathing with an effort and forced his body to relax. Damn these tight spaces: he had never liked them.

Rémi checked the straps on his leather armour to keep his mind occupied.

Strange how the darkness seemed to shift and swell, almost like the sea on a cloudless night. Faces kept emerging from those shadow-waves to break against his composure: Maura and the children, of course;

Bertrand, ever serious but no longer doubting his worth; Salome, with that look on her face that said she was not fooled; even old Everard when he had died, straining to deliver one final command.

Boots scuffed against stone. Rémi tensed. For a moment, he heard nothing. Then he caught the faint sound of whispered instructions.

In French.

Come this way, you son of a whore, he thought.

Rémi once overheard old Thibauld saying that he wrote from left to right on his parchments. If the French commander was educated, perhaps he would think the same way.

Metal scraped against stone. The sound of booted feet echoed down his tunnel. Rémi bent and closed the shutter on his lantern. The darkness was blinding, but he could not afford even a glimmer of light giving away his position.

How many approached? How many would he have to slay before he could gut their leader? That was their one chance: kill the French commander and the mercenaries might flee.

They were coming closer. Rémi kept his breathing shallow and tightened his grip on the haft of his axe. Light wavered around the sharp bend. Close now.

The glow brightened until individual veins in the rock became visible. Every step, every creak of armour, was exquisitely clear.

Rémi grinned. *That's it, you mangy curs. I'm waiting.*

Rémi squinted as his eyes adjusted. The tip of a sword rounded the corner.

Fool. A long blade designed for chopping was useless down here.

The soldier rounded the bend just as Rémi lunged. He rammed the sword aside with his shield and buried his axe in the man's chest. The soldier collapsed and dropped his lantern. Wild shadows climbed up the walls as shouts erupted in the tunnel.

Rémi wrenched his axe out in a spray of blood. He side-stepped and swung his axe in a low, back-handed blow around the corner. The axe head swung beneath the bottom of a shield and crunched into bone. A man screamed. Rémi yanked on his handle and the second soldier collapsed on top of the first. He finished the poor fellow with a blow to the neck and retreated.

Two down. How many more?

"That was well done," a voice said in a cultured French accent. "But really, how long do you think you can last?"

Rémi waited in a half-crouch, his shield ready. Did they have any fire-pots? He was finished if they carried crossbows.

"Come join me and we'll see," Rémi replied.

"Ah, so you're not one of those meddling English. Judging by your accent, you must be the loyal sergeant, not the chevalier who can barely grow a beard." An amused note entered the voice. "Is this some kind of pathetic attempt to defend the boy and his wench?"

Rémi bit back his reply. Was this merely an officer or the commander who had led the attack at the Marne? He prayed silently for the latter.

"Silence is its own answer."

Surely only the aristocracy could possess that kind of smugness? "Can you fight as well as you talk?" Rémi taunted.

"It need not come to that." The man must have retrieved the fallen lantern as the light in the tunnel steadied. "I'll give you a choice. You tell me what you're looking for in these caves and I'll let you go. Refuse and I'll have you hacked into unrecognisable pieces before I send instructions to have your family suffer the same fate."

"There is nothing down here except your foul stench," Rémi replied.

"I don't believe you," the man snapped. "And Maura shouldn't have to suffer for your mistakes, should she?"

Ice wedged between Rémi's ribs. How did he know her name?

"And you have three children, I believe. The Baron confessed as much before we burned him as a heretic. We'll find them if you don't tell me what I want to know."

"There's nothing here," Rémi said in desperation. "You can see that for your cursed self."

"Can I, now?" The man stepped cautiously into view. He held the lantern in one hand and gripped a long dagger in the other. Rémi recognised his cruel face with its sharp eyes and neatly trimmed black beard.

"There you are, at last. You've given me quite a chase since the Marne. But that's over now, isn't it?"

Rémi's knuckles cracked around the shaft of his axe, waiting for the right moment. "We've found nothing, I tell you."

"Don't lie to me!" the man screamed. "There must be something down here. *He* is afraid of this place. Give it to me now, or your children will curse your name as they roast upon a spit."

Rémi frowned. Had the man gone insane? What was he talking about?

"Please. Tell me where it is. Before *he* comes." The man gestured back towards the tunnel. "I'll let you go. All of you, if you just give me something to fight him with. Ahh!" He staggered against the tunnel wall.

Rémi shifted his weight. If he killed this man, would it truly end the threat to his family?

"Before who comes?" Rémi asked cautiously.

"The demon," the man spat through his teeth. "He's—" The man shivered and pushed away from the wall. "Where are they? The boy and the woman." His voice and tone had changed. Even his fevered expression had turned cold and superior.

What was going on?

Rémi shifted into a fighting stance. "Long gone. There's nothing to be had down here."

"You don't lie to a Lord of Severity and live." He lunged with his dagger. Rémi deflected the blow with his shield and chopped downwards. His axe thudded into the man's thigh.

Rémi returned to guard stance. The commander would bleed out in a few minutes from a wound like that.

The man stared at his injured leg. "Your impertinence will be punished." He lurched forward and slashed at Rémi's neck. Rémi blocked again with his shield and buried his axe in the man's face.

The man convulsed on the end of his axe. Rémi tried to pull it free, but it wouldn't budge. He pulled harder. The two of them lurched about in the tunnel in a horrific parody of a dance.

Tendrils of black mist curled about the shaft of Rémi's axe. He stared in astonishment as they unfurled towards him. What in the name of the blazing angels was that?

He let go just as the longest plume brushed against his wrist.

CHAPTER 35

8 August 1099

The bride of Baphomet

Hugues hesitated in the narrow passage below the āl-Aqsa mosque. The air down here was steeped with ancient secrets, yet it failed to excite his imagination as it once had. He raised his lantern and the light wavered as his hand trembled. His nerves had not steadied yet, even four days after their ill-fated visit to the necropolis.

"What are you waiting for?" Godefroi asked gruffly. He and Achambaud were following Hugues in single file.

Hugues sighed. "I was thinking of Etienne." Not exactly the truth, but not a lie either.

"What of him?"

Try as he might, Godefroi's abrupt manner could not disguise his weakness. Like Hugues, he had not fully recovered from his encounter with Gamaliel. Frequent bouts of dizziness left Godefroi grasping for balance. According to his Chamberlain, Godefroi had soiled his bed-sheets last night, and Hugues had quietly arranged to have them burned. At some point, he would need to discuss these night terrors with Godefroi, but they had more pressing concerns.

"Etienne loved secrets," Hugues replied, "but he loved problems even more. The mystery of this woman is one he would've enjoyed unravelling."

"That's true," Achambaud said in quiet voice. He still wore his arm in a sling and had not regained feeling in his left hand. According to the physicks, the damage was likely irreversible. Yes, they would all carry scars from their search for the keystone.

"I had no choice," Godefroi said defensively.

"No one blames you," Hugues replied. "From what you've told me about your experience with the Fallen, Etienne died long before his body did." Hugues turned in the narrow corridor to face the other two men. "I'm grateful for what you did, Godefroi. I'm especially thankful to have you both here after...everything." Hugues lifted his hand to make the sign of the cross, but let it drop. "God bless you both."

"I kept my vow." Godefroi shrugged, as if that explained everything.

"You're welcome, Hugues." Achambaud's smile held a hint of pain.

"I'm expected back at court soon," Godefroi prompted.

"Of course." Hugues removed the large brass key from the pouch that hung from his waist. He approached the one door that was locked in the passageway. Candlelight glimmered around the timber frame. Hugues unlocked the door and it swung open on oiled hinges.

Salome was on her feet in the centre of the small cell. Even though she stood still, Hugues had the impression of movement, as if she had just come to a stop as the door swung open. A sling of thick linen supported her left arm. They had set her broken collarbone as best they could. Salome held Hugues' battered Bible in her good hand. "You have questions," was all she said.

"We do." Hugues moved into the cell, followed by Godefroi. Achambaud closed the door after him and leaned against it.

Salome was dressed in a plain woollen gown to ward against the chill. Hugues studied her web of scars as she moved to the edge of her sleeping pallet. She still wore the silver netting of stars in her dark hair. A handful of candles glimmered in various niches around the small cell.

"Please accept my apologies for the poor accommodation." Hugues indicated the cramped cell. "When it's safe, we'll move you somewhere more comfortable."

"It will never be safe for me. That's the first thing you must understand." Salome sat on the rough pallet. "When do you propose to move me?"

"In a few days." Godefroi shifted on his feet. "These are hostile lands, and not everyone in Jerusalem can be trusted."

"I'm sorry your beloved was injured," Salome replied. "Does she live?"

The muscles in Godefroi's jaw bunched as he ground his teeth together.

"Godwera lives," Hugues replied before Godefroi said something regrettable. "Our physick believes she'll recover, although it will take time."

"That's good." Salome's gaze shifted to Godefroi. "You blame me."

"I blame myself," Godefroi replied. "First, for letting her accompany us to your tomb. Second, for not heeding her warning when she begged us not to disturb it."

Hugues grimaced. Yet another mistake to tally against his conscience.

"You would not have reached me without her." Salome shifted her unnerving stare to Hugues and Achambaud. "The Pentemychos contains five chambers. It always requires five to unlock its secrets."

"Who are you?" Achambaud demanded.

Salome gave him an apologetic smile. "You cannot read me, Seer. I'm beyond such things." Addressing the three of them, she said, "I won't answer any further questions until one of you swears to act as my advocate and defender against the powers of Severity. Part of my curse dictates that I may only impart my knowledge to one who is prepared to bind their fate with mine."

Achambaud grimaced. "How can anyone, in good conscience, make such a vow to a total stranger?"

"Did you not seek me out?" Salome asked. "All of you?" She regarded each of them in turn. "Wisdom cannot be bestowed. It must be earned, otherwise it loses all value."

Hugues recalled Umayr saying something similar.

Godefroi shook his head.

"I'll do it," Achambaud said heavily.

"No," Hugues replied. "I've asked enough of you both. Besides, I made a promise to Enoch that will last well beyond my lifetime." Enoch's command to protect Salome had sunk deep into his mind, so that thoughts of her were never far, whether he was waking or sleeping. "What do you require?"

"Kneel." Salome took Hugues' right hand. Her skin was warm, and despite the faint scars, smooth to the touch. She placed her free hand on Hugues' head. "You simply need to state your full name and vow before God to act as my advocate, and to defend me from the forces of Severity, until the end of your days. This you must swear in the name of the Holy Shechinah."

"And this is the only way you'll trust me?"

"It is," Salome replied gravely.

"Very well." He drew in a slow breath. "I, Hugues de Payens, do solemnly swear before God that I will act as both advocate and defender of the Lady Salome, until the end of my days. In the name of the Holy Shechinah, Amen."

Pain stabbed his hand where Salome held him. He pulled free to find a faint rose had been etched into his flesh between his thumb and index finger.

"That's my mark," Salome said. "It signifies that we're bound, for as long as you draw breath."

Hugues examined the brand. "Now tell us who you are."

Salome sat on the edge of the pallet with a sigh. "As I said before, my name is Salome. I am the daughter of Herodias, the former Queen of Chalcis, and step-daughter to Herod Antipas."

Salome's pronouncement was met with stunned silence.

Hugues tried to make sense of her words. "Are you claiming to be the same woman whom the Old Testament tells us danced before Herod and in return, asked for the head of St John the Baptist?"

Anger twisted Salome's mouth and she thumped the Bible sitting in her lap. "That is a lie! The true gospels never claimed such a thing. John was my mentor and friend."

Hugues gaped in shock. "Scripture states that—"

"It's wrong," Salome snapped. "I sought John's wisdom, his knowledge, not his head." She held up Hugues' Bible. "This scripture of yours has twisted the truth until it's almost unrecognisable."

"But how can such a thing be possible?" Achambaud asked. "Almost a thousand years have passed since that woman lived."

"I am the Bride of Baphomet." Salome pulled up the sleeve of her gown and brandished her scars. "You all witnessed it."

"The bride?" Hugues frowned in confusion.

"You've heard of the ten spheres of the Holy One, yes?" Salome asked.

Hugues nodded. "We know them as the Sephirot."

"Ah, the Hebrew name." Salome rolled her sleeve back down. "Baphomet is the wisdom of the spheres, the Holy Word that breathed life through them."

"I don't understand," Hugues said.

"Thank heaven I'm not the only one," Godefroi muttered.

"None of the Rabbis spoke of this," Hugues protested.

"In Arabic," Salome explained, "*Abufihamat* means 'Father of Wisdom'. In Greek, combining the words *Baph* with *Metis* results in 'Baptism of Wisdom'. The word is even recognised in Hebrew. Once converted into that language, applying the Atbash cipher produces *Sophia*, which is also the Greek word for wisdom. Baphomet is the universal name for the wisdom of the Holy One, the divine Word that flashed through the ten spheres and came to rest in the keystone."

Hugues felt as if the floor had dropped beneath him. "So you're saying—" He paused. Even to utter it was a blasphemy of a greater order than any he had contemplated before. He cleared his throat. "If I understand you correctly, you claim to carry the Word of God writ in your flesh."

"One half. The part that belongs to Mercy." Salome's solemn gaze flicked to Achambaud. "It's that power which has sustained me through the long years since the fall of the Essene."

Hugues ran a hand across his stubble. Could her claims be true? A thought suddenly occurred to him: Salome had been mentioned elsewhere in Scripture. "In the Book of Mark it says that Salome, younger sister to Mary the Madonna, and mother of the Apostles St James and St John, was present at the crucifixion of Christ. Do you claim to be this woman too?"

Understanding dawned across Salome's face. She laughed, the sound cold and bitter. "I see what they've done now. The truth lies buried deep within your Scripture, wrapped in metaphor so that only those initiated in the mysteries can unearth it."

"Would you care to explain it to the rest of us?" Achambaud asked.

Salome smoothed the grey fabric of her gown with her good hand. "I was there when they nailed him to the cross. The Salome that you speak of, the younger sister of his mother, was also there." Amusement sparkled in her eyes when she looked up. "I can see that explaining my presence would inconvenience those who translated your Scripture, yet I'm named nonetheless."

"I would consider it a courtesy," Godefroi said in a strained voice, "if you'd speak plainly. Given the cost we have paid to find you, it seems only fair."

"Of course." Salome inclined her head towards Godefroi. "The Essene revered a figure called the 'Teacher of Righteousness'. That teacher was whoever carried the collective knowledge of the Essene. For a time, it was John. After his death, his legacy passed to me. That's why your Scripture names Salome as being present at the crucifixion: it's a subtle message to indicate that I am linked to the Apostles. In the same way, the ridiculous accusation that I sought the Baptist's head is a metaphor for my inheritance of his knowledge."

"This is your idea of plain speech?" Godefroi said in disgust. "You're as bad as Hugues."

"Godefroi," Hugues said, "I carried this essence within me. You saw her draw it from me. Is what she claims so extraordinary?"

"And let's not forget," Salome said, "the keystone that pierced my flesh. You, Godefroi de Bouillon, have felt its searing touch. Can you doubt me after everything you've witnessed?"

Godefroi folded his arms across his chest. "None of that explains how you came to be hidden beneath the necropolis, locked in a crystal rose. It struck me as a prison more than a tomb."

"That's a fair point," Hugues said. "How did you come to be there?"

Salome gave them a brittle smile. "Pride. In the decades after Christ's death, the Jewish people came to believe the time had come to cast off the Roman yoke. A great revolt spread across the land. The Roman garrison in Jerusalem was slaughtered. However, it soon became apparent that Rome's reprisal would be swift and brutal. In the days before the Emperor Vespasian's legions arrived, the elders of the Essene secreted me in the necropolis. I was much older than I appear now. I don't understand how they drew Baphomet from me, but it preserved my body and concealed me from the forces of Severity. Since then, my slumber has only been disturbed once before your arrival."

"Umayr," Hugues guessed.

Salome nodded. "Along with the other members of his cabal. You can imagine my surprise at being woken by Moslems...or Franks, for that matter. Tell me, what's become of my people?"

Godefroi ignored the question. "What did they seek from you?"

"They didn't seek me," Salome replied. "They were compelled. It was the time of testing and their cabal was chosen."

"Testing," Hugues repeated with a questioning note. "Enoch mentioned this, but I didn't understand the reference."

"You don't know," Salome breathed in astonishment. Her dark gaze darted between the three men facing her. She shook her head in amazement and said something in her native tongue.

"Explain," Godefroi commanded.

Hugues saw pity in her eyes and he suppressed a shiver at her expression.

"Please," Hugues said, "what is this test?"

Salome's shoulders dropped and a weary note entered her voice. "Every few centuries, the five chambers of the Pentemychos—or the five elements of the human soul, if you prefer—are tested to determine whether they cleave to the Pillars of Mercy, Severity or Unity. The outcome of this test shapes the age that follows."

"An artefact that shapes the course of history," Hugues whispered. "It's a test that weighs the human soul, balancing it between the virtues of Mercy and Severity." He finally understood. All that the Salt Lines had learned, all the risks they had taken, were finally validated.

"This test," Godefroi said, "is not for us."

"No," Salome replied. "Enoch said that time is not yet upon us."

"Yet we still woke you," Godefroi pressed. "Why was that allowed to happen?"

For the first time, Salome faltered. "I can't explain it. Perhaps the two halves are finally to be reunited."

"What two halves?" Achambaud wore a look of frustration.

Salome looked at the ceiling of her cell. "Ein Sof give me strength," she muttered. "When the Holy One breathed the divine Word down through the ten spheres, he needed a keystone upon which Creation could rest. That keystone was an enormous block of sapphire. The gem was split into two halves to symbolise the division between Mercy and Severity, or life and absence. One half binds the bodies of the Lords of Severity to Abaddon in the core of what your Bible calls hell. The second half was cast into the world and has been guarded by the great civilisations of antiquity. It became known as Baphomet."

Salome hunched her shoulders. "The Lords of Severity wish to reunite the two halves to escape their prison. If they succeed, the spheres will crack and the emptiness between the spheres will pour into our world. It was for this reason that Baphomet was merged with my flesh: I'm charged with keeping it from Severity until all five chambers of the human soul cleave to the middle pillar. Now that Severity knows that I've woken, they'll hunt me without respite. My only hope is to reach Mount Heredom."

"Mount Heredom," Hugues said. "I've never heard of it. Where is that?"

"I don't know," Salome replied. "All I can tell you is that it's described as the 'Mount Sion of the far north', but I've never seen it on any map."

"Didn't the crystal shard destroy Gamaliel?" Hugues asked.

Salome shook her head. "He's diminished, but you can't kill emptiness."

"So he'll come back," Godefroi said, looking pale.

"They'll all come," Salome replied. "Sooner, rather than later."

◆━━━━━━━━━━━━━━━━━◆

"What do you think?" Godefroi asked. "Is she telling the truth?" The three men had retreated from Salome's cell and reconvened on the ground floor of the empty mosque. Godefroi had found much of Salome's revelations difficult to follow, although he did not doubt her sincerity. Not after having experienced Gamaliel's hunger for what she possessed.

"I believe her." Hugues pinched the bridge of his nose between thumb and forefinger. "I sense only...honesty from her. And great fear. We've exposed her to enormous danger."

"Perhaps your judgement isn't completely objective." Achambaud stared at the rose on Hugues' hand.

"Perhaps not," Hugues admitted.

Godefroi sat on the tiled floor with his back pressed to the wall. While his leg was healing slowly, he was always tired. "We must decide quickly. Rumours have reached court." He dropped his voice for fear of eavesdropping. "Al-Afdal, the Egyptian Vizier, has sworn to retake Jerusalem. Even now, his army is on the march. I've summoned Raymond and Robert of Normandy, but they are yet to respond. Without their troops, I fear Jerusalem will fall."

"As the new Patriarch of Jerusalem, Arnulf has sent emissaries to them and Constantinople," Achambaud said. "Perhaps they'll heed the call of the Church instead?"

"Perhaps," Godefroi said, "although they are unlikely to arrive in time. I've decided to march out at dawn tomorrow with every available soldier to force Raymond to come to our aid. Preparations have commenced. If we're defeated, Raymond will be isolated and outnumbered. He'll have to join us to ensure his survival, but even with his numbers, the outcome is far from certain."

"Regardless, we can't leave Jerusalem yet," Hugues replied. "All the ports will be watched, including Jaffa."

Godefroi didn't need to ask who would be watching. Gamaliel's touch was not an experience he would ever forget.

"Besides," Hugues continued, pretending not to notice Godefroi's sudden shiver, "it will take time for the Salt Lines to prepare a place to hide Salome. The Cistercian Order they have just established at Cîteaux Abbey is in its infancy. Even if they were ready to receive us, they're expecting a relic, not a person."

"Like the rest of us," Achambaud muttered.

"I need time," Hugues said to Godefroi. "Time to plan our return to Lorraine and to find this Heredom. Achambaud can go ahead, with letters of introduction from us to the Count of Champagne. He will be well received at Troyes and can convey what we have learned."

Achambaud glanced at Hugues in surprise.

Weariness settled over Godefroi. "Do as you must. My main priority is the defence of Jerusalem. And before you say anything, I know I must leave the fighting to others. All of our efforts will amount to nothing if the city falls to the Egyptians."

"Perhaps Edessa," Achambaud suggested.

"The Syrian frontier is hardly secure," Hugues replied. "Nor will I trust our fate to Baldwin. He must never know of what we have done here."

"Agreed," Godefroi said. "However, he will rule after me. Establishing good relations with him now will serve you well in days to come."

Godefroi glanced between the two men. "Achambaud, if you're returning to Troyes, I want you to take Godwera with you. She must not stay here. Especially if Baldwin succeeds me."

"I would be honoured," Achambaud replied. "Hopefully she'll recover enough to travel."

Godefroi clasped Achambaud's forearm. "Thank you. I know you'll keep her safe."

"With my life."

Godefroi saw his feelings for Godwera mirrored in Achambaud's expression. The recognition was both cruel and comforting.

"Your time has not arrived yet, Godefroi." Salome emerged from the shadows in the corridor.

Achambaud frowned at Hugues. "I thought you locked the cell?"

"I did," Hugues replied in confusion. "The key is right here." He fumbled at his belt.

Salome held up the key in the palm of her hand. "You swore an oath, Hugues de Payens. Locking me in a makeshift dungeon is hardly acting as my defender and advocate."

A look of chagrin spread across Hugues' face. "The only way I can protect you now is to keep your presence hidden."

"My presence is known, so subterfuge is pointless." Salome studied Godefroi. "It is given to me, at various times, to glimpse something of the road that lies ahead. If you will allow it, Godefroi, I offer this gift in compensation for what you have endured."

Godefroi hesitated, and he glanced at the mark on Hugues' hand.

Salome caught the look and shook her head with a rueful smile. "No, I will not brand you. Hugues has become my Shroud. I do not need another." She glanced at Hugues. "Besides, I already know his fate."

"And what is that?" Godefroi asked.

"He will establish a great order of warrior-priests named after the temple beneath us, along with you, Achambaud de St Amand." Salome touched the cross stitched into Godefroi's bliaut. "The Salt Lines will grow more powerful and prosperous than any kingdom."

"How can you know such a thing?" Godefroi demanded.

"It does not matter." Salome tilted her head. "Will you accept my offer?"

"I know where my journey ends," Godefroi replied. "I saw it written in a Saracen's face beneath this very mosque." He offered her his hand anyway.

Salome smiled. "It gladdens me to see that your courage has not fled with your strength."

Godefroi made no reply.

Salome's grip on his hand tightened and she closed her eyes. Her breathing slowed and deepened. Godefroi counted his heartbeats that had suddenly accelerated. Salome became the centre of his focus: the strange scars that lined her face, the netting of stars woven through her hair, the hollow of her neck, and the rise and fall of her breath.

Nothing else existed except their connection.

"Āl-Afdal is close," Salome said in a remote, flat voice. Her lips barely moved, as if she was speaking from some place deep within. "Egypt is emptied of its warriors."

Godefroi tensed, but Salome's grip remained tight.

"You will meet them on the plain before Ascalon. Your allies will come, albeit almost too late. Accept the lesson in humility and be reconciled. I see you attacking at dawn, with the sun behind you. It conceals your lack of numbers." Her lips trembled.

"One of your Princes drives for the Vizier's banner," Salome said. "Āl-Afdal flees the field. His army breaks, splintering into tribes. I see the cross raised overhead, golden and victorious."

Salome released his hand, took a step back and drew in a shuddering breath. Godefroi had the impression that she had just returned from some distant, incomprehensible place.

Salome raised her palm in a formal gesture of farewell. "The triumph will be yours, Godefroi. Then you may finally rest. Be comforted in the knowledge that history will remember you with favour."

Godefroi read the regret in her face. "How long do I have?"

"Less than a year," Salome replied without any hint of emotion.

That was more than he had hoped for, although it might not be a mercy. He had seen other men linger horribly from wounds they could never recover from.

"I hope that you find this Heredom," Godefroi said calmly. "Perhaps we'll see each other again at the Lord's table." He marched up the stairs, ignoring the trembling in his legs and the stricken looks on the faces of his companions.

CHAPTER 36

25 December 1307

The Halls of Mercy

Salome lifted her lantern to reveal their tunnel had been blocked by a cave in. Bertrand peered over her shoulder. They might be able to move some of the smaller rocks, but the larger boulders buried beneath would be far too heavy.

"We need to go back," Salome muttered. "There must be another way." She tried to push past. Bertrand placed a restraining hand on her shoulder.

"This is the fifth, maybe sixth, tunnel we've tried," he said in a low voice. "I thought you knew the way."

Salome bit the inside of the lip. "I was not expecting so many branches. We just have to keep looking."

"We're running out of time." Bertrand nodded in the direction they had come. The distant clash of weapons echoed faintly down the tunnel. He hated leaving this battle to the others, but he knew the fight would find him eventually. He wondered how Rémi and William were faring.

"Then we should stop arguing and keep moving." Salome pushed past and backtracked down the narrow tunnel.

"It would help if I knew what to look for," Bertrand murmured as he trailed after her.

"This place was worshipped once, so look for signs of devotion. Perhaps symbols carved into the stone. Maybe even an altar. Whoever ransacked this place didn't get past the gate, so the markers should still be here."

The tunnels twisted through the rock, often rising sharply before dropping unexpectedly. It was impossible to tell how deep they were or how far they had travelled from the portcullis. He felt like they had entered some vast catacomb where all light eventually died.

How could the Lords of Mercy possibly reside in a place like this if they represented life?

Salome stopped at a juncture. "This way." She pointed towards the second fork.

"Are you sure? It all looks the same to me."

"I'm accustomed to being underground," she replied. "That's the tunnel we came from."

Bertrand listened. Yes, the sound of fighting was slightly louder in that direction.

Salome moved down the second fork and he followed her pool of light. Darkness rolled in behind them. Who knew what it might conceal?

Bertrand counted their steps to keep his mind occupied. He had taken thirty-seven when Salome stopped again. She lifted her lantern and gasped. The tunnel abruptly opened into a circular chamber. Light from the lantern revealed a stone sarcophagus in the centre. A woman had been carved into the lid, her arms crossed over a long sword that pointed towards her bare feet. The seal of Solomon was partially visible surrounding her head before disappearing behind her long tresses.

Salome lifted her lantern higher. Shadows retreated to reveal five alcoves carved at intervals into the curving rock wall. Surrounding the sarcophagus, each alcove contained a statue dressed in long robes. Their heads were strangely elongated, while their features were narrow and austere. Beneath the dressed stone of their robes, their limbs were unusually long and lean. Each of the statues gazed down upon the sarcophagus, their expressions difficult to read, although Bertrand sensed a measure of grief.

"This is the place," Salome whispered in awe. "We must—"

Bertrand gripped her arm. "Quiet," he breathed into her ear. Listening intently, Bertrand caught the sound of something scraping against stone. Salome closed the shutter of her lamp until the light was little more than a dim glow and she backed away towards the sarcophagus. Bertrand adjusted his shield and drew his dagger. His long sword would be a liability in this narrow tunnel.

The shuffling was accompanied by the sound of panting. Could it be one of their allies fleeing from the battle? The footsteps stilled and Bertrand pictured the man pausing at the fork in the tunnel, trying to decide which way to go. If he chose the wrong fork, they might elude whoever it was.

The panting grew louder. Bertrand shifted to one side of the entrance to the chamber. He crouched down, his blackened shield hiding most of his body. With luck, he might be able to identify who it was before they saw him.

Light glimmered in the tunnel and the darkness retreated into cracks in the walls. Bertrand's pulse throbbed and his grip on the hilt of his knife tightened until it became painful.

A man rounded the bend. Bertrand lunged forward, shield raised and dagger poised to strike at the man's unprotected thigh. He recognised Rémi at the last possible instant. Bertrand stared in astonishment.

"Rémi! By God, I nearly stabbed you." Bertrand sagged against the wall in relief.

Rémi raised his lantern and peered past Bertrand. Seeing a friendly face, Salome unshuttered her light.

"What happened back at the cavern?" Salome asked. "We heard fighting."

A leer spread across Rémi's face. "They're all dead." His gaze flickered between Bertrand and Salome. "And you're cornered at last." Rémi swung his axe and Bertrand ducked on instinct. Sparks flashed as the axe struck stone.

Bertrand stumbled backwards. "What are you doing?" His training took over despite his shock and he raised his shield.

Rémi's axe slammed into the shield. The force of the blow sent Bertrand staggering.

"Rémi, what are you doing?" Bertrand cried again.

Rémi laughed and his next blow struck the top of the shield, wrenching Bertrand's left arm.

"Severity has taken hold of him," Salome cried. "You must kill him, Bertrand."

Rémi raised his axe for another strike. Bertrand charged and drove his shield into Rémi's chest. The impact forced Rémi backwards and he dropped his lantern. Shadows leaped and danced where flames licked at the spilled oil.

"Stop this!" Bertrand cried. "In Christ's name, how can you do this after everything we've been through?"

Rémi's eyes rolled and he shuddered. It lasted for a fraction of a moment. "You should hear him screaming in here," Rémi replied in a deep, gravelly voice. He tapped the side of his head.

Bertrand dropped into a half-crouch to present a smaller target. Salome chose that moment to throw her dagger. It whistled past Bertrand's shoulder and scored the side of Rémi's head. Rémi leaped forward and grappled for Bertrand's shield with his free hand. His sheer strength forced Bertrand's guard down while he raised his axe.

"Stop!" Bertrand cried.

Rémi's axe reached its apex and Bertrand realised he had no choice.

He plunged his dagger into Rémi's armpit, hoping to incapacitate him. Rémi barely seemed to notice and his axe swung down in a diagonal stroke. Bertrand released the dagger and twisted away from the blow, but his arm was still strapped to the shield. Instead of slicing into his neck, the axe smashed into the back of his ribs.

CHAPTER 37

12 August 1099

The plain of Ascalon

Godefroi waited in his saddle as his troops were quietly deployed. Dawn was not far off. The sun would rise behind them, just as Salome had predicted.

He suppressed a flicker of impatience. The armour he had worn since leaving Lorraine, once so familiar that it had felt like a second skin, now felt loose and awkward, and chafed the burned skin on his right arm. Gaston had tried to convince him to wear something more befitting his status, but he had refused. This armour had absorbed his blood and sweat. It had shaped the man he had become. If he was to die upon this field, then his armour would become his tomb. He couldn't think of anything more fitting.

Godefroi examined his troops. His infantry had massed into rough lines, seven or eight deep. Soldiers carrying long spears formed the first row, followed by unmounted chevaliers, milites and rag-tag pedites, many of whom carried Saracen weapons. Archers and javelin throwers remained at the rear. Godefroi had forbidden the use of standards in the hope of maintaining surprise against the over-confident Egyptians. He had even banned raising the golden cross until battle was joined.

With no cloud cover, the air was cold and carried a hint of salt. The sea was only a league or two distant. Egyptian galleys kept pace with the Vizier's army, but they would play no part in this battle.

His gaze shifted to the Christian centre. Count Raymond and Robert of Normandy had only arrived at dusk the day before, while their infantry had trickled in throughout the night. Many of their pedites would not have slept at all.

Raymond had taken the right flank, leaving the left to Godefroi. Al-Afdal must be supremely confident, as he hadn't set any scouts. No doubt he expected the Christians to huddle behind the walls of Jerusalem at the news of his thunderous approach.

Only a few mounted chevaliers remained with Godefroi. Most of the horse he could muster was concentrated in the centre under Robert where they could be used to maximum effect. Only a handful were left in reserve.

Godefroi's personal banner, a large golden cross quartered by four smaller crosslets on a field of white, waved at the head of the army. The honour of carrying Godefroi's standard into battle had been bestowed upon Robert of Normandy.

He should be leading these men into battle, not these other lords.

The massed ranks of soldiers under Robert commenced their march towards the slumbering Egyptian camp. Godefroi waited for a count of thirty and then signalled his infantry forwards, galloping along their line with his sword raised overhead. None of his troops cried out or beat their shields. Those that had survived this long pilgrimage were superbly disciplined. They knew they were outnumbered, perhaps three-to-one, possibly more. Even so, they marched forward, grim-faced, and silent. He brimmed with pride at commanding such men.

They topped a low rise to find the Egyptian camp was spread out on the plain below. Countless tents dotted the flat ground and long plumes of smoke rose from cooking fires. Groups of horses were tethered next to clusters of tents, as was the Saracen way.

The different factions of āl-Afdal's army were obvious even to Godefroi. While the army was primarily composed of Egyptians, he spotted Bedouins, Berbers and even the fearsome, black-skinned Ethiopians. A large tent dominated the centre of the camp. Godefroi did not recognise the dark blue standard emblazoned with a silver crescent and Arabic script that fluttered next to the entrance, but he assumed it must belong to āl-Afdal.

Godefroi urged his troops forward and cast a quick glance to gauge the progress of the rest of the army. Incredibly, the Saracens did not realise the danger until the Christians were almost within bowshot.

A belated cry of alarm swept through their camp. Saracens stumbled from their tents at the commotion. A volley of arrows curved over the Christian infantry and landed amongst the Egyptian camp. Warning cries turned to screams as arrows found their mark. Godefroi signalled a similar barrage. A hail of burning arrows arced over Raymond's flank.

Robert had timed his attack to perfection. The sun had just risen over the rise that had concealed their position as the Christians reached the outskirts of the camp. Saracen warriors squinted into the blinding sun as volleys of arrows and javelins decimated their ranks. Many died before they could muster a counter-attack.

The Egyptian camp erupted into chaos. Pockets of warriors struggled with their rearing horses. Panicked camp followers dashed through the bedlam, dodging fallen bodies. Tents caught fire as Raymond's archers used their superior elevation to pepper the Egyptian forces.

A group of large Ethiopians wielding deadly flails charged towards Godefroi's line. With spears levelled, his troops rushed forward to skewer the large warriors. Then Godefroi's troops were inside the camp and cutting down every Saracen that dared oppose them.

Godefroi held back, knowing he was in no condition to join the fight. A massed charge of chevaliers smashed through the densest part of the camp. The Provençals fell upon the right flank of the Saracens, scattering all before them.

Robert of Normandy enjoyed the most success. He and a group of mounted chevaliers drove towards āl-Afdal's tent. A knot of Egyptian infantry tried to make a stand, but they were trampled by the armoured charge. All attempts at resistance crumbled as āl-Afdal and his bodyguards fled the field in panic.

Godefroi watched the Saracen army splinter into its components just as Salome had foreseen. Each faction tried to withdraw with minimal losses, ignoring their allies as they were routed. The Ethiopians and Berbers fought a hopeless rear-guard action, while Egyptian warriors fled in waves, many heading towards the port of Ascalon. The Bedouins mounted their camels and slipped away into the dry inland wastes.

The victorious Christians tore down āl-Afdal's standard and raised the golden cross in its place. After this crushing defeat, it would be months, if not years, before āl-Afdal could threaten Jerusalem again.

Godefroi tried to savour the triumph, but he found no joy in it. His mouth was dry and the smell of smoke stung his nostrils. He knew this would be his final victory, yet it belonged to others, as did the fate of Christendom in the Holy Land.

Now that Salome's vision had come to pass, he knew without question that his death approached. Godefroi shifted in his saddle. Perhaps he had been granted the time that remained to live a new life, one not governed by the Salt Lines.

Surely he had earned it?

Victorious cheers broke out across the battleground. Godefroi smiled beneath the faceguard of his helmet. Anyone watching would assume he was exulting in their victory. In truth, he was marvelling at this first, tentative taste of freedom.

CHAPTER 38

25 December 1307

The Halls of Mercy

"**B**ertrand!" Salome's scream echoed wildly through the tunnel. He couldn't breathe.

All the air had been smashed from his lungs. Each attempt to draw breath felt like heated barbs were pulling his chest apart, and blood ran down his side where the axe jutted between his ribs. Bertrand collapsed against the foot of the nearest statue. He stared at Rémi in disbelief.

"He's crying like a child, cub," Rémi said in that terrible, rasping voice. "Imagine how he must feel, being the one to strike you down. The final Shroud cut down by a man who thinks of himself as your father." Rémi wrenched the dagger from his armpit and turned to face Salome.

"You'll come with me." Rémi pointed Bertrand's bloodied dagger at Salome. "The Lords of Severity will reunite you with Mercy's half of the keystone and this whole charade," he said with a gesture that encompassed the chamber, "can finally end."

Gasping, Bertrand rolled onto his good side. Salome needed him, but his body refused to comply. Air rasped through his throat and his strength was ebbing. Would it be so wrong to let exhaustion finally take him? He had done everything Salome had asked and still they had failed.

"You presume too much." Salome backed away and put the sarcophagus between her and Rémi. "These are the Halls of Mercy. Severity has no place here."

Rémi laughed. "Your precious archangels withdrew in disgust from this place long ago. They're no longer here to save you." Rémi took a step towards her. "Submit or I'll hack off the parts we don't need, starting with your ears."

Bertrand panted. If he could just get his knees beneath him. He shifted position and Rémi's axe grated against his ribs in a blaze of agony.

Salome drew her belt knife and glanced at Bertrand in desperation.

Seeing his plight, her face hardened with resignation. "I won't let you take me."

"You have no choice," Rémi replied. "Your Shroud lies dying. The Salt Lines are broken, and Mercy refuses to heed your call." He beckoned with his free hand. "No help remains for you, Salome, daughter of Herodias. Severity is all you have left."

Bertrand gathered the remnants of his strength and tried to stand. The walls of the tunnel blurred and a subtle, silver light glimmered through the veins in the rock. It reminded him of the net of stars Salome had worn in her hair at Rooklyn Abbey. Neither Salome, nor Rémi, seemed to have noticed. He traced the source of the light back to the pool of blood oozing from his wound. There, etched into the wall of the chamber beneath the statue, was a symbol he recognised.

A five-pointed star inside two circles. The Seal of Solomon.

"I won't allow you to unmake the tree," Salome said to whatever had overtaken Rémi. "That's not what He intended."

"Don't flaunt your ignorance," Rémi growled. "Submit. I'll not ask again."

Bertrand shifted his weight to get a better look at the seal. Spots swarmed across his vision. Dipping his finger into his blood, he traced the outer circle of the seal. The silver light glistened where his blood touched the rock. He completed the inner circle and then started on the intersecting lines of the star.

"Better that I never existed than become a tool of Severity." Salome shot a despairing look at Bertrand before turning her dagger and driving the blade upwards beneath her ribs.

"You whore!" Rémi jumped onto the sarcophagus and caught Salome as she sagged. Her head lolled and her hair brushed against the floor.

"No!" Rémi pulled the blade from her body and shook her. "You can't die. It's impossible!"

"Salome!" Bertrand tried to cry out, but all he could muster was a groan. After everything they had suffered, he had been unable to protect her. He slumped against the rock in despair.

Rémi threw Salome to the ground. The familiar face contorted into a snarl as he swung around to face Bertrand. "You'll have to do. You're her Shroud after all."

Bertrand closed his eyes. *Please Lord,* he prayed, *let me die now. If I am indeed a heretic, I beseech Thee to forgive my trespasses against you.*

Rémi's fist closed around Bertrand's hair.

Finish the seal, Bertrand, a voice replied inside his mind. *Such depravity should not go unpunished.*

He opened his eyes with great effort. Rémi stood over him, his eyes wild and cursing in an unfamiliar, guttural language. Bertrand glanced at the seal. The inner and outer circles glimmered silver, but the star remained inert. He had only traced three of the five points. Ignoring Rémi, he smeared his blood across the two remaining lines to complete the pentacle.

"What's this?" Rémi peered at the symbol Bertrand had drawn. His eyes widened. "No."

Shafts of silver light burst forth from the seal. Bertrand squeezed his eyes shut against the blinding radiance. Intense heat washed across his skin and the tunnel throbbed beneath his dying body.

Rémi screamed and all went still.

Bertrand squinted. The seal remained painfully bright. Rémi had let go of him and backed away to where he had dropped Salome's body. A look of absolute horror had transformed his face into that of a stranger's.

The star turned within the inner ring. Slowly at first, but accelerating. With each rotation, the star expanded, forcing the two circles to widen. In a few moments, the seal reached the roof of the chamber.

The star was a blur of light, spinning so fast Bertrand's eyes could no longer follow it. A loud crack echoed through the chamber and pieces of stone fell from the statue. Bertrand gaped in astonishment as a figure emerged from the alcove. It was tall and dressed in a brown robe of samite. A strange, golden-hued face stared down at Bertrand. The apparition had no hair to speak of, not even eyebrows. Its head was an oval shape and its eyes colourless. Thin lips drew back in a smile as it knelt next to Bertrand.

I am Sandalphon, Lord of the Ishim and Custodian of Malkuth, it said into Bertrand's mind. *Do not pass through the veil just yet.* Sandalphon removed the axe from Bertrand's ribs and touched the wound. Bertrand's pain immediately receded and he could breathe again.

The remaining statues splintered and four more figures stepped down from their alcoves. Each was identical in appearance to Sandalphon. One knelt down and picked up Salome's limp body. The other three faced Rémi.

"You cannot interfere." Rémi stabbed a finger at the robed figures. "You swore to withdraw from Malkuth, to let mankind choose its own path. The two of them belong to me."

One of the figures confronting Rémi spoke. *This is not true, Gamaliel. We swore to let mankind determine its fate, but this Shroud summoned us. With his courage and sacrifice, and his very blood, he calls to us. Sammael's plan has failed, yet again. Baphomet is beyond your reach and none remain to carry it for you.*

Rémi spat at the speaker. "Twist your words however you may, Gabriel. You've broken your vow. There's no escaping that."

You are the trespasser here, Gabriel replied. *Heredom was given unto us and I will not suffer your presence a moment longer.*

A spear of light appeared in Gabriel's hand. Rémi screamed in defiance. As Gabriel drew his hand back to cast the spear, Rémi sliced his throat open with Bertrand's knife. Blood poured down his chest.

"Rémi!" Bertrand struggled to rise. Sandalphon held him in place with firm but gentle pressure.

Gabriel's spear pierced Rémi's chest and flung him backwards, pinning him to the far wall. A black mist writhed out of Rémi's mouth, ears and nostrils. It wailed and moaned, cursing in French and a dozen different tongues. The impression of a horrible, twisted face stretched through the vile fog. Most terrifying of all, it was identical in appearance to Sandalphon, apart from its agonised expression. The mist imploded with a sudden rush of air.

The silver spear also faded and Rémi's broken body slumped against the hard stone.

Sandalphon gently lifted Bertrand in his long arms. Rémi and Salome were both dead. Tears streamed down Bertrand's face.

"Let me die," Bertrand begged. "I can't bear another moment of this."

Not yet, Sandalphon replied. *While you hover at the outermost boundary of life, there is something you must witness first.*

"Why?" Nothing mattered anymore. Everything he cared about had been taken away.

You have brought us back into this world, so now we ask you to enter ours.

Sandalphon strode through the alcove, followed by the four remaining Lords of Mercy. Bertrand endured a moment of nauseating disorientation then they were...elsewhere.

A huge cavern surrounded them. Bertrand gazed upwards, following the curve of rock as it soared far overhead. They had arrived in the centre of an enormous natural dome. Strange, pale blue light illuminated the vast space.

Sandalphon set Bertrand on his feet. Bertrand's armour had disappeared, along with his wound. He wore the simple white habit of a chevalier with a cord of woven gold wrapped around his waist instead.

"Is this purgatory?" Bertrand asked in a hushed voice.

A full head taller than Bertrand, Sandalphon smiled down at him. *No, think of it as an outpost. And a new beginning, we hope. Be at peace now, as there is something we must do.*

One of the other Lords had laid Salome out on a low circular dais carved from black marble. In death, her face was pale and she seemed younger. Grief twisted through Bertrand. He was the one who should have died, not her. If only she had seen the seal. Why didn't the Lords save her?

We could not. A faint tone of admonishment entered Sandalphon's voice. *We had sworn to stand aside until humanity demonstrated its worth. It was your dedication to her, and her denial of Severity at the cost of her life, that compelled our return. She will be honoured for all time.*

The five Lords of Mercy surrounded Salome's body. Gently taking her hands and feet, they spread them wide, imitating the star of Solomon's seal. Sandalphon smoothed the charcoal hair from her face and adjusted the silver net of stars upon her head.

What were they doing?

Touching the five cardinal points of Salome's body with one hand, the Lords bowed their heads. The surface of the marble rippled outwards from Salome, like a pebble striking a still pond at night, and a chime echoed through the vast cavern. The Lords lifted their free hands and the marble encased her body. Within moments she was contained within a gleaming black sarcophagus that captured every detail of her features.

Bertrand choked back a cry of grief. He would never touch her or speak with her again.

The Lords turned outwards from the sarcophagus and pointed. Deep fissures cracked through the floor of the cavern. They widened as they spread outwards, becoming trenches wide enough to accommodate a horse and cart. They raised their hands upwards and rock groaned as it rose up from the cavern floor. Bertrand staggered as the earth shook.

Impossibly smooth walls of stone, at least twenty yards in height, surrounded them. Broad pillars strained from the earth where the Lords stood, encasing them in stone. The five columns guarding the approach to Salome's sarcophagus sprouted curved arches. The roof closed in overhead, blocking out the cavern. Floor tiles knitted together seamlessly beneath Bertrand's feet.

The ground stilled and an expectant silence settled over the enormous hall that had risen around Salome's remains. This place dwarfed the great cathedrals in Troyes and Reims.

For a terrible moment, he thought he had been entombed alone. Then Sandalphon emerged from the pillar nearest Salome's head.

The Temple is complete.

Bertrand stared. "I...don't understand. What is this place? A sepulchre?"

In time, it may become many things, Sandalphon replied. *A sanctuary, a library, a temple dedicated to advancing understanding of the five parts of the human soul. But first and foremost, it is a fortress.*

He didn't know how to respond.

This Temple exists on the boundary between the world that you know and the ninth sphere of possibilities.

"I'm sorry," Bertrand apologised. "I don't understand."

Sandalphon placed a comforting hand on Bertrand's shoulder. His touch radiated warmth and peace. *I understand this must be confusing. Let me explain. We have created this place because we wish to found a new Order. One dedicated to the great restoration between Ein Sof and his countless children. We would be honoured if you would accept the title of Grand Master.*

Bertrand stared in astonishment. "Me?"

Who better than the Shroud who finally guided Baphomet safely to rest? Even more astonishingly, Sandalphon bowed to Bertrand. *My brothers and I owe you a great debt.*

"I don't wish to seem ungrateful, but what if I choose to go back? To my homeland." The very thought of such a journey was exhausting, yet he had promised he would take care of Rémi's family. And he still had Justine to answer to.

The Halls of Mercy end at the portcullis. If you choose to step beyond that boundary, it would mean returning to your physical existence in Malkuth. Your wound has been suspended, not healed.

"You mean I would die."

Yes.

Bertrand considered this. Did he still wish to live with nothing but Salome's sarcophagus for company?

Elements of the Salt Lines have survived Severity's purge, Sandalphon said. *You could offer them sanctuary here, and learn about your heritage.*

And he would not be alone. Another thought occurred to Bertrand. "Can I send messengers?"

Of course.

"Even as far as France?"

Sandalphon's smile widened. *Your reach will stretch far beyond that.*

EPILOGUE

18 July 1100

Sunset

Godwera hurried into the antechamber in a flurry of linen and silk, her sandals slapping across the marble floor. Hugues was struck by how much her time in the Holy Land had changed her. Gone was the pale, secretive woman who had bound her figure and disguised it beneath a cassock. The woman that rushed towards him was darker of skin and possessed a determination that bore no resemblance to the former wife of Baldwin de Bouillon. It was unlikely that anyone would ever connect the two women. Still, she was wise enough to cover her head and face with a veil.

"How is he?" Godwera asked.

"It's almost time," Hugues replied gently. There was little point in sparing her feelings. Better that she accept the reality of what was happening now, than suffer the shock of it when she entered the royal bedchamber.

"Is he really that bad?" She kept her distress in check, although Hugues could read it in the tight lines of her face. "Your messenger only told me he was ill and that I must hurry back from my pilgrimage."

"There is little more to tell," Hugues replied. "He collapsed during a feast held in his honour by the Emir of Caesarea. Naturally there is talk of poison in the souks." Hugues spread his hands. "People will always arrive at the worst conclusions."

Godwera nodded. The true source of Godefroi's illness must never come to light, even if the inevitable recriminations cost Christian or Moslem lives. She glanced over her shoulder at the two members of Godefroi's personal guard whom she had passed when entering the antechamber. Seeing they remained at a discreet distance, Godwera removed her veil.

"Let me see him." Godwera strode towards the double doors that opened into the main bedchamber of Godefroi's palace.

235

Hugues caught her arm. "Prepare yourself. He is not the man you remember."

"I know that," she replied with a catch in her voice.

"When he arrived in Jerusalem, they had to carry him on a palanquin. Even the slightest jolt caused him pain. Now he hardly stirs."

Godwera shook off Hugues' hand. "I have seen people I care about die before, as you well know."

"Not like this," Hugues warned. "The physicks can do nothing for him. He may not...know you."

Godwera's eyes filled with tears. "We did this to him," she said in a low, fierce voice. "If only we had made different choices."

Hugues avoided her gaze. "There was no way to know it would turn out like this. His fate weighs heavily on my conscience."

Godwera's lips twisted in a mixture of anger and disappointment. "It weighs heavily on my *heart*." Her gaze bored into him. "You would make the same choice again, wouldn't you? Knowing the outcome, you would still sacrifice Godefroi and poor Etienne for *her*."

How could he answer that? Salome was always in his thoughts. He could almost feel her standing at his elbow. Thankfully Salome had agreed not to accompany him today. "He'll be pleased to see you," Hugues replied. "Waking or dreaming, your name is always upon his lips."

Godwera choked back a sob and swept past Hugues. She pushed the double doors open and hurried inside. Taking a moment to gather his composure, Hugues followed her inside.

Godefroi's bedchamber was a large rectangular room that abutted a large balcony overlooking the roofs of Jerusalem. Thick velvet curtains had been drawn against the glare of the late afternoon sun. A narrow gap allowed a light breeze to stir the air in the chamber.

The bed was huge with four bedposts that supported a silk canopy. Littered with brightly coloured cushions and sheets of silk, Godefroi de Bouillon was almost lost within the finery.

Godwera had rushed to the side of his bed and must have fallen to her knees at the sight of him. One of her hands was outstretched, almost touching Godefroi's elbow. Her body trembled and Hugues caught the sound of short, hitching sobs at the back of her throat.

"Messire," Hugues said in something approaching his normal voice. "You have a visitor."

Godefroi stirred. His skin was so pale it was almost translucent, revealing the web of veins and capillaries. Every time he saw him like this, Hugues relived the moment when he plunged the shard of

Baphomet into Godefroi's thigh. That memory, and the associated guilt, would haunt the rest of his days.

Godefroi's ribs were clearly visible through the silk of his gold-coloured shift. The bones in his wrists and shoulders jutted beneath his skin. His thick beard was gone, a victim of the physicks' most recent attempts to revive him. He looked younger, more vulnerable, without it. Dark crescents underlined his eyes and his cheeks were hollow.

Godwera dabbed at the sweat that glistened across Godefroi's forehead with her sleeve. Hugues watched as she fought for control. He might as well be watching a mirror.

"Godefroi?" Godwera said as she stroked his cheek. "I've come to see you." She sat on the side of his bed and took his hand. It had taken Hugues most of the first day after Godefroi returned from Caesarea to muster the same courage.

"Godwera." The name was little more than a moan. Godefroi's eyes remained shut and he was deathly still.

"Yes, I'm here. *Really* here." She squeezed his hand for emphasis.

Godefroi opened his eyes with obvious effort. Even the blue of his eyes had faded, leached of life so that they had almost become colourless, just like the crystal rose that had encased Salome.

It was obvious he did not have the strength to turn his head. Godwera slid across the sheets until she could look down upon him. "I almost didn't recognise you."

A smile touched the corners of Godefroi's mouth.

"Hugues?" Godefroi breathed.

"I'm here." Hugues moved to stand behind Godwera. Godefroi had not been this lucid in at least two days.

"Almost...time," Godefroi whispered. His eyelids fluttered. Hugues feared he would lapse back into delirium.

"Not yet, my love." Godwera clasped his hand to her chest and held it tightly. "You can rest soon, but not yet." Her tears ran freely and Hugues' cheeks were wet too.

Godefroi moaned. "Achambaud?" he breathed.

"He should have reached Troyes by now," Hugues replied. "He might even be on his way to Lorraine with the letters you wrote, depending on how quickly the Salt Lines could gather. Don't fret, Godefroi. They'll know what you have achieved here."

The drawn lines in Godefroi's face softened. "No...hurt...any... more. Can't...feel."

Godwera gave Hugues a querying look.

"It's the final stage of his illness," Hugues explained. "He has become numb to the pain as his body falters. A small mercy."

"Will God...forgive me?" Godefroi murmured.

"Of course He will," Hugues replied with all the fervour he could muster. "Your life has been lived with piety and humility, and in the service of God. How could He not embrace one of His greatest soldiers?"

Godefroi sighed and his eyelids drooped. Godwera kissed his fingers and stroked his burned forearm. He drifted for a time, but not as long as Hugues had feared. Eventually, he opened his eyes again and spoke in a stronger voice. "Baldwin."

"Your brother has been summoned from Edessa," Hugues confirmed. "Arrangements are in place. He will inherit your title."

Godwera suppressed a shudder.

"Salome?" The name held a sharper edge to it.

"Baldwin will never learn of her existence," Hugues replied. "We'll have her in Lorraine before he is anointed. Don't worry. Everything is arranged."

It was hard to tell whether Godefroi was satisfied with this response. His features were so still they gave nothing away. Only his eyelids fluttered, as if he was having trouble focusing. Or perhaps he was already gazing upon the next kingdom, and Hugues' words were like the wind at his back, ruffling his hair and clothes but conveying no meaning.

"Don't...stay." Godefroi's gaze settled on Godwera.

"I won't leave you," Godwera replied in a broken voice. "Not now. Perhaps I was wrong to deny us. Perhaps I allowed fear to rule my heart. But I have always loved you, Godefroi. Never doubt it, my dearest. Carry it with you...wherever you may go."

The raw grief in Godwera's voice was like the blow of a mace. A single tear slid from each corner of Godefroi's pale eyes. Hugues drew back from the bed. He should not be witness to this parting. He lacked the fortitude to endure it.

"Go...home," Godefroi whispered.

Hugues met Godwera's anguished look. The pain she was enduring to comfort Godefroi humbled him. He backed away from the bed and moved quietly to the double doors. Hugues could not offer them anything other than privacy.

"I'll always remember your kindness, Godefroi." Godwera smiled through her tears. "I won't stay. I don't think I could stand it." She squeezed his hand again. "I'll offer a prayer for your soul at your family's chapel."

Godefroi sighed and his face became peaceful. His fingers brushed against Godwera's wrist, the movement so slight that Hugues almost missed it. Her face crumpled into grief. Hugues could take no more. The sight of the two of them joined like that tore at the seams of his soul. He slipped through the double doors and quietly closed them behind him.

The sun was low on the horizon, glinting between the rooftops of Jerusalem and across the parapets of the Tower of David. Hugues tried to pray, but his heart and mind rebelled. He paced the antechamber and remembered all of those who had died: Firyal, Umayr, Etienne and countless soldiers paraded mercilessly through the endless halls of memory.

Hugues could find no peace. So much death and destruction had been wrought in his quest for the Salt Lines. He could not undo them, much as he might wish to. Only the future remained. Protecting Salome was the only way he could atone for his sins.

The double doors opened. Godwera stood trembling in the doorway. Behind her, the velvet drapes had been thrown open so that the setting sun glared through the balcony. Her hair was dishevelled and her eyes were like gouges in her face. She teetered, as if on the verge of fainting.

"He's gone," she said tonelessly.

Hugues dropped to his knees, the strength severed from his legs, and lay flat on the floor. He pressed his face against the cool tiles and wept.

---

28 August 1308

Sunrise

Bertrand waited impatiently just inside the portcullis. The tramp of feet echoed down the stairwell that led up to the ruined fortress of Mount Heredom. Snatches of conversation reached him. He listened avidly, trying to discern both tone and meaning. Some voices were low and filled with wonder, others fearful or heavy with exhaustion.

William was first to emerge into the narrow cavern. The English knight still limped from his battle with the mercenaries, yet he grinned broadly at the sight of Bertrand.

"How many?" Bertrand asked in English. His impatience bordered on rudeness. Fortunately, William did not take offence.

"And good morrow to you," William replied. "We number just over two dozen, if it pleases you. More would have come, but a large party draws attention."

Bertrand nodded. William's caution was well-founded. Members of the Templar brotherhood were still being persecuted in France and apparently the mood in England was turning against them.

"And?" Bertrand lifted his lantern to peer at the group of people shuffling into the cavern.

"And what?" William feigned ignorance.

"Are they here?" Bertrand asked in exasperation.

A broad smile broke across William's bearded face. "Of course. They were the first I chose."

"For heaven's sake. Bring them to me."

William laughed and strode into the growing knot of people spilling into the cavern. Men and women gazed curiously at Bertrand, perhaps wondering why he did not come forward to greet them. A few children peeked around their parents' legs.

Anxiety tightened inside Bertrand and soured his mouth. He had imagined this moment for months. Words seemed so inadequate, yet he felt compelled to say something. He had lost count of how many speeches he had composed and discarded.

William re-emerged from the milling crowd with a woman and three children in tow. The woman was short, with iron-grey hair tucked neatly into a wimple and a sturdy grey kirtle. While her clothes might be modest, her bearing was proud. The eldest boy followed her, holding hands with a girl who had not yet seen seven summers. The youngest struggled to keep up, his brown eyes wide as he took in their strange surroundings.

William stopped in front of Bertrand. "May I present Madame Maura," he said in French.

Bertrand swallowed a lump that had not been there moments ago. He bowed. "Do you know who I am?"

Maura scrutinised his face. "I believe I do," she said carefully.

Bertrand knelt. "Then I beg your forgiveness." All speeches forgotten, he spoke from the heart. "Please believe me when I tell you that Rémi was my only true friend for many years. The best parts of me were all learned from his example. I loved him dearly, and I grieve at his loss every day."

Maura and her three children stared at Bertrand.

God help him. He could see Rémi in the children's features. Renier had the same bristling hair. Already little Gueri was tending towards the same stocky build. But it was Aude, clutching her little brother's hand and staring at him with Rémi's dark brown eyes, that nearly undid him. Strangers they might be, yet they were the only family he had left.

"He asked me to convey a message to you," Bertrand said in a hoarse voice.

Maura raised an open palm. "Don't." She squeezed her eyes closed in pain and shook her head. Tears trickled down her cheek. "He's been gone so long, it's easier to let it stay that way."

"Maman," Renier said, "I want to know what Papa said."

"Me too, Maman," Aude chimed in. Little Gueri nodded vehemently.

Fresh grief tore through Bertrand. He should have insisted Rémi remain in France. How could he, of all people, allow a man to be taken from his family? These guilty thoughts were a well-worn path. He doubted that he would ever be free of them, nor would he wish to be. Perhaps Maura saw that in his face. Her stern expression softened as the children plucked at her sleeves.

Bertrand chose his words carefully. "I know what it's like to have an absent father. If you'll permit it, I will tell your children about the kind of man Rémi was. And I know he would want them to visit his grave, which is not far from here. From time to time, if that is acceptable."

Maura's face crumpled in pain. She clutched her children to her skirt and gave him a fierce nod over their heads. She seemed incapable of words and Bertrand understood this only too well. He rose to his feet, feeling lighter than he had in months.

I'll take care of them, Rémi. As if they were my own. I promise.

The other pilgrims were silent, watching this strange exchange.

More people had filed into the cavern. Bertrand wished he could greet them properly. William approached as Maura gathered her children to one side. "There is someone else who is most anxious to see you."

"Who?"

William indicated a cloaked figure. The pilgrim approached slowly, head lowered as a petitioner might approach the throne of a king. Bertrand frowned. The hood of the pilgrim's cloak hid their face.

"Welcome to the Halls of Mercy," Bertrand said uncertainly.

The pilgrim lifted the cowl. Bertrand stared into familiar, blue eyes. Bertrand sank to his knees. "You came. I didn't think you would."

"William found me in Troyes," Justine replied. "He explained why you could not come in person." She glanced at his side uncertainly.

"Roustan is dead. Rémi killed him."

"Good," Justine said with a fierce look. She glanced around the cavern. "And Salome is gone too?"

"Yes. She has finally found her rest."

Justine took his hands and drew him to his feet. "Bertrand, was it worth the sacrifice in the end?"

"It was...necessary." He stared into Justine's face. While Salome had always aroused his desire, she had never invoked the tenderness he felt for this woman. "I know I have no right to ask anything of you. My life is still yours to claim, as I promised. But let me show you what we have achieved before you decide." He gestured back down the tunnel. "Let me show you why our lives were destroyed...and how they might be rebuilt. Together. If you wish it."

Justine's eyes narrowed. "I won't let you hurt me again."

"After all the suffering I have inflicted, my purpose is to heal now, not harm." He gazed longingly at her uncertain, worried face. "Everard, my Preceptor, once told me not to bring my past with me when I became a chevalier. I ask the same of you now. Please, Justine, let us begin anew."

"I'm not sure I can ever forgive you, Bertrand."

"I'm not asking you to. Just give me the chance to make amends."

Bitterness twisted Justine's mouth. "I have lost so much."

"Then let me offer something to replace it," Bertrand urged. "Please, I beg you."

Justine nodded slowly. "Last chance," she said softly.

And that was enough. Her presence was more than he could ever have hoped for. Gratitude swelled in his heart and he fought back tears of relief.

Frightened and curious faces stared at the two of them. He grinned at little Gueri, who ducked his head but smiled back when he thought Bertrand wasn't watching.

Bertrand turned to the remaining pilgrims and spread his arms wide. "Welcome to the Order of the Dawn. Be at peace, for you are finally home."

CAST OF CHARACTERS

THE HOLY LAND, 1099

Hugues' five sacred points:

Achambaud de St. Amand	A knight and bodyguard to Godefroi de Bouillon.
Etienne de Champagne	An engineer and designer of Godefroi's siege tower.
Godefroi de Bouillon	Duke of Lower Lorraine and one of the principal nobles commanding the siege of Jerusalem.
Godwera de Bouillon	Former wife of Baldwin de Bouillon. Believed to have died while travelling south from Constantinople. Disguised as a monk called 'Gondemar'.
Hugues de Payens	Chaplain to Godefroi de Bouillon.

The Christian Nobility:

Baldwin de Bouillon	Younger, ambitious brother of Godefroi de Bouillon.
Diederic	A Flemish knight appointed to act as Godefroi's bodyguard during the siege of Jerusalem.
Gaston de Bearn	A minor noble charged with the responsibility of overseeing the construction of Godefroi's siege tower.
Raymond de Toulouse	Born Raymond St Gilles, now the Count of Toulouse. Godefroi's fiercest adversary in the struggle to rule Jerusalem.
Robert de Normandy	Duke of Normandy and cousin to Robert of Flanders. One of Godefroi's most important supporters.

Robert de Flanders — Duke of Flanders and cousin to Robert of Normandy. One of Godefroi's most important supporters.

The Christian Clergy:

Arnulf de Chocques — Chaplain to the Duke of Normandy.

Peter Desiderius — A priest who claimed to have divine visions. Supporter of Count Raymond.

Peter de Narbonne — One of the most senior ranking clerics. Made Bishop of Albara by Count Raymond in September 1098.

Umayr's Arabic Cabal:

Ālim Sharif — An elderly Saracen warrior whose title translates roughly to "learned noble".

Firyal — An elderly Saracen woman known to her people as The Seer.

Jalāl — An old Saracen man known to his people as The Alchemyst.

Tahīr — An old Saracen man known to his people as The Physick.

Umayr — A mysterious Saracen known to his people as the Qādī, which translates as a combination of "judge" and "master of the law".

FRANCE AND ENGLAND, 1307

The Templar Commanderie:

Arnaud — A senior knight or chevalier.

Bertrand de Châtillon-sur-Seine — A newly made knight. Third, and much maligned, son of the Baron of Châtillon-sur-Seine.

Everard de Chaumont — Preceptor (i.e. commander) of the Templar Commanderie in Brienne-le-Château.

Laurent — A Chaplain at the Templar Commanderie in Brienne-le-Château.

Rémi — A sergeant and lifelong mentor to Bertrand.

Roland — A senior knight or chevalier.

Thibauld — Everard de Chaumont's Seneschal.

Characters in France:

Guillaume de Nogaret	Keeper of the Seals for King Philippe and the king's principal adviser.
Guillot	Abbot of a Cistercian Abbey.
Huon	A gamekeeper for Justine de Fontette.
Justine de Fontette	Former lover of Bertrand and widowed ruler of the estate at Fontette. Justine's deceased husband was a vassal of Bertrand's father, the Baron of Châtillon-sur-Seine.
King Philippe le Bel	Philippe the Fair, King of France, and fourth of that name.
Malbert	Captain of *Le Blanc Écume,* a cog out of the port of Fécamp.
Maura	Rémi's wife.
Roard	A large knight and bodyguard to Salome.
Roustan de Toulouse	A ruthless agent of Guillaume de Nogaret.
Salome	A mysterious woman protected by Roard and Everard de Chaumont.

Characters in England:

Edwyn	Abbot of Rooklyn Abbey on the edge of the Yorkshire Dales.
Tristan	A merchant in Portsmouth and a broker for Abbot Guillot.
Sir William of Salisbury	An English Templar knight leading a band of their brethren north to escape an expected purge of the Order in England.

MERCY AND SEVERITY

The Lords of Mercy and Severity:

Gabriel	One of the five Lords of Mercy. Leads the angelic choir of the Cherubim.
Gamaliel	One of the five Lords of Severity. Opposes the archangel Gabriel.
Haniel	One of the five Lords of Mercy. Leads the angelic choir of the Elohim.
Lilith	One of the five Lords of Severity. Opposes the archangel Sandalphon.
Enoch	According to Scripture, Enoch, the son of Cain, was raised bodily into Heaven and became an archangel.

Michael	One of the five Lords of Mercy. Leads the angelic choir of the Malachim.
Orev Zarak	One of the five Lords of Severity. Opposes the archangel Haniel.
Raphael	One of the five Lords of Mercy. Leads the angelic choir of the Beni Elohim.
Sammael	One of the five Lords of Severity. Opposes the archangel Raphael.
Sandalphon	One of the five Lords of Mercy. Leads the angelic choir of the Ishim.
Tagiriron	One of the five Lords of Severity. Opposes the archangel Michael.

GLOSSARY

Abaddon	Prison for the bodies of the Lords of Severity. Located in the seventh, and deepest, layer of Hell.
Adonai Melech	The divine name used to invoke the power of the tenth Sephirah called Malkuth.
Aloah v'Daat	The divine name used to invoke the power of the sixth Sephirah called Tipheret.
Baphomet	A mysterious term with a range of possible meanings, all of which derive their root from the ancient word for "wisdom".
Bascinet	A helmet, typically worn over the top of a chainmail hood. The knight would usually wear a leather cap to protect his skull from chafing.
Bliaut	An over-gown worn by men and women during the Middle Ages. Typically, the men's version was shorter in the hem, while women wore theirs to ankle length.
Ceinture	A thick belt worn around the waist, often with a bliaut.
Chevalier	"Knight" in French.
Compline	The evening devotion, usually held around nine in the evening. Forms part of the Liturgy of the Hours and is observed by monks and brothers of the Templar Order.
Elohim Tzabaoth	The divine name used to invoke the power of the eighth Sephirah called Hod.
Ein Sof	Translates roughly as "God the Unknowable" — that is, the aspect of God that is beyond human comprehension.
Franj	A collective term used by the Saracens to refer to all Franks and other Christian invaders.
Hod	Translates from Hebrew as "Glory" or "Splendour". Hod is the eighth Sephirah in the Tree of Life and corresponds to reason, abstraction, logic and communication.

Holy Sepulchre   Located in Jerusalem, this is the most common name for the church built over the sites of Christ's crucifixion and resurrection.

Jehovah Tzabaoth   The divine name used to invoke the power of the seventh Sephirah called Netzach.

Kabbalah   The word "Kabbalah" literally means "to receive or accept". Historians disagree over the timing of the emergence of the Kabbalah, but most agree that it derives its origins from rabbinic Judaism. Over time, the Kabbalah has been incorporated into Western mysticism.

Lords of Mercy   Five archangels who cleave to the Pillar of Mercy and fight for the restoration of the unity between Ein Sof and all His children.

Lords of Severity   Five archangels who cleave to the Pillar of Severity. Responsible for the expulsion of humanity from the Garden of Eden.

Malkuth   Translates from Hebrew as "the Kingdom". Malkuth is the tenth Sephirah in the Tree of Life and corresponds to the material world, practicality and stability.

Matins   The morning devotion held at dawn. Forms part of the Liturgy of the Hours and is observed by monks and brothers of the Templar Order.

Menhir   An upright stone often with carved markings. Menhirs were used in ancient times as markers for sacred sites or meeting points.

Messire   From Old French, translating roughly as "My sir" or "sire".

Milites   A Roman term the Franks borrowed to describe professionally trained infantry.

Mount Heredom   Referred to in Isaiah 14:13 as 'the mount of assembly in the far north'. Thought to be Schiehallion in the geographic centre of Scotland.

Netzach   Translates from Hebrew as "Victory" or "Endurance". Netzach is the seventh Sephirah in the Tree of Life and corresponds to intuition, emotion and sensitivity.

Pedites   A Roman term the Franks borrowed to describe foot soldiers. Typically, poorly equipped compared to chevaliers and milites.

Pillar of Mercy	The right Pillar of Mercy belongs to the Tree of Knowledge that Adam and Eve ate from. It represents life, purity, and abundance.
Pillar of Severity	The left Pillar of Severity belongs to the Tree of Knowledge that Adam and Eve ate from. It represents death, corruption, and absence.
Pillar of Unity	The middle Pillar of Unity is an aspect of the Holy Shechinah and represents the one true path to God.
Saracen	A term used by Christians during the First Crusade to refer to all Moslems.
Seneschal	A senior official, or servant, in charge of a noble's household.
Sephirah	Singular usage of Sephirot.
Sephirot	The Ten Sephirot are manifestations of God, often represented by medieval Kabbalists as spheres emanating outwards from Him through the Tree of Life. The Ten Sephirot are the source of life in the universe, moving from the abstract concept of Ein Sof that humanity cannot comprehend to the physical matter comprising our existence.
Shaddai el Chai	The divine name used to invoke the power of the ninth Sephirah Yesod.
Shechinah	The Holy Shechinah is the manifestation of God in the lower worlds separated from His direct presence, symbolised by the Pillar of Unity. In Christianity, the Holy Shechinah might correspond to the Holy Spirit.
Tafurs	Vicious peasants who participated in the armed pilgrimage to take Jerusalem from the Saracens.
Tipheret	Translates from Hebrew as "Beauty" or "Compassion". Tipheret is the sixth Sephirah in the Tree of Life and corresponds to individuality, personality and the mind.
Tree of Life	The Tree of Life is a pictorial representation of the Ten Sephirot, showing the process of Creation. The Tree of Life is divided into three pillars: the left Pillar of Severity, the right Pillar of Mercy, and the middle Pillar of Unity.

Vespers	Devotion held at sunset. Forms part of the Liturgy of the Hours and is observed by monks and brothers of the Templar Order.
Yesod	Translates from Hebrew as "Foundation". Yesod is the ninth Sephirah in the Tree of Life and corresponds to imagination, dreams and instinct.

Acknowledgements

To say *The Salt Lines* has endured a long and difficult gestation would be quite an understatement. So, first and foremost, thank you for persevering with this story until the end.

While the two books of *The Salt Lines* contain elements of fantasy, a large amount of historical research underpins both timelines, and many of the cast are documented historical figures. In the pursuit of a ring of authenticity, I must thank my wife Liz for supporting my trip to Jerusalem and France to conduct research whilst she was pregnant with our second daughter. I'd also like to thank Matt Filkins for his assistance in criss-crossing France in search of fortified chateaus, one of the few remaining Templar commanderies, and the original Cistercian Abbey.

A number of other people have played key roles in helping me craft *The Salt Lines*. I'd like to thank Gillian Pollack and Wendy Waring for their insights into the Kabbalah and the lives of those dedicated to the *Ordre du Temple*.

Additional shout outs must go to members of the Thorbys writing group—both past and present—for not only their kind and thoughtful critiques, but also their encouragement: Chris Barnes, Karen Beilharz, JK Breukelaar, Steve Denham, JJ Irwin, Karen Maric, Anne Mok, DK Mok, Emma Munro, Rivqa Rafael, Angie Rega and Susan Wardle.

To my agent, John Jarrold, thank you for your incisive comments, encouragement, and most of all, patience. To my editors—Maria Kelly for Book 1, and Gregory Stewart for Book 2—thank you for your care and attention to detail.

I'd also like to acknowledge Dr Karen Brooks for her gracious words about *The Salt Lines* saga. If you're yet to discover her wonderful historical novels, then I encourage you to visit https://karenrbrooks.com/

And finally heartfelt thank yous to Gerry Huntman at IFWG Publishing for ushering this story into print, and to Greg Chapman for the wonderful cover gracing each book.

Nathan Burrage
September 2023